PRAISE FOR

TIME OUT OF TIME

§ BOOK ONE §

BEYOND THE DOOR

BOOKLIST TOP 10 SF/FANTASY FOR YOUTH

"Open this book and step into a dazzling world of wonder. Enter, and be enchanted!" —MARGI PREUS, AUTHOR OF THE NEWBERY HONOR BOOK *HEART OF A SAMURAI*

"Seeing the Wild Hunt confidently and beautifully brought into the twenty-first century is exciting indeed. A timeless and compelling tale!" —BRIAN AND WENDY FROUD, AUTHORS OF *TROLLS* AND OTHER FAERIE BOOKS

★ "McQuerry's compelling narrative races forward, immersing the reader in its lyrical mysteries." —*BOOKLIST*, STARRED REVIEW

"McQuerry smoothly blends adventure, coming-of-age, and mystery with a mythological world where special academic and problem-solving talents are required assets rather than nerd-bait for bullies. The characters are charming, and the quirky, supernatural good guys are compassionate and forgiving." —*VOYA*

"A promising start to a fantasy series mines the rich ore of Celtic mythology and propels a young boy into cosmic battle." —*KIRKUS REVIEWS*

"A sense of wonder and worry permeates the narrative, evocative of *The Dark Is Rising* or the work of Neil Gaiman, and the cliffhanger ending will leave readers clamoring for more." —*PUBLISHERS WEEKLY*

"Fantasy addicts will find plenty to like." —*SCHOOL LIBRARY JOURNAL*

MAUREEN DOYLE McQUERRY

AMULET BOOKS
NEW YORK

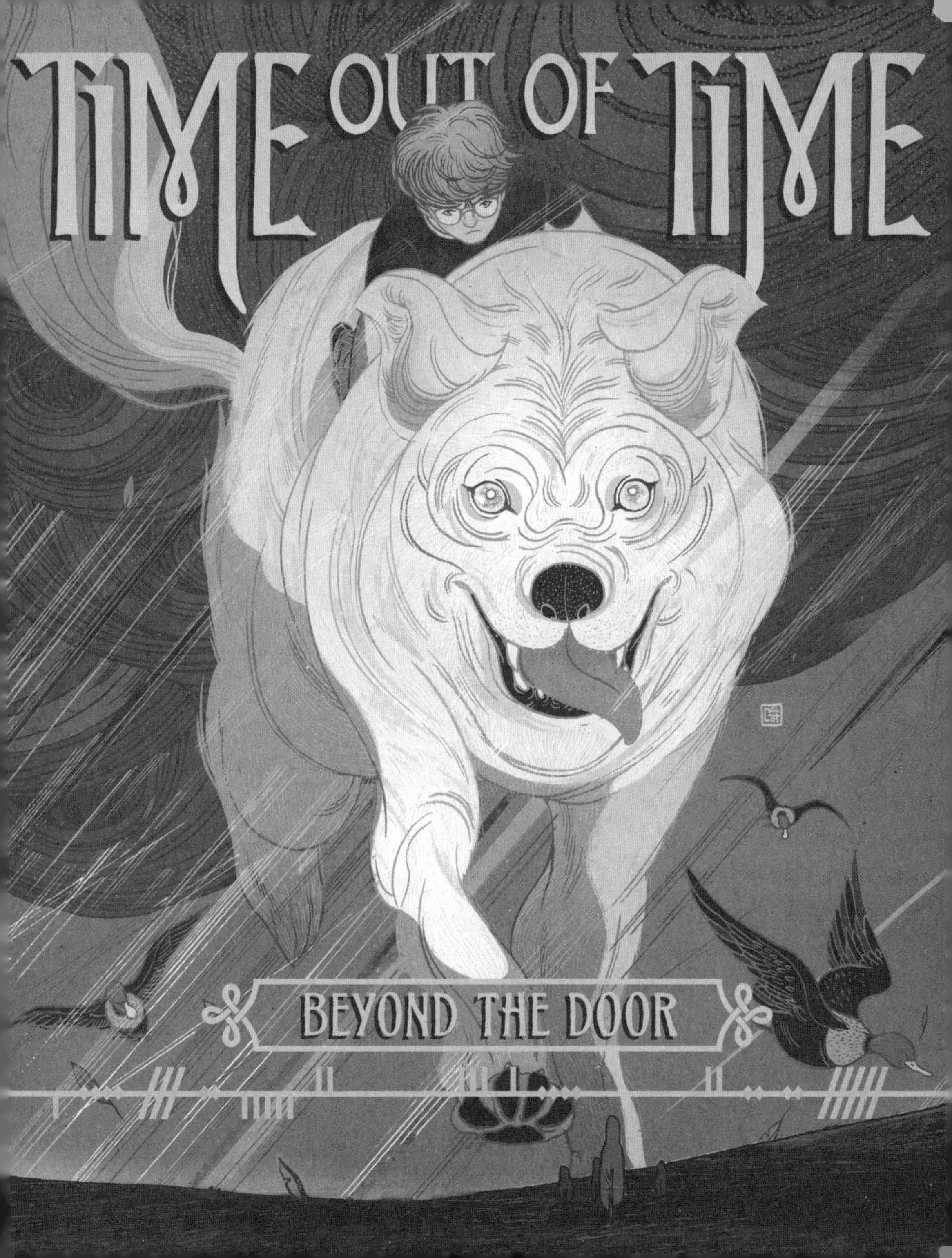
TIME OUT OF TIME
BEYOND THE DOOR

The Library of Congress has catalogued the hardcover edition of this book as follows:

McQuerry, Maureen, 1955–Beyond the door / Maureen Doyle McQuerry.pages cm.
— (Time out of time ; book 1) Summary: When mythical creatures appear, a mystery of
unparalleled proportions begins to unfold for Timothy, his sister Sarah, and school bully
Jessica, who must defeat the powers of the Darkness.
ISBN 978-1-4197-1016-2
[1. Adventure and adventurers—Fiction. 2. Brothers and sisters—
Fiction. 3. Mythology, Celtic—Fiction. 4. Space and time—Fiction.
5. Magic—Fiction. 6. Animals, Mythical—Fiction.] I. Title.
PZ7.M24715Be 2014
[Fic]—dc23
2013025513

ISBN for this edition: 978-1-4197-1493-1

Text copyright © 2014 Maureen Doyle McQuerry
Book design by Sara Corbett and Kate Fitch

Printed and bound in U.S.A.
10 9 8 7 6 5 4 3 2 1

Amulet Books are available at special discounts when purchased in quantity for premiums and
promotions as well as fundraising or educational use. Special editions can also be created to
specification. For details, contact specialsales@abramsbooks.com or the address below.

ABRAMS
THE ART OF BOOKS SINCE 1949
115 West 18th Street
New York, NY 10011
www.abramsbooks.com

FOR BRENNAN AND GLAIRE, WHO LOVE STORIES

SEE PAGES 374–75 TO LEARN ABOUT THE SEGRET GODE IN THIS BOOK.

PROLOGUE

STOOPED AND SHUFFLING, the man slipped sound-lessly through the shadows of night. His hair was long and shaggy, his clothes ill-fitting and unremarkable except for the many pockets of various sizes that covered his jacket and trousers. Wherever he walked, the streetlights dimmed. It seemed to make the man stand a little taller and his stride lengthen. He gazed hungrily into well-lit windows of houses, and his pale skin began to itch. It was only mid-March, but spring was coming. The daylight lasted longer; the air carried the first faint scents of new life. Soon, very soon, the change would come.

He stood hidden in shadow outside the windows of a small house on Willow Street. Silhouettes moved back and forth behind the curtains. The windows blazed, but this was not the house he was look-ing for. When his scalp began to tingle, he raked his fingers through his hair. A single leaf had sprouted from the back of his head. The change was beginning. A tabby cat rustled through the laurel bushes. Pausing to stare warily, it inched closer to the man, then rubbed against his ankles. As he bent to scratch its ears, he thought of the lengthening days ahead. Every year he waited for the days to grow longer, for the short days of winter to change to summer. This spring would be different. He could feel it. He could even hear it in the voices of the trees.

He hurried toward the outskirts of town, past the road to the forest's edge, where the houses became more scattered, hidden behind hedges and large trees. He was in search of a particular house where two particular children lived. He had been waiting for this spring for many years. The boy should be almost twelve; his sister, two years older. Their house was half-hidden by a large clump of birch trees, white and shining in the moonlight. A wide porch wrapped around two sides. The green front door had been left ajar.

It was time to begin.

✢ ✢ ✢

The rough bark of the sycamore dug into the girl's back. She was not used to sitting in trees, and she had been in this tree for what most people would consider a very long time. Above her, the stars burned in the night sky and the distant moon looked as if it were tangled in the uppermost branches of the tree. Occasionally, she swung her legs or ran a comb through her long pale hair. Her job was to wait and watch, and as she waited, she sang. The song had no melody, but it spun out into the night like a silvery ribbon. As she watched, the front door opened tentatively: a slender slice of light, and a boy's face appeared, and then disappeared. Surprisingly, the door stayed open. She continued to sing as minutes passed. Finally, there was movement in the darkness and her back relaxed against the tree. A man came shambling across the wide lawn, moving purposefully toward the open door.

✛ ✛ ✛

The girl's song carried itself on the wind through the night and spread out in the four directions of the compass. In the north, it disturbed the sleep of a pack of white hounds; they stirred restlessly, whimpered, and barked. Their master looked at the sky and wondered why they should travel so soon. Nevertheless, the hunt would ride when and where it was summoned. He saddled his well-muscled horse, black as the night sky. Then he hooked a polished hunting horn to his belt. The hounds would be glad of some exercise, and he wouldn't mind some himself.

In the east, the song reached into the sleep of the one-eyed man and gave him horrible dreams. A striped orange cat, held in a small trap by his bedside, hissed, longing for freedom. Only hours before, it had been hunting for a morsel of food or water. In a cage next to the cat, a gray rat hunched miserably, rubbing its paws over its pointed face. The man snorted loudly and called out in his sleep, but because he lived alone, nobody came. In the next room, other animals growled or mewled piteously. Those without voices merely shifted, seeking comfort in cages that gleamed like jewels.

STRANGE
VISITORS

AT THE DOOR AND INTO THE HOUSE

S TRAY GUST OF wind howled down the chimney, sending a spray of last fall's leaves out of the hearth and scuttling across the living room floor. Timothy James Maxwell jumped up with a start from the book he had been trying to read. It wasn't a windy night. Leaves had never blown down the chimney before. He went to the fireplace and peered cautiously up the chimney, but all he could see was the blackness of the flue. A puff of air blew directly in his face, and he pulled out his head, smacking the back of it on the bricks. "Ouch!"

Fortunately, neither the leaves nor his cry awakened Mrs. Clapper, who had fallen asleep in the recliner at least half an hour ago. She slept soundly, with her legs, thick as tree trunks, sprawled in front of her, head thrown back, mouth gaping like a trap. Her nose whistled with each deep breath, and her full lower lip quivered. She wasn't really too bad, as babysitters went, Timothy thought, but the fact that she was a babysitter was a problem. At eleven and three-quarters, he was quite sure he no longer needed a babysitter. Unfortunately, his parents didn't agree. And even though they tried to pass her off as a companion, he wasn't fooled. So when they had taken his older sister, Sarah, to a ballet audition in the city, Timothy was left, alone, with the Clapper.

"We'll be home Sunday night as soon as we can—promise," his mother had explained. Timothy looked down at the carpet and drew his eyebrows together.

"Buck up, son. Clapper's a good sort, and she'll probably play Scrabble with you to your heart's content." Timothy considered this to be nothing more than bribery because his father knew how much he loved Scrabble: the smooth wooden tiles, the random surprise of letters, and, of course, the fact that he usually won.

"I don't think I need a babysitter anymore, now that I'm almost twelve," Timothy replied with dignity. "I can take care of myself just fine. What could happen? Nothing ever happens here. If you really don't want me left alone, then one of you should stay. It doesn't take two people to see an audition." He knew he was being unreasonable, but he couldn't stop the words.

"We know that you're very capable," his mother had replied, bending close so that he caught the minty fragrance of her soft brown hair and a faint whiff of turpentine. "We just want you to have some company, and Mrs. Clapper has already agreed. Do be kind to her, Timothy."

At that point, Timothy had known the battle was lost. He thought of the word *conquer*. A handy word to use in Scrabble, but a miserable word when it was directed at him.

Over the years, Mrs. Clapper had stayed a number of times, but always when he and Sarah were home together. He didn't like the idea of having Mrs. Clapper to himself. He'd always counted on Sarah to divert most of the babysitter's attention. And he was still haunted by some of the strange stories she had told them, stories about people who shape-shifted into animals, about changeling children or creatures that came in from the dark if you left a door or window open.

The evening hadn't passed as slowly as he had feared. They had played Scrabble, and he'd won every game but one, and she'd let him play WarGames on the computer for an hour. But even this couldn't make up for tolerating a babysitter. Then Mrs. Clapper had made a batch of ginger cookies and begun one of her stories. It was about a stone that had been missing for many years, a stone that cried out loud when the right person put a foot on it.

"How can a stone cry out?" Timothy popped a warm cookie into his mouth.

"This one has a voice, but it's not a human voice. A cry rings out when a just leader places a foot on it. Of course, there are those who'd rather the stone was silent."

"Why?"

"Because they're not interested in justice."

"Are you sure there isn't a sword in this stone?" Timothy asked, thinking of the story of King Arthur.

"No, there is no sword in this stone. But there is a missing sword in the story, and a missing spear and cauldron as well." She handed Timothy a dish towel and the wet mixing bowl. "Like Arthur's stone, one specific person is intended to find it."

Timothy considered. "A good story should have battles."

"Oh, there are battles, fearsome battles, and if the Dark wins them, the Dark grows stronger."

"The Dark?"

"Of course, the Dark. The Dark wants the stone and is willing to do all kinds of terrible things to prevent anyone else finding it. That must never happen. Just as the Light longs for everything to be free, the Dark longs to control everything."

The story was definitely getting interesting, Timothy thought. A chill passed up his arms. "What kinds of things?" He set the bowl aside and bit into another of Mrs. Clapper's ginger cookies. Crumbs cascaded to the floor.

"Things that are better left unspoken. They'd give you worse nightmares than the wolves you're afraid of."

Timothy cringed. He never should have told Mrs. Clapper about the wolves in his nightmares.

"Before I say anything more, close the drapes. You never know who might be watching us. And lock the door. You never know what might wander in." She barked out a laugh, and went into the living room. Settling into the leather recliner with a sigh, she pulled the plaid tartan throw over her legs and closed her eyes.

"This throw is from your mother's family, isn't it? The O'Dalys."

"Yes, I guess so, but who would be looking in here? There's nothing very interesting in our house."

"Sometimes ordinary things turn out to be more interesting than you think."

Timothy drew the drapes. "So where is this stone?"

Mrs. Clapper opened one blue eye and peered up at Timothy. "Only the Stewards of the Stone know that, and maybe not all of them. But the stone *is* meant to be found. By the right person, of course . . . *If he survives.*"

Her words hung in the air. Timothy breathed them in. "It's a quest, isn't it?"

But Mrs. Clapper's breathing had become deep and regular. She had fallen asleep. Timothy had picked up his book on magic tricks and tried to read, but the story of the stone distracted him. A talking stone would definitely be spectacular.

That was when the leaves had blown down the chimney.

⊹⊹⊹

Now rubbing the knot forming on his head, he took one more careful look up the chimney. Nothing. Too bad real adventures were so hard to come by. He looked at the snoring Mrs. Clapper. Once she was in bed for the night, he could spend more time on the computer. He could stay up all night if he wanted to.

He grasped Mrs. Clapper's sweatshirt-clad shoulder and shook: no response. This time he grabbed her shoulder more firmly and spoke directly into her ear. "Mrs. Clapper, I'm going to bed now."

She snorted loudly. "Oh, my goodness, it's past eleven. At least you don't have school tomorrow." She pushed up her reading glasses to the top of her head. "Time for you to get ready for bed, and I think I'll be heading that way myself." Easing herself up out of the overstuffed chair, she cocked her head to the side, and her clear blue eyes peered sharply at Timothy. "Is there anything you need?"

For a moment Timothy felt as if she knew he was planning to stay up most of the night. "No." He feigned a yawn. "I'm just really sleepy."

"Well, good dreams, then, Timothy, good dreams." And she wandered down the hall to the guest bedroom. "And turn off the lights on your way to bed."

Timothy set off in the direction of his bedroom. He stopped in the bathroom and made sure to let the water in the sink run at least three minutes to simulate brushing his teeth. Then he flushed the toilet and checked the hallway. No Mrs. Clapper in sight, and the door to the guest bedroom was firmly closed. Now for the computer.

As he passed the front door, Timothy couldn't resist opening it and peering out into the dark. The night was warm for mid-March, and the wind that had blown the leaves down the chimney seemed to have completely disappeared. And, of course, there was nothing waiting to come in as Mrs. Clapper had suggested. If only life were more like the stories she told. He could hear the night noises, the shuffle of trees getting comfortable, the soft trill of a screech owl, and could smell the mustiness of the river a few blocks off. Maybe he should try an experiment. What if he kept the door open a few inches and waited to see if anything came in? He had all night to get to the computer.

Timothy left the door open just a crack, grabbed his book, and climbed halfway up the stairs to wait.

Scientists had to be open to all possibilities. This was a data point. He didn't believe any of Mrs. Clapper's stories, but it was best to be objective. He opened his book and began the chapter about sleight-of-hand tricks. Every few minutes he looked up. Nothing happened. Timothy finished the chapter and stood up, feeling foolish. What had he expected? He'd never tell anyone about this little experiment. Time for the computer.

Two steps down the stairs, and the door moved. A strange thumping began in Timothy's chest, as if his heart was trying to escape the cage of his ribs. Slowly, the door swung inward. Timothy drew back into the shadows of the stairs and held his breath. He thought of Mrs. Clapper's words, *Things that are better left unspoken.* A long face followed by a long, spare frame sidled into the living room. Beneath his shaggy black hair, the man's face was as pale as moonlight, his eyes the startling green of new leaves. Timothy froze. Should he call out and try to scare him off? He checked his pocket for his cell phone. Empty.

He leaned forward and let his breath out slowly, quietly, so he wouldn't be heard. He'd watch for a few minutes and see what the man was after before calling Mrs. Clapper.

The man grabbed at the air. The light in the hallway dimmed. As Timothy watched, the man stuffed his hand into a large pocket of his coat. The pocket glowed.

It was impossible! No one could grab light as if it were a solid object; all the laws of physics were against that happening. But that is exactly what the man did. When one pocket was full, he filled another, and the light in the room grew dimmer. Timothy could see light spilling out over each pocket's edge like a moon just brimming above the horizon. If the man moved too quickly, the light would spill on the floor.

Timothy crouched down and concentrated on keeping his breath quiet. Now that his initial terror was gone, he felt . . . He wasn't sure how he felt. *Intrigued*, he thought to himself . . . No, *mesmerized*. Scrabble tiles popped into his mind. *Mesmerized*, twenty-four points, a good choice because of the *z*.

The man continued filling his pockets. The light in the living room dimmed even more. Something rustled in the doorway. Timothy clenched his hands.

A girl came in, and with her came the smell of snow. She was a little older than his sister, Sarah, and moved with the grace of a dancer.

Timothy was leaning so far forward now that he almost lost his balance and tumbled down the rest of the stairs. The girl, shining with a faint light, walked through the living room, picking up books, flipping the pages, and setting them down again. Every now and then, she ran her fingers through her white hair—hair even longer than Sarah's—and Timothy heard a faint tinkling sound. Wherever she walked, she left footprints of silver-white dust on the blue carpet. Timothy bit his lip. This really couldn't be happening.

By now, the man's pockets were full of light and the room was almost dark. Timothy inched farther down the steps. What should he do next? Suddenly, dogs howled in the yard.

Timothy didn't move. Mrs. Clapper must hear them. She'd be here any minute. She didn't come. His heart beat wildly.

A large head thrust itself into the room, a man's head with thick curly brown hair and a disorderly beard. The rack of antlers that sprouted from his hair scraped across the door lintel. A silver hunting horn swung from his belt. His eyes roved back and forth. Timothy made himself as small as he could. A cold sea sloshed in his stomach. Something about the man felt dangerous, unpredictable. Timothy shuddered and tucked his chin into his chest.

The howling was closer; he could hear claws clacking on the porch. The wolves of his nightmares, rangy beasts with glittering eyes and snapping mouths, popped into his mind. Timothy began to sweat. Why didn't Mrs. Clapper wake up? The situation was definitely out of control. The dogs were sure to have very large teeth!

The horned man spoke in a rumbling voice. "You've summoned the hunt early this year." Once more, his eyes raked the shadows. Then he leaned forward and sniffed. Adrenaline surged through Timothy. If he moved, he'd be discovered. With every clenched muscle, he wished for the horned man to go away.

"There are rumors that Balor and the Dark are on the move again. Events are unfolding that require haste. The *Filidh* must discover his role and his strength. Cerridwyn assures me he is ready." The pale man's voice rustled like the branches of trees in the wind.

Timothy ran his moist palms down his jeans. What he was hearing made no sense at all. The Dark? Was this the same Dark from Mrs. Clapper's story?

The horned man nodded his great head, the antlers knocking a lamp shade sideways, clattering a picture to the floor. "Dark or Light, you know that the hunt takes no side in the battle. Who is the prey?"

At the word *prey*, Timothy flinched. Why did the man ask *Who* instead of *What*?

"It remains to be seen," the pale man answered. "I don't know what choices will be made, but you and your hounds are free to hunt lawful prey. Know this: I will do whatever it takes to defend the Filidh. And Balor will do whatever it takes to destroy him." The pale man was standing taller now. He opened one of his pockets. The light inside glowed. "I have captured some of the light of his house. It will call him to me."

The girl said nothing. She watched and listened.

The horned man turned to leave, ducking his antlers under the door. The baying of the hounds receded. Then the glowing girl followed him out the door, trailing the fine silver dust like the tail of a star.

Timothy pressed his face against his hands. He didn't like the word *prey*. The pale man looked around. His pockets bulged with light, and his green eyes peered into the shadows. They settled on the stairs where Timothy hid, as if he sensed his presence. Then the man turned and left, taking most of the light from the room with him.

In the dimness, Timothy leapt from the bottom step. He slammed the door shut and locked it. He leaned against the familiar solid wood while his breathing slowed. Should he get Mrs. Clapper, or call the police first? But what would he tell them? No one would believe his description. What did the man plan to do with the light? And how could light call someone?

He ran one hand through his hair and looked around his perfectly ordinary living room: a layer of fine silvery dust powdered the carpet, the lamp shade hung askew, and a picture lay on the floor. Nothing else, except the dimness, gave a clue that anything out of the ordinary had occurred.

If he woke Mrs. Clapper, he'd have to explain. She'd tell his parents. The questions would never stop. And he'd be doomed to having babysitters for the rest of his life. Nothing had been stolen. Timothy straightened the lamp shade, hung the picture back on the wall, and looked at the footprints with dismay. He'd sweep the silvery dust up. But first, he scraped some of it from the floor into a plastic bag, which he slipped into his pocket. Evidence. He'd save it to show Sarah. She could keep a secret. Then he hurried to the broom closet. In the distance, the dogs bayed. Timothy thought he could still smell their damp doggy odor. The silvery dust came up easily, leaving the floor just as it was.

For a long time, Timothy gazed out the living room window, his heart still tap-dancing in his chest. Question after question bubbled up. He felt like a shaken bottle of soda, about to explode. If only Sarah were home!

Reluctantly, he climbed the stairs to bed, but it was many hours before he fell asleep.

✛ ✚ ✛

Rosemary Clapper sat on the edge of the guest bed, looking at her watch. March 15, way too early for the horned man to be out and about, she thought, unless there was something unusual, something worth hunting. She had watched Timothy and Sarah grow over the years, and now it appeared the time had come. She got up and pushed her feet into a pair of pink slippers. She shivered and tightened the flannel bathrobe. The temperature always dropped by at least ten degrees after a visit from a star.

EVIDENCE

WHEN TIMOTHY AWOKE, the sun had already slipped under his bedroom shades and crept across the foot of his bed. He looked at the clock and sat bolt upright: 11:00! This was absolutely the latest he had ever slept. Sleeping late made Timothy feel like he was missing something. He remembered it was Sunday and that Mrs. Clapper was still there. Sarah and his parents wouldn't be home until evening. And then he remembered *them*— the strange man stealing light, the silvery girl, and the threatening man with his hounds. In an instant he was wide awake, heart pounding. He pulled on jeans and a crumpled T-shirt from the pile on the floor, then bounded down the stairs, the plastic bag of evidence still in his pocket.

In the morning light, the living room was undisturbed. The carpet showed no remnants of the silvery dust from the girl's feet, and the front door remained firmly closed. Timothy exhaled and went into the kitchen.

Mrs. Clapper was seated at the table with a cup of coffee and the newspaper. She was wearing the same green sweatshirt she had on the night before, and on her feet were a pair of fuzzy pink slippers.

"I'm glad to see you're finally awake. I always think morning is the best part of the day, although night can have its own charm." She got up from the chair and began to beat some eggs into a frothy mixture. "I hope you slept well." She poured the eggs into a large frying pan.

Timothy found that he couldn't meet her eyes, and once again his heart danced to a staccato beat within his chest. "I slept fine."

"That's good because there's a lot to be done today. Your mother asked me to get you started on raking the winter debris out of the flower beds to get them ready for spring. Right after the ides is the best time to start."

"What are the ides?" he asked, munching a piece of cold toast.

"Hmm, and I thought you were so advanced." Her eyes twinkled as she scooped a steaming pile of scrambled eggs onto his plate. "The ides of March were yesterday, March fifteenth. It's the day Caesar was betrayed."

"I know who Julius Caesar was—emperor of Rome."

"I should hope you know. A soothsayer warned him to 'beware the ides of March,' but he must not have taken her seriously because the senate happened to be meeting that day, and his good friend Brutus stabbed him in the back at the foot of Pompey's statue. Anyway, the ides are a day when you need to be careful because surprising things can happen."

The toast stuck in his throat. "What do the ides have to do with raking the flower beds?"

Mrs. Clapper began washing out her coffee cup in the sink. "I like to think of them as the end of the winter. It helps me remember when to get started cleaning up the yard."

He thought that this year the ides had proved more surprising than she knew, and pushed his eggs around his plate. "Why didn't he believe the soothsayer?"

"Well, that's a good question, Timothy. Sometimes people only believe what they want to believe, and sometimes people have trouble believing anything they can't see for themselves. It could be that he just didn't know what to beware of, or whom to trust." She cleared his plate, clicking her tongue over the wasted eggs. "Now, go get the rake while I put on my shoes."

Timothy didn't really mind yard work. He liked being outside, but today he wanted to be at the computer, looking up information about the strange horned man. He was sure that he had seen the horned man's face before as an illustration in a book. It had given him the same thrill of dread he felt last night, when the rough antlers scraped above the door and the shaggy head appeared. The door frame! Why hadn't he thought of it sooner? The antlers would have left a mark on the painted woodwork. He rounded the side of the house at a run, rake in hand, but Mrs. Clapper was on the front porch, washing windows. He'd have to wait to check that, too.

As he dragged the rake through the flower bed, he tried to convince himself that it had all been part of a very realistic dream. The dirt, still soggy after the last of the snow had melted, muddied his shoes and the cuffs of his pants. Dead leaves were caught in the spiny branches of shrubs lining the bed, and some had formed wet piles covering the bulbs he and Sarah had planted last year. Sarah was wild for flowers, particularly daffodils. They had spent hours digging bulbs into the beds all across the front of the house.

He wished she was home now, so he could show her the bag of silvery dust. He stopped, the rake still poised in the air. In the mud of the flower bed were the prints of hounds. Very large hounds. The bed had been crossed and recrossed by several large dogs. He could hear their baying as clearly as if they were still in the yard, and with a shiver remembered the scrabble of their paws on the porch. Worst of all, he pictured their sharp teeth and slavering mouths. Timothy knelt in the mud and spread his hand across one of the paw prints. It measured almost the same size as his hand.

"Timothy!" Mrs. Clapper called from the porch. "It looks like a neighbor's dogs got loose last night."

Timothy stood up and walked over to the porch steps. He should have thought of the paw prints before Mrs. Clapper found them. She poured the soapy water left in the window-washing bucket over the wooden boards.

"They appear to be unusually large dogs." She peered at him over the top of her glasses.

Timothy felt as if his tongue were stuck to the roof of his mouth. He couldn't think of a single thing to say in response. Mrs. Clapper had just removed an important piece of evidence. He shrugged in her direction to let her know he heard, and then he returned to the flower bed and began raking furiously, stepping carefully so that he didn't muck up another piece of evidence.

Half an hour later, when he finished raking and walked in through the front door, Timothy was not surprised to find two ragged scrapes in the shiny paint above the door. The marks were visible only when the door was open; maybe no one would notice them before he could find some paint in the garage. On the other hand, they were more evidence for Sarah. In the meantime, there was one more thing he needed to do. He slipped cautiously into the kitchen, no Mrs. Clapper in sight. He opened the trash can and took out the garbage bag. He couldn't chance Mrs. Clapper discovering the silver powder and asking questions. And he still had the small bag of dust in his pocket as evidence for Sarah.

Timothy dipped his finger into the fine powder in the garbage bag. It clung to his skin, coating it in silver. What was this strange stuff made from? He sniffed it. There was no odor.

"And just what are you up to?" Mrs. Clapper stood in the doorway of the kitchen, hands on ample hips, a dish towel flung over one shoulder.

Heart pounding, Timothy dropped his hand and thought fast. "The garbage is full, and I just thought I'd take it out." He didn't sound convincing even to himself.

"Very thoughtful, Timothy." Mrs. Clapper opened the dishwasher, still shaking her head.

But Timothy was already out the back door. To be extra sure that the bag wasn't discovered, he held his breath and rooted down under soggy paper sacks, old cardboard boxes, and a putrid bag of chicken leftovers. Gagging on the smell, he stuffed the garbage bag underneath the trash. The bag of chicken was wet and gooey. It came apart as he was holding it and left long, smelly streaks when he wiped his hands on the legs of his jeans. He sighed. Now he'd have to change his pants. Being sneaky was complicated.

SECRETS

SUNDAY EVENING, SARAH sailed through the front door and did a neat pirouette in the entryway. At thirteen, she resembled one of the porcelain dolls in their mother's china cabinet so closely that their father had started calling her "doll baby," a name Timothy was sure he would have found disgusting if he were a girl. Sarah, as she explained to Timothy over and over, would someday be a principal dancer with the New York Ballet—if she didn't become a pirate first. He noticed that she mentioned being a pirate less and less these days, and he found this disappointing. In his opinion, it would be much more interesting to have a pirate for a sister than a dancer.

"I have a scholarship!" Sarah announced. "A scholarship for two weeks this summer for dance classes with *the New York Ballet!*" She said the words with such reverence that Timothy imagined them floating above her head in capital letters.

"Congratulations!" Timothy jumped up, spilling Scrabble tiles across the floor. Mrs. Clapper beamed. His parents followed in close behind.

"Tim, she was amazing! We missed you. How was your weekend?" His mother ran all the sentences together and threw her arms around him at the same time. He breathed in her minty scent and ducked out of her embrace.

"Son," his father said, ruffling his hair.

The next few minutes were filled with the type of jumbled questions and answers that people share when they have adventures to relate. Somewhere in the chaos, Mrs. Clapper said her good-byes, his mother pulled a new book out of her purse and gave it to him, and his father went back out to the car for their bags.

"What happened here?" He frowned, looking up at the frame above the door. "It looks like something scraped the paint off. Timothy, what have you been dragging into the house? Not starting any more science experiments, are you?" he asked almost hopefully. He was sure that Timothy had a future as a research scientist, especially after he won the science fair last year.

Timothy squirmed under his father's gaze and tried not to look at the deep scrapes in the shiny green paint. "No, I didn't bring anything in."

His father only rubbed the marks and raised his eyebrows.

✛ ✛ ✛

When Timothy finally had Sarah to himself, it was late. Already dressed in pajamas, they were sitting among the family of toy bears on Sarah's bed. Sarah did not pay much attention to the bears anymore. She knew, however, that Timothy still talked to them sometimes when things at school were particularly difficult—like the time when Jessica Church, the most popular girl in seventh grade, called him "genius boy" and "nerd brain." Sarah also knew he would rather die than admit talking to the bears.

Sarah had told her story, in detail, twice, and now sat stretching one leg above her head and yawning sleepily. "How was the Clapper? What exactly did you do while we were gone?"

Timothy knew that now was the time to tell Sarah everything, but suddenly he was reluctant to let his secret go. He wanted to stretch it out and savor the importance of his news. And there was the chance that she wouldn't believe him. After all, he wasn't quite sure he believed it himself. Still, she was his sister, his best friend, and she was usually tolerant of his ideas, even when other people found them odd. Most important, she never laughed at him, including the times when some of his ideas didn't work out as smoothly as planned.

Take, for example, when he was seven and decided that he needed to simplify his normal routines so that he could use his time more efficiently. To save extra minutes, on Sunday night he put five pairs of underpants on under his jeans. He would have put on seven, but that made the jeans uncomfortably tight. Every morning he would peel one off. His plan lasted three days until his mother caught him and explained that the pants he needed to change were the ones on the inside. That night he heard her tell his father over dinner and they both laughed, but Sarah never did. She merely said, "Good thinking, Timothy. Too bad it didn't work out." That was what he liked about her, that and the fact that she never complained when he won at Scrabble or chess, and she never called him Tim, just Timothy.

Now he shifted self-consciously on the bed and stretched out on his stomach so that he would not look Sarah directly in the eyes. "You're never going to believe what happened. I don't know if I even believe it myself."

Sarah listened intently, not interrupting, while Timothy described the events of the previous evening.

"Right . . . a horned man and a glowing girl."

"I know it sounds crazy, but it's true! You saw the scratches on the door!"

Sarah raised both eyebrows and folded her arms across her chest. Timothy knew that skeptical look too well. "That's where the scrapes came from, his antlers?" she asked. "Were you scared?"

"Yeah, at first. But then the pale man started grabbing light, and I forgot about being scared until the horned man showed up. And his dogs." His voice faded out. "They were vicious dogs. At least, that's how they sounded."

Sarah frowned in concentration. "Like wolves. No wonder you were scared. Why didn't you call the police?"

"And tell them a man was stealing light?"

"You've got a point. Timothy, you'd better not be lying to me."

"I swear this is absolutely true. Besides, I have evidence." He dashed into his room to retrieve the bag of silver dust from the pocket of his jeans. But the jeans were gone! He looked under the bed, in the back of his closet, and even in the bathroom hamper. Dread settled like a weight on him. He raced into the laundry room. On the top of the washing machine was a neatly folded stack of laundry, his jeans on the top. Grabbing them off the pile, he thrust his hand in one pocket and then in the other just to make sure. Nothing.

"What took you so long?" Sarah demanded when he returned empty-handed.

"I saved some of the silver dust the girl tracked in. I put it in a bag in my pocket, but Mom must have done the laundry and washed my jeans."

Sarah rubbed lotion on her feet. "Well, I need more evidence than scratches on the door. You have to admit, this is pretty hard to believe. Did these people of yours say if they'd be coming back?"

"I told you, they didn't talk to me. How am I supposed to know if they'll be back? And there *is* more evidence. I swept the rest of the silver stuff off the floor and put it in a garbage bag. The only problem is, the bag's buried in the trash. But I can dig it out. We can get it right now."

"It's too late. Besides, Mom and Dad will wonder what we're doing. You can get it first thing in the morning."

Timothy expelled a long sigh. He had counted on the evidence to impress her. "Sarah, have you ever heard of the ides of March?"

"Sure, in *Julius Caesar*." She ran a brush through her hair and gathered it up into a ponytail. "Why?"

"Oh, nothing important—just something the Clapper said, that's all."

"Do you think they'll come back? And what did they mean about the Dark?" Sarah glanced over her shoulder at the curtained window.

"I don't know, but it reminded me of one of Clapper's stories." Timothy picked at a loose thread on the blanket. "We could try another experiment: open the door and see if they'll come back."

He looked up to gauge Sarah's response.

She raised her eyebrows.

She hadn't written him off completely, he thought. Sarah really was an okay sister.

"I'm going to assume this actually happened and it wasn't a dream or something," Sarah said.

"It did."

She nodded. "Remember that gallery opening where Mom is showing paintings in a couple of weeks? That's when we can try your experiment again. With both of us home, we won't need Mrs. Clapper. Now, get out of my room. I want to sleep." She slid down under the covers. As Timothy left, she called out, "And I want to see that garbage bag in the morning."

UNDESIRABLES

THE MORNING STARTED OFF badly. Timothy had never paid attention to the trash schedule, but it seemed they picked up garbage early, very early, Monday mornings. So when he and Sarah hurried out to the driveway, all they found was an empty can.

Timothy insisted on showing Sarah the evidence in the flower beds, but the paw prints, according to Sarah, could have been left by any very large dogs. Deflated again, Timothy had left for school without breakfast.

"Hey, Timothy!" Kenny Anderson was already at the bus stop, his trombone case resting against one leg. "We've got a band concert tonight. Are you coming?" He ran his tongue across his new braces.

Timothy shrugged. The bus rides to and from Enterprise Middle School were not his favorite times of the day. In fact, the twenty minutes seemed interminable now that Sarah rode an earlier morning bus to take French classes. For the first time, he was forced to find a seatmate. At least Kenny got on at the same stop, which gave Timothy someone to talk to while he waited, but Kenny was considered as much of a nerd as

Timothy. Once on the bus, they followed the unspoken rule of separating and searching for empty seats. Because they were one of the last stops on the route, every available seat had at least one other person already in it. Timothy dreaded the inevitable eye roll from the older kids—or worse, their condescending sneers.

As they climbed up the steps of the bus, Steve, the ponytailed bus driver, greeted Kenny and Timothy with a hearty "Morning, boys!" and the doors shut with a groan behind them.

Jessica Church sat in the front seat with Tina Salcedo. Jessica always sat in the very front, which as everyone knew, was the second-most desirable spot on the bus. The most desirable spot was the back, but that was the special province of the eighth-grade boys. Timothy tried to slink past Jessica without being seen, but this was impossible. Jessica had curly brown hair; round hazel eyes; a small, perfectly shaped nose; and breasts. Several of the seventh-grade girls had magically changed shape during the last few months, while everyone else was going about their daily business. The girls had transformed into different beings who talked about makeup, clothes, and boys, giggling in a way that let you know you were excluded from their discussion. Jessica made Timothy extremely nervous.

"Brain boys have arrived. How are the alien implants doing?" Jessica smirked. This sent Tina off into a fit of giggles. Tina, Timothy noticed, had somehow missed the transformation, but she wore an enormous amount of jewelry and black fingernail polish to compensate.

Fortunately, there was a seat open halfway back in the bus.

Unfortunately, it was right in front of Justin and Trevor, the sixth-grade spit-wad kings. Timothy pulled up his sweatshirt hood and prepared himself for another day of school, that alien planet where he had difficulty even breathing the air. The other inhabitants knew a secret language that he could never master. It was a certain way of joking, of moving, of carrying your head, a code he could not crack, and this was strange because Timothy James could break almost any real code he had ever encountered. It was just this human code that gave him problems.

At school, Timothy headed straight for the library. Twenty minutes until the first class. If he hurried, he could see if the new book on magic tricks was in. He'd been practicing the ones he knew on Sarah, but her cooperation came at a high price, usually taking her turn at cleaning the kitchen.

"Timothy, just the person I was hoping to see. Look what we got in." Mrs. Goldberg, the school librarian, held up a glossy new hardcover. *Chaos Theory.*

"Thanks." Timothy tucked it under his arm and looked for an open chair. No one bothered you if you were reading. Teachers found reading an acceptable activity and never interrupted you with pep talks. Even other students ignored you for the most part. Books were like a magic invisibility cloak.

As he made his way to the last open chair, Jessica and a large eighth-grade boy rounded the stacks. The boy raced Jessica to the chair, trying to pull her into his lap.

"Don't, Brian!" Jessica squealed, and then she caught sight of

Timothy with his bulging backpack and *Chaos Theory* displayed promi-
nently under his arm.

"Nerd alert! Nerd alert!" She pointed one glittery fingernail in his
direction. Several heads turned to watch. Brian threw his head back,
guffawing so loudly that his baseball cap fell to the floor. Timothy could
hear snickering spreading like fire as he stood clutching the oversized
book, wishing he could sink right through the floor and out of sight.

Now was the time for retreat, he told himself, a dignified retreat.
Don't let them smell fear or shame, ever. His legs wobbled. He stumbled
awkwardly to the back of the reading room and sank to the floor. Sitting against the wall, his face prickled with heat. He opened the book as
a shield. For a few minutes, the words squiggled on the page like snakes
refusing to come into complete focus. When the letters formed more conventional shapes, he found himself reading a definition:

> *Chaos theory is finding the underlying order in random data or*
> *events. Just a small change in initial conditions can potentially result*
> *in huge transformations.*

Underlying order in random events . . . What if there was no underlying order? Timothy wondered. What if random was just, well, random?
He forgot about his recent humiliation as he puzzled over the last few
days. Maybe there was a pattern that he couldn't see in the series of
random events happening in his own life. But no matter how hard he
thought, he still couldn't see one.

WISHES

THAT NIGHT, SARAH AND TIMOTHY sat in their pajamas on the slope of the roof under a wide band of starlit night. It was their favorite place, right outside Sarah's bedroom window, the one place where they could talk in absolute privacy.

Sarah's quilt was tucked up around them, but they could still feel the last bite of winter right through the blanket, and they huddled close for warmth.

"That's Orion's Belt, and over there is Betelgeuse." Timothy held his flashlight over the star chart.

"It doesn't look like a belt to me," said Sarah. "It looks like part of the Big Dipper. Did you know that you can have a star named after you? A girl in my class got a star named for her on her birthday. It came with a certificate, and everything said 'Amanda Jane' on it. Somewhere out there is a star named Amanda Jane Robbins."

"That's crazy. Stars shouldn't be named after people. Stars don't have human names."

"What kind of names should they have, then?"

Timothy thought seriously for a while. "Cold names, faraway names like Trillium or Evealene."

"Timothy, did you wish on the first star tonight? I did. I wished I could be Clara this year in *The Nutcracker.*"

Timothy shook his head.

"Well, wish something now. What do you wish?"

Timothy didn't take long to answer, and when he did, Sarah was surprised by the sincerity of his voice. "I want to be wolfproof."

She knew that this was not a time to laugh. "What do you mean 'wolfproof'?"

"Well, wolves are dangerous beasts."

"Go on." Sarah thought she knew where this was heading. After all, it was her bed that Timothy used to visit after one of his bad dreams.

"Wolfproof, so that I wouldn't have to dream about them anymore. I could look wolves right in their fierce eyes and tame them. But it's more than that. You know how when something is waterproof, it's resistant to water? The water just beads up and runs off?" Sarah nodded. "Well, I want to be *resistant* to scary things. I want to be brave."

"That's a weird wish. Most people wish for *things* that they want or for lots of money," was all Sarah said.

"Well, I'm not very brave. I'm tired of having wolves in my dreams, chasing me, and I don't want to worry about their teeth," said Timothy, remembering the mat of paw prints in the flower beds. "But then, I'd also like to fly, and I really wish I was taller. I hate being one of the shortest kids in seventh grade."

"I think one wish would be all we'd get," Sarah replied. "I'd want to be the best ballet dancer in the world, and dance in New York, and have everyone throw roses at my feet."

Timothy nodded. He felt slightly disappointed that her wish had nothing to do with pirates, but he could understand wanting to do something very well. If he was that good at something, anything, then people like Jessica Church would respect him. He might even be able to sit on the backseat of the bus.

"The gallery opening is in two weeks and we can try your experiment again when the parents are out of the house. I just wish it was sooner," Sarah said.

Timothy looked thoughtful. "I went online and looked up the horned man."

"And?" Sarah knew it was pointless to hurry Timothy along when he wanted to explain something, but she often tried.

"There are lots of horned men in different mythologies from different countries. Cernunnos and Herne are both from Celtic mythology, Pan is Greek, and then there's Pashupati and he's Hindi. They're all hunters, but I'm not sure what exactly they hunt. Herne and Cernunnos hunt with dogs. So maybe our horned man is British. I don't know about the others. Some of them were even worshipped."

"So, why was he at our house?"

Timothy shook his head. He could still hear the horned man's rumbling voice. "He was looking for prey. He asked the pale man who the prey was."

"What prey could be in our house?"

Timothy was silent.

"Don't be ridiculous. Why would anyone want to hunt you? Tell me again what the pale man said."

Timothy's voice cracked. "He said, 'It remains to be seen.'" But Timothy didn't tell Sarah the thing that was bothering him the most. The way the pale man had looked directly at him before he left.

✛ ✛ ✛

Sarah scooted closer to him. "That doesn't mean he was looking for you." She looked back up at the sky. "How do we know when wishes come true? What if I do dance in the New York Ballet some day? The whole time I'll be wondering if it's because I wished it to happen or because I worked really, really hard to get there."

"Well, if you wished for something you couldn't get yourself, like pirate treasure, and you got it, I guess you'd be sure. How would I know if I was really wolfproof or if I just got braver because I got older?"

Sarah laughed. "Then we should stick to wishing for impossible things."

But Timothy wasn't ready to relinquish the thought. "Maybe part of wishing is that it makes it easier to keep going."

"What do you mean?"

"It's like when you hear a rumor about something. If you hear a rumor that there's a hidden treasure in your yard, you'll work harder to find it than if you just hope there is hidden treasure. Maybe our wishes are rumors of things we're supposed to do." And secretly Timothy hoped it was true, that he really was supposed to be brave, as long as he didn't have to do anything too difficult to prove it.

THE MAN IN
THE LIBRARY

T HE REST OF THE WEEK passed quickly between school, homework, and chores, but the mysterious visitors were never far from Timothy's thoughts. Sarah left the house Saturday mornings by nine for three hours of ballet practice, and he stayed behind, with a handful of chores to do. The lawn wouldn't need mowing yet, but he did have windows to wash and the garage to sweep out. Usually he hated these jobs, but today they gave him some uninterrupted time to think. He and Sarah had finally put a plan in place late last night, long after his parents had closed up the house and turned out the lights for the night.

Sarah had crept into his bedroom and curled up on the foot of his bed. "I think you need to go to the library tomorrow." She shook Timothy until he was fully awake and paying attention. "I went to the library website and wrote these down." She pulled a crumpled sheet of notebook paper out of her pajama pocket. "These books have more information about mythology and the horned man. This one looks the best." She pointed at a book about British mythology.

Timothy sat up, pulling the quilt up around his neck like a sack. "Okay. I'll go after I finish my chores, if you think it will help. I still want to know why they came here, and that won't be in any book. What if it never happens again?"

"Then I'll know you're crazy!" Sarah looked hard at Timothy. "If this is one of your jokes, I'll find a way to make you suffer for years." She yawned broadly and stood up. "I'm counting on you to get the information."

Saturday morning, after finishing his chores, Timothy found himself in front of the public library. He'd been going to the library for as long as he could remember, first to story time when he was quite young and then to get one of his prized possessions, his first library card. Since then he had been a regular visitor, but today was different. He was on a mission. He had supplies: a notebook, mechanical pencil, extra lead, a granola bar, Sarah's book list, and several computer printouts stuffed in his backpack.

He claimed a table near the reference section and spread out his notes. Sarah had listed three possible books, and his own research had turned up several others. First stop was one of the computer stations to confirm that the library carried the books he wanted. He was in luck; two of them were listed as checked in and on the shelf. One was checked out. The others were not listed in the library holdings, but might be available through interlibrary loans. He set off among the stacks to retrieve the two books. He was able to find the first one, but the second was in a different set of numbers entirely. In fact, that whole section of shelf seemed to be missing. Puzzled, he returned to the table with the one volume and began reading.

After thirty minutes, Timothy was sure that the book would be no help at all and pushed the volume away in disgust. He had also looked at several reference books, including an encyclopedia of British mythology. These were more useful, and Timothy took careful notes of any relevant information.

> *Herne, in legend a horned hunter and leader of the wild hunt, was a real huntsman associated with Windsor Great Park in England who was mortally wounded when protecting his master. He was saved from death when a strange magician named Urswick tied a stag's antlers to Herne's head. In return, Herne had to give up all his skills at hunting and woodcraft. Unable to live without hunting, Herne hanged himself and now rides through the park with a pack of hounds chasing his prey, the Bent, to the ends of the earth.*

Timothy changed his pencil lead, all the time wondering what these stories had to do with him. He knew nothing about hunting, had never heard of Windsor Great Park, and didn't believe in myths like the wild hunt. Still, the story made him uneasy. Who were the Bent? It was easy to imagine his horned visitor, with his roving eyes, chasing animals and humans across the sky with a pack of killer hounds . . . He closed the book with a snap.

Perhaps Mrs. Torres, the reference librarian, could direct him to the book he had been unable to find; she was very helpful when he needed information about sulfides for his science-fair project last spring. But the person behind the desk today, with his long, narrow face and shaggy hair, was someone Timothy didn't recognize. The nameplate just read: *Julian.* He was, Timothy thought, approachable. Not all people were, but Julian seemed as though he wouldn't mind being interrupted in the middle of whatever he was searching for on the computer.

"Excuse me. Could you help me find this book?" Timothy thrust the call number toward Julian. "Its shelf seems to be missing."

Julian looked up and raised one eyebrow until it was hidden by a thick lock of curling hair that had tumbled down over his forehead. Timothy thought he detected Julian's lips twitching as if he were about to smile, but he carefully looked at the call number and then at Timothy. "Oh, I see. Celtic mythology."

A low-pitched giggle Timothy would recognize anywhere broke the silence of the library. It was the giggle of Jessica Church, a sound he had heard too often and usually at his expense. What was she doing here on a Saturday? He felt his face flush tomato-red and turned away from the reference desk, muttering "Never mind" under his breath. He tried to slink away, but it was too late. Julian was already on his feet, saying, "If you'll just follow me." So Timothy followed, head down and examining the slate-gray carpet, desperately hoping that (a) the glow had disappeared from his face and (b) Jessica had not heard Julian's declaration of "Celtic mythology."

Julian led him between stacks of books, through the periodicals, past the audio books, to a far corner of the library. They stopped in front of a small, plain wooden door that Timothy had never noticed before. Over the door a bronze plaque read *Special Collections*. Jessica's giggle faded from his mind. His heart began to dance. An undiscovered, secret library room!

The small room was lined from floor to ceiling with wooden bookshelves, some so high that an oak ladder on rollers was needed to get the books down. In the center of the room were four empty library tables with wooden chairs. Timothy followed Julian into the small room. He was in the very heart of the library; he could almost hear the heartbeat of books. Two overstuffed chairs commanded opposite corners of the room, one empty, and one occupied by a man with a bristly brown mustache. He wore a blue sweater over a blue-striped shirt with blue pants and even, Timothy couldn't help noticing, electric-blue socks. He tried not to stare, but the very blueness of the man was so deliberate and startling that he could hardly pull his eyes away. He noticed with satisfaction that while everything else matched completely, the socks had a touch more green.

Julian was pointing to the labels on the shelves: "Architecture, Art History . . . What we have on the subject should be here." He indicated the mythology section. Timothy nodded, but Julian didn't move. The blue man cleared his throat and noisily flipped a page. Julian ducked his head and looked directly at Timothy. "Is this a school project?"

"No, not really."

"I thought not."

"I'm just kind of interested." Timothy again remembered Jessica and was glad she was nowhere in hearing range. Kids didn't just do research for the fun of it.

Julian seemed to be reading his mind. "Of course, if you want even more information you might talk with Mr. Twig over there. He's quite an expert on mythology." Julian paused. "And quite approachable as well." Again Timothy suspected that he was about to smile but at the last minute changed his mind. Julian quietly shut the door, leaving Timothy alone with the special books and the very blue Mr. Twig.

The book Timothy had been looking for was there on the shelf. He was able to get it down without using the rolling ladder, which he found disappointing. Immediately, he could see why the book was housed in Special Collections. The edges of the pages were gilt, and the pages themselves were thick and creamy. He closed his eyes and discreetly held the book near his face, breathing in the inky smell of it. Throughout the book were illustrations by various artists. Timothy pored over a delicate drawing by Arthur Rackham. He stared at the pictures for a very long time, imagining what it would be like to be able to draw that well. Then he remembered that he had a mission.

Flipping to the index, he located the section on Cernunnos. Once again Cernunnos was listed by various names, but it was the illustration of him that made Timothy catch his breath. Staring back at him from the lower corner of the page was the same bearded face, burning eyes, and curling hair that he had seen in his own house just a week ago. The same rack of antlers sprouted from the man's head, but the mouth was open wide with laughter. The caption underneath read *Herne, the Hunter.* And Herne was surrounded by a pack of wolflike dogs called the yell hounds. Timothy could tell that the dogs loved the hunt just as much as the laughing man and reveled in the pursuit of whatever they chased. He looked at their mouths bursting with sharp teeth and knew he would never want to be their prey.

The text said that Herne and his hounds pursued souls across the sky to the very ends of the earth. That any beast left untethered on the nights Herne rode would be driven mad or chased unto death. Timothy shivered; his arms prickled. In the corner, Mr. Twig noisily turned a page in his book. Suddenly, Timothy was very glad he was not alone in this heart of the library. When he looked up, he was almost sure he caught Mr. Twig staring at him over the rim of his silver reading glasses.

The text said Herne typically rode on May Day and again in the fall on Samhain, around the time of Halloween. Then why had he been in my house in March? Timothy wondered. And then his mouth grew dry. What if Herne was searching for his soul? Was Timothy *Bent?* He didn't want to read any more and shut the book with a firm thump. Mr. Twig cleared his throat and looked up.

"Had enough, have you?"

Timothy startled. "Excuse me?"

"I asked if you have had enough history for the time being." He looked directly at Timothy, and Timothy, managing to ignore the man's extreme blueness, stared back right into Mr. Twig's gray eyes.

"I wasn't reading history, just some mythology," Timothy replied.

"Same thing. Where do you think myths come from? History, of course."

"Myths are just stories people make up to explain the way the universe works." Timothy had known this ever since third grade, when he read all the Greek mythology books in the children's section of the library.

"Most people believe that, but I'm surprised you haven't seen through it. Did you know that every culture has some common elements in their mythology? Oh, they might call the creatures by different names, but the same things are at work. For example, almost every mythology has dragons—Chinese, British, Norse, even West African legend. Why do such common images exist across cultures and time if there isn't an element of truth?" He took a deep breath and his mustache bristled. "And 'little people,' as the Irish call them: faeries, sprites, and brownies, what have you. Obviously, there must be some reality behind that story. We just choose to lock them up in books because it's safer that way. Besides, we all have a very hard time believing that things now are not the way things have always been." And Mr. Twig shut his mouth with such finality that Timothy didn't know whether to respond or not.

It was certainly one of the most interesting conversations he'd had in a long while. The word *enigmatic* popped into Timothy's mind. It was a word he had just discovered and been longing to use. It seemed to fit Mr. Twig very well. He'd just decided to tell Mr. Twig about his strange visitors when the man rose from his chair and walked out the door.

"But—" Timothy snapped his pencil lead in frustration. Mr. Twig was a primary resource, and Timothy had missed his chance.

He hurried to the door. A small white rectangle on the seat of Mr. Twig's chair caught his eye. It was a business card embossed with gold letters: *Robert Twig, Professor Emeritus, Mythology*. A phone number and an e-mail address were listed. Timothy slipped the card into his pants pocket and checked his watch. Sarah would be home soon.

He was well beyond the periodical section and almost to the front door when he passed a table with a familiar-looking head bent over an open book. Jessica Church sat at one end of the long table, surrounded by a clutter of books. Timothy remembered their latest research assignment, a report about a U.S. state, but it wasn't due for another week. He walked quickly, hoping to sneak by the table without being seen, but Jessica stretched and raised her head just as he passed. He felt himself shrink into his jacket and despised himself for it.

"Oh, hi." Jessica looked up in surprise.

"Hi," he muttered.

"You're in the wrong section. Nerds are under *N*."

Timothy slouched deeper in his jacket and kept walking. Didn't she ever let up?

"Tim, wait."

He paused.

"Have you started the state project yet?" She looked at him with a small furrow between her eyebrows.

He wondered if it was a trick question. "No, it's not due for another week."

"Yeah, well, I thought I might get a head start." She looked slightly embarrassed. "Don't tell anyone."

Timothy remembered that Jessica was the only other person in their middle school to pass the state math challenge. But being smart definitely wasn't considered cool. "What state do you have?"

"Rhode Island. My dad was born there."

"I've got North Dakota, but I don't know anyone who's ever lived there. I haven't started yet."

"So, why are *you* here, then?"

He had been hoping to avoid that question. "Looking up some information for my sister."

"What kind of information?"

Now Timothy frowned. Why did she care? "Nothing important."

Jessica bit a fingernail. "Never mind." She didn't continue.

His backpack slipping off one shoulder, Timothy stood awkwardly. He didn't know what to say next. "Well, bye."

Jessica looked down, but as Timothy walked away, he was sure he heard her say, "Good job on the chess tournament."

Timothy shrugged. He thought no one but other nerds ever paid attention to the chess scores. He and Jessica had just finished a conversation about normal things like school projects, and still he felt awkward. Maybe it was because they had never had a conversation before that didn't leave him feeling humiliated. His hand slipped to the card in his pocket. Mr. Twig's number was still there. Timothy wasn't sure which event was more surprising, the conversation with Mr. Twig or his exchange with Jessica.

As Timothy walked toward the door, his notes safely stowed in his pack, he noticed that Julian had left the reference desk. Even his name card was gone. Mrs. Torres was there, busily thumbing through a catalog.

✛ ✛ ✛

Sarah sat on her bedroom floor, bandaging her right foot. It was the second time she had lost a toenail in the last month. Timothy couldn't bear to watch. Her feet were long and knobby, red and sore. Ballet had made goblin's feet of them, he thought. The audience watched dancers gliding across the stage as if it were no effort at all, but Timothy knew their feet hurt and that dancers sweated just like other athletes. At least, he thought, pirates had decent feet. He noticed with satisfaction that the Jolly Roger still hung on Sarah's bulletin board, although now surrounded by a flurry of dance pictures. Two long-stemmed red roses hung above them, dried and desiccated mementos of a recital.

"Hold this." Sarah thrust a wad of gauze into Timothy's hands. "Put it right here against the toe." She began to wind tape around her foot to hold the toe in place. "Tell me again what that book in Special Collections said."

Timothy sighed. They had been over this already. He had shown Sarah his notes, told her about the color-coordinated Mr. Twig, but left out any mention of his encounter with Jessica. Now she insisted on going over every detail meticulously, in case he had forgotten something important.

"That's what detectives do in books. They make witnesses repeat their stories for accuracy, in case it jogs their memories."

"There was a picture of Herne in the book. He definitely was the horned man that was here, in our living room. In the picture, he had his dogs with him, big white wolflike dogs with red eyes." He didn't know how to explain that even in the picture the hounds' ears glowed transparently. "They were hunting." His voice faltered there, and Sarah looked up.

"Okay, what bothered you about the picture? Was it that the dogs looked like wolves?"

"They hunt souls across the sky. The souls of traitors." Timothy felt the same sense of dread in his stomach when he said these words as when he first read them. He thought of Scrabble and the word *anxiety* with its lovely eight-point *x*. "I'm not sure whose souls they hunt or why, but one of the books said something about traitors." He stuffed his hands in his pockets. "Wait a minute! The Twig man left this." Timothy pulled out the crumpled business card from the lint of his pocket.

"Why didn't you show this to me right away?" Sarah snatched the card from his hand.

"I forgot about it."

Sarah nodded with satisfaction. "Good thing I made you explain it all again."

Timothy held his tongue while she continued. "We'll have to call him. He must have left it for you to find."

"Maybe we should just forget about it all, pretend it never happened." Timothy hated calling people he didn't know.

"I'll call him tomorrow," Sarah said decisively. She had finished bandaging her foot and did a few hamstring stretches for good measure. "I think we should do it soon, before he has time to forget you. Let's see what happens when Mom and Dad are at the gallery opening. We might have more to tell him."

"I think we should set up everything just like last time. I want to see if this experiment is reproducible." But Timothy hoped his sister didn't hear the hesitation in his voice as he worried about what exactly Herne did with souls and why the pale man was stealing *his* light.

THE GIRL ON THE LAWN

HICH DO YOU THINK? The first one is maybe too loud. This seems more suited to a gallery opening." Timothy's mother held a flowing black blouse in front of the lime-green shirt she was already wearing and peered into the living room mirror. Sarah sat perched on the sofa arm, her brow furrowed in concentration.

"Elegant . . . You want to look elegant yet artistic, and the black one does." She nodded with a certainty that amazed Timothy. Where had she learned this secret language, this strange assurance? He looked at her thin shoulder blades protruding through the back of her sweater as if they were the beginning of wings. He would never have thought to offer his mother the word *elegant* to help make her decision. *Elegant* was only an eight-point word in Scrabble, unless you could command a double- or triple-scoring letter space. Timothy thought hard: *stylish*. The same number of letters but worth thirteen points. He could see the warm toffee-colored tiles spread across a table and pictured being able to hand them to his mother as a gift to speed her departure.

The magic word seemed to work. His mother cast one more anxious glance at the mirror and then disappeared into the bedroom, murmuring, "If you really think so," as she shut the door behind her. At the same moment, their father walked in, adjusting his tie. "Time to go! Elizabeth! Don't want the famous artist to be late for her show!"

Timothy checked his watch. He predicted it would be at least ten more minutes before his parents were safely out the door. Sarah seemed to be waiting calmly, but his insides turned crazy somersaults. They had gone over their plan in detail, but what if something went wrong? What if the horned man came again, peering through the doorway, searching for Timothy's soul, or what if the snuffling pack of hounds broke into the house? Timothy fidgeted and scratched his back. Maybe this wasn't the best idea. On the other hand, it was the only way he could make sure Sarah believed him. It had taken quite a bit of convincing to get his parents to agree to leave them home alone.

"We won't be too late. You're sure you'll be all right?" His mother's anxious gaze scanned the room as if checking for potential threats. The black sleeves of her blouse floated gauzily as she reached out to give them both hugs. Timothy thought, *sophisticated*, more letters than *elegant*, and was about to add up the points when he realized that his father was addressing him.

"Remember that Sarah is in charge. What she says goes. You've got our cell phone number, right?"

"Of course we do. You need to go or you're going to be late," Sarah replied firmly. And then, in a swirl of perfume and aftershave, they were out the door.

Sarah collapsed in the rocker. "I thought they'd never leave. What time is it?"

"Don't worry, we have a little while before it gets dark."

"Good, because I need to find the camera."

Timothy looked at her in alarm. "The camera? I never said anything about taking pictures!"

"We need a record of them . . . *if* they come." Sarah already had her head buried in the nearest cupboard, rummaging through binoculars, old umbrellas, and crumpled winter scarves.

"I don't know if we should take pictures. Maybe they wouldn't like it. Besides, it will skew the experiment. I didn't have a camera last time. I thought that maybe we should just try talking to them." Timothy felt the somersaults begin again and sat down in the middle of the floor. "Besides, I wouldn't want to do anything to upset the horned man."

Sarah pulled her head out of the cupboard long enough to fix him in her gaze. "We need evidence. You should know that with your obsession for the scientific method. Besides, talking to them would change the experiment, too. Here it is, the digital one!"

"Okay," Timothy agreed reluctantly. "We need to be on the stairs."

Sarah aimed the camera at him and snapped a trial shot. "Battery is still good. Now we wait."

Timothy surveyed his ordinary living room in his ordinary house, and he wondered once again why anyone would want to come and explore here. A polished wood entryway with a coat rack opened onto the living room with a blue-gray rug, striped couch, the leather recliner and tall white bookcases flanking a fireplace. In the corner was an old upright piano that his mother played sometimes when she was thinking up a new idea for her art. It was just like any of a hundred other living rooms in a hundred other houses. Why choose theirs?

+‡+

As soon as it was dark, Timothy opened the front door. Overhead, a thin slice of moon floated like a pale melon wedge. More than anything, he wanted Sarah to see what he had seen. He'd confront the silver girl and the pale man.

He sat next to Sarah on the stair landing and pulled a crumpled paper out of his pocket. The horned man Herne, or Cernunnos, had more names than Timothy could remember. But in every account he was wild and unpredictable. Timothy focused on feeling wolfproof.

Sarah breathed over his shoulder. "Who do you think will come first?" The camera was stuffed into the pocket of her carpenter's pants, and she sat curling and uncurling her pink-polished toes.

They waited for fifteen minutes.

Timothy checked his watch. Half an hour had crept by. Nothing.

He willed the door to open wider. He could feel Sarah's patience stretched tightly like a wire about to snap. Even snarling hounds would be better than silence. "Let's wait just a little longer."

"Okay, you got me. I fell for it this time. Why do I always believe you?" She unfolded her legs to stand.

"Wait!" Timothy grabbed her arm. "Not all experiments are reproducible. There are anomalies. Just because you don't see anything now—it doesn't mean it didn't happen before." He could hear the note of desperation in his own voice and cringed.

"I can't believe that I wasted my time this week looking up answers for your stupid mythology questions." She stood.

Timothy jumped up and blocked her from going down the stairs. "Have I ever lied to you before about anything important?"

Sarah gave him a long, slow look. "No. But there's always a first time. Look—maybe you really think something happened. Maybe you dreamed it. But things like you described don't happen in real life. They happen in movies or in books. Sometimes I wish life was more exciting, too."

"*I didn't make this up!*" His words exploded. "Quit being so, so . . . condescending!" He hated the way she talked down to him. Even worse, he hated that Sarah, who always believed him, was questioning his credibility.

"That does it. I tried to be nice to you. I'm going to watch TV. Don't bother me unless there's a horned man in the living room."

She pushed Timothy aside and stomped down the stairs, flipping on the light at the bottom.

Timothy stopped short of punching his fist in the wall. Sarah was the one person he could say anything to. She should know he'd never deliberately mislead her. He ran down the stairs and slammed the front door closed.

What if she was right? What if he had invented the whole episode? Timothy leaned against the door. Was it possible to imagine hearing an entire conversation? He puzzled over the pale man's last words, "The light will call him to me." Had the man been talking about him? He didn't feel drawn anywhere.

After two hours on the computer, he was still angry. He rattled around the house and ignored Sarah in the den. Outside, an owl trilled. One of the living room windows was open. Timothy tugged on the raised sash. The window was stuck. Beyond, the yard was a dark expanse.

And in that darkness, someone was humming.

Timothy stuck his head out the open window. A flicker of movement at the edge of the lawn caught his eye. A girl's silhouette.

His breath came faster. She was watching the house. A faint glow surrounded her. It was her, he was sure of it—the silver girl from the other night. He ran to the den.

"The girl's on the lawn! The one who was in our house."

Sarah looked up from the television. Her face was icy. "Timothy, stop it."

"Now. You have to come now! Please!"

She looked away.

Timothy grabbed her by the arm.

"Ouch! I said—" Sarah paused.

Timothy's breath came in great gulps.

Her face softened. "Okay. Show me."

Timothy prayed the girl was still there as he dragged Sarah out to the porch.

Sarah peered into the dark. "Timothy! You're right! There's a girl staring at our house. And she glows!" she whispered.

"Told you!"

Headlights swung into the drive.

"It's Mom and Dad." Timothy's voice trembled. "They can't come home now!"

The car doors slammed. The headlights died.

"Timothy, Sarah, what are you doing outside? Is everything all right?" their father called.

Timothy stared across the black, empty lawn.

"Fine. Everything's just fine," Sarah said, and shot Timothy one of those looks, the kind that meant "Play along."

✣ ✣ ✣

Star Girl ran her fingers through her hair and wondered how humans could stand to live in such a crowded place. She looked longingly back up at the sky and thought of cold, black nights, the vast emptiness of space, and her sisters singing in the moonrise. Humans called Electra and her sisters the Pleiads. People made up stories about them, but the stories never captured the whole truth. Electra's job was to bear witness to the events that would soon unfold. She had been on earth for one cycle of the moon, watching and waiting. She had witnessed the Greenman and Herne's visit to the boy's house. She'd heard their conversation, and returned to watch the house night after night, but there had been nothing more to observe.

Now there were only several weeks until May 1 of human time: Beltane, the spring fire festival. Human time was linear and very confusing, not at all like time as she knew it, which was more like water pouring off a tabletop, flowing in all directions at once.

✝ ✝ ✝

With each hour, the Greenman's movements had become stiffer. It was difficult to hold objects; he could no longer button his coat. His skin was changing, growing rough and peeling like sycamore bark. It was time to return to the forest, to his favorite clearing under the hornbeam tree. The dogwoods would be in bloom now, blossoms large and as white as his hand.

This was always the most difficult part, knowing what was to come. How he longed for the rustle of leaves, the birds sorting through his hair, the feel of the earth itself rising in his veins. Best to be gone from the town before anyone could notice how wooden his voice had become. It was as strained as the voice of a creaky old man. Best to be gone before his joints sealed.

DO YOU BELIEVE IN EVIL?

TIMOTHY AND SARAH rode the bus across town to an unfamiliar neighborhood. Every Sunday afternoon, their mother painted and their father golfed. When their mother had asked where they were going, Sarah patiently explained that Timothy was interviewing a professor of mythology for a project and that she was going along to keep an eye on things.

It wasn't really a lie, Timothy reasoned. They *were* going to meet a professor of mythology. Still, their mother had insisted on talking to the professor on the phone and writing down his address. Mothers were not conducive to the detection process.

Sarah barely spoke during the ride across town. She stared out the window and absently drummed her fingers on her knee. Timothy's mind wandered back to the library and his only real conversation with Jessica. He liked her better when she was alone. Of course, *tolerated* was a better word than *liked*; it was worth ten points if you could play off an *e* and *d*. *Enjoyed* would be even better, but that was stretching his intent. He couldn't quite say that he enjoyed Jessica. She had even looked different last Saturday—no jewelry and her curly hair pulled back tightly in a ponytail. Jessica was smart, he knew, and somehow in the library, away from school and surrounded by books, she seemed less dangerous.

Mr. Twig's street was lined with old ash and maple trees. The houses were set far back on their lots, often hidden behind hedges and over-grown shrubs.

"He's at number twenty-eight," Sarah said for the fourth time as she twisted the golden chain at her throat round and round in her fingers. Timothy had come prepared. His notebook was tucked under his arm and he had two mechanical pencils, each filled with fresh lead, peeking from the pocket of his shirt.

Number twenty-eight was a gray-shingled house with narrow bay windows and a bright green door. A hedge of laurel separated the house from the street, and an iron gate opened onto the brick path.

"Now it's time to walk the plank," Sarah cackled as she swung open the gate.

Mr. Twig took a long time to answer the door. Timothy thought about how easy it would be to turn around and flee. But before he could act on his thoughts, the door swung inward and there stood Mr. Twig, dressed from head to toe in shades of brown. Timothy caught Sarah's eye as if to say, "See, what did I tell you?"

But Sarah had already extended her hand. "Sarah Marie Maxwell," she said very distinctly.

Mr. Twig's nose twitched as he offered a hand freckled with age spots. "Robert Twig, at your service. Won't you and Timothy please come in? I was delighted you called."

He led them into a small, dim living room. A large, dark piano sat in one corner, brooding over the rest of the formal antiques. The chairs were the type that never looked comfortable to sit in and always made you think about your posture. Two things immediately caught Timothy's eye. The first was the rug. It was woven into a dense mat of flowers, with colors so deep and rich that he felt he could reach his hand in and pull up a bouquet. The second was a tapestry that covered much of one wall. In it, a young woman stood with her hand on a unicorn's mane.

A tray with glasses of lemonade and small plates of cookies rested on the coffee table, but Timothy felt like his mouth was stuck shut. Sarah's obviously was not. She balanced her plate of cookies on her lap, held her lemonade, and talked—all at the same time.

"We are hoping that you might be able to give us some information about mythology," she said.

"What type of mythology?"

"British, I think. Herne, the hunter, and Beltane and—"

Mr. Twig leaned back in his chair. "That is most definitely British, but there have been hunter stories in a number of cultures." He rubbed his hands together and nodded his head. "But let's start with Beltane."

Timothy could almost see the older man start to glow as he began to lecture. It was like being in school, but more interesting, Timothy thought as he pulled out a mechanical pencil and opened his notebook.

"The ancients in Ireland and Britain celebrated the four fire festivals —Beltane, Samhain, Imbolc, and Lughnasadh. Beltane, May first, was one of the most important of these festivals, a welcoming of spring and life. It's coming up in a few weeks. It was a time for reveling." And then he looked somber. "Despite the death. There is always a death."

Timothy looked at Sarah. He didn't like the way Mr. Twig had tacked death onto his explanation, but before he could ask anything about it, Mr. Twig was talking again. "You've heard of Dionysus, haven't you?"

Timothy nodded. "Yes, but about the death—"

"That's a story for another time."

Timothy could tell by the finality in Mr. Twig's tone that for some reason the subject was closed.

"What do you know about Dionysus, eh?"

Timothy could answer this question easily. "He's the Greek god of wine and revelry."

"Right. His presence could drive a whole community mad. People would take to wandering off into the forest for days. But most people haven't heard of another god associated with him: Cernunnos." Here Professor Twig stopped, sipped some lemonade, and stared at Timothy from under his curling eyebrows. "He's lord of the forest in Britain. People used to leave carved heads in doorways on Beltane in his honor.

The heads were decorated with flowers and antlers. That's where we get our tradition of leaving flowers for May Day."

After hearing "antlers," Timothy couldn't focus on anything else Mr. Twig was saying. A question leapt from his mouth. "Antlers? Why antlers?"

"Because Cernunnos is one of the Celtic stag men! He has antlers growing from his head like a stag. Sometimes he gets confused with Herne, the leader of the wild hunt. I suspect you may have heard of Herne."

Now he had Timothy's full attention. Sarah, too, leaned forward in expectation, almost spilling the second serving of cookies from her lap. "What's the wild hunt?"

"The wild hunt usually happens in the fall on Samhain—Hallow-een, as you know it—and in the spring on Beltane. But Herne's been known to ride at other times, before a great catastrophe or significant event. He rides across the sky with his pack of Gabriel hounds, fierce-looking white beasts. It's said that any animals left out on those nights go mad. The hounds will pursue them to the ends of the earth. But surely you've felt it in the fall? Nights when the winds fly, there's a sound of baying like wild geese overhead, and there's a touch of something in the air that sends a shiver down your spine."

Timothy knew exactly what Mr. Twig was talking about. He'd felt it mostly in autumn, when the season was about to change, the feeling of something about to happen. And he shivered in the warm room.

"Do you believe in evil?" Mr. Twig paused to let the question settle like dust. The sun moved behind a cloud and a shadow was cast across the floor. He continued, "People tend to fear the wrong things. You see, Herne's not malevolent; he's a hunter and he hunts. But Balor of the one eye—that's another matter entirely."

The name Balor roamed around in Timothy's head like something he should know, but it found no place to settle. He was sure he had heard it somewhere before.

"Is he more frightening than Herne?" Sarah asked.

Mr. Twig stared off into space and rested his chin on his fingers. "You've asked the wrong question. He doesn't always look frightening. Sometimes Balor is very beautiful, and he's a master craftsman. Sometimes he changes form entirely and becomes an animal, a shape-shifter, but that's another subject. The question you should ask is, '*If* he's evil . . .'"

"Is he?" Timothy asked.

Mr. Twig didn't hesitate. "Oh, yes, and he is never true. Remember that—evil is never true." And he tapped his index finger on one bony knee for emphasis.

"What does he want?" Sarah asked.

"Balor?" Mr. Twig gave a dry chuckle. "What we all want at times— our own ending to the story. He wants power, but he is already powerful. Like all emissaries of the Dark, he wants to destroy the Light, to take truth and bend it to his will. And unlike most people, he is not bound by time. But it's wiser not to talk about him too much. The Dark has eyes and ears everywhere. And Balor, himself, can show up in the most unexpected places."

The Dark. The horned man and the pale man had talked about the Dark. Timothy closed his eyes, trying to remember their exact words—something about the hunt riding because the Dark was on the move again. And the pale man had used another word, one Timothy had never heard before, *Filidh*. The pale man had vowed to protect the Filidh.

When Timothy opened his eyes, Mr. Twig was leaning forward, his bright eyes fastened on Timothy. "How else can I help you?"

The shadow had passed. Timothy shifted in his chair. "What is a Filidh?"

"A keeper of the word and wisdom. A Filidh is an ancient title. It is hereditary, rather like a king or emperor. Filidhs are tasked with reminding people of the true stories, and in that way the Filidh is a guardian."

"But I've never heard of one before." Timothy looked at Sarah, and she shrugged her shoulders.

"A true Filidh is chosen. You don't hear of them much in this world anymore."

"In this world?" Timothy's voice came out in a squeak.

Before Mr. Twig could respond, Sarah voiced a question. "In the wild hunt, what are the dogs hunting?"

Again Mr. Twig lowered his brow. "Souls. Herne and his hounds hunt souls."

Timothy's voice was still tight. "Who are the Bent?"

"*The Bent* is an old term. It describes a person who is in the process of becoming more Dark than Light, who is *choosing* darkness over light." Mr. Twig's eyes shifted from Timothy to Sarah and back again. "Eventually, a person will become what he or she chooses."

✠ ✠ ✠

School. The last weeks of April limped slowly forward. Timothy was counting out the days until May 1. Daily he replayed Mr. Twig's warning that the wild hunt rode on Beltane.

On Tuesday morning, Timothy sat at a table in the corner of the commons with his friends before classes started. His group of friends was small: Jay and Caleb from the chess team and Gillian Oliver, who had been born in Holland. She spoke three languages and was captain of the chess team. Every now and then Gillian read out loud a particularly good line from the book she was reading. It really didn't seem to matter if anyone was listening or not. Jay and Caleb huddled over a computer magazine, arguing about the best way to maximize graphics on a small screen. But today, even they were irritating. Timothy had been up most of the night before, worrying about Herne and what he might want with his soul. Ever since his visit with Mr. Twig, Timothy's nights had been restless. In his dreams, the horned man returned with his pack of hounds.

Souls were not anything Timothy gave much thought to. When he was younger, his parents had started taking him and Sarah to Sunday school, but the concept of a soul never seemed adequately explained. Deep down, he assumed that everybody had one. But as to the old stories of people selling their souls to the devil or trading their souls for some unusual talent, well, he wasn't convinced. He had read somewhere of an experiment in the early 1900s that concluded that the weight of a human soul was twenty-one grams. But, as far as he knew, no one had ever scientifically verified a soul; it couldn't be seen, tested, or duplicated. So why did the thought of Herne hunting souls seem so terrifying? He was still stuck in the web of these sticky thoughts when he heard a voice over his shoulder.

"I know why you were at the library." Jessica Church sat down next to him. Today her hair was a cloud of ringlets with something that glittered all over her curls.

His friends backed away, far enough for safety but close enough to listen. They'd all been her victims at one time or another.

Timothy turned to look at her. "What did you say?"

Jessica lowered her voice so his friends wouldn't hear, but Timothy noticed that Caleb and Jay had stopped talking and were leaning in. "I said, I know what you were looking for at the library. The man at the reference desk told me."

This was the last thing Timothy wanted Jessica to have, ammunition against him. He certainly didn't want to discuss his research with her. What about his right to confidentiality? How could Julian the librarian give him away?

Jessica widened her eyes innocently. "I just told him that we were working on the same project, and I needed to know what part you had already looked up."

"Why do you care?" Timothy felt more annoyed than intimidated by her.

It took her a long time to respond, and then her voice was so quiet that Timothy almost missed the answer.

"Because of the note."

MYSTERIOUS LETTER

J ESSICA OPENED HER BINDER and slid a perfectly folded piece of blue paper from an envelope bearing her name. Timothy thought of the crumpled wad of papers in his binder and knew he was dealing with an altogether different species of person. A faint smell of something familiar rose from the paper as she unfolded it. It reminded him of the woods, damp and earthy. The penciled writing was small and cramped, as if the person writing had difficulty forming the letters. He made sure his back blocked the curious stares of his friends as he read.

Time out of time
the horned man rides
with the forest queen,
the Greenman dies,
the heavens bear witness,
the great wolf flies,
and Timothy James stands alone.

Timothy stared without speaking. The sight of his name on the pale blue page sent his heart racing.

"So what does it mean? Is it some kind of joke?" Jessica looked him directly in the eye.

Timothy stared back into the mosaic of green and brown in Jessica's eyes and almost lost his train of thought. "I have no idea."

"Then why were you looking up stuff about British mythology? And why is your name there?" The old belligerent tone crept into Jessica's voice.

"Tell me where it came from, and maybe we can figure it out. And keep your voice down unless you want everyone to hear." He glared over his shoulder at his friends until they reluctantly moved away. Then he pulled out one of his mechanical pencils and began copying the words on a crumpled piece of paper he pulled from his pocket.

"Well, that's what makes it so strange. It was just there with the rest of our mail. But the envelope didn't have any postmark."

"You didn't show it to anyone, did you?" Somehow Timothy knew that the strange poem was not intended to be read by just anyone.

"Of course not! I'm not that stupid! I picked up the mail. But I want to know how it got there."

"Did anything else strange happen that day?" Timothy asked casually and thought of his own unexpected visitors. Could they have come to Jessica's house, too? Was she testing him in some way?

She wrinkled her forehead. "No, nothing—unless you call my

great-aunt Rosemary strange. She comes to visit pretty regularly, but she wouldn't be writing mysterious poems. And it does have your name in it! So what's the deal?"

Timothy wondered just how much he should tell her. Maybe he could stall and talk it over with Sarah. He looked up at the clock and realized with relief that the bell was about to ring. "Look, I didn't write the note, but I might be able to find out more about it. I want to show my sister the poem. We've had some weird things happening at our place, too—" The bell shrilled. "I guess I'll have to tell you about them later." He shoved his copy of the poem into his front pocket and hefted his backpack off the floor. "Gotta go. Don't want to be late for class."

Jessica frowned and carefully refolded the blue paper, tucking it neatly in the envelope before slipping it in her binder. Timothy could tell she was curious about what else he had to say, but she didn't press him. Probably, he thought, because she didn't want to be seen walking with him to class.

✠ ✠ ✠

Math. Science. He puzzled over the poem through every subject until lunch. He'd come up with a few more questions about the note and decided he might even feed Jessica a little more information. But as soon as he walked into the cafeteria, he knew any communication would be impossible. Jessica and Tina sat at the table with the popular kids. Timothy walked past, making sure to avoid eye contact with them. It was a survival skill he had learned early. Andy, the tallest boy in the seventh grade, put his thumb and forefinger to his forehead in an *L* for "loser" just as Timothy passed. He thought he could hear Jessica's laugh above all the others, high, tinkling, and cold.

✛ ✛ ✛

On Thursday, an assembly was held in the gym during sixth period. Timothy tried to avoid pep assemblies whenever possible; the pushing, yelling crowds of students gave him a headache. He knew he was supposed to like the adrenaline rush as each grade tried to out shout the other grades. He wasn't sure he even knew what school spirit was. It had something to do with sports, winning, being the best. He thought of a *National Geographic* special he had watched as the members of a tribe shouted, shook spears, and banged on drums to frighten away evil spirits. He pictured the bleachers full of spear-shaking students and felt a little better. At least the school week was almost over.

Timothy walked as slowly as he could toward the gym, hoping for a seat at the edge of the crowd. In the general jostle of bodies, Jessica appeared at his side and whispered to him quickly, without ever making eye contact. "Come over to my house today at four. We need to talk, because you know something you're not telling me." And without waiting for an answer, she flowed on in the current of students carried toward the gym. Timothy ran his hand through his hair, took his glasses off, put them on, took them off again, and eventually stopped walking altogether. People like him were never invited to the homes of popular people. It was an unspoken rule; the way things were. He knew where she lived, definitely biking distance. But, whatever would he say one-on-one to Jessica Church?

Timothy crowded onto the edge of the nearest bleacher. His friends were scattered somewhere in the sea of bodies. As soon as he sat down, he realized he had chosen exactly the wrong spot.

"Did I just see you talk to Timothy Maxwell?" Tina's voice hovered high and sharp a few rows behind him.

Timothy's heart sank. He strained to hear Jessica's mumbled reply but couldn't catch it.

"No way! Timothy Maxwell wrote you a poem?"

Timothy closed his eyes in resignation, scrunching down as far as possible. Maybe nobody would notice him here.

"Was it a love poem? Read it to me!"

"It was a dork poem. I threw it away." Jessica's voice was clear and biting. "Pathetic what some people will do for attention."

Timothy hunched his shoulders as a volley of guffaws and whistles were launched from behind.

✠ ✠ ✠

By the time Timothy arrived at Jessica's on his bike, he was sweating. Anger and fear warred in his stomach, creating the same kind of knot he always got before giving a presentation in class. Why visit his tormentor? He'd said he would help her, and then she had lied to everyone about the note. She couldn't be trusted. He hated her. But he had to know about the poem. It was tied, he was sure, to the strange happenings at his house. And information was the most important thing.

Jessica, sitting on a rope swing, was waiting for him on the front lawn as if she had never considered that he wouldn't show up. This made Timothy even madder. He had decided on the way over to explain just enough about the mysterious visitors to keep her interested, get the information he needed, and then he'd be out of there. After dropping his bike on the grass, he walked straight up to her and began with, "This is what I know."

Jessica listened while the scowl on her face deepened. "I don't believe you. You're crazy." She scuffed the toe of her shoe into the lawn. "There are no people like that."

"I'm not making this up!" Timothy felt his voice crack in frustration.

"You don't believe in fairy tales and things you can't see. You're smarter than that!" she retorted.

He sat down on the grass next to the swing. "I believe in all kinds of things that I can't see. I can't see electricity, but I believe in it. And so do you."

"I'm not talking about the kind of things you learn in school."

"Okay. Are you scared of the dark?" Timothy asked.

"What do you mean?" A note of suspicion crept into Jessica's voice.

"Just what I said. Does anything in the dark scare you?"

Jessica twisted a long, brown curl between her fingers. "Not anymore. Maybe when I was a little kid, but all little kids are afraid of the dark."

"You'd walk through the graveyard on Hollis Hill by yourself, at night, without a light?"

She was frowning now. "So what's your point?"

"It's just that it's not an intellectually honest position to take. If you're afraid in the dark, it's because you believe that there's something scary there that you can't see, even if you only believe it until you turn the light on. And ghosts are definitely not something you learn about in school."

She ignored his explanation. "If you really saw these people, what did they want and why did they come to you?"

"You tell me. You're the one who got the note. You still didn't tell me how you got it." Timothy felt his confidence growing. So far, talking to Jessica had not been as bad as he'd feared.

She pushed off with one foot from the tree trunk and swung away from him in a slow arc. Her brown curls blew back from her face, and she didn't say anything at all as she swung back again.

For a moment, even though he despised her, Timothy thought Jessica looked almost pretty, with her wild hair flying behind her and her cheeks flushed in the breeze. The thought caught him off guard. He reminded himself of what she had said at school.

"I found it Monday. There was nothing special about that day at all except that Great-Aunt Rosemary came to dinner."

"Did she bring it?"

Jessica shrugged as she swung by. "It was just stuffed in the mailbox with all the other mail."

Now she was flying away from him again, her feet pointed up toward the sun. He thought he caught a glimpse of silver at her belly button as her flowered shirt rose above her waist. Was it pierced? He stood up and climbed onto the top rail of the fence that bordered the yard.

"Tell me about your aunt."

Jessica dragged one long leg through the grass to slow herself down. "Great-aunt, but not really. Her name's Rosemary Clapper, and she's an old friend of the family. I just call her my great-aunt. She's ancient and wouldn't write a note like that."

Timothy almost tumbled from the fence. "Clapper? I know her!"

"You do?"

"Yeah. She used to babysit us." Inwardly he cringed, hoping Jessica wouldn't guess how recent "used to" was.

"Really? Well, then, you know what I mean. A normal old lady."

Normal was not the word he would choose for Rosemary Clapper. Maybe *conventional*, seventeen Scrabble points. And yes, it did appear that Jessica had a ring in her belly button.

She noticed him staring and bunched her shirt higher. "Like it? Tina and I got them pierced, and I thought my mother was going to have a stroke. Now I think she's gotten used to it."

Timothy tried to pull his eyes away from the shine of silver against the creamy curve of her stomach and unexpectedly blushed. He needed to get the conversation back under control. "Is there anyone else who could have put the note in the mailbox?"

"No one. It has to be some kind of joke."

"Well, 'When you eliminate the impossible, whatever is left, no matter how improbable, is possible.' Sherlock Holmes said that." Timothy blushed again. Jessica was right. He was a nerd.

"I think we need to focus on what the poem means. It sounds like a riddle—that is, if you really didn't write it. Maybe you were just trying to get my attention," Jessica said with a smirk.

"You were a real jerk to say that I sent you a love note at school. I told you everything I know. If you don't want my help, just say so."

Jessica narrowed her eyes and then she looked away.

Timothy pointedly looked at his watch. It felt good to stand up to her. "Let's both think about it and try to come up with some ideas. I'll ask my sister—she's good at things like this." He picked up his bike. "For now, I wouldn't say anything to anyone else."

Jessica smiled and two dimples appeared. "Oh, I won't. They'd think I was crazy. Call me if you see those people again."

He wasn't quite sure if her last words were tinged with sarcasm.

THE HORNBEAM

FOR HUNDREDS OF YEARS, the hornbeam tree, *Carpinus betulus*, had ruled over his part of the forest. His weathered bark was fluted and muscular, gray and hard like iron. He was an imposing sight, sixty feet tall with a trunk at least nine feet around—not the tallest tree in the forest but the strongest and broadest. His branches flexed like well-muscled arms. He had seen five hundred Beltanes come and go. In all that time, the Greenman had come to the forest. Trees have their own way of telling time. Their leaves act as sensors for detecting changes in rainfall, in sunlight, in the temperature of the air. Their roots burrow into the soil, feed on the change of seasons, drawing cold nourishment in winter, sending sap flowing in spring.

And so Hornbeam was not surprised when the Greenman came limping stiffly to shelter under his wide branches. Already, leaves were curling from behind the man's ears. They were the new lime green of spring, almost translucent in the sun, and they wreathed his head like a mane. The man's fingers were thickening, growing scaled and hard like

Hornbeam's own bark. The next part, the tree knew, would be the worst: foliage bursting from the man's mouth and ears, his eyebrows shooting out viny tendrils. Hornbeam shuddered; the transformation was always so painful for these half-creatures. To be neither man nor tree was a terrible fate.

Sheltered under the great branches, the Greenman felt his coat split open down the back seam as his shoulders spread. Then the terrible rushing in his head began. Although he had been through this transformation many times before, he was never fully prepared for the scratchy feel of stems pushing up through his throat, out his ears. He writhed in pain. Soon, he would lose his human speech. Only when the sap ran fully through him would he be limber enough to move freely again. He shook his head, threw it back, and shouted with the last of his speech, "All things are made new!" The forest rippled with his words, waiting for time itself to burst into bloom, time out of time.

Hornbeam looked out over the length and breadth of his land. Spring is a festive time in the forest. Small leaves unfurl in every shade of green. Dogwoods show off their pink-and-white blossoms, and animals celebrate with new litters. The Greenman crouched in agony, waiting for the sap to run. Hornbeam listened carefully to the wind, alert for even a faint baying of hounds. They were a faint rumbling in the distance. A storm would arrive with them, but his leaves did not yet detect a drop in temperature or an increase in humidity. Below Hornbeam's branches, the Greenman trembled and shook. The tree knew, just as the Greenman did, that new life always required a death of some kind. Hornbeam bent low and soothed him noiselessly with his leaves.

✝ ✝ ✝

On the bus ride home from ballet, Sarah sat by the window and watched the familiar landscape of trees and houses pass by. She was thinking about Timothy and wondering if he had made any progress on the case. Sarah liked the phrase—"progress on the case"—and thought that maybe she should train to be a detective in case dancing didn't work out. It would definitely be less dramatic than being a pirate, but possibly just as lucrative. She cupped her chin comfortably in her right hand and imagined the life of a private eye. For a moment, she caught a glimpse of her own reflection in the window, yellow hair slicked back into a perfect bun; a small, tilted nose; and wide-spaced eyes.

She was startled from her daydreams when a figure on the sidewalk captured her attention. A girl, just a few years older than Sarah, stood looking up into a fir tree. Her white-blond hair hung past her hips in a single braid. Her long blue dress skimmed a pair of bare feet. She was so out of place on the residential street that Sarah turned to watch her. She had the uncomfortable feeling that she should know her.

Just then Mrs. Clapper walked out from one of the houses and began talking to the girl. Then Sarah knew: The girl standing on the sidewalk talking to their old babysitter was the girl Timothy had described. She was the girl who had come into their house with the pale man and Herne. She was the same girl Sarah and Timothy had seen watching their house.

If Sarah could get off the bus, she could find out more. In her excitement, she knocked over her backpack, spilling the contents across the floor.

"Clumsy," the bald man in the seat behind her muttered. Behind him, two little girls giggled. Sarah felt her face flush as she scrambled to collect an escaped water bottle and a tube of lip gloss. Even worse, her roll of foot tape began to unravel beneath the seat. The bus rumbled on without stopping. Sarah ducked under the seat to gather and rewind the tape. Why was Mrs. Clapper with Star Girl? And who was the girl, really?

THE HORNED MAN

I N T H E B L U S T E R Y land of the north, dark clouds dragged their bellies across craggy hills and storms brewed at a moment's notice, spring was always late, and sheep outnumbered people. Here, Herne, the horned man, lived with his dogs. In this remote land, the dogs could run fast and free, chasing one another along the mountain faces, their yaps and howls only part of an afternoon storm. But now their restless pacing and constant yapping stretched his nerves. They wrestled and rolled, nipping at one another's legs, a white mass of fur and haunting red eyes.

They annoyed him, but he understood them. He, too, longed for the hunt, to feel his horse move beneath him as the fields of spring spread out below. In the hunt was the only place he was content, stirring a storm and then riding the edge. Spring was coming, and they would ride. The Greenman had called him early and had promised that this would be an exceptional Beltane. A new Filidh would be tested.

Herne stood at the open door and lifted his face to the wind. He could catch a faint whiff of it now, the scent of quarry. Breathing deeply, he inhaled the scent of wild animals: deer, fox, and badger, as well as the different scents of domesticated cat and hound. And mixed in the wind was the distinctive odor of humans.

✞✞✞

Sarah exploded from the bus and ran, shedding hairpins across the lawn. She flew through the front door. "Timothy, I've got news! I've seen her!"

But unlike most afternoons, Timothy didn't appear from the kitchen, happily munching a snack, or come bounding down the stairs from his bedroom, book in hand. She dropped her backpack on the floor and listened to the rise and fall of muffled voices coming from the kitchen. Curious, she pushed open the door and found her mother seated with Mrs. Clapper, enjoying a cup of tea and some cake. The late-afternoon sun gilded the scene, and Sarah felt her stomach rumble. But how could Mrs. Clapper be here when she had seen her not twenty minutes ago with the girl?

"Sarah, look what Mrs. Clapper has brought by—some of her apple cake. Come have a piece." Her mother beamed up at her, and Sarah noticed a streak of cerulean blue smeared across one side of her nose. She must have been in the middle of painting.

Mrs. Clapper smiled welcomingly, and Sarah was sure she saw her eyes twinkling. Her senses prickled to full alert. It was time to be cautious like any good detective, sleuthing for all she could while not giving herself away.

"Sit with us, Sarah, and have some cake. You can tell me about your dancing classes," Mrs. Clapper said.

Sarah didn't need a second invitation. She poured herself a glass of milk and reached for a piece of cake. She felt her sore muscles begin to relax. As she ate, the conversation swirled around her. They were discussing neighbors who had moved away, and Mrs. Clapper's friend's operation. Nothing to take notes on, just normal grown-up conversation. Sarah licked the crumbs off her fork and pondered how to get Mrs. Clapper on a subject of more significance. She couldn't ask if Mrs. Clapper happened to know a star girl who trailed silver dust wherever she walked. Sitting here in her family's ordinary kitchen, listening to the two women talk, Sarah began to wonder if she had imagined what she had seen. The afternoon sun made her feel drowsy.

She turned toward Mrs. Clapper. "I thought I saw you this afternoon from the bus. You were talking to a woman in a beautiful blue dress." Sarah realized that she had interrupted the flow of conversation and caught a slight frown from her mother. Did she see a flicker of something in Mrs. Clapper's eyes?

"Well, you might have done. My niece has been visiting from out of town." She turned toward Sarah's mother. "She's always been one for interesting dresses. For a while, she was wearing only vintage clothes, but now I think it's long dresses. She never got over playing dress-up."

Sarah sighed. If only everything didn't sound so perfectly normal. She would need to try another tactic. But before she could form a question, the back door swung open and Timothy came in, red-faced, as if he had been running. Whatever he had been about to say died on his lips as he saw the group gathered around the table.

"Timothy, you're just in time for cake," his mother said, reaching for the cake knife. "I hope you enjoyed yourself at your friend's. What was her name?"

Timothy stared right at Mrs. Clapper. "Jessica. Jessica Church."

"Oh, my goodness—Jessica. I've known the Church family since before Jessica was born. She's always called me her great-aunt, and I'm as fond of her as if I was."

Sarah noticed that Mrs. Clapper's smile didn't reach her eyes. She was watching Timothy intently in the same way that Prank, their pumpkin-colored tabby cat, eyed squirrels just out of her reach. In fact, she could almost imagine a twitching tail. And perhaps strangest of all, Timothy smiled back smugly—not to mention, he had just spent the afternoon with a girl!

ADDITIONAL EVIDENCE

TIMOTHY CRUNCHED a large mouthful of cereal and looked at the clock. It was almost midnight, and he was starving. He seemed to be hungry all the time these days. Cereal was fast and always on hand. The upstairs hall was dark, and he didn't bother turning on the light. The sounds of his parents' voices had faded into sleep, but a bead of light shone out from under Sarah's bedroom door. He liked the house at night, when everything was hushed. When he was younger, he'd imagined objects taking on a life of their own after everyone was asleep, chairs and tables moving around the house, his toy soldiers and Legos staging battles on the dark field of his bedroom floor.

As Timothy padded across the hall in bare feet, he stumbled over something soft. It wiggled. He lost his balance. The cereal bowl flew up in the air, spattering the walls with milk. *"Meeoow!"* It was only Prank, waiting to get into Sarah's room. Timothy scooped up the bowl with its few remaining bits of soggy cereal, knocked on the door, and then burst into Sarah's room. Prank scooted in behind him.

"Shouldn't you be in bed? It's a school night." Sarah sat cross-legged in a pool of light on her bed. Around her were spread dozens of pictures and random scraps of colored paper. She was frowning over two shades of sheer green tissue paper.

"What about you? I was hungry."

"Well, don't wake Mom and Dad."

Timothy surveyed the mess in her room. Sarah was in the middle of another collage. One wall of her bedroom was a kaleidoscope of papers: yellows, reds, brilliant blues, and soft violets. Dressed in a white nightgown with her yellow hair loose on her shoulders, Sarah looked like a wingless angel. For a brief instant, Jessica's dark hair and mocking face passed before his eyes.

"Have you come to consult the master detective?" she said without looking up.

Timothy sailed sheets of red and yellow tissue paper to the floor as he cleared off a corner of the bed and climbed on. "You know Clapper has to be involved in everything that's been happening."

"That's obvious, Watson. She was with the suspect this afternoon. It's too bad I didn't get off the bus in time."

Timothy remembered that Sarah had been reading *The Hound of the Baskervilles* in school.

From under the bed Sarah pulled out a yellow notebook and flipped it open to the first page. "Tell me everything Jessica said."

When Timothy finished, she printed *Suspect #1: Clapper* in the notebook. Below, she made a bulleted list of evidence. "It's time to analyze the facts."

And she began to read out loud: "'Number one: She was babysitting the first time *they* appeared. Number two: She was seen with the star girl at her house. Number three: She claimed the girl is her niece. Number four: The mysterious letter came to Jessica when Clapper visited.'"

Sarah looked up. "Those are the facts, Watson."

"So, what do we do now, Holmes?" Timothy asked around a mouthful of the dregs of cereal left in the bowl.

Sarah bit her nails. "Question the suspect? But I think she's sly. Maybe we should spy on her first. In *The Hound of the Baskervilles*, Sherlock Holmes hid in a hut, watched the suspects, and took notes. Even Watson didn't know he was there."

"Maybe everything to do with the Clapper is coincidence." Timothy used the edge of the sheet to wipe his mouth.

"'The world is full of obvious things which nobody ever observes,'" Sarah quoted. "That's from *Hound of the Baskervilles*, too. I say we need to look for the little things that will give her away." She carefully lifted the drying sheets of paper and placed them on the floor and then folded the rest of the colored paper into a large envelope. "Tell me what day it is, Watson."

"Friday, now," Timothy replied, looking at the clock.

She added the day to a new column in the notebook and then wrote: *Spy on Clapper.*

"But what exactly are we looking for?" Timothy tilted his head back to drain any milk left in his bowl.

"Anything that seems peculiar, anything out of the ordinary. Also, evidence about the girl. Who is she?"

Next Sarah added a column for deductions. Prank leapt nimbly onto the bed, circled once, and then lay purring against Sarah's back. "Tell Mom you're meeting me tomorrow at five o'clock outside ballet. We'll stake out Clapper's house on the way home."

✛ ✛ ✛

Thursday night, Jessica couldn't sleep. The waning moon shone like a streetlamp seeping in between her bedroom curtains, striping the room with a pale silver light. Under her pillow, the note burned into her thoughts.

The genius boy, Timothy, seemed to take the note seriously, even when she suggested that it might be a joke. Could it be a hoax he was playing on her? She turned restlessly under the sheets. Did it really have anything to do with Great-Aunt Rosemary? They had been close when she was little; many nights, Jessica had begged for a story before she went to sleep. But then Jessica had gotten older, and her great-aunt seemed frumpy, obsolete—a tiresome older woman. Jessica sat up, throwing her sheets on the floor; she drew the smooth note out from under her pillow. A cool gust stirred the curtains and made the paper flutter in her hand like a living thing.

Timothy wasn't that bad, she thought, once you got to know him.

He was the only one who could outscore her in most subjects—not that she wanted the rest of her friends to know how well she did. This weekend, she and Tina had big plans. Once her parents were asleep, she would slip out her bedroom window, climb down the ash tree, and be off to a high school party. The type of party someone like Timothy would never be invited to.

She got out of bed and pulled the curtains wider. The moon was tangled in the branches of the rowan tree. The tree had been a house-warming present from her great-aunt when her parents first moved in many years ago. Her mother said it was one of the strangest gifts they had ever received, but one of the loveliest. Great-Aunt Rosemary always referred to it as a rowan tree, but her mother said it was nothing more than a mountain ash. Perhaps tomorrow she should make a long overdue visit to her great-aunt.

THE STAKEOUT

STAR SAT IN A TREE in Mrs. Clapper's yard and watched the night deepen. As the sky darkened from blue to black, a screech owl called softly above her, his feathered horns dark silhouettes against the sky. From her perch, she could identify her sisters, the six stars of the Pleiades, glowing just above the horizon. Tonight the astronomers would wonder about the missing seventh star, the lost Pleiad. Few would know which star was missing, and even fewer would be able to give the name of the missing sister: Electra. Only a chosen few astronomers would ever connect the missing star in the Pleiades to her, in the form of a girl, sitting in a tree. The Pleiad sisters had been called many things over the millennia: doves, maidens, flames. Each description captured a part of the truth, but none could describe them entirely. Now scientists peering through ever-evolving telescopes defined them as an open star cluster and determined that they were four hundred light-years from earth. But many astronomers still used the old names from Greek mythology when referring to them individually: Alcyone, guardian of the winds; Merope, the eloquent sister; swarthy Celaeno; Maia, the eldest; twinkling, young Sterope; Taygeta of the long neck; and Star Girl's own name: Electra, bright and shining. There had been names before these; those were given when the world was new. On any particular night of winter in the northern hemisphere, six or all seven of the sisters were visible from earth. And that variability had led to the myth of a missing sister.

Soon the moon would be nothing but a silver sliver in the sky. Star Girl missed the sky and the ability to look down at earth from a great height. In the distance, she saw the roofs with humans dreaming beneath. She looked up once more into the sky and began to sing. The melody wound its way into the darkness of night until she could no longer see even its faintest glimmer. Her job was to watch and wait, and that is what she would do.

✝✝✝

Friday afternoon, Sarah and Timothy approached the Clapper's house cautiously, having decided that a large lilac bush would serve as the perfect screen. From behind the bush they could glimpse the backyard through the slats of the fence and peer through a kitchen window. Sarah had a notebook and pencil ready.

"But what do you do on a stakeout?" Timothy asked.

"Watch," said Sarah. "You just watch for a very long time and write down everything that happens, like if anyone comes or goes or if you hear anything."

They both determined that they would look for any evidence of the girl's silvery strands of hair or the glowing dust of her footprints. But there was no evidence in sight. Timothy felt his nose and throat begin to itch. Lilacs irritated his allergies. He pinched the end of his nose just as Sarah jabbed him in the ribs. "Listen, someone's talking in the backyard."

Timothy pushed farther into the bush to get a better view, but whoever was talking was standing too close to the fence to be seen. The voice sounded familiar. "It's Jessica," he whispered. "She's talking to Mrs. Clapper."

Sarah raised her eyebrows and began to write furiously in her notebook. "Get closer and tell me everything they say."

Timothy was on his hands and knees now, between the bush and the fence. He burrowed farther in and could feel his eyes itching and his nose start to run. If he strained, he could just make out a few words.

"Do you remember the story you used to tell me about the girl who got mysterious messages from a talking crow?"

"Yes. Crow Girl. Of course I remember, Jessica. You asked me for it every time I babysat you."

"You don't suppose people might get mysterious messages in real life, do you?"

"I don't see why not. Most stories, at least the best ones, the ones that last, have something of truth in them."

"But not talking crows!"

"Maybe and maybe not, but what's on your mind? Surely you haven't come here to ask me about old stories?"

Timothy could feel a sneeze building like a tidal wave. Not now!

"Well, what if you got a message that didn't make too much sense, and you didn't know where it came from, and it had the name of someone you knew in it? What would you do?"

The sneeze exploded out of Timothy with all the force he had used to hold it in.

He lost the beginning of Clapper's reply, and now there was complete silence on the other side of the fence. He heard Sarah's terse whisper. "Don't move."

"What was that?" asked Jessica.

Timothy thought he heard Jessica climbing up onto the fence. He pulled himself into a tight ball and shut his eyes.

"I don't see anyone," she said.

The voices faded, and Timothy heard the back door slam.

"Come on!" Sarah tugged his arm.

Just then Timothy heard something above him. It was almost music, but not quite—at least, not any music he had ever heard before. He uncurled and opened one eye, peering up through gray-green leaves into the limbs of an apple tree just on the other side of the fence.

There she was.

The girl sat in the crook of one of the highest branches, dangling a long white leg. She was staring down at him with her silvery eyes and no expression at all on her pale face. But Timothy had no doubt that she saw him—in fact, she was looking right at him. He inched out from under the shrub. Bits of leaf and twig scratched his face and stuck in his hair. Sarah tucked the notebook and pencil into her pocket.

"Timothy, let's get out of here!"

"Not yet. She's there, up in that tree." He wiped his nose on his sleeve.

But Sarah had stopped listening. The front door swung open, and Jessica Church stood on the steps, bidding her great-aunt good-bye. Sarah and Timothy froze, completely exposed on the side lawn. There was nowhere to go. Jessica looked straight at them, and in that moment, nose dripping, twigs and leaves sprouting from his hair, Timothy knew that any hopes he'd had of ever seeming normal were gone. All because of Sarah and Sherlock Holmes. What a fool he was! He wanted to curl into a ball on the grass, sink a million miles into the earth.

"Run, Timothy!" said Sarah, and she dashed across the street and up the sidewalk. Timothy swiped his arm across his nose again. Lungs wheezing with every stride, he ran after his sister. He knew that running would make him look even more foolish, that he should have come out with some clever remark instead. But he ran anyway, as fast as he could with a tight fist squeezing his lungs.

A STORM
BUILDS

SNOOPS AND SPIES! You could at least tell me why you were there!" Jessica angrily bit off each word. "Were you following me?"

Timothy was hunched in the coat closet with his cell phone pressed to his ear. She had called at exactly the wrong time. His family had been sitting down to dinner. Timothy had left his phone on the kitchen counter, and his father of all people had answered it!

"Just a minute, young lady. I'll get him . . . Timothy, there is a female person on your phone."

Timothy watched his mother and father exchange looks, and Sarah kicked him under the table.

"Keep it short," his father added. "It's dinnertime."

This was the ultimate invasion of his privacy, his father answering his cell phone! He mumbled a hello into the phone. Then he excused himself from the table. He was sure Sarah would be listening from the kitchen, so he'd slipped into the closet. It was stuffy, and his voice was muffled by the press of coats.

"We were doing just what you were, trying to get more information. And no, we didn't have any idea that you were there."

"How do you know where my great-aunt lives?" Jessica sounded suspicious now.

"Sarah passes her house on the bus, but I told you—she used to babysit for us." Then Timothy remembered the girl. "Did you see her?"

"See who?" Jessica still sounded angry.

"The girl with silver hair; she was up in the apple tree."

"All I saw was Great-Aunt Rosemary. That girl was there? Are you sure?"

"Of course I'm sure. She was in the apple tree in the side yard, looking at me." Timothy wondered if he sounded like a lunatic. There was no answer on the other end for several seconds. Jessica had ended the call, he was sure. His stomach clenched. He knew the story would be broadcast all over school on Monday. Then he heard her voice speaking quietly.

"I think I found something. Strands of something silver, like very long hair. They were on the floor in the kitchen. My great-aunt was sweeping up some kind of glittery powder when I came in. I don't think she knows I saw it."

"That's from her, the star girl." Jessica hadn't hung up, didn't think he was completely crazy! His mother's winter wool coat tickled his face. "I can't talk any more now; we're eating dinner."

"If you weren't following me, explain why you ran away."

But Timothy couldn't think of anything to say. Seconds unraveled, and he shifted uncomfortably. "We didn't want Mrs. Clapper to see us—it was a stakeout."

Jessica laughed, and Timothy's heart sank. "Well, you're not very clever detectives, are you—getting caught and all."

"Did she tell you anything?" Through the muffle of coats, Timothy could hear his mother calling.

"Not much, except to say that I should pay more attention to her fairy stories. She didn't admit leaving a note or anything. I told you, she's just your average old lady."

"Try to remember everything she said, exactly as she said it." Timothy hesitated again. "I think we're going back tomorrow night to look for the girl. It will be Beltane. Professor Twig said Beltane is significant. Do you want to come?"

"'Significant'? Who talks that way? And I've got more important things to do on a Saturday night than play detective. I've been invited to a party." Then she added quickly, "But let me know if you find out anything, okay? And don't follow me again."

"Sure, bye." Timothy ended the call feeling like a fool. Now he would have to face his parents' questions, too. But when he came out of the closet, Sarah was in the middle of a lively story about that afternoon's ballet class. By the time she was done, the phone call was forgotten. He shot her a grateful look, and Sarah smiled back, kicking him again in the shins and wiggling her eyebrows. He knew what she meant. They'd talk later. But for the rest of Friday night, his mother had a family Scrabble game planned. Whoever won would get to choose a movie to watch. He'd have to put aside the plans that were just beginning to take shape in his mind.

Timothy was just about to use all seven of his letters in one audacious move when the house phone rang.

"Just let the answering machine get it," his father said. "If they want us, they can leave a message."

But Sarah was already halfway to the phone. "Mom, it's for you." Sarah handed her the phone and shrugged when their dad mouthed, "Who is it?"

His mother was on the phone a very long time. When she returned, her face was flushed and her eyes sparkled. "Well, I've had some good news."

"Out with it, then. We're in the middle of a game."

But Timothy could tell that his father was curious.

"I won the juried competition from the art gallery opening!"

Timothy thought his mother immediately looked younger, fresher, in her triumph.

"Hooray for you, Mom! You *are* good, you know." Sarah beamed at her proudly.

"Well, that's really something, Liz! We're all proud of you!"

"There's one problem. The reception is tomorrow night; I hadn't planned on going, since we went to the opening, but now . . ." Her voice trailed away.

"Of course we're going. The children will be fine for a few hours."

And suddenly Timothy and Sarah were faced with the prospect of being all alone on Beltane. Nothing could have made them happier.

IN THE DARK

T WAS LATE Friday night.

Something thumped against his window. Timothy sat up in bed. The room was thick with darkness. It was cold, much colder than it should have been, and the thumping continued. He knew he should get up and check it out, but he didn't want to get out of his warm bed. Everything seemed sinister in the darkness. Familiar things took on strange shapes. His model airplane hung from the ceiling like a bat; across the room, his coat on a chair became a human hunkering in the corner.

Timothy forced his legs over the side of the bed. The window felt miles away as he crossed the room one trembling footstep at a time. This was not the friendly dark of a familiar place but a deeper, menacing darkness. His heart raced, and still he forced himself forward. A cold blast of air stopped him at the window. His blinds banged against the sill.

"I didn't leave the window open," he said out loud just to hear a voice. But his voice sounded small and tinny in the darkness. He would have to lift the blinds to close the window, and suddenly he was filled with dread. What if something was outside, watching and waiting for a chance to come in?

Slowly, he pulled the cord, lifting the blinds. The wind was blowing out of the north, and clouds scuttled across the sky. He struggled with the stubborn window sash. Something on the roof above his window moved. It was a dense shadow in the shadows of night. Timothy froze and held his breath. The shadow took the shape of a cat, and Timothy slowly exhaled. It must be the neighbor's cat looking for Prank. The cat came closer, slinking across the roof toward the window. Its fur was the light cream of a Siamese; the neighbor's cat was a calico. Puzzled, Timothy was just about to call out to it when the cat raised its head and made a final dash toward the windowsill. A scream strangled in Timothy's throat.

The cat had only one eye, a cloudy blue eye, and the eye was set in the middle of its head. The animal gathered itself to spring, then froze in midleap, paws extended. It fell back onto the roof. A tree bough rested on the ledge of the open window, and the cat seemed unable to cross it. Timothy slammed the window shut. With its back arched, the cat spit and hissed, its grotesque eye shining straight at Timothy.

He pulled the curtain closed and ran to Sarah's room, but her door was locked. He stood in the hallway, taking deep breaths, trying to calm himself. No cats had eyes in the middle of their heads. He crept back into his room and turned on the bedside lamp. He didn't look at the window. The wind howled around the house. Slipping deep under the bedcovers, he listened for the sound of claws on the glass. Although he listened for a long time, he never heard the cat scrabbling to get in. Just before daybreak, he finally slept after convincing himself it was all part of a very bad dream.

✢ ✢ ✢

The day was blustery and clouds were speeding across the sky on Saturday morning. Sarah had forgotten to close her blinds and the sunlight played across her blankets, shining full in her face. She wrinkled her nose and muttered, "Okay, okay, I'm up."

Stretching, she walked over to the window. Despite the sun, the weather looked as if something might be brewing. On the windowsill, something caught her eye. A tree bough. There was no tree near her window. How did it get there? She wandered into Timothy's room. Timothy was usually the first one up in the family, always afraid that he might miss something if he slept too late. This morning he was still a lumpy form under a worn blue comforter.

"Get up." She poked at the lumpy shape and crossed to his window. "Oh, look—you have one, too."

Timothy managed to open a sleepy eye. "One what?"

"A piece of tree on your windowsill. Did you put it there?"

Timothy was fully awake now. All the fears of last night came rushing back. He pulled his comforter around his shoulders and reluctantly followed her to the window. Sure enough, just as in his dream, a branch lay across the sill. He felt his hands grow cold. Making sure there was no cat in sight, he opened the window. The end of the branch wasn't rough and jagged like one broken off in a storm. It was smooth, as if it had been cut. Leaving the branch in place, he closed the window. He thought he recognized the type of leaves but struggled a minute to remember the name of the tree. "Rowan boughs."

Sarah glared at him. "Mother should never have let you take that community ecology class last summer."

"They're placed in windows and doorways to keep witches away."

"That wasn't in the class! How do you know?"

"It was in one of the books I was reading to get information about *them*. May Day used to be called Beltane, and rowan boughs are a tradition. They were put on window sills to keep the people in the house safe on Beltane—and last night was Beltane Eve."

"Like flowers on doorsteps?"

"Mmm, older than that." Timothy wondered if he should tell Sarah about his dream and the one-eyed cat.

Sarah opened the window and pulled at the branch.

"Leave it! I didn't put it there, but whoever did must think we need protection." The idea that they might need some type of protection made Timothy uneasy. He decided to keep the dream to himself, at least for now.

Sarah looked at him strangely. "Timothy James, do you know more than you're telling?" She flopped down on the rumpled bed. "I think we need to go back to the library today or talk to your Mr. Twig. Who would have put these branches on our windowsills anyway?"

"Don't you have ballet?" Timothy dropped the comforter, glad he didn't have to answer her question. He was wearing gray sweatpants and pulled on the first T-shirt he could reach.

"Not today. Some of the dancers are out of town for a workshop." Sarah frowned. "I don't like the idea of people sneaking around our house at night. It gives me the creeps."

✟ ✟ ✟

Once again Timothy found himself at the library on a Saturday, but this time Sarah was with him. He hadn't paid much attention to Beltane when he was researching earlier, but ever since visiting Mr. Twig, he'd both looked forward to and dreaded the day, and now it was here.

Before leaving the house, Timothy and Sarah had checked all the doors and windows. At each entry point, they found a tree branch. Timothy couldn't shake the fear his dream left behind. It paced him like a shadow.

Herds of preschool-age children stormed the library for story time. Sticky with paste, they cut brightly colored strips of construction paper to weave into May Day baskets. Sarah did not like little children—they made her edgy—but Timothy could still remember being one and felt a certain empathy with them. He wanted to tell them to enjoy themselves now because things only got harder as you got older.

He noticed that the same long-faced, floppy-haired Julian was sitting behind the reference desk. Sarah was headed right toward him. Timothy wound through the stacks back to the Special Collections room to look for the book with the pictures of Herne and the long description of Beltane. As soon as he entered the small room, he relaxed. *Sanctuary*, he thought, seeing the word arranged as Scrabble tiles. Today he was the only one in the room. No Mr. Twig snorted in the corner.

He was just getting settled when Sarah appeared. "The librarian said you would be here. Look what he found for me! I asked him about Celtic traditions, and he gave me this book." She slapped a book down triumphantly on the table next to him. "It talks about Beltane." She flipped through the pages and paused. "Morris dancers!"

A glossy photo showed a troupe of dancing men bedecked in bells and ribbons, twirling flaming sticks.

Timothy raised an eyebrow. "So?"

"I know about them from dance class. It's an old tradition of dance in the British Isles. But look what it says." She pointed at a caption under the photo. "'They dance on Beltane, or May Day, when the Jack is slain.' It might be important because of Beltane. And didn't Mr. Twig say something about a death?"

Timothy looked up at Sarah. "Who is 'the Jack'? And why do they kill him?"

Sarah read on. "'Sometimes the Jack is a real person covered with vines and leaves. Sometimes it's just an effigy, a dummy.'"

Timothy stared at a photo of a man covered in foliage.

Sarah continued. "'The dancers pretend to kill him, and then the Jack comes back to life.' It must have something to do with spring coming."

"Well, I can't see what it has to do with us," Timothy said, but the fear was back, making his heart race.

COME INTO THE STORM

THE KNOCKING AT THE DOOR was insistent, although it was difficult to hear over the wail of the storm. Saturday night, Beltane. Timothy and Sarah were home alone. Their parents had left hours ago for the artists' reception. Despite the date, it had been a normal Saturday, and Timothy wasn't sure whether to be grateful or disappointed. And then the wind had started blowing. It never stormed like this in the spring! Who would come knocking on a night like this?

"I don't think you should open that!" Sarah's voice was sharp.

Prank arched her back and hissed.

Timothy looked through the peephole in the door, straight into the face of Mrs. Clapper. Why was she out in this storm? He opened the door, and the wind pushed in like an uninvited guest howling its displeasure. Disheveled, Mrs. Clapper stood on the step, wisps of gray hair wild about her face. She was wearing a long cloak, and she carried a willow basket on her arm.

"Your parents are going to be late. They called and asked me to check on you two." Her voice was calm and her eyes gleamed.

She likes this storm, Timothy thought.

Sarah looked over his shoulder.

"Come in," Timothy offered.

"Oh, no, I think it is far better that you come out," Mrs. Clapper replied.

Then Timothy saw it peering from behind her cloak: a golden-furred wolf! He took a step back, right onto Sarah's toes.

"Come into the storm; we haven't had one like this in years!" Mrs. Clapper continued. "And we have business to attend to."

Timothy's mouth opened and he swallowed a gulp of air. Did he just see what he thought he saw?

"What's wrong with her?" Sarah hissed into his ear. "Okay," she said more loudly, looking right at Mrs. Clapper.

Didn't Sarah see the wolf? wondered Timothy.

Sarah grabbed a sweatshirt from the hook by the door and ran outside.

Timothy tried to hold her back, but his voice failed him. Mrs. Clapper turned to stare out across the lawn. The wolf was gone, but strapped on her back was a quiver full of arrows and a bow. Mrs. Clapper had lost her mind; there could be no other explanation. He couldn't let Sarah go out there alone with her.

As soon as he stepped out on the porch, the door slammed shut behind him. The wind swirled with voices. Clouds scurried across the sky, covering and then revealing a sliver of moon. He shivered in his T-shirt. The temperature was dropping fast. "I think you should come in," he pleaded. And then the wolf with gleaming yellow eyes poked its head out from under Mrs. Clapper's cloak and growled.

Sarah leaned against the porch rail, looking into the storm. "It's wonderful, isn't it? Come on, Timothy, let's go for a storm walk!" She danced a few steps across the porch and pulled the sweatshirt hood over her hair. Sarah had lost her mind as well! He needed to warn her about the wolf!

"Come with us, Timothy," Mrs. Clapper urged.

High above the storm's moan, Timothy caught the faint sound of a voice, singing. It was the same voice he'd heard before in his front yard and in Mrs. Clapper's apple tree. Then he saw the girl. She was standing across the lawn, under the hawthorn tree. Her hair, caught by the moonlight and wind, swirled around her in a silver mist.

This was his chance to talk to her.

Keeping his distance from Mrs. Clapper and the wolf, Timothy crossed the lawn. Walking was harder than he thought. It was like stepping into a swiftly moving river. The wind was the current, and it took all of Timothy's effort to move against it. Behind him, he heard Sarah calling, but he had to reach the girl before she disappeared again. Then Mrs. Clapper was at his side. How did she get there so fast?

"Don't mind my dog, Timothy. He won't harm you."

Timothy shot a glance at the beast loping at her side. She could call it a dog, but it looked like a wolf to him. His heart revved.

"Who is the girl under the tree?" Timothy shouted into the wind.

"She is a star, one of the Pleiad sisters. Her name is Electra, but she is known by other names, too. She's come to bear witness to the events of this Beltane." Mrs. Clapper moved agilely through the storm.

A star! So she really *was* a star girl? Timothy decided that described her perfectly: her cold remoteness, her silvery hair, the fine dust of her footsteps.

Up ahead, Electra, the star girl, stood still, watching as they approached. She didn't try to leave. Her face, Timothy thought, showed no emotion.

"We mustn't lose your sister, Timothy James." Mrs. Clapper put a hand on his arm to slow him. But Timothy kept his distance; he had no intention of getting close to the beast. "Your sister has a role to play, too," she said as she waited for Sarah to join them.

"Is that a wolf?" Sarah's face was pink with the cold wind, and her eyes shone.

Mrs. Clapper only said, "He is Gwydon, and he is very wise."

Timothy hurried forward until he stood face-to-face with Star Girl under the hawthorn tree. He had no idea of what to say to a star. She was beautiful in a terribly cold way.

When Sarah and Mrs. Clapper reached his side, the girl spoke:

"Time out of time
the horned man rides
with the forest queen,
the Greenman dies,
the heavens bear witness,
the great wolf flies,
and Timothy James stands alone."

"Hey, that's the poem in Jessica's note! How do you know it?"

But the girl didn't answer.

"Yes—Jessica," Mrs. Clapper said. "She is part of our business tonight. It seems that she could use a friend or two right now. Perhaps we should head in that direction."

"What do you mean?" Nothing was making any sense to Timothy.

"She isn't at home," Star Girl spoke again. "She's out in the storm."

Jessica was out in the storm? She had said she was going to a party. And why did she need a friend? She had lots of friends.

Mrs. Clapper and the others had already moved on. As the clouds hid the moon again, Timothy suddenly felt lost. He hurried to catch up. The landscape had changed. There were more trees in the distance than he recalled.

When he reached Sarah, he grabbed her hand. If they were going to follow a star and a crazy old woman with a wolf into a storm, they'd do it together.

┼ ┼ ┼

Jessica had her plans worked out. The party started at nine but would go on for hours. Her parents were already in bed. She'd wait to make sure they were really asleep and then climb out the window and down the rowan tree. Tina and her older brother would meet her and he'd drive them all to the party. She'd be back home before her parents ever woke up.

She had used the tree as an escape before. She was good at climbing, but tonight the weather was bad. She looked out her bedroom window. A tree branch had broken off and was now lodged on her windowsill. She opened the window and impatiently tossed it off. A cold wind blew in. She'd need both hands free for climbing. She looked at her new sandals. Silver with two-inch heels. She couldn't climb in them. She held their straps with her teeth and looked regretfully at her purse. No way to carry that, too. Then she leaned out and circled the nearest limb with her arms, and threw one leg over the branch. Careful not to rip her new jeans, Jessica pulled herself up to standing. Then, using her bare feet and hands to balance, she picked her way down through the branches, her sandals swinging from her mouth. She swung from a low branch and dropped the last few feet to where Tina and her brother, Jimmy, waited at the base of the tree.

"Ready for a little partying?" Jimmy asked.

A thrill shot through Jessica from the top of her curly head to her bare toes.

"Can't wait!" She'd never been to a high school party before, and she hoped she didn't sound as nervous as she felt. Nervous and excited. Jimmy, with his short dark hair and teasing eyes, looked good in his tight black T-shirt. She leaned one hand on Tina's shoulder and pulled on her sandals.

She ran her fingers through her hair as she slid onto the bench seat of the pickup truck, next to Tina. Jimmy didn't say much, but he hummed during the drive. Tina chattered with excitement. Jessica was glad she didn't have to say anything. When Tina talked, nodding was enough. She didn't exactly know whose house they were going to, but that didn't really matter; what mattered was that she was attending her first real high school party.

When they arrived, it was just as she imagined it would be. Music throbbed through every door and window. People were jammed into the front room, laughing and talking in a smoky haze. Jimmy disappeared almost immediately, leaving Tina and Jessica to look around.

"So, who are all these people?" Jessica had expected to see more people she knew.

"It's not just people from Jimmy's high school. There are people here from everywhere—that's how you can tell it's a good party," Tina said. But she wasn't really looking at Jessica. She was busy checking herself in the entryway mirror.

A tall redheaded boy came by and handed them each a drink in a large plastic cup. "Welcome to my humble home." He laughed and melted back into the crowd.

Jessica took a careful sip and tried not to make a face. Maybe if she just held the cup, people would think she was drinking.

She and Tina wandered through the rooms, clutching their drinks and looking for familiar faces. Tall bookcases lined one room where several couples were trying to dance. They had pushed back a couch and were crowded into one corner while a noisy group sat playing cards in the middle of the floor. As Jessica watched, a girl gestured widely, spilling her drink on an Oriental rug. The room smelled of incense and sweaty bodies, and something sweeter that she couldn't identify. She found a table under a large family portrait to put her cup on. There was the same redheaded boy, posed with two younger sisters, who appeared to be twins, and his parents. His mother had hair as red as his. Jessica wondered where they all were now as the party filled their house. For a while, Jessica and Tina watched the card game, and then they continued to wander from room to room. The crowded house began to give Jessica a headache. Someone had handed her another drink, but other than that she was ignored.

"Tina, this is really boring. Let's go," Jessica said.

Tina looked at her curiously, as if she didn't know her. "You've got to be kidding. This party is the best! See that guy over there? He's been watching me since we got here." She patted her hair. "Well, what do you think? I think he's pretty hot!"

Jessica looked across the haze of smoke at a blond, pimply faced boy with a snake tattooed on his forearm. He was weaving ever so slightly as he stood there, but he was definitely looking their way. Well, Tina could have him. Jessica tried to look unself-conscious and sloshed down the drink in her cup. This one tasted like soda, but it was mingled with another taste. It made her tongue curl. Tina walked—no, slithered, Jessica thought—across the room to the snake boy. There seemed to be couples everywhere she looked: on the couches, in the hallways, on the stairs. There was nothing worse than being alone in a group of people who weren't alone. Suddenly, the room felt oppressively stuffy. She fled back to the card game and sat watching until she could stand it no longer. Not a single person talked to her.

Jessica found the kitchen. It was one of those dark-toned, high-tech kind of kitchens she saw in pages of magazines. At last, there was someone she knew. Jimmy sat on a granite counter, surrounded by a group of guys all trying to balance spoons on their noses. On his head he wore a wreath of leaves taken from a table centerpiece. Every time one of the boys got a spoon to stay, the group cheered and handed the boy another drink. The air was humid and sticky the way it gets before a storm. Jessica lifted her hair off her neck; she could see the beads of sweat on Jimmy's upper lip. His black hair shone as he carefully placed the spoon on the end of his nose. It stuck. The group cheered and handed him a drink. Jessica began to giggle and couldn't stop. Several of the boys turned to look at her and Jimmy scowled, his wreath askew. "The kindergartners are in the other room. Isn't it past your bedtime?" he asked, straightening his leafy headpiece.

The group laughed loudly and Jessica felt herself flush red. Suddenly, her new clothes seemed overdone. In the corner of the kitchen, one boy sat alone. His hood was pulled low over his head, keeping his face in shadow. He smiled at Jessica's discomfort.

Without turning, Jessica backed into a large boy in a stained T-shirt. Laughter erupted even louder as he made kissing noises at her retreating back. Her head began to spin and she looked frantically for Tina, the sound of the boys' laughter still in her ears. But Tina seemed to have disappeared with snake boy, and Jessica found herself alone, her face hot and her head throbbing. She made a dash for the front door and fresh air.

Outside, the wind howled and tore at the house. The smell of rain was in the air. The hooded boy followed her out and onto the porch. Jessica watched him nervously, but he didn't stop. He walked down the steps and paused to look at the sky. As his hood slid back and the streetlight illuminated his face, Jessica noticed a strange tattoo. A single eye right in the middle of his forehead. The boy jammed his hands into the pockets of his jeans and sauntered into the storm. Jessica watched him as long as she could, past the parked cars, past the last streetlight, until he disappeared into the dark.

She shivered through her thin blouse. It was after midnight, and she wanted to go home. She would walk; there was no way she would ask Jimmy for a ride—or for anything ever again! If she called her parents, they'd be angry. No, they'd be furious. They'd pick her up, but she'd be grounded for the rest of her life. She reached in her pocket for her cell phone. Nothing. She'd left it at home in her purse.

The walk home would be long, but she could do it and get in before her parents discovered she was gone. She looked down at her jeans and high-heeled sandals; better to be off in the storm than stay here where she was unappreciated. With a vague idea of the way home, Jessica started out.

✦ ✦ ✦

It was time. The dogs were prancing with anticipation, and their master eagerly watched as the storm grew. As Herne blew into a silver horn, raising the cry of the hunt, his horse strained and pawed the ground. Herne urged it forward. Horse, rider, and dogs burst into the night with the wind at their backs. The white hounds yapped their delight. Together, they swooped through the sky, low over the hills and down into the valleys. People in the outlying farms who knew the old legends kept their livestock sheltered on Beltane. When they heard a noise like the cry of geese passing overhead, they knew the hunt was abroad. Only in towns where the old stories were forgotten did stray dogs or prowling cats feel the fur rise on their backs and run panicked, until they were caught up in the swirl of the wind. In the Maxwells' kitchen, Prank cowered under the table, every sense alert. The wind screamed its fury. Herne shouted with delight, the wind in his antlers, and the world swept before his hounds.

GREENMAN

TALKING WAS IMPOSSIBLE in the noise of the storm, so Timothy trudged along silently beside Sarah. With each stride, the streets of his neighborhood became less and less familiar. Trees crowded close, obscuring the sidewalks, and he ducked his head to avoid being scraped by low branches. By now they should have reached the mountain bike trails that ran through the woods on the edge of town, but the trails had disappeared. They followed the faint glow from Star Girl through the shifting dark.

Timothy was afraid to go farther but even more afraid to stop. What if the changes around him were real and not part of his imagination? Geese cried harshly overhead. Sarah barely seemed to notice. Her face held that grim look of determination she wore when practicing a difficult dance combination, with all her energy focused on the task ahead.

Timothy stumbled and looked down. The sidewalk crumbled into a dirt path, uneven and rocky in places. It was like being caught in a really bad dream. But in dreams he was never so tired.

✛✛✛

At the edge of the clearing, the Greenman was fully awake, no longer living in a painful half-world; the transformation was complete. Movement was easier for him now. The stiffness of a few hours ago was gone. He leapt and swayed, moving with the assurance of wild things, perfectly at home in the forest. Spring had come! He could feel it through the storm, hear it calling to bulbs and seeds buried under the ground. The smell of it was in the blossoms—new life bursting forth. Trees mumbled at the wind, the fierce oak, thickets of alder. They were his brothers now, and he could understand their individual voices. But there was something else besides spring in the wind tonight. The small and scurrying things of the forest had all taken cover. No voles or rabbits, mice or skunks were abroad. They had burrowed deep into their dens or tunneled underground. Overhead, the clouds blew across the moon. The night became black. And the Greenman heard the first cries of hounds in the distance. Herne was riding. It wouldn't be long before the boy and his sister arrived. The Greenman still carried the light from their house. It shone in his leaves and glowed from a hole in his bark.

✛✛✛

Several things happened at once, which caused Timothy to become even more disoriented. The single-lane track they had been following disappeared completely in underbrush. As he swiveled his head frantically in several directions, looking for a sign of something familiar, he noticed that the dog by Mrs. Clapper's side had grown. Gwydon was now the size of a pony, and he turned his enormous head, fixing Timothy with gold-flecked eyes. Timothy felt all his old panic rising in his throat; he fought to hold back a scream. The wolf's thick golden fur bristled, and his tail looped up over his back as he trotted at the woman's side. Timothy darted a quick glance at Mrs. Clapper to see if she had noticed the wolf's transformation. The Clapper herself had changed. She was taller, and her short gray hair had lengthened. Were his eyes playing tricks? It was difficult to see anything clearly in the darkness.

Sarah had dropped his hand and was now several strides ahead of him. He shot another glance at Mrs. Clapper. Her hair was longer still, streaming over the shoulders of her cape! There was no mistaking it this time; the hair flowed almost to her waist. Timothy couldn't look away. This couldn't be real! There was no explanation for such things. Even worse, the bushes and undergrowth on the path didn't scratch his arms or legs but parted as they walked deeper into the woods. His heart felt cold and coiled like a spring. Sarah was now far ahead of him. He tried to hurry to her side, but his legs were weighted with fear.

✝ ✝ ✝

As Sarah kept her eyes on Star Girl, she found it easier to move through the trees and scrub bushes. They were in a forest now, and as the trees grew denser, the bushes thinned. Wherever they were being led, it was to something important. She was sure of that. The storm, the dark, the star girl—all added to the sense of mystery. She looked back over her shoulder at Timothy; he was far behind, but she didn't worry.

Mrs. Clapper was near him. How could an old woman like Mrs. Clapper move so easily through the storm?

Sarah followed Star Girl to a clearing hidden by the branches of a very large tree. The tree's trunk was gray and muscled like human flesh. Underneath the tree, the ground was bare and smooth, devoid of bushes and undergrowth, like a secret room protected by stout arms. Star Girl waited under the branches until Sarah caught up. Together they waited for Mrs. Clapper, Gwydon, and Timothy.

✛ ✟ ✛

When they reached the clearing under the tree, Timothy decided to do what he had been dreading. He turned and looked fully at Mrs. Clapper. He was staring at someone he did not know. She turned her face toward him. In the moonlight, he saw that the wrinkles and age spots were gone. In their place was a young, unlined face. Her glittering blue eyes appraised him coolly, fiercely. Timothy held his breath. She was taller and broader of shoulder than before, and the bow and arrows looked as if they belonged on the back of this new person. Mrs. Clapper's dark cloak was the dim green of the deepest forest. A skirt, the color of a ripe plum, swirled when she moved, and instead of good, sensible walking shoes, Timothy glimpsed sandals on her feet. He let out a shaky breath and wondered if this was what it was like to lose one's mind. He squirmed under the gaze of this stranger and her fierce dog. He cleared his voice to speak, but it caught in the back of his throat. And then she smiled.

Her smile opened as slowly as the sunrise does on foggy mornings, and it dazzled him, chasing away all the confusion. At once, she was less forbidding. He noticed that Sarah was staring, too, her mouth open, in a cartoon O of surprise. Good, he thought, at least I'm not losing my mind alone.

"Don't you recognize me, Timothy?" Mrs. Clapper's new voice was very clear, like an ice-cold stream. "Tonight I am—"

"Artemis, goddess of the woods and hunt!" The words burst from Sarah, and she looked surprised to have said them out loud. "I read about her in mythology."

"Yes, Artemis, but also many other names. Tonight, in this place, I'm Cerridwyn. That is how they know me here, just as you have known me as someone else."

"But what happened to Clapper?" Timothy was afraid that his voice was quavering.

"You will see Mrs. Clapper again, just as you knew her. We're all part of a larger story written in the trees and stones. You, Timothy, and you, Sarah, are part of that story, too. Everyone I am is a reflection of that story. Before all things and after all things, the story is."

"What story?" Sarah asked.

"One in which you two will play a very important part tonight." At her side, Gwydon's ears twitched. He looked into the dark and whined.

"He's bigger," Timothy almost whispered.

"He's in his true shape now. In your world, he was a doglike creature, but now he is a different creature altogether."

Timothy did not like her use of "your world," as if they were in some other place. Before he could say anything more, Gwydon whined again and a shadow moved out from the trees.

At first, Timothy thought it was just a tree moving in the wind, but this tree walked into the clearing where they were standing. He looked more closely. As the tree approached, Timothy saw a human face encircled by a wreath of leaves. Vines draped from his eyebrows and leaves grew from the corners of his mouth. Light glowed from a knothole in his side. His eyes were kind and merry all at once, and suddenly Timothy recognized this creature with the body of a tree and the face of a man.

Timothy slipped close to Sarah's side. "It's the pale man," he whispered in her ear.

"What?"

"I can tell by his eyes. And something else. I know we can trust him."

"Greetings, Greenman." Cerridwyn spoke with formality. In reply, he bowed very low, then stood and jumped like a jester. Sarah laughed out loud. This seemed to please the Greenman, and he swayed and dipped until she laughed again.

Suddenly, hounds howled. Their cries were right overhead. Sarah pressed her hands over her ears. Timothy felt gooseflesh rise on his arms as he ducked and covered his head. The Greenman stood absolutely still, and Gwydon howled, an ancient cry that filled the night. Timothy, looking up, could see small red pinpricks of light moving through the dark.

All he wanted to do was hide, somewhere safe, anywhere away from the piercing lights.

✛ ✚ ✛

A squirrel dashed from the bushes. It ran to the Greenman, climbed one of his massive legs, and disappeared into a hole in his side, safe at last. A deer crashed through the undergrowth, eyes wild and sides heaving. Again the hounds called. They were closer now, and the deer, breathing heavily, ran blindly on. Timothy thought he could feel the hot whisper of the dogs' breath as they passed overhead.

"The hunter rides." Star Girl looked up at the sky. Her voice was calm, but Timothy shivered as though he might never be warm again.

"Who is that?" Sarah's voice was tight and high.

Cerridwyn looked fierce once again. "Herne and his hounds ride tonight."

IN THE SHADOWS

AT FIRST, the wind seemed to be her friend, echoing her anger and embarrassment. Jessica walked quickly, barely thinking where she was going. She was just glad to be away from the party. She would show them all—how dare they treat her that way!

She headed west, in the general direction of home. She had a good sense of direction, and she was confident that she could find her way, even though she knew the walk would be long. These streets were unfamiliar, but she remembered the car ride here. Once she was out on the main road, everything would be easier.

The wind tore through her light top and scoured her arms. No matter which way she turned, she seemed to be walking into a headwind. She couldn't remember it ever being this cold at the beginning of May. Her toes in her high-heeled sandals felt numb. And the wind kept the clouds scurrying across the moon, changing the landscape from dark to light.

She shivered and thought of her conversation with Timothy. *Aren't you ever scared of the dark?* he'd asked. Tonight might make her change her mind. Twice she felt as if she were being followed. The back of her neck prickled and she turned around quickly, but no one was there. It's just the wind, she said to calm herself. If only she had remembered to bring her cell phone!

In the distance, she heard geese honking. Did geese fly at night? Jessica looked up, but saw nothing but clouds scudding across the moon. Her sandal straps rubbed her ankles raw. They definitely weren't made for long walks. Ahead was a large park.

She decided to cut straight across it to the main road.

The people at that party were all losers, especially Tina and Jimmy. Why hadn't she noticed it before? They tried too hard; they knew a few popular people, but they'd never really be popular themselves. If Jimmy thought he could humiliate her in front of his friends, then he was wrong. At the memory of everyone in the kitchen laughing at her, her face grew red again. She would find a way to make him regret embarrassing her.

Jessica slowed to a stop. Shouldn't she be at the edge of the park by now? Maybe she had cut across it diagonally. It was too dark to tell. She adjusted her direction, and wished again for her cell phone. The call of geese, harsher this time and right overhead. Their cries sounded like dogs, angry dogs, barking and snapping. She huddled close to a large willow until the noise passed. When she stepped forward, something grabbed her hair! Her heart jumped to her throat.

"Who's there?"

Silence. The grip on her hair didn't lessen. Slowly, she turned her head and looked behind. Willow branches had snagged her hair. The more she moved, the tighter her hair was caught. She tried to reach back and untangle it from the branches, but it was impossible. Her fingers were numb with cold. She yanked harder; a few strands ripped. In a panic, she closed her eyes and gave one swift tug. The remaining strands of hair tore away; her eyes stung with tears.

The trees were thick in this part of the park, willows and ash. They crowded in around her. She came to a small, muddy stream and jumped over it, sinking into the bank on the other side. Ahead, the ground rose steeply. She climbed the first few feet, only to slip backward in the wet grass just as she neared the top. Her sandals sank into the mud. She pulled them off, gripped the straps with her teeth, and used her hands to pull herself up the last few feet. The legs and knees of her pants were heavy with mud and grass. At the top of the bank, she stopped to catch her breath, wiping the mud from her hands on her jeans.

The clouds parted, letting the moon silver the tops of trees. Instead of arriving at the edge of the park as she expected, she was on the verge of deeper woods. A narrow path led into a dense jumble of trees and then disappeared.

Jessica dropped her sandals and sat on the grass in frustration. Mud caked her sandals and was packed under her fingernails. Her new shirt offered no protection against the chill. And worst of all, she was completely turned around. There were no woods she knew of near this side of town. She wrapped her arms around herself and shivered. She'd have to go back the way she'd come, but when she turned to look behind, her way was blocked by trees. They stood like sentinels crowding the stream, and all she could see now were more trees in every direction.

Dogs again. Their cries rose to a deafening pitch right above her. How could the sound of dogs be coming from the air? She looked up into the sky. Small red lights, the size of laser pointers, were coming toward her. Instinctively, she ducked her head, tucking herself into a ball. The baying became a furious clamor, a sound that made her heart beat cold. She had to get away, before whatever they were saw her. She pulled herself to her feet, left her sandals, and ran along the path into the woods. Tree roots twisted across the path, and she fell, skinning her palms and twisting her ankle. The fury of the dogs came closer.

Crouched on her hands and knees, she looked desperately for a place to hide. Not far from the path, she noticed a bulky shape among the trees. She crawled toward it. There, among the stands of beech and oak, was a small stone building no larger than a garden shed. Ivy twined over the top and sides, but the door stood open, and with a grateful whimper, Jessica scuttled in, pushing the door closed behind her. Inside, it was pitch black. She didn't move. Was there anything else in here with her?

The barking dogs were all around now. She drew her knees in close, buried her face in her arms, and huddled against the cold wall. The mustiness of the forest floor rose around her. She held very still. Finally, their calls grew distant, and then silence surrounded her.

Flying hounds? Impossible. But she had no other explanation for what she had heard. She couldn't shake the feeling of being hunted, of being prey, a rabbit pursued by a fox. A great shudder passed through her. She was completely lost in woods she hadn't even known existed. Her pants and blouse clung to her in cold, wet patches. Her hands stung and her ankle throbbed. Tears welled up in her eyes, and she swiped at them with the back of her hand, leaving a broad streak of mud across one cheek. If she didn't keep moving, she might freeze and never be found here in the stone hut. The hut must mean she was close to other houses. The woods must form a greenbelt, blocking the sight and noise of the road.

Jessica opened the door and stepped outside, pressing her back against the hut's wall. She listened again for the hounds, but their noise was gone. The clouds had swallowed the moon. There was nothing to do but limp along the path in her bare and blistered feet. A path must lead somewhere. And feeling slightly more optimistic, she hobbled into the woods.

⚜ ⚜ ⚜

Once the hounds had passed, Timothy realized he had been holding his breath. The Greenman moved again, but Sarah and Star Girl still remained motionless, as if they were still listening to something.

"Can't you hear it, Timothy?" Sarah asked. "Music."

Timothy listened carefully, and he could just make out something that might be the faint sound of flutes. The music came closer. Nothing else could surprise me tonight, he thought. Mrs. Clapper—or Cerridwyn, or whoever she called herself—ignored them all as she talked in low, hushed tones to the Greenman. Timothy was cold and hungry, which seemed silly things to worry about at a time like this. Still, his body persisted in sending these ordinary signals, even when nothing else was ordinary at all.

"Sarah, should we try to get away?" He spoke in a whisper, but he had the feeling Star Girl could hear every word.

"Why? Didn't you hear that we're part of the story, too? And—" She stopped midsentence. "Morris dancers, Timothy!" Timothy's knees grew weak as if he needed to sit down. Here in the middle of the woods, six dancers appeared, all dressed in white. Bright red ribbons hung from their arms, and small bells tinkled as they danced. One of the men played a tin whistle. The last dancer walked solemnly, bearing a pole at least eight feet long. At his signal, the rest of the men stopped while he wrestled the pole into the ground. Timothy forgot about his growling stomach as he watched. Bright streamers floated from the top. A maypole! He had danced around a smaller one in elementary school. Each of his classmates held on to a ribbon, and they danced in a circle around the pole until the teacher stopped the music. Then they reversed direction and danced the other way. But that maypole was only a shadow of this tall one.

While the one man played the tin whistle, the others wove in and out between each other, and as they danced, the ribbons on the pole became braided. The swiftest dancer of all was the smallest. Timothy found it almost impossible to track him in the dance. He moved like a high and intricate melody that wound itself among the other dancers.

Timothy looked at his companions. Star Girl watched without expression. Gwydon, the wolfhound, lay by Cerridwyn's side, with his nose on his enormous paws. The Greenman swayed in rhythm to the music, and Sarah laughed as if she were delighted to be lost in a storm with a group of insane people. Only Mrs. Clapper wasn't watching the dance; her eyes were focused on something at the edge of the clearing, something that waited in the shadows.

SWORDPOINT

MORE THAN ANYTHING, Jessica wanted to find help. She had given up hope of braving it outside by herself and finding her own way home. So when she heard the music, she limped toward it, despite the branches that snapped her face.

The music came from a clearing under a massive tree. She ducked under low limbs, swatting leaves from her face. A tall, fierce-looking woman, with long red hair and arrows on her back, was staring straight at her. By the woman's side was a very large wolf. Jessica swallowed hard and took a step back. And most terrifying of all was a dancing tree. Beyond the woman and wolf, a group of men in funny clothes danced around a maypole to the music of a tin whistle. And outside the circle of dancers were Timothy and Sarah Maxwell! They stood next to the most beautiful girl Jessica had ever seen.

Jessica called to Timothy, but only faint rasping sounds came from her throat. The redhaired woman continued to stare at her. Why didn't the woman say something? Couldn't she tell that Jessica needed help? Her ankle throbbed, and she shivered from the cold and wet.

✢ ✢ ✢

Sarah jabbed Timothy in the ribs. "Look—isn't that Jessica?" She pointed across the clearing. There, under the edge of a tree, Timothy saw a disheveled Jessica. Her curls were tangled and plastered against her head, her jeans were muddy, and her feet were bare. Her face was pale and her eyes wide. He thought of Mrs. Clapper's statement that Jessica could use a friend. He'd completely forgotten the reason they had set forth.

"Jessica!"

He started to walk toward her when Cerridwyn gripped his arm, hard. "Ouch!"

Cerridwyn didn't say a word, and she didn't let go. Didn't she see Jessica?

"What are you doing?" Timothy tried to jerk his arm away, but she held him back.

The dancers broke their circle, the music stopped, and one man stepped forward. In his hand was a simple crown: gold vines were woven together with a single gold leaf at the center. He walked toward Cerridwyn, and she inclined her head, finally dropping Timothy's arm. The dancer nested the crown in her red hair. It gleamed in the moonlight with a glow greater than that of Star Girl.

The dancer with the tin whistle called out in a loud voice, "Spring has come, the winter is past. The earth awakes!"

Cerridwyn looked so much like a queen standing there with the gold leaf crown that Timothy felt as if he should bow down. As if she could read his thoughts, she turned to him. "Never mistake the creature for the Creator." And Timothy turned away, embarrassed to have someone read his mind.

Quick as an eyeblink, the Greenman began to dance. The whistle player blew a lively tune. The Greenman's leaves rustled, his branches dipped and swayed. He stopped and bowed toward Sarah, who flushed, took hold of a long knobbly branch, and joined him in the dance. The other dancers shook their bells and clapped.

As Timothy watched, he forgot all about Jessica. He forgot his fear and found himself longing for something he couldn't name. It was the same kind of longing he felt when he looked out his window in the very early morning when no one else was awake. The feeling he got just before Christmas, of something wonderful about to happen. If he had looked across at Jessica, he would have seen that she felt something very different.

✛ ✛ ✛

Jessica also watched the Greenman turn and bow to Sarah and then, for the first time, she saw his face. It wasn't quite the face of a man, but it was a face that she recognized. She saw Jimmy Salcedo peering back at her from under a fringe of leaves. She could see the mocking look in his eye, the disdainful curve of his lip. All the shame and anger from the party flooded back. He chose Sarah to be his partner and not her! The dancers were laughing at her, too. Laughing and clapping! Her breath came in short gasps. She wouldn't let them mock her! She wouldn't be the fool! Timothy was talking to the beautiful girl, and they both looked in her direction. Jessica's hands clenched and unclenched. A trickle of sweat rolled down between her shoulder blades. Slowly, she crept toward the dancers.

✝ ✝ ✝

The pace of the dance slowed. From the sidelines, Timothy watched each dancer reach under his white tunic and draw out a short wooden sword. Time for new tricks. Would they juggle the swords or fence with one another? The Greenman dropped Sarah's hand, and she slipped out of the circle.

Then the mood changed. The Morris men turned toward the Greenman. They held up their swords. The lead dancer shouted and leapt, his sword pointed at the Greenman. The treelike man backed away. Timothy didn't understand. What was going on? The dancer chased the Greenman round and round and in and out between the braided ribbons. The other dancers cut the Greenman off at every chance. Two dancers grabbed him, one on each side. As he struggled, they tied him to the maypole with the braided ribbons, wrapping him as tightly as an insect trapped in a spider's web.

The pursuer dropped his wooden sword and reached under his tunic. From a leather scabbard, he withdrew a short sword. Its silver blade gleamed in the moonlight.

Flickers of fear ran down Timothy's spine.

"Stop!"

Cerridwyn, Star Girl, Gwydon—nobody paid any attention to Timothy's shout except Sarah. Sarah was crying.

✛ ✛ ✛

Jessica stood just outside the circle. With both hands clenched into fists, she stared at the sneering face of Jimmy. Anger jolted through her. Finally, Jimmy was getting what he deserved. Solemnly, the dancer handed his short sword to her.

Without hesitation, Jessica ran forward. The Greenman, still bound by ribbons, watched her. He didn't struggle and kept his sorrowful eyes on Jessica's face.

"No!" Timothy shouted.

But Jessica barely paused before plunging the sword into the Greenman's side. His leafy face crumpled as if in dismay, and Timothy heard a low groan. Within moments the woody arms were limp, and his body sagged, supported only by the colored ribbons.

"Greenman!" In a rush, Sarah was at his side, supporting his head.

Timothy followed, stopping a few feet from Jessica.

"Jessica?" his voice cracked.

Her face was twisted in anger.

"How could you?" His voice was stronger now. Disgust and pity rolled together into one. He balled his fists, but his feet remained rooted to the ground. "Why did you do it? What's he ever done to you?" His face felt hot. "I hate you!"

With two hands, a dancer pulled the sword from the Greenman's side. Then the Morris men stepped up to the Greenman, one by one. Each dancer plucked a leaf from the limp form and stuck it in the band of his hat.

His face is empty, Timothy thought as he stared at the Greenman. All the life gone. He was slumped like a felled tree, just like the story of the Jack in the Green. This was Jessica's doing. She killed the Jack! This was worse than being a bully at school. She was Bent, just like Mr. Twig described.

Overhead, hounds bayed again. The wind suddenly revived and spun into a frenzy.

Jessica shook herself as if she were waking, and looked around. Her eyes fastened on Timothy. They held his for a moment, as if asking a question. Timothy dropped his gaze.

Jessica backed away.

"Look!" Sarah pointed up at the sky.

Pinpoints of red grew larger, drew closer.

The Morris men sheathed their swords. With a swift stroke, a dancer freed the Greenman from the web of ribbons. Sarah tried to cushion his fall, but he was too heavy, too stiff. The men lifted his still body from the ground, three men on each side, and without a word, they bore the lifeless form of the Greenman into the woods.

"Where are you taking him?" Sarah's voice cut sharply through the clearing, but there was no answer.

As his sister began to sob, Timothy looked across the clearing to Cerridwyn. She looked so stern and fiery that Timothy turned his eyes away.

Jessica had paused at the edge of the clearing. Timothy looked at her terror-filled face. Her shoulders were hunched; her body shook. He'd never seen anyone look as alone as she did. And through the night, the hunt drew closer.

✝ ✝ ✝

Jessica knew with certainty that the hounds were coming for her. She could imagine their hot breath on her neck, the great slobbering mouths, and the sharp bite of their teeth. Timothy and Sarah, the only people she knew here in the woods, looked at her with horror and pity. She had to get away, but where could she go?

Cerridwyn extended her bare arms wide. She reached one hand out to Timothy. With the other, she gestured in Jessica's direction. As Timothy looked at Jessica, his anger warred with pity. He couldn't forget what she had done, but she was so alone and miserable. "The hunt is coming. Soon it will be upon Jessica. Tonight she is the hunt's rightful prey. Timothy James Maxwell, you have the chance to rescue your friend, but it is a choice that only you can make."

"What?" A coldness crept up from Timothy's toes. "What do you mean?"

"You can save her."

Timothy shook his head. "My 'friend'? Why should I help her?"

Cerridwyn looked at him silently for a moment. "If you choose to go, Gwydon can aid your flight." Timothy looked at the ground. Cerridwyn was asking for some kind of choice. Was she asking him to be hunted instead of Jessica? Why him? Jessica wasn't anything like the popular girl who tormented him at school. No, she was a mess. It was impossible not to feel sorry for her. "What will happen to me?" He swallowed hard.

"I can't tell you how your story will end, because I don't write the stories. I can only tell you that you will be hunted across the skies. Gwydon is swift, and I suspect there are others who will come to your aid." Nothing she said sounded in the least reassuring to Timothy. "I can also tell you that if you take her place, Jessica will go free and return home safely."

Timothy thought of being chased across the sky by the very things he feared the most—the large wolflike hounds. It was worse than any nightmare. He looked at Sarah. She'd stopped crying and was standing by his side, listening to everything Cerridwyn said. He looked at Jessica again.

Star Girl now stood next to Jessica, watching them all. Jessica was pale, trembling, and covered in mud. Timothy remembered all the times she had made fun of him in front of her friends at school. But he also remembered talking to her in the library and visiting her at her house, another Jessica. Was it enough to make him risk his life? Would he even do that for a very good friend?

Timothy shuffled his feet. No one else spoke. He felt as if the entire world was waiting for his decision. He remembered the strange note with his name in it. *And Timothy James stands alone.* That poem had his name in it. Was it about saving Jessica? He felt as if this was something that he and he alone was meant to do, some purpose especially designed for him. He had wanted to be brave, to be wolfproof. He looked up at Cerridwyn. Her smile was reassuring, and he felt the first glimmer of hope. She thinks I can do this.

"I want to go with him," Sarah said, as if she could tell what he was thinking. "He's my little brother and I'm supposed to watch over him." She looked as fierce as any pirate in the middle of a storm.

"It's not your task. Your story goes in another direction," Cerridwyn said in a firm voice. "But quickly now; soon it will be too late to decide."

When Timothy looked up, he could see the red eyes of the hounds and the darker silhouette of antlers against the sky. He looked straight at Cerridwyn. This was his task; if he looked away, he would lose his nerve. "I'll go," he said, even though his legs shook and his heart pounded so hard, he thought it might explode from his chest.

Cerridwyn took the gold leaf crown from her head and placed it on Timothy's. "My crown goes with you. Whoever wears it has some of my power, and great strength against adversity. It's not something to be given, or worn, lightly."

Timothy put his hand up and touched the crown. He felt his back grow a little straighter, and for a moment, he almost felt brave.

Cerridwyn signaled to Gwydon, who padded over and stood by Timothy's side. Timothy knew he was meant to climb on the wolf's back. He closed his eyes and tried not to think of all forty-two teeth in the wolf's mouth.

"Why does he have to go?" Sarah's voice was shrill. "Jessica is the one they want!"

Timothy knew Sarah was afraid for him. For a moment, his own fear made it impossible to move, but Gwydon lowered his head, and Timothy, with his eyes closed, put his arms around the thick fur of the wolf's neck. Sick with fear, he swung a leg across Gwydon's back. He could feel the wolf's muscles bunch and gather. In one tremendous bound, they were off, skyward.

20

THE HUNT RIDES

ARAH STOOD, lips slightly parted, watching her brother disappear into the storm on Gwydon's back. There was nothing she could do. Hot tears of frustration spilled down her cheeks. She looked at Jessica, who still cowered. "If anything happens to my brother—"

But Cerridwyn cut off her words. "It wasn't your choice. This night will be long, and we still have much to do before we see your brother again."

"How can you know that we *will* see him again?" Sarah met Cerridwyn's eyes with a challenge. "I should have gone; I'm the oldest."

"Age has nothing to do with it; he is the one who was called. We also have a job to do." As she spoke, she removed an arrow from her quiver and tested its strength.

The word *we* offered Sarah a glimpse of hope. "Please, I'll do anything to help him."

The wind rustled and moaned through the tops of the trees. Sarah looked across the clearing. Both Jessica and Star Girl were gone.

Cerridwyn spoke. "Can you use a bow and arrow? Can you ride?" She looked closely at Sarah, and Sarah was acutely aware of how tall and imposing Mrs. Clapper's new form was.

"I won a prize for archery at summer camp two years in a row."

"At least you know how to shoot, but the conditions will be very different tonight," Cerridwyn said. From under her cloak she drew out a bow, smaller than her own, made of yew wood. She handed it to Sarah, along with a quiver filled with some of her own arrows.

Sarah held the bow in her hands and was surprised how light it felt. She fumbled nervously, trying to fit an arrow into the bow.

"Watch me now." In one smooth motion, Mrs. Clapper demonstrated how to pull back the bow, aim, and fire, sending an arrow flying into the canopy of the hornbeam tree. Sarah heard it fall through the branches, and there, lying on the ground, was a seedpod pierced through by the arrow.

"Pay close attention and follow me, and you'll do fine. But it will require all your concentration."

Sarah wasn't so sure that she would be fine at all. But the job gave her something to think about other than her brother. Her fingers felt thick and clumsy. The wind whipped her hair into her eyes, making it difficult to see; the cold seeped into her bones. Her fear for Timothy kept rising like a tide.

Cerridwyn drew another arrow into her bow, this time aiming into the open sky between the canopy of trees. Her wild red hair gleamed.

The wind lifted her cloak; underneath, her bare arms were strong and muscular. She let the arrow loose into the night sky. Sarah waited and watched and tried to concentrate, as Cerridwyn had asked. For some minutes, she saw and heard nothing; then there was another sound in the wind. Something was coming toward them with great speed. Sarah half hoped it would be her brother returning on Gwydon, but what came instead took her breath away.

✦ ✦ ✦

Timothy opened one eye. Before him, the night sky streamed by; clouds and stars were all a frightening blur, and the wind made his eyes tear. His arms were locked around Gwydon's neck, his face almost buried in the shaggy fur. Slowly, he opened his other eye and looked down. They were high enough above the treetops that his feet cleared them by a yard; they were low enough to see every house, every lawn, in detail when the moon was unobscured. The first glimpse sent waves of terror washing over him. The ground was so far below! By the second glance, he felt exhilarated! This was better than any of his flying dreams, better than anything he had ever imagined!

Gwydon was steady in flight, and as Timothy gripped the wolf's sides, he could feel the beast's muscles working to propel them through the night. He steadied the crown on his head. The exhilaration didn't last long. The wind lashed out with sudden force, and in its gusts Timothy could hear voices, the baying of hounds, and a deeply bellowed laugh. He pictured the red-eyed hounds chasing him. Worst of all, he pictured the horned man who hunted souls. The wave of fear was so strong that he almost slipped from Gwydon's neck. Bile rose in his throat, and he was afraid he was going to be sick. He closed his eyes again and hung his head over the side of the great beast. The cold wind bit his face and raked through his hair.

Gwydon heard the calls, too. His speed increased. He rose higher into the sky, and his path became more circuitous as the sound of the hounds grew closer. Below him, Timothy heard the scream of a horse that had been left out to pasture, and he braved a look downward. In the moonlight, he saw a dark coat with a blaze of white across the horse's chest. Two hounds sped downward toward the horse. Again the horse screamed. Then, gathering his strength he bolted over the fence. The hounds did not let up. Timothy could see the tops of their white backs disappear through the trees, in pursuit. Then the horse was in the open again, running with a wild fury; the hounds gained on him. Timothy could imagine the heaving sides, the sweat-flecked neck. In an instant, the hounds were upon the horse, the first ripping at the Achilles tendon so that the noble animal would stumble and fall. The second hound tore at the horse's throat, and the dying beast let out a final, piercing scream. Timothy buried his face in Gwydon's fur, but this time images of the dying horse filled his head. A sob shook him as he realized that he, too, was their prey.

Why had he agreed to do this? The choice had seemed clear earlier; it was something that he was called to do, something that had less to do with being a hero than obeying whatever was calling him. And now he was sure to die: falling from Gwydon's back, or on the ground, savagely attacked by dogs; it really didn't matter how. He just knew that he wasn't ready to let that happen. There must be some way to survive. He summoned all his willpower to focus on that thought. But it wasn't enough. Turning his head, he saw the gleam of the hounds' eyes, the silhouette of antlers tearing through the night behind them. Help me, he thought, and then he shouted the plea out loud. It echoed emptily through the night.

✚ ✚ ✚

Two white-tailed deer came bounding out of the sky and skidded to a stop near the feet of Cerridwyn. Sarah thought they were the most beautiful creatures she had ever seen. They were a perfectly matched pair in both size and coloring, a soft brown with white markings. Each sported a full rack of antlers above a long, arching neck. Sarah timidly reached out a hand to stroke the velvety fur. The stag quivered under her hand, but its eyes were focused on Cerridwyn, who bent to whisper something in each of the stags' ears. Then, without speaking a word to Sarah, she mounted one of them with ease. Sarah swallowed, guessing that she was expected to do the same.

She slung her bow from one shoulder as she had seen Cerridwyn do. The deer's back seemed to be a long way off the ground. When Sarah threw one arm around the stag's neck, he shifted his feet uneasily. There was no saddle or stirrup to help her pull up when she tried to throw a leg over his back. How was she supposed to mount? One leg was almost over when she slid in a heap to the ground. *Ouch!* Her tailbone collided with a rock. Rubbing her backside, she tried again. Again she fell. Cerridwyn said nothing, but her stag pranced impatiently.

"I need help."

Cerridwyn looked down at her from the back of her deer, and in the half-light her face, terrible and beautiful, softened. She spoke several words in a language Sarah did not recognize, and the deer knelt down, bending his forelegs under him. Now Sarah easily slipped onto his back. She threw her arms around his slender neck just as he bounded into the sky. Toward Timothy, Sarah hoped.

21

REGRETS

T HE BLIND FEAR and panic subsided, leaving in their place a strange vacantness, a feeling Jessica knew well, one she always tried hard to keep at bay. It was the same emptiness she felt in the dark hours of morning when the rest of the world slept. It was the feeling she got when she was alone for too long and unwanted thoughts circled like flying insects. This time there was no escaping her thoughts. Her mind replayed the last hour and the awful thing she had done. Striking out at Jimmy had felt good, repayment for mocking her, but the crumpled form on the ground had not been Jimmy at all. Instead, it was a forlorn thing, part man, part tree. It wasn't as if she had hurt a human, she tried to reassure herself, but then the dancing men had come and borne him away as if he were a human after all. And she had seen the look of horror on Timothy's face and on his sister's face.

The hounds came then. She could almost feel their hot breath, hear the snapping of their jaws. Just as she was about to run, Timothy had mounted something . . . a giant wolf. And the hounds turned and chased him instead. The emptiness came over her like a howling wave.

Just as she felt as if she would drown, the beautiful girl touched her arm, and the burn of her touch forced Jessica to focus on the pain and kept her mind from being swept away. She knew that Sarah blamed the entire course of events on her. And if anything happened to Timothy, Jessica knew that she would always blame herself.

All she wanted to do was escape. When the star girl left the clearing and climbed a great ash tree, Jessica followed—anything to avoid Sarah's accusing eyes. They climbed silently through the leafy branches, feeling the muscled bark of the tree beneath them, climbing higher and higher until Jessica was sure there could be no branches above. Still they continued to climb. If a tree could be said to straighten its back, then that was exactly what the ash was doing; branches that hung down toward the ground were lifted and straightened. Just once, Jessica looked down; the ground was a dizzying drop below. She felt her head swim, and she threw both arms around a stout branch and refused to move. Without speaking, the girl stopped just above her, settling into the vee of two leafless branches. Jessica's hands were raw from gripping the ridged bark so tightly. Her arm burned from the girl's touch, and her twisted ankle throbbed.

"Who are you?" Jessica asked.

Star Girl looked down at Jessica, her bright hair like fine spiderwebs among the branches and twigs. "I am here to bear witness. It is my job to watch and remember."

"What do you mean 'to bear witness'?" Jessica was sore and tired. She felt a flicker of anger return.

"It means to carry along something you have seen, to pay attention, to keep the knowledge alive. Look." Star Girl gestured downward, and for the second time that night Jessica looked down.

Below her stretched the expanse of the forest, and she could see it all, border to border. And beyond the forest to the west she could see a great span of water with no farther shore. She couldn't tell if she was looking at a very wide river or the ocean. To the east were fields, some with fences and a house, that ran into the feet of saw-toothed mountains. The farthest mountains were capped with snow. None of this was the land Jessica knew. She was not on the edge of a wooded greenbelt bordering the highway. She could see a road, but it was dirt and faint in the moonlight. The entire world that she knew was gone, and as she looked out over the strange land, an overwhelming feeling of nausea shook her. She closed her eyes and wrapped herself tightly around the branch.

"Where are we?"

"The land you see is still your land, but tonight we are in time out of time." As the girl finished speaking, the wind began to scream again. Fresh gusts blew in from the north. The branches swayed, and Jessica looked up into the night sky. Two white-tailed deer appeared out of the darkness. It couldn't be! Sarah and the huntress were riding them! When she heard the hounds barking, Jessica moaned and hid her head.

✛ ✛ ✛

The quarry had changed. Herne could smell the change before he saw it; a boy riding a large wolf was leading the hounds. Herne peered across the backs of his dogs. He knew that wolf, Gwydon. Cerridwyn must be involved. He dipped low over a pond; the hounds had caught a scent below. A pair of geese flew up, panicked. Startled, they honked their way skyward, wings beating furiously. The hounds howled their satisfaction, urging the geese forward. The geese would not be able to last long. Herne raised the silver horn to his lips and blew. The baying of the hounds was answered by something else, an older cry, the forlorn voices of wolves howling at the moon.

SUMMONING
THE WOLVES

TIMOTHY WAS SLOWLY growing accustomed to the motion of powerful Gwydon's legs surging forward. It was a strange sensation, as if the huge wolf were running across the ground rather than through the night sky, but the roar of the wind filling Timothy's ears and the billowing clouds were more like navigating an ocean. He needed all his concentration to balance, holding on to Gwydon's shaggy neck. Every now and then he allowed himself short glimpses over the wolf's flanks to the land below. Where were they, Sarah, Star Girl, and Cerridwyn?

He remembered the words in the Celtic encyclopedia, *Herne hunts souls.* Timothy thought of his own soul and wondered what Herne could want with it. And what did Herne do with the soulless body? Was it cast away on the ground like the crumpled form of the Greenman? Timothy tried not to think of the gentle Greenman lying in a heap on the forest floor. He thought instead of the strange poem with his name in it, and tried to remind himself that this was his great adventure, something that only he could do. But it didn't help much. He lost all sense of time, and his body ached as if he had been riding for hours, shoulders clenched in fear and legs cramping where they gripped Gwydon's sides. He tried to flatten himself along the wolf's back to reduce the wind resistance and keep himself warmer.

Tired and buried in Gwydon's warm fur, Timothy dozed off. He had no idea how long he drowsed, but a flash of jagged lightning and the crack of thunder startled him awake. The second flash split a black pillar of clouds as the hounds' voices grew to a crescendo. Timothy buried his face deeper into Gwydon's fur, hoping to block out the noise of his pursuers, but another sound caught his attention. The blast of a horn was immediately followed by the harsh and lonely howling of wolves. It was a sound both like and unlike the call of the hounds, chilling Timothy's heart. Gwydon dipped low, and Timothy brushed the crown of an oak tree with his legs. A pair of mallards flew up through the leaves, desperately flapping their wings. Timothy turned and watched in horror as the white hounds surrounded them, almost trampling them in their flight. Neck askew, one plummeted to the ground, a hound in pursuit.

Lightning flashed again. A pack of gray wolves appeared, slavering and running to join the hunt. All of Timothy's old fears rose like a great wave about to suffocate him. *If only we could be wolfproof!* His eyes burned and teared, from the wind or fear he didn't know. And still Gwydon ran on.

✤ ✦ ✤

From the back of her deer, Sarah watched her brother's flight for what seemed like hours. For the first time in her life, she was unable to help him. The deer easily kept pace with the hunt, and as she rode, her stomach was curdled with fear. The two animals glided silently, unnoticed through the night. Cerridwyn looked grim and beautiful, her red hair streaming behind her and her cheeks flushed in the wind. If it had been any other time or circumstance, Sarah would have loved the wild ride through the night sky, but her fear for Timothy kept her mouth dry and her heart pounding.

The quiver of arrows pressed into her back, and she worried whether she would be able to use them well when the time came. Over and over again, she told herself Timothy would escape. On the other hand, the Greenman hadn't escaped, and she shuddered, as if an icy finger traced her spine. Ahead, the white hounds ran without tiring, followed by the awful man with horns, the man Timothy had called Herne. But on Gwydon, Timothy managed to stay in the lead, keeping a safe distance beyond the snarling and the snapping jaws.

Suddenly, from behind, Sarah heard wolves howling. As she looked over her shoulder, she saw the pack break through the clouds! The deer swerved to avoid them. She slid sideways until only one leg was across the stag's back. She tightened her arms around his neck and inched herself upright. Would the wolves pursue the stags?

†✝†

Herne had called in the wolves, but it was no more than Cerridwyn had expected. He would follow his prey to the ends of the earth, but she would do what was necessary as well. She looked across at the deer that kept pace with her and nodded in approval. The girl, Sarah, was coping remarkably well. She looked frightened but determined. It was almost time. Cerridwyn could feel it in the wind, in the pace of the storm. Far below, she had seen the white forms of the Morris men moving slowly, carrying the Greenman. She knew they would stop near the river. She would have to act swiftly and accurately. She thought about Herne; she had known him from the beginning of time beyond time. He lived for the hunt and his hounds. The wolves were gaining on Timothy. Even Gwydon would have difficulty outrunning them for long. For the first time, she would need to interfere with Herne's task. The death of a wolf would be of little consequence to Herne, but he would not easily forgive the death of a beloved hunting hound.

TRAPS AND SNARES

THE RAIN BEGAN in harsh bursts that blew sideways across the sky. Timothy felt the drops sting his face, and he closed his eyes as he rode face-forward into the storm. Gwydon continued running closer to the ground; he was barely skirting the tops of the trees. His fur grew slippery and wet, and Timothy slid from side to side. The smell of wet fur surrounded him like a heavy blanket. Water plastered his hair to his head; droplets ran down his neck and into his shirt. He was thoroughly miserable.

Another bolt of lightning struck, close enough to make even the hair on his arms stand on end. His ears rang with the clap of thunder. Directly ahead, a small section of sky opened, a ragged tear in the night. Light seeped out. Gwydon, with the hunt close behind, lunged forward and into the opening just as it was closing. The wolf's desperate leap carried them up and through an open window. The terrible clamor of the hunt, the baying of the hounds, the shriek of the wind—all went silent. They had found sanctuary.

✛ ✛ ✛

When the prey vanished, the hounds began to howl. Herne, who had ridden with his dogs for time out of time, had never seen prey vanish into the sky as the boy and wolf had done. Blowing the silver horn, he tried to rein in the hounds while they circled and pawed the air. The company of wolves snapped and growled alongside them. They had lost their prey and would not be consoled.

✛ ✛ ✛

Timothy looked back over his shoulder for Herne and his pack but saw only darkness. Gwydon had eluded the hunt. They landed with a thud in a dimly lit room. A faint mechanical whine and Gwydon's claws clacking on a wood floor were the only noises.

They appeared to be in some kind of workshop. The whirring and clicking sounds came from an amazing array of mechanical devices that covered every surface. Cages of fine woven metal, intricate silver nets, braided tethers, and jeweled boxes. Cage doors and the lids of boxes whirred open and clicked closed of their own volition. Ornate and plain, all were made with skilled workmanship—even Timothy could tell that. Gwydon stood at attention, his sides still heaving. His ears flicked forward, a low growl vibrating his chest.

Out of the shadows stepped one of the most striking men Timothy had ever seen. He was tall and muscular; his bronzed skin glowed. Golden hair curled around the tops of his ears, and each feature on his face was perfectly carved, so that his nose looked like the very definition of *nose*, and his eyes gleamed as all eyes should gleam. He wore a deep-red velvet vest. It was buttoned over a white shirt with a stand-up collar. The sleeves were pushed up to reveal the muscular forearms of a workman. His black pants were tucked into a pair of fine leather boots.

"Well, hello there. Whom do I have the pleasure of addressing?"

The fur rose along Gwydon's neck, and his growl was louder now.

"Hush." Timothy placed a palm on Gwydon's head. "I'm Timothy, and this is Gwydon." And he felt his body relax just the tiniest bit.

"It's not often I encounter a boy riding a wolf in my workshop."

If Timothy found it remarkable to be suddenly out of the storm and in a workshop, it was no more remarkable than any of the other confusing events of the night. By now his mind felt so thick with weariness that he no longer tried to make sense of it all. He was only grateful to be away from Herne, his hounds, and the pack of wolves. And was growing warmer every minute. The fear of the hunt was behind him, and he could think again.

"What are these?" Timothy gestured toward all the strange devices. His legs still vibrated with Gwydon's low growl.

The golden man laughed. "They're beautiful, aren't they?" He held up a silver net so fine that it ran like water through his fingers. "Here, try to tear it." He tossed the net to Timothy.

Timothy tugged and pulled at the silvery metal. It was flexible but impossible to break. *"Magnificent,"* he said and couldn't help mentally adding up the Scrabble points for each letter, nineteen total.

The man beamed with pleasure. "I make snares and traps, cages for hunting, or capturing, or protecting things. I see you appreciate fine workmanship." He gestured at the small crown Timothy wore.

Timothy reached up and felt the slim circlet still nestled in his hair. He had forgotten all about the crown. "Where am I, and how did I get here?"

Again the man smiled, and his smile dazzled Timothy. He found himself wishing that this man could be his friend. "Well, you are in my workshop. You and the beast entered through my window, but where you've come from and why, I can't say."

Gwydon growled loudly and bared his fearsome teeth. He paced back and forth across the workshop floor while Timothy still sat on his back. Timothy placed a restraining hand on the wolf's head.

"Perhaps you and your wolf would like some water. Why don't you slide down?"

And suddenly there was nothing that Timothy wanted more than cool, sweet water. His throat felt parched and the air too warm. As he tried to slide from Gwydon's back, the wolf turned his large head and snapped at Timothy.

"Here, here, we can't have that." The man strode over to a large wooden chest, opened a drawer, and took out a large collar and leash that twinkled and gleamed. The collar was studded with red and green jewels. Timothy wondered if they were rubies and emeralds and immediately thought of Sarah. She would love this place; it would remind her of pirate treasure. "Do you think this will suit him? You can tether him here while we have some refreshment, and you can give him a bowl of water."

"Yes, that's a good idea, tethering him," Timothy found himself saying, even though he knew in his heart that Gwydon would despise being tethered. But it might be the only way to get some of the cool, sweet water, and his legs ached so from riding on the wolf's back. Why couldn't Gwydon see that they were safe now?

Timothy slid off the wolf's back, and his legs quivered as they hit solid ground. He took the collar from the man and fastened it around Gwydon's neck. Then he clipped the leash to a hook on the floor. Gwydon dropped his head and shoulders but looked at Timothy with eyes full of reproach. With unbearable thirst, Timothy watched the man pour some water from a pitcher into a silver bowl.

"Perhaps we can make a trade. Some water for that circlet you are wearing." Again he poured a stream of sparkling water into the bowl.

Timothy's eyes never left the bowl. His tongue felt thick, and it stuck to the roof of his mouth. If he didn't drink soon, he was sure he would die. Cerridwyn's stern face flashed before him, but he pushed the image aside. Surely she would understand how much he needed water. "All right," he said, though his tongue felt so swollen, he could barely form the words. He reached up and removed the simple crown.

The man grabbed the crown from Timothy's hands and thrust the bowl at him. The man stuffed the crown into a deep pocket of his pants.

Timothy took a small sip. The water was just as cool and sweet as he'd imagined, and he drank in greedy gulps. Water trickled off his chin and dripped on the wood floor. But his thirst was not satisfied.

Just as Timothy was about to ask for more, he heard a cat cry. The cry came from across the room, and even Gwydon lifted his dejected head, his ears twitching. On one of the long wooden shelves, a gray cat crouched under a small dome. The cage was too small for the hunched creature, which reached one soft paw out through the silver gridwork as if pleading for freedom. But the cat wasn't the only caged animal. Timothy spied more animals: other cats, birds, reptiles, and rabbits, each one confined in a different cage. The cages were works of art. They gleamed and glowed. Each had intricate patterns of mesh, some silver, some copper. "Why do you have all those animals in cages?" Timothy asked.

"Cages and snares," the man corrected him. "I use the animals to test my workmanship."

The gray cat continued its mewling. The man looked up and drew his eyebrows together. The cat cried louder.

"Silence!" In one bound, the man was across the room. He lifted the cage from the shelf and swung it through the air, dumping both cat and cage into a large wooden barrel. Timothy tried to get closer to see what was inside the barrel, but his legs wouldn't move.

"I suspect you are still thirsty," the man purred. "There is nothing like riding to dehydrate a person."

And Timothy found that he was indeed thirsty, so thirsty that he couldn't speak, only nod.

"I'm so glad *you* came, but I was expecting a young lady. She was to be my assistant. The hounds should have delivered her here. I was hoping to enjoy Herne's expression when he lost her." The man pulled a pocket watch from his vest pocket and impatiently checked the time. His other arm was still in the barrel. "That should do it." He pulled up the cage, dripping wet. The gray cat lay in a limp huddle, paws extended through the grid . . . drowned.

Gwydon growled deep and low. Timothy's stomach lurched.

"Where is she?" the man asked impatiently. "The girl I was expecting?"

Jessica's face filled Timothy's mind. He was sure that she was who the man was looking for. "I took her place," Timothy found himself saying. "I was chased here by hounds with red eyes."

"How very noble! But I would expect no less from the boy with the crown. I knew we would meet sometime. But I never expected you to come to me." The man opened a drawer and pulled out a silver belt. It shimmered and sparkled and snaked through his hands like something alive. "I had a present for her."

Timothy reached out one hand to touch the belt. But the man dangled it just out of his reach. Even more than he wanted the next drink of water, Timothy wanted that belt. All thoughts of the drowned cat were gone. He longed to let the slippery silver run through his hands.

"Perhaps the belt will fit you." The man bent toward Timothy.

Timothy held his breath.

With a terrible lunge, Gwydon thrust his neck and shoulders forward, straining the tether. Surprised, the man dropped the belt. It fell to the floor in a silver curl.

Snakelike, the belt unwound and slithered across the floor, disappearing under a tall dresser. Timothy threw himself to the floor. The simple wooden dresser stood on long curving legs, the bottom clearing the floor by about two feet. There was just enough room to crawl under it. The belt gleamed in the darkness just beyond his fingertips, and Timothy scooted under the dresser. He was close enough to grab it, but it slinked away, out of his reach. He inched forward. The belt slithered beyond the back of the dresser. Timothy crawled closer and made a quick grab for the belt. With a whir and click, something dropped down behind him and snapped into place.

Startled, Timothy looked back over his shoulder. A metal door with an intricate grid pattern had dropped between him and the back of the dresser. He swiveled his head; on all sides were metal bars of the same intricate pattern. The dresser was merely a few inches deep, a false front for a large trap. His heart sank. The metal bars were thicker than those on the animal traps but no less ornate. He was in a cage, caught, just like one of the animals. And the silver belt was gone.

The cage was not tall enough for Timothy to sit upright. He crouched on his knees. Just like the animals, he had been lured into a trap. The intricate cage was nothing more than a trap with a door that dropped down and latched. His father had used one to capture a raccoon that had taken up residence under their front porch last summer. The latch and bolt made the door impossible to open from the inside.

Timothy pushed as hard as he could against the door, but it didn't give. He rolled onto his side. There was no room to straighten his legs. He thrust them against the side of the cage as hard as he could. Nothing gave. From somewhere behind him, he heard a laugh.

"Set the trap and bait it well. The prey follows; it always will." The golden man stood looking at him, hands on his hips, his eyes gleaming.

"Let me go!"

"But I've forgotten my manners. My name is Balor."

The man paused while the name settled in the air. Timothy stared through the bars of his cage. He'd heard that name before. Mr. Twig's words came rushing back to him. "The question you should ask is, If he's evil." Fear made it difficult for him to breathe.

"What do you want?" Timothy's voice was tight. He was afraid he already knew the answer. Trapped in this cage, he would be held for Herne and the hunt.

"I confess you were a surprise—but a valuable one. You've already given me your crown." Balor dangled it from one hand. "You have no rowan branch for protection this time."

How could he have trusted this man? Timothy shot a glance at Gwydon. The wolf's eyes were locked on Balor. Gwydon bared his teeth.

"There are many portways between worlds. Even the noble Gwydon didn't know this one. He was so desperate to save you from the wolves, he carried you right into my workshop." Balor laughed with delight and strode from the room.

"Wait, you've got to let me out!"

But there was no one to hear his cry.

Gwydon whined again and then lunged. He lay back down and worried at his hind leg.

Timothy was a prisoner in a world of elaborate cages. Unless he looked carefully, it was almost impossible to see the doors and wires that held them closed: sliding wires, pivoting wires, and some that seemed to be simple snares, a loop of silver on a length of line. Timothy remembered finding a dead rabbit in the woods near his house. It had hopped into a loop of wire, releasing a trigger bar that tightened the wire around the rabbit's leg, lifting it off the ground. When Timothy came across it, the rabbit was long dead. One leg hung at a crazy angle, obviously broken, and no one had ever come to claim the prey. He had wondered what bait had drawn the rabbit into the trap, or if the rabbit had simply wandered in the wrong place.

He thought ruefully of the silver belt and felt his face flush with shame. He had been caught as easily as the rabbit. How quickly he had handed over Cerridwyn's gift, the golden crown. What would she think of him? And Balor had tethered the faithful Gwydon! His eyes watered, and his shoulders, already sore from bending over Gwydon's back, burned from being hunched.

All around him, the traps and snares gleamed. Their beauty and craftsmanship made them even more horrible. An exotic bird with yellow and red feathers looked down from an upper shelf. Cats of all sizes and descriptions cowered in small traps, and something with red eyes and a sinewy body of thick fur hunched near him. Across the room, Gwydon whined again and continued gnawing at his paw.

The floor was cold and hard; Timothy was hungry and the water had only intensified his thirst. If he concentrated on the problem of escaping, he could forget about his discomfort for a few minutes at a time. Most important of all, concentrating kept him from giving up. But he was tired, and his mind couldn't or wouldn't obey him for long. It ran in useless circles. He had failed the one adventure set before him, failed Sarah, Jessica, Gwydon, and Cerridwyn. He'd been taken in by Balor, dazzled by him and his glittering cages. This is what came of trying to be heroic.

Timothy rolled onto his back, knees drawn up to his chest, and let despair wash over him.

TIMOTHY'S PLAN

ERCHED IN THE TREETOP, Jessica watched the mad flight across the sky. She should have been the one struggling to ride the wolf, would have been the one if Timothy hadn't taken her place. It was as if she were watching through binoculars, forced to view a scene she would rather not see, but at the same time, she couldn't look away. Timothy was slumped low, shoulders hunched and head almost pillowed in the wolf's fur. Herne and his hounds were gaining on them, the wolves and hounds howling in chorus. A small wolf pulled ahead of the pack, lunging at Gwydon's left hind foot. The great wolf swerved to miss the snapping jaws and, in that instant, Jessica saw Timothy slip sideways.

"No! Timothy, hold on! I'm sorry!" But her screams and her tears were lost in the wind. She looked to the star girl for help, but the girl sat calmly on her branch, watching the event as one might watch a movie. "Do something . . . anything!" Jessica hissed.

"It is not my place to change events, only to observe them," she replied without once glancing in Jessica's direction.

✛ ✛ ✛

Timothy must have slept, because the next thing he knew, the room was darker and he was colder. But his mind seemed clearer. There had to be a way to escape. It was up to him; nobody was going to rescue him.

He carefully examined the locking mechanism again. If he could just understand it, then perhaps he could work backward and release the latch. He knew a little about snares and traps. When his father had set up the box trap to catch the raccoon last summer, Timothy had read everything he could on the computer about traps and snares. His obsession for information came in handy now. He knew that most snares grew tighter the more you struggled. Traps had a moving part that was triggered by a release, grasping or closing around the victim. Some doors were held in place by gravity, but some actually locked. By lying on his side he was able to see how his cage closed. When the door dropped, a bolt or pin slid into place. So, no matter how hard he pushed against the door, it wouldn't budge. The only way out would be to release the latch pin from the outside, but the space between the bars was too narrow even for his fingers. Besides, he would need two hands to raise the door once the pin was released.

The weight of the door had caused it to fall, and in the upper-right-hand corner of the cage were the bolt and latch pin. The latch was held in place by a spring. He rubbed his hand across his nose, which had begun, annoyingly, to run. To open the trap, he would have to find a way to reach out of the cage and release the spring, then lift the door so he could slip out.

The odds were not in his favor. He needed something long, thin, and fairly strong to push back the pin. Turning onto his side, he slipped his hand into one pocket of his jeans. He tried the right pocket first: gum, string, a flat skipping rock—nothing at all useful. He carefully rolled to the other side, trying to remember what he had stored in his pockets. He used to carry a pocketknife, but those had been outlawed at school, so his knife sat at home on his dresser.

If only he could straighten his legs. He forced his hand into his left pocket and tugged out a badly bent playing card, the ace of spades, followed by a wad of rubber bands. He burrowed his hand down farther and felt it scrape against the very thing he had been looking for, his mechanical pencil. He had stuck it in there when he dressed because his shirt didn't have a pocket. Never had anything seemed as perfect as his old blue pencil.

Just as he had hoped, the pencil slid smoothly between the bars. Gwydon gave a low growl, and Timothy froze, listening for footsteps. All was quiet. His hand shook, so it took several minutes before he could line up the tip of the pencil with the bolt. He had forgotten to draw in the lead; with a small snap, it broke off. If only the pencil was strong enough! Timothy pivoted the pencil against the bar, pushing the latch pin as far as he could.

Now came the delicate part. With his left hand, he inserted the thin metal clip between the pin and the bar, so that it would hold the pin in place until he could insert the pencil between the next two bars. His hand was so unsteady that it took two tries. He quickly pulled out the pencil; the clip held. Carefully, he stuck the pencil between the next two bars. He had to hurry! Every moment, he expected to hear Balor's footsteps. Even though the room was cold, a bead of sweat appeared along his upper lip.

Bar by bar, Timothy worked the pin, using the pencil, out past the edge of the door of the cage. Finally, he reached the point where the pin was released from the latch and no longer locked the door; the spring was fully compressed. It would take two hands to lift the door, and the pencil would drop as soon as he lifted it. He would have only one chance.

If the pencil could hold just long enough! He arranged himself the best he could to lift the heavy door, but it was difficult in his crouched position. It was awfully cold now; his fingers were stiff and clumsy as they gripped the bottom of the door.

He thrust the door up with all his might. It was even heavier than he expected. As the door slid up, it dislodged the pencil, which tottered for a moment on a horizontal bar, then dropped outside the cage, rolling out of reach!

Timothy wedged one leg under the door. The metal scraped the heavy denim of his jeans. Twisting and sliding, he forced himself under the door, inch by inch. Now just his shoulders and head remained inside the cage. His arms trembled from the weight of the door pressing down. The metal bar scraped the side of his face and nicked his ear.

Finally, he lay free, scraped and exhausted. He was outside the cage! Gwydon watched intently.

Timothy pushed himself to his feet and crouched down by the wolf, ready to undo his tether. "Let's go. I'll help you."

Then he saw why Gwydon no longer moved. His hind leg, held in a bear claw trap, was matted with blood where the teeth of the trap bit through the thick fur.

"Don't worry. I'll get you out." He tried to sound more hopeful than he felt. Gwdyon growled deep and low, and then licked Timothy's hand. The bear trap was held by two springs, one on each side. Timothy needed to release each one to open the jaws. Hoping his weight would be enough to compress the springs, he stomped one foot down on each. The jaws shuddered, and sprang apart.

Gwydon tentatively lifted the injured leg up and out of the trap. It was a pitiful sight. The golden fur was stiff with blood. Timothy ran his hand down the leg, feeling gently through the stiff fur and hoping against hope that it wasn't broken, that Gwydon would be able to bear them both to safety. The wolf flinched as Timothy's hand passed down the length of his leg. It seemed intact, but his hand came away sticky with fresh blood. The wolf watched patiently as Timothy pulled off his shirt, ripping off a strip of cloth to bandage the leg. He had never bandaged anything before and, once again, felt totally inadequate for the job. Trying to remember the way Sarah wrapped her feet for dance, he tucked the loose end into the top of the wrapping, hoping it wasn't so tight that it would cut off Gwydon's circulation.

Gwydon stood stiffly and nudged Timothy with his nose. Timothy unfastened the collar. "Do you think you can still carry me?" he whispered.

From overhead, he heard a sharp hiss. Timothy jumped to his feet. A striped orange cat with mangy tufts of fur and an ear that looked as if it had been chewed up in a fight crouched in a cage. This cat didn't plead for release. Instead, it fixed Timothy with its green eyes, demanding freedom, compelling him to help. Once more, Timothy looked around the workshop at the sad, trapped animals. A puppy whined and pressed itself against the bars. There might not be time to free all of them, but he couldn't leave without trying to release as many as he could, even if it meant having to face Balor again. He'd start with the old cat. It was difficult to reach the cage, even when standing on tiptoe. When he finally slid the bolt open, the cat sprang to the floor, hissing and shaking as if throwing off a terrible indignity.

As quickly as possible, Timothy began to open cages: the exotic bird, a large iguana, the cowering puppy. Some of the animals milled around his feet, rubbing against him and tripping him up, while others disappeared immediately.

He had to hurry. There were still many more traps and snares. The more he opened, the more he noticed. A small fox dragged a leg broken by a snare, but there was no time to tend to any injuries. Once the animals were freed, they were on their own. He worked steadily, occasionally pinching a finger, but becoming more adept with each cage he opened. Timothy was so intent on his work that he didn't hear the soft tread of steps from behind.

Gwydon growled. A strong hand gripped Timothy's bare shoulder. Spinning around, he was face-to-face with Balor.

"Cutting your visit short? You passed my test magnificently, like I knew you would." A compelling smile spread across his handsome face. "I've been looking for an intelligent assistant like you for a very long time. You are even more valuable to me than the girl I expected. You must understand, I had to take every precaution. I couldn't let just anyone be my assistant." He paused to let the word *assistant* soak in.

Timothy stood still.

"You, Timothy, are worthy of learning my secrets, of changing the world. You're capable of great things, things you've never imagined. You don't often get an offer like that, do you?" And Balor smiled his heart-breaking smile.

For a moment, Timothy wavered. He could learn Balor's secrets. Maybe he had misunderstood. Maybe this had been nothing more than a test. He looked into Balor's deep eyes and imagined what it would be like to be his assistant, remembering the silver belt.

"*Yee-ow!*" The orange cat's yowl cut through the workshop. It arched its mangy back and hissed. With an effort, Timothy pulled his eyes away from Balor. The spell of Balor's words was broken.

A movement in the shadows caught his eye. A small man with tufts of gray hair and a scraggly beard was creeping out from one of the opened cages. Hunched over, he paused and sniffed the air. Catching Timothy's eye, the man gave a nod and smiled, showing a mouthful of yellow teeth. Silently, he slinked away into the darkness. In the cage lay the split pelt of a rat. Did the man come out of the rat's skin?

Timothy shuddered as Balor's hand tightened on his shoulder. He tried to twist from Balor's grip as Gwydon nudged his legs. How to make Balor loosen his grip? If Timothy could distract Balor, even for a moment, he and Gwydon might have a chance. Otherwise, he would find himself back in one of the cages, or worse.

"If I was your assistant, would you give me something like this?" Timothy swiped at an ornately carved glass bowl. It tottered and fell from its stand, and Balor loosed his grip as he grabbed for the bowl.

In an instant, Timothy had flung one leg over Gwydon's back. With a swift bound, the wolf was airborne, heading straight out the window. Timothy slipped and then tightened his hold as he pulled himself onto the wolf's strong back.

Once free of the workshop, he couldn't help looking back. Balor's face was framed in the window. As Timothy watched, the beautiful features melted like wax, leaving gray skin stretched tightly over bone. In the very middle of Balor's forehead was a single socket filled with a milky eye. The eye was roving through the darkness and light streamed from it. Timothy knew the eye was seeking him.

He pushed his face into Gwydon's neck. He remembered another one-eyed creature, the cat at his bedroom window. Mr. Twig had said Balor could take many forms. Had Balor been searching for him even then?

Timothy and Gwydon flew into the dense chill of clouds. He shivered without his shirt and burrowed down into the wolf's fur. Once more the clouds parted. Beyond, the storm still raged. Timothy thought of the animals he had set free, and hoped that they, too, had made their escape. And who was the man who had escaped from the cage?

The ground was very far away, and a strange thickness in his head made Timothy dizzy. And over the rain and wind, he heard the thing he dreaded: the call of hounds. He had not escaped the hunt; it had waited for his return. And behind him, in the dark, Balor's eye was still searching.

A WILD SHOT

ARAH HAD NOT GIVEN UP. She continued to squint desperately into the wind and rain. She couldn't lose Timothy; he had to be out there somewhere! Cerridwyn was nowhere to be seen. They'd been separated in the storm. The hounds bayed, the wolves howled. Sarah could still see the red lights of their eyes circling above her where Timothy had disappeared.

And then she saw him. Timothy appeared on Gwydon as if he had just burst from a cloud. And he was close.

"Timothy!" Her voice was swallowed by the wind.

The hounds and wolves spotted their quarry as well. As Sarah watched, the hounds snarled and dove. In a moment, they would be on Timothy. Where was Cerridwyn?

In desperation, Sarah fit an arrow into the bow. She gripped the stag hard with her thighs to steady herself. The rain had almost stopped, but the wind continued to wail. As Sarah drew back the taut string, her arms trembled. This was nothing like archery at camp. The stag slowed, but he still moved, and she had to adjust for the wind. Taking a deep breath, she aimed for the lead hound. Then for good measure, she shot two more arrows.

✛ ✛ ✛

A sudden pain and fire coursed up Timothy's leg. One of Herne's hounds had bitten him! He grabbed for his calf, expecting blood. Instead, the butt of an arrow stuck out from his leg. He bent to tug at it and slid sideways. "Help, Gwydon! I'm falling!"

He clutched at the wolf's densely furred neck. But he slid farther. The leg with the arrow dangled as the other leg slid across Gwydon's spine. Timothy's fingers lost their grip, one by one. They scrabbled desperately at the slick fur but found no purchase. Hot rivers of pain shot up his leg. He was falling! He flailed his arms, but there was nothing to grab.

Wind shrilled in his ears. Trees rushed up from the ground. All around was black, empty sky. Branches tore at his face, slashed his bare chest and arms. The hard bed of earth waited just below.

✛ ✛ ✛

Jessica could no longer sit in the tree with the silent girl. Timothy needed help! She saw him slide from the wolf's back. He was falling! She marked the spot where he would land and began a frantic climb down through the branches. The others might get there before her. They might not want anything to do with her. But it didn't matter. This was all her fault, and all that mattered now was finding Timothy.

Timothy fell straight into a copse of elms. They were farther away than they'd looked from the tree. Jessica hunched against the wind and ran. As she ran, she tripped over tangles of roots and branches blown down by the storm. Flashes of lightning split the dark. Her ankle throbbed, but fear for Timothy drove her forward. When she looked up, Jessica found that she wasn't running alone; the star girl traveled silently beside her.

✛ ✚ ✛

Sarah screamed! One of the arrows she fired had struck Timothy's leg. She urged the stag toward the ground just as Timothy tumbled into dense foliage. Cerridwyn appeared at her side as she descended. She raised a pale arm and called out a strange word in a language Sarah did not know. Cerridwyn's voice seemed to be directed to the trees below them. Then she raised her bow and took aim.

The wolves and hounds dove down toward Timothy's plummeting body. Sarah knew that the slow, the injured, and the weak were the first to be attacked by any wolf. Wounded prey were easy marks, a fast meal for hungry predators. Cerridwyn's aim was sure. Her shot dropped the lead wolf with an arrow to the throat. Wolves and hounds scattered, unsure whom to follow. Cerridwyn fired again. Her shot went wide. The next lodged in a wolf's haunch. Timothy disappeared into the trees. The hunt lost sight of the prey. A horn sounded high above them. Amazed, Sarah watched as the hounds and wolves drew back as one.

Then a roar shook the sky, a roar filled with anguish and rage.

Herne's voice bellowed. "Cerridwyn, you have broken old laws by interfering with my rightful prey! Don't think I will forget this night!" Then he and his pack of hounds and wolves swept away.

Gwydon dove past Sarah. His large frame maneuvered between the elms. Cerridwyn followed close behind, and Sarah did likewise. The Greenman lay pale and silent on the ground, surrounded by the Morris dancers. But Sarah didn't see Timothy.

ALONE

SMALL UPPER BRANCHES ripped and tore at Timothy's body. Then larger branches, like arms that flexed under his weight, passed him downward, limb to limb, softening his fall but never breaking it completely. The arms that caught him were hard and rough, the hands clawing, but they never let him plummet completely to the ground. He could smell the damp earth, the leaf mold, the ancient smell of the forest floor. And then, a sharp whack to the back of his head. Darkness rushed in. Above, thunderheads gathered, spilled open, and turned the rain into a deluge.

⊹ ⊹ ⊹

As soon as Sarah and Cerridwyn landed in the clearing, Sarah jumped from the stag's back. Gwydon was already there, pacing and sniffing. But there was still no sign of Timothy. The Morris dancers, one by one, walked silently to the Greenman. Each dancer took a leaf from his hat, and laid it on the Greenman's chest. Sarah watched, remembering the story of the Jack in the Green. Rain clung to her lashes, dripped down the back of her neck. She had never felt so miserable. She swiped at her eyes with a wet sleeve. A breeze stirred the leaves on the Greenman. A murmur swept through the group of Morris men.

The Greenman's branchlike arms were waving! Then he was sitting and pushing himself to stand. His roar of laughter shook the leaves on every tree and his own viny foliage danced.

Sarah froze, her mouth open in disbelief. The poor, broken Greenman was alive! She turned to Cerridwyn. "I thought he was dead!"

"He *was* dead; that wasn't an illusion. But death doesn't always have the final word, even though the Dark would like us to think so. Things are not always as they appear—sometimes, not even death. The Greenman reminds us of that each year," Cerridwyn replied.

All his stiffness was gone. In fact, the Greenman seemed taller, stronger, and leafier. It was no longer a question of tree or man; the two had become a new creature brimming with life.

Gwydon paced forward and nuzzled the Greenman's hand, and the Greenman bowed to him. Again the furious baying hounds passed overhead. The deer pawed the ground and fled. The Greenman paused, looking up into the sky. "An evil older than the hunt is abroad tonight. But he has no power here." At the sound of his voice, Gwydon sighed and lay quietly alert at his feet, nose twitching and eyes following every move.

Difficult as it was to take her eyes from the Greenman, Sarah had a more urgent mission in mind. Where was Timothy?

✛ ✛ ✛

I didn't kill him. I didn't kill him. The refrain ran through Jessica's mind like a fresh wind. She had finally reached the clearing, with the star girl at her side. They had run the entire way, and now Jessica sucked in great gulps of air, feeling as if her lungs might burst. Before her, the Greenman stood, whole and alive. A terrible weight rolled from her shoulders.

Jessica stared at the Greenman. Up close, he was taller and more magnificent than she had expected.

"Come, child." The Greenman's voice was tender, but his words were a command.

She limped forward. Her ankle was hot and swollen. Unsure, Jessica looked into his merry eyes. He extended two branches in her direction. They reminded her of arms. And then she was hugging his ridged trunk and burying her face in the leaves that sprang from his fingertips. "I'm so sorry, so very sorry," she murmured into his damp bark.

The Greenman looked down at her from his great height and brushed her face gently with his twiggy fingers. "I know," was all he said in a voice filled with the life of the forest: birds and deer, trees and vines, and all the small and scurrying things. And Jessica was sure that he did know.

"But where is Timothy?" Her voice was muffled against his side.

The Greenman gently put her aside. He walked to the edge of the clearing, stopping under one of the elms. He cleared away shrubby undergrowth and, there, nestled like a baby, was Timothy. His face was badly scratched and bleeding. He was missing his shirt, and his jeans were torn and muddy, and the shaft of an arrow stuck out of one leg. But Jessica was sure that he was still breathing.

✢ ✢ ✢

Sarah tried to run to Timothy, but Cerridwyn held her back. "It's not time yet."

"I shot him. That's why he fell!" Sarah struggled in her grasp. "Please, I'm so afraid I killed him."

The wind shrieked. For the second and final time, the hunt passed overhead. Flickers of fear ran down Sarah's spine, but the hunt continued past them. Herne and his hounds sought new prey.

"The Greenman lives, and Timothy James stands, but not alone," Star Girl said. As she spoke those words, Timothy opened his eyes and sat up. He looked around bewildered, but he smiled at Sarah across the clearing. Then his face clouded as if he were remembering something terrible.

The Greenman lifted Timothy from the bushes and laid him at Cerridwyn's feet.

"You've been shot, but it was this arrow that saved you." Cerridwyn bent and, as gently as possible, pulled the arrow from his leg. Timothy winced. Sarah threw herself at her brother, hugging and crying. Cerridwyn bandaged Timothy's leg with a strip of cloth from her own cloak, and Sarah wiped the dirt from his face.

Soon everyone was talking. It was a strange gathering: Sarah hugging Timothy, the Greenman talking to the beautiful star girl with a wolf at their feet, and the redhaired huntress watching over all. Even the Morris dancers had regained their spirits and danced around the circle. But Sarah noticed that Gwydon was not relaxed. He frequently looked up, toward the tops of the trees, the fur on his neck bristling.

✢ ✢ ✢

Only Jessica stood alone on the outside of the circle. Her eyes were fastened on Timothy, and she felt a great lump growing in her throat that made it impossible to talk or even swallow. She looked out between the trees into the forest, and considered slipping away. It would be the best thing to do. She wasn't part of this celebration; they didn't want her. She was the reason Timothy was injured. She took a few steps on her throbbing ankle, but suddenly the wolf was there, blocking her path with a low growl. Trembling, she backed up, and he growled again. "What do you want?" Jessica asked.

"He knows it's important that you stay." Cerridwyn appeared out of the shadows. She towered over Jessica, and on her head was a crown with a single gold leaf, identical to the one she had given Timothy. "Aren't you the one who received the poem?" she asked.

Jessica nodded.

"Then your story isn't over, either. It wasn't sent to you by mistake or by coincidence. You play a central part in all that happened tonight."

"Yeah—I caused it all," Jessica said bitterly.

"No, you don't get that much credit. What happened tonight is only one small part of a larger story that began before you were born and will continue for many years to come. You're a part of that story." Cerridwyn looked fiercer now, and then her face softened. "You can change *your* part in the narrative, though."

Jessica let herself be led, limping, back into the circle. Gwydon followed, wagging his tail now—if wolves' tails could be said to wag.

GIFTS

"T HE GREENMAN'S ALIVE!" Timothy shouted as he
peered over Sarah's shoulder.

"Yes, and so are you!" Sarah squeezed him so tight
that he winced. Every inch of his body hurt. And he was
still worried. He couldn't forget the image of Balor with
his terrible eye. What if Herne's hounds came back?

At the edge of the clearing, Timothy saw another familiar face. Cerridwyn held Jessica's arm in a firm grasp as she dragged her back into the clearing.

Sarah followed his gaze and narrowed her eyes. "This was all Jessica's fault!"

Releasing Jessica, Cerridwyn stepped into the center of the circle. When she spoke, the wind stilled and the trees stopped their noisy rustling. "We have come to a place, time out of time, where we have all been summoned." She paused and looked around at the many faces. "Jessica Church, step forward."

Even as her heart dove to her toes, Jessica raised her head and met the gaze of the others in the circle. This was it; things could not get any worse. Sarah glared in her direction, but Timothy only looked curious. She shuffled forward. The eyes of the huntress burned into hers.

"I have been watching you for many years."

Jessica furrowed her brow. This was not at all what she had expected to hear. Who was this woman who had been watching her?

"You have taunted others; you have bullied, lied, and betrayed."

Jessica bit her lip but didn't say anything.

"Tonight you saw how your decisions affect others. You have the chance to make new decisions, to take on a new role." Cerridwyn changed in the blink of an eye to old Mrs. Clapper.

Jessica gasped.

"Perhaps you recognize me better in this form."

"I don't understand," Jessica said. "How can you and the huntress be the same person?"

"Appearances can be deceiving. I have many forms and have lived many years."

Jessica looked down. Her voice was very quiet. "I've made so many mistakes. What new role are you talking about?"

"You *were* the hunt's rightful prey."

Jessica shuddered as she recalled running through the woods with the hounds overhead.

"But," Cerridwyn continued, "there's more to you than meets the eye. You're capable of great kindness and courage. You just rushed to help Timothy, even though you were in pain. You can use your intelligence to help many others, if you choose to. It's not what you've done in the past but what you'll do in the future that matters now. Think of a new start as a kind of gift. And I will help you by passing on some of my skill and wisdom."

It sounded too good to be true. Jessica looked at Timothy. His face was covered in scratches. He had no shirt. His glasses were askew and streaked with dirt. When he had fallen from the wolf's back, she was sure he would be killed. He had risked everything so that the hunt wouldn't chase her. And now she was being given another chance. Who wouldn't take that offer? She worried her lip.

"But what if I can't do it? What if I mess up again?" It would be easy if she were like Mrs. Clapper, a goddess on the side.

"You probably will. But what matters now is your intention." Mrs. Clapper's eyes never left Jessica's face.

The silence in the clearing was complete, as if the night had paused to listen. Sarah stood with the bow hanging from one hand, her fair hair plastered to her forehead. Her eyes, Jessica thought, are still accusing me. But when Jessica's eyes met the Greenman's, something in her melted.

Mrs. Clapper reached under her cloak and drew something out of her pocket. A necklace with a single blood-red ruby on a golden chain dangled from her gnarled fingers. "This is to help you remember." She extended the necklace to Jessica, who reached for it with trembling fingers.

Jessica slipped the necklace over her head. The chain lay gleaming along her collarbone. Two things happened right away: Jessica seemed to grow taller, and Mrs. Clapper was Cerridwyn again, tall, proud, and beautiful.

"There are times coming when people will forget the old stories. Myth and all it represents will remain locked away in dusty books. All myth is a reminder of things people have forgotten they know, and of things yet to be. For many years past and many to come, I have been a signpost, a symbol of truth. We"—Cerridwyn gestured to the Greenman, Gwydon, and Star Girl—"are all reminders of true things. My time in your world as Mrs. Clapper is ending. I will have other forms in other places, but in your world it is time for you to carry on part of my task."

"I don't know how," Jessica said in a very small voice.

"No, I don't expect you do yet. But you'll learn, and you'll have friends to help you." Cerridwyn smiled at Timothy and Sarah. "And I will help you as well."

☩ ☩ ☩

Sarah felt her face flush. It didn't seem fair that Jessica, who Timothy said was never nice and never did the right thing, was receiving this honor. She wasn't sure exactly what the honor was, but it did involve a spectacular necklace.

As if he could read her thoughts, the Greenman spoke. "Remember, Sarah, that you can't always know the inside by looking at the outside." He placed a twiggy hand on Gwydon's head. "You and Timothy have important work to do also, and have already proved that you can do it well."

Sarah thought of her stray arrow that almost sent Timothy to his death. "But I failed. I hit Timothy and almost killed him."

"Killed him? As Cerridwyn said, yours was the shot that saved him. If not for your shot, he would have been caught by the hunt. His fall from Gwydon prevented Balor's eye from reaching him."

"Balor? The evil man Mr. Twig warned us about?" Sarah asked.

"Yes, Balor of the evil eye. He will go to very great lengths to destroy friends of the Light and stop at nothing to eliminate a future Filidh, once he has gotten what he needs from him." The Greenman's voice grew very grave. "Balor's eye can kill with a glance, but only at a great cost to himself. Once he kills with his eye, Balor is at his weakest. His power ebbs for a time. If he had used his eye against Timothy, even Gwydon could not have protected your brother. Your shot made him fall out of the path of Balor's eye. So, you see, even mistakes can be redeemed."

Sarah felt happiness creep quietly in. But every time she heard Balor's name, she trembled. She tried hard to remember what Mr. Twig had said about a Filidh. "Who is the Filidh?"

"Someone who will learn his place in time." Leaves rustled as the Greenman spoke. He crossed to Sarah. With twiggy fingers, he withdrew something from his side. It was a long, slender core of wood, fragrant and crossed with many rings. A small hole remained in the side of his trunk where the core had been extracted. "The heart of a tree, to help you remember what others have forgotten."

He extended the core to Sarah. "Loyalty and bravery are qualities that many in your world no longer value, or they confuse them with blind obedience. You have been very brave. Keep this near you; you will need it in the adventures to come."

At the words "the adventures to come," Sarah felt her resentment toward Jessica slip away like a shadow into the night.

"And Timothy, who sacrificed his life for a friend," the Greenman continued.

Timothy felt suddenly confused. Blood rushed to his face. "No, I just did what it was important for me to do. I didn't think about sacrificing anything." And then in a very quiet voice he added, "In fact, at first I really didn't want to help Jessica at all."

"Where is the crown given to you by Cerridwyn?" asked the Greenman.

Timothy's heart sank. Perhaps he could pretend it had fallen off on his wild ride. But the Greenman was staring at him with solemn eyes.

"I traded it, for a bowl of water."

"And did that water satisfy you?"

Timothy's voice was almost a whisper now. "No, no it didn't. But I thought it would, and I was so thirsty."

The leaves on the Greenman's head trembled and shook. "You have opened the door to danger, for the crown can be misused and cause you regret."

Timothy felt as if his heart would break.

"But," the Greenman continued, "you have also done a remarkable deed by riding in the place of someone who has bullied you and taunted you, someone who was not yet a friend. More, you've been given unusual intelligence and unusual grace. Use them well." He shook his wild head, and a single leaf drifted down. He caught it between his rough fingers and handed it to Timothy. The leaf appeared to be as clear as glass, but it glowed a deep blue as Timothy took it in his hands. It was almost weightless, and, as he watched, the blue changed to red and then back again. "As you know, a leaf, even a simple leaf, has many layers. This leaf will help you know whom to trust and warn you if danger is nearby. Watch as the color changes. As long as the leaf glows blue, you are safe. If the color changes, you must be wary. If the leaf grows hot, you know trouble is near. And one more thing." He whistled, and Gwydon was at his side. "You have the friendship and loyalty of a noble beast. He will always be there when you call."

From all sides, Timothy heard a great rustling of leaves, almost as if the trees were applauding. He bent over and buried his face in Gwydon's fur. He felt no fear of the great wolf now, only a deep trust. Timothy turned the glowing leaf over and over in his hands and ventured a shy smile at Jessica, and was pleased when she returned it. All the while, Jessica had been changing. Somehow, even though the dirt, the mud, and the scratches were still there, Jessica glowed. She looked like a princess dressed as a peasant. But later neither Timothy nor Sarah could ever say why. *Jewel*, Timothy thought, fifteen points with only five letters. He shook his head and tried to focus. Sarah gave him a hug, and his stomach rumbled. How long had it been since he'd eaten?

"There is still much to say, but now you must return to your own time." Gwydon limped over and stood by Timothy's feet. "He's ready to take you two home. Herne and his hunt have passed; you will be safe." Cerridwyn spoke to Timothy and Sarah, but she looked at her great-niece.

"But what about"—and here Timothy's voice became thin—"Balor? He's still alive!"

"Did you really think you could defeat evil in one night?" Cerridwyn smiled. "You, great-niece, will travel with me, for there are things we need to talk about." And Jessica blushed with pleasure and looked remorseful all at once.

Then the Greenman bent low over Gwydon, so low that his leaves brushed the wolf's legs. And when he straightened, Gwydon was able to rest all four paws soundly on the ground.

Timothy climbed onto Gwydon's broad back. The fur was dry now, and softer than anything he had ever felt. Sarah climbed on behind. In one agile leap and without time to say good-bye, they were in the air. Timothy looked around for Electra, Star Girl, who had been quietly observing all that happened. She was sitting on a branch of an elm, and he thought he could hear her singing.

WOLFPROOF

THE NIGHT BLAZED with stars, more than he had ever seen from town; some red, some green, but most a dazzling white. Timothy imagined each one as a person, like Electra, watching over his world.

From Gwydon's back he watched the trees below make way for roads and the outlines of houses, shining rectangles of light in the night. Sarah rode behind him with her arms around his waist, her head resting on his shoulder. They had been gone so long; how would they explain everything to their parents? He pictured their father phoning the police to report his children missing; his mother standing on the porch calling their names. Had they been gone for days? Time out of time. So many things had happened, too much for one night. He thought of asking Sarah, but by her deep and regular breathing, he knew she was asleep, and he didn't want to wake her. And in the back of his mind, there was another worry. Balor. Just thinking his name made Timothy's heart pound and his hands sweat.

As the roads became familiar, Gwydon ran lower in the sky, just above the treetops. Signs of the storm were everywhere. Small branches and thick limbs littered roads and yards. A fence was blown over, and stray shingles punctuated lawns. Then Timothy's own house was below him. No one waited on the front porch. The only lights burning were in the living room, where he and Sarah had opened the door to the storm so long ago.

Gwydon landed in the front yard just beyond the birch trees, his front legs touching down first, followed by his strong haunches. The landing jarred Sarah awake, and she squealed at the sight of their home. Timothy reluctantly slid off the big wolf's back. He remembered sitting on the roof with Sarah and wishing to be wolfproof. Gwydon shook his massive head, with jaws that could break a human femur in a single bite. Timothy looked into the wolf's golden eyes, and reached out to stroke the soft fur, but Gwydon backed away. He was not a pet, and with a long, backward look, he was off at a trot into the trees.

Sarah was already on the porch, cautiously peeking inside the front door. "It's only a little after midnight!" Sarah said. Timothy wondered which midnight it was. Was it still May 1? The headlights of a car swung into the driveway. His mother and father climbed out, looking pale and tense. His father was talking rapidly into his cell phone. His mother came over to them, and smiled brightly. But it was a fake smile. Timothy could tell.

"I'm sorry we're so late, but what are you two doing up? You should have been in bed an hour ago!" Her voice strained to sound cheery. Then all her brightness crumpled. "Oh, something very sad has happened. On the way home, your father and I passed an accident. Mrs. Clapper . . ." And here her voice faltered. "Mrs. Clapper was out walking her dog in the storm, and she was hit by a car. Your father stopped when he recognized the dog. It was just a few blocks from here."

"What happened to her?" Sarah asked.

"Oh, baby, she didn't make it. I'm so sorry."

Timothy gasped as if the air had been squeezed from his lungs. His eyes prickled with tears. He looked up at the sky where the canopy of stars still winked. Hadn't Cerridwyn said they would see her again in another form? He inhaled deeply. The old Clapper was gone, but not Cerridwyn. He was sure of it. He'd miss the Mrs. Clapper he'd known for so many years, and he would miss her stories.

At his side, Sarah cried inconsolably, all the tiredness, strangeness, and sadness pouring out at once. In the distance, geese called in flight. Timothy and his father looked up. Then his father slung an arm around Sarah, and together they walked into the house.

"What happened to your face, Timothy?" His mother gently stroked the scratches.

Prank meowed and rubbed against his leg. Timothy sighed with relief. "Tree branches. I couldn't find Prank in the storm." At least it wasn't a complete lie, he thought.

Pleading exhaustion, Timothy hurried off to bed as soon as he could. He lay awake, wondering about time and how it worked. Was Jessica safe, home in her bed? And what did Cerridwyn say to her? He thought about the Greenman's words to Sarah as he gave her the heart of a tree, "for the adventures to come." He pulled the leaf out from under his pillow. It was still a clear blue. He curled his hand around its smooth surface. *Awesome*, he thought, worth twelve points.

PART 2

THE FILIDH

WATCHMEN

OCTOBER.

Timothy sat in the hammock suspended between the Carolina poplar trees and chewed on the end of his mechanical pencil. The days were ending earlier now; soon it would be dusk. Digging his hand in his jacket pocket, he palmed the small glass leaf and drew it out. Just as he expected, a cool, clear blue.

For six long months he had waited, expecting something—anything—to happen. For six months he had carried the leaf with him every day. It never changed. Only he had changed. Last spring's adventure had complicated—Timothy mentally deleted the word—no, *terminated* any hopes of ever feeling normal again. If it hadn't been for Sarah and Jessica, he would have been tempted to discount the entire adventure as a dream, but every day Sarah reminded him of the Greenman's words, "for the adventures to come." But no adventures had come. Summer passed to autumn and a new school year.

What did remain complicated was his relationship with Jessica. They were friends outside of school, but Jessica was still in another social group entirely. He looked in the old notebook open on his lap at the list he had made two years ago, after his first week in middle school. "Ways to Be Normal":

1. *Pretend you don't know the answer.*
2. *Never run between classes with your backpack on, even if it is the most efficient way to get somewhere.*

The list filled two pages, and now he added one last rule: *Never let it slip that you once rode a wolf through the sky in the middle of the night.* Timothy sighed. Blending in took a whole lot of work, and he was still failing miserably. If only he could learn to keep his mouth shut when he knew the answers at school and pretend that he was interested in sports as much as science. He shoved the leaf back in his pocket.

He shivered. The air was sharp with the promise of frost. Halloween was just a few days away. Closing his notebook, he swung both legs over the side of the hammock. Time to take it down for the year. The sound of something very large flapping right over his head made him duck. It was as if someone were shaking out a very large sheet. Instinctively, he threw his arms up to cover his head as a dark bird with a wingspan of at least six feet swept onto a high branch of one of the old trees. The bird's head glowed white.

A bald eagle, right here in his yard!

Before he completed the thought, another eagle wheeled in to roost on a dead branch in the same tree. One eagle was unusual enough,

Timothy knew, but two *roosting* together? Eagles were solitary birds, preferring to hunt and roost alone.

Moving quietly now, Timothy crossed the porch and slipped through the front door, being careful not to let it slam.

"Eagles in the yard!" he cried as he ran into the kitchen. "Two of them!"

"Are you sure?" Peering at him over his newspaper, Timothy's father looked doubtful, but his mother was already groping through a cupboard for the binoculars. Sarah was out the front door in an instant, Timothy right behind.

Their parents followed. Sure enough, two dark blobs, very large blobs, hunched in the treetop right above the porch.

"I wouldn't believe it if I hadn't seen it," Timothy's father said. "We've never had eagles before."

"I think one is a juvenile." Timothy's mother handed her son the binoculars. "His head is still dark. Maybe we can get a better view from the upstairs window." His parents returned to the warmth of the house.

It was hard to get a good look at the eagles. Timothy was standing right underneath them, and, through the binocular lenses, the birds were just dark shapes. He backed out from the under the tree. Something hot pressed against his side. Timothy shoved his hand into the pocket. It bumped against the glass leaf. It was almost too hot to touch! Gingerly, he drew it out. The leaf glowed bright red.

"Sarah!" He held the leaf in his open palm.

She poked the leaf with her finger and quickly drew back. "It's hot! Finally!"

They locked eyes. Timothy did a quick scan of the yard. Nothing. Now that something was happening, he didn't know what to expect.

"What does it mean?" Sarah looked up at the dark shapes hunched in the tree.

Timothy shook his head. "I don't know what it means, but I know it's a warning."

"Do you think it has anything to do with the eagles?" Sarah lowered her voice as if they might hear her. "They look like watchmen," she muttered into his ear. "Maybe they're watching our house."

The thought made him nervous. Dusk was coming quickly. Already it was growing difficult to see the eagles. As the dark crept in, the name Balor of the One Eye crept into his mind. "Watchmen? If you're right, I hope the birds are on our side." He dropped the hot leaf back into his pocket. The problem is, he thought, I have absolutely no idea what the warning means.

✢ ✢ ✢

Is he the one?

Andor's question arrived black and spare in Arkell's mind, for eagles shared an economy of words. Speech was seldom necessary during long, solitary days of hunting.

Yes. The smallest one and all that is his. Arkell lowered his great wings. The shadows of the two eagles were a mere thickening in the growing darkness as they hunched in high branches of the Carolina poplar.

Arkell lifted his white head and sensed the wind. It was blowing from the east and carried the first scent of frost. He needed to convey the urgency of their mission to Andor, but the words were difficult to form after days of silence. He thought of vast, lonely places in the shadow of the mountains, and of the killing cold that came with winter. He thought of harsh seasons when food was impossible to find and hunger was a constant presence. He thought of man as predator. This was the urgency he sent through the night to young Andor.

And Andor seemed to understand. He raised his head and sent a silent reply: *The next few nights will be difficult. We will watch through the darkness.*

Arkell settled himself on the branch, his head dropping between hunched shoulders.

Yes. Watch and wait with him. Watch and wait, and keep the Dark at bay.

✛✛✛

There was someone else watching Timothy's house. Star Girl saw the eagles arrive. But no one noticed her as she settled into a tree at the edge of the yard. The boy's leaf was hot now and glowing. It was time for her to witness the events that would soon unfold. Unlike the eagles, she would offer no protection. She would merely watch and witness.

✛✛✛

The doorbell rang for the fifth time that evening. Timothy finished off another candy bar and poured the rest of the bag of candy into the large bowl by the front door. Every year there were fewer and fewer trick-or-treaters. It was already after nine, late for little kids to be out, even if it was a Friday. Still, they had gone through only one bag of candy; three more bags were open and ready on a chair by the door.

Timothy looked at the candy with satisfaction: mostly chocolate and he'd have it all to himself, since Sarah always complained that chocolate tasted like mud. Besides, she was off at a Halloween slumber party tonight, and his parents had left him and Jessica in charge of answering the door while they watched a movie in the family room.

Timothy smiled to himself. Just six months ago, he and Jessica could never have been friends. Now they had joined forces, at least outside of school.

She came in from the kitchen with a steaming bag of popcorn in her hands as Timothy answered the door.

"Trick or treat!"

There were no princess gowns or superhero capes in this group of trick-or-treaters. In the front of the group were two boys Timothy thought he recognized; they were dressed in dark baggy clothing, their faces smeared with black smudges. A younger girl was with them, all in black with pointy cat ears and a long tail pinned to the back of her pants.

"I didn't know you two were friends," the girl said to Jessica.

Jessica smiled and took the bowl of treats from Timothy. "Open your bag. You're probably the last people tonight, and we might as well get rid of all this candy."

Timothy was about to protest, but his attention was caught by the fourth person on the porch.

Like the others, the figure was bundled in black, but his face was disguised by a rubber mask. A dark hood shaded the mask from the porch light. Most disturbing of all, Timothy couldn't tell if the figure was male or female. At first, he thought the masked figure was part of the group, but when the others melted into the shadows, clutching their bulging bags of candy, the hooded shape lingered, a pillowcase extended like an offering.

The night grew still, without wind or noise. Timothy felt his scalp prickle. Jessica drew a deep breath behind him.

Timothy grabbed the last handful of candy from the bowl and leaned forward, deliberately dropping it piece by piece into the pillowcase so he could steal a closer look under the stranger's hood. In the dim light, the trick-or-treater's rubber face was gray and puffy, the nose a misshapen blob.

Above it was a dark-rimmed opening for a single eye.

Timothy jumped back and Jessica gasped.

The hooded figure took a step toward the lighted living room. A raspy hum rose like a swarm of bees from behind the mask. Something squirmed in the pillowcase.

Timothy's mind screamed for him to shut the door, but his arms refused to obey. The figure shuffled forward, one foot raised to cross the threshold, then stopped, abruptly, as if it had run smack into an invisible barrier.

The figure shuddered and dropped the sack.

At the same moment, a large shape swooped down across the porch, followed quickly by another. The eagles! The stranger flung his arms across his face.

"Shut the door!" Jessica cried.

Finally, Timothy's arms moved. He flung the door closed, but a moment too late: a large brown rat darted out from the pillowcase and scampered across the threshold into his house.

The eagles screamed in frustration.

"What was that . . . that *thing* on the porch?" Jessica shrieked. She jumped onto the bench in the entryway, knocking over the bags of candy in her rush to escape the rat. Miniature chocolate bars and packets of gum skittered across the floor.

"You're supposed to be the one with powers!" The mask had one eye! All he could think of was Balor! He looked at Jessica standing on the bench. "And by the way, rats can climb." He hoped Jessica couldn't hear how frightened he felt.

He couldn't see the rat anywhere in the long hallway, but he was *sure* it was there somewhere, lurking, watching them. "The *thing* couldn't come through the door! The eagles tried to stop it."

"It might be the rowan I hung over the door." She climbed off the bench and walked to the entrance. "I hung it there when I came in, to keep away evil, like Great-Aunt Rosemary used to do." Jessica stood on tiptoe to touch the small cluster of leaves that hung just above the threshold. Her face was white, her hazel eyes enormous. "I wasn't sure it would really work."

"Then how could the rat still get in?"

"Maybe rowan only works against people." She turned toward Timothy. "Check your leaf. I bet it's hot!"

Timothy felt inside his sweatshirt pocket. Jessica was right; the leaf blazed. He pulled it out, and it glowed red in his open palm. "We have to find the rat before anything happens!"

"Don't worry," Jessica said grimly. "I think it will find us."

✛ ✛ ✛

Andor landed heavily on a branch; Arkell swooped in behind. *Evil has entered the house.*

Arkell's words appeared in Andor's mind, and they were dark with despair.

NO ORDINARY RAT

J ESSICA'S PARENTS PICKED her up late, long after the last trick-or-treaters had come and gone. Despite searching the house, neither she nor Timothy saw any sign of the rat. Timothy decided not to say a word to his parents, who would overreact, like parents always did. Any explanation might involve sharing more about the adventures of last spring than he was prepared to discuss.

The rat was waiting—waiting until they were asleep and vulnerable. As Timothy prepared for bed, he pictured it peering out from his closet, with gleaming yellow eyes and a skinny tail. Rats could climb, maybe even jump. He got the baseball bat from his closet. If the rat attacked him in the night, he'd be armed. Then he pulled his blanket up so no edge touched the floor. He wasn't going to make it any easier for the rat to get to him. The leaf still glowed a dull red, and he placed it under his pillow. He checked the batteries in his flashlight. Working. Stowed it under the covers. Time to watch and wait. But by early morning, his eyes were too heavy to hold open any longer. Around four, he drifted off, sleeping deeply and plagued by nightmares.

✛✛✛

A scream splintered his dreams. He sat up fast and confused. The rat! Like a piercing whistle, the scream went on and on.

He grabbed his baseball bat, leapt from his bed, and pounded down the hallway to the stairs. The scream came from his mother's art studio, on the first floor in the back of the house. He flew down the stairs and slid into the studio, almost knocking over his father.

His mother was bent over, clutching her calf.

"It bit me! A huge brown rat came out of nowhere and bit me!"

"A *rat?*" His father bent down to look at his wife's leg. "Liz, are you sure?"

Timothy's heart sank. He should have said something last night! Should have searched for the rat all night, if necessary!

"It looks like a bite all right," his father said. "But a *rat* . . . We've never had rats in the house. And they don't usually bite people."

"Well, it bit *me*," his mother sobbed, "and I know what I saw!"

While his father went to get some ice, Timothy picked up his mother's paintbrush from the floor and mopped up the splattered oil paints. The small puncture wounds on her leg were surrounded by an angry red welt.

"Did you see where it went?" he asked.

"It was all so fast. But I think it went in there." She gestured toward the utility room. "Be careful!"

Timothy cautiously pushed the utility room door open and turned on the light. Washer, dryer, shelves of canned goods . . . Everything looked normal. But the rat could be hiding anywhere, waiting and watching with its beady eyes.

His father came back with a bag of frozen peas in his hand. "This should help the swelling. We'll have to take you in for a rabies shot. Then I'll call the exterminator."

Timothy's father always rallied in a crisis, issuing orders as if he were a military commander. Usually, it made Timothy feel safe, but this time it was different. He knew that even his father couldn't find *this* rat, not if it didn't want to be found.

As soon as his parents left for the emergency room, Timothy traded the bat for his flashlight and dropped down on his hands and knees. He crawled around the base of the washer and dryer, shining his flashlight under and behind them.

Nothing.

Then he shone the light behind all the shelves.

Still no rat in sight.

He stuck the flashlight into the waistband of his sweatpants and got his cell phone. He needed to tell Jessica what had happened. Maybe there was something that Cerridwyn had taught her that might help him. Cerridwyn had given Jessica a book of mythology before leaving last May. But Timothy was skeptical. Would myth be of any use in this situation? And would an exterminator be of any use against an evil rat?

Jessica's voice mail picked up on the first ring. He left a message.

Then he sent her a text. Now there was nothing to do but wait until the rat showed itself again. Timothy went into his bedroom to get dressed, and then he remembered his leaf. When he slipped his hand under the pillow, he knew even before he touched it that the leaf would be glowing and hot to the touch. Now a murky red, the leaf looked as if it were filled with smoke.

Dropping the leaf into the pocket of his jeans, Timothy went into the kitchen to pour himself a bowl of cereal. And think. As he lifted the bowl to drain the last of the milk, he heard a faint scuttling noise. Slowly, he lowered the bowl. Across the room, from between the legs of the maple china cabinet, two yellow-flecked eyes shone.

Timothy hurled his spoon at the eyes, splattering milk across the floor. He didn't know what he expected, but he hoped it would at least scare the rat or flush it out of hiding.

But nothing happened. The rat didn't flinch. It continued to stare at him boldly from the cover of dark.

"*Bold*," Timothy grumbled aloud. Only seven points. But he knew this rat was worse than bold. It was *malevolent*.

"Get out of our house!" he yelled, sure that this very unordinary rat could understand what he said.

But still the eyes did not move. Only watched.

Timothy could feel his anger growing. Okay, if the rat wasn't going to move, he'd *force* it out.

He retrieved the baseball bat, and rooted in the kitchen junk drawer, through the string, coupons, and glue sticks, finally closing his hand over a small box of wooden matches. It took three tries to get the match lit—just enough time for Timothy to realize that he didn't want to be only one match length away from the creature, even if it was lit. A fire extinguisher—that was it!

Timothy flung open the pantry door and grabbed the extinguisher from its bracket on the wall. Crouching, his hands shaking as much from anger now as fear, he squeezed the trigger. With a loud *whoosh*, foam jetted out, and the rat, larger than any normal rat should be, ran straight toward him. He grabbed the bat and swung. But the rat was too fast. The bat thwacked hard against the floor, sending a jolt of pain through Timothy's shoulder. The rat disappeared under the cabinets.

"Timothy James! What are you doing?"

THE RATCATCHER

IMOTHY JUMPED. Bubbles of foam cut a swath across the kitchen floor, and the fire extinguisher lay on its side.

"Is there a fire?" Sarah dropped her sleeping bag to the floor.

"Watch out! There's a rat under there, an evil rat!" Timothy gestured wildly at the bottom of the cabinets. "It bit Mom, after it crawled out from some trick-or-treater's bag! I tried to chase it out with the fire extinguisher, and it rushed me!"

Sarah spun around to survey the room. "Bit Mom?"

"I think it was sent by Balor!"

✠ ✠ ✠

Sarah ate a slice of toast with peanut butter while Timothy mopped up the floor and explained everything in chronological order, describing the terrible one-eyed mask, the raspy hum and wheezing laugh, and the rat's dash into the house. He tried not to leave anything out.

His cell phone rang just as he got to the part about the matches.

"Timothy, I called a rodent exterminator on the way to the ER," his father said. "They don't usually come out on Saturdays, but they're making an exception. If he gets there before we get home, let him in to do his thing. Is Sarah home yet?"

"She just got here."

"Good. We shouldn't be too long, but you know how things are at the ER." And he disconnected.

"Dad called an exterminator," Timothy told his sister as he hung up the phone.

Sarah lifted her sleeping bag off the floor. "Maybe an exterminator will help."

"This isn't a normal rat, Sarah. I think *we* need to do something. Otherwise, it won't leave until it gets what it wants."

Sarah shuddered. "What does it want?"

"I don't know. But the leaf's been burning-hot the whole time."

"I hate rats. They have nasty yellow teeth and those naked tails! If it was an ordinary rat, we could set Prank on it. But I don't think she'd be any match for the rat you described," Sarah said.

As soon as Sarah mentioned Prank, Timothy felt a jolt of fear. Where was their cat? He dashed out the front door to call for her just as an old pickup truck lumbered into the driveway. The blue paint had long since faded and peeled away, leaving the truck covered with scabrous blotches. Wire cages and wooden boxes were stacked precariously in the bed, looking as if they might topple out at any minute. Even the headlights were askew.

A small man in overalls climbed out of the truck. He moved so stealthily that Timothy couldn't hear the gravel crunch under his feet as he carried a metal trap up the driveway. Every few steps, he paused to look furtively around. There was something vaguely familiar about his slinking walk and hunched posture.

"I think I've seen him before," Timothy whispered to Sarah, who had joined him on the porch.

The little man stopped at the base of the steps and looked up, his long nose twitching, as if smelling the air. Gray hair sprouted in tufts from under a red cap and bristled on his chin, and his small, bright eyes fixed on Timothy and Sarah. Then he turned his head and spat.

Timothy felt Sarah flinch.

"Ratcatcher," the little man announced, climbing the steps and extending one bony hand. "Name's Nom."

His hand was gray with old dirt, but Timothy shook it anyway. The ratcatcher's nails scrabbled against Timothy's hand as he withdrew it. Then the little man smiled, showing a jagged row of long yellow teeth and pale gums.

Now Timothy was *sure* he had seen this man before, but he still couldn't place him.

The ratcatcher leaned forward. "I hear you got a rodent problem. Well, I'm yer man, then! No one knows rats like me."

Sarah drew back in distaste. "Our parents said to expect you. They'll be home any minute."

"This isn't any ordinary rat," Timothy muttered.

"Eh? Rat's a rat. There's good uns and bad uns, just like people. Oh, some of them's tricky, but I knows a few tricks meself." The rat-catcher rubbed his bony hands together, and his nose twitched again. Flecks of yellow glinted in his beady brown eyes. "Gonna let me in, then?"

Then Timothy *knew*. The last time he had seen this man, it had been in Balor's workshop, where he had been held prisoner. The man had escaped from one of the cages Timothy opened and had scuttled across the floor. The ratcatcher moved in the same hunched way, and had the same sinewy build.

Sarah motioned for the ratcatcher to follow her into the house. Timothy hurried to catch up.

They were met at the door by Prank. She crouched low, her tail whipping slowly from side to side, a hunter's metronome.

The little man's step faltered. "Cats!" he cried. "Can't abide 'em. Nasty, sneaking creatures."

Timothy scooped Prank up in his arms and took her to his mother's studio. She hissed, struggling to free herself.

"If you can't behave," he scolded her, "I'll have to leave you in here." He closed the door.

"The last time my brother saw the thing," he heard Sarah telling the ratcatcher when he entered the kitchen, "it was in here."

The ratcatcher stood motionless in the middle of the room, as if listening for something. As if smelling for something. "Not here now, is he?" he said finally.

Sarah looked at him skeptically. "How can you tell?"

"Rats got an odor, subtle-like," he replied as he scurried from room to room, sniffing as he went. "You get to know it. This one smells a bit different, though. Smelled that smell before, I have."

Timothy was thinking furiously. If this *was* the same man he had helped escape from Balor's workshop, and he had no doubt that it was, why was he *here*, in *their* world? And how could Timothy let him know he recognized him? Was he supposed to *say* something?

"Got to attract 'em, that's what you got to do," the little man continued, still nosing around. "You say this ratty bit someone?"

"Our mother," Sarah said.

"Oh, that's not good. Not good at all. Dangerous critters, rats. Got to know how they think. They move along the edges of things, you know. Safer than crossing a room. Always look in the corners!"

Timothy tried to catch the man's eye. "This rat doesn't seem to be afraid of anything," he said quickly, "and it has yellow flecks in its eyes."

"Cheeky, is he? Not afraid of anything? Unnatural, that it is."

The ratcatcher was down on his hands and knees in the utility room, sniffing along the baseboards. "He's been here, all right." He raised up on his knees and looked right at Sarah. "You got something to attract 'im, young lady. Piece of tree in your room, in't there? Go get me it."

Sarah froze. She looked at Timothy. He could almost hear her ask, How could the ratcatcher know about the piece of tree that the Greenman gave me last spring?

Timothy's mouth was dry. This proved it; he *was* the man from Balor's workshop!

But before he could say anything, Sarah asked, "What piece of tree do you mean?"

"Don't think I don't know things. I do. Why do you think *he* gave it to you? If you want this ratty caught, better fetch it."

Sarah didn't say another word as she ran off to her bedroom.

"I remember you," Timothy said finally, squatting down next to the ratcatcher, who was sniffing along the baseboard near the washing machine. "You were in the workshop. Balor's workshop."

"And I'm owing you, aren't I?" the little man said matter-of-factly. "You got me out of there, you did." The ratcatcher smiled again, a slow smile that showed all his yellowed teeth. "So now I'm doing *you* a favor, disposing of the ratty. Smells like he's here. Behind yer washing machine."

"But how did you get here, in this world?"

"What, you think no one's looking after you? Do you think the Light would leave you on yer own, unprotected-like? You seen the two eagles in the tree outside yer house, didn't you?" The little ratcatcher sniffed.

Watchmen! Sarah was right. "Well, they didn't do a very good job if they let the rat into the house," Timothy said.

"Wasn't their fault. They can't come in the house. How was they to know there was something in the bag?" Nom shook his head. "You'd think the council would be smarter."

"Council?" Timothy felt the conversation spinning out of control.

Sarah dashed back with a small glass cylinder clutched in her hand. Inside was the core of wood from the Greenman's side.

"That's right, princess," the little man said approvingly. "Keep it closer next time." He licked his lips. "Open it up now."

Sarah drew out the slender piece of wood. "From the heart of a tree," the Greenman had said. She held it out to the ratcatcher.

The little man snatched it up, pressed his pointy nose against it, and inhaled deeply till his nose quivered. "Just what I thought," he announced. "We'll only be needing a tiny piece." Then he put the end in his mouth and bit it off.

"Stop that!" Sarah grabbed the remaining piece of wood.

The little man drew back his lips: A tiny piece of wood protruded from his stained teeth. Removing it, he pulled a vial out of his shirt pocket, opened it, spit into it, and then dropped in the piece of wood. "Got any peanut butter?" he asked, as if he did this sort of thing every day.

Sarah stood transfixed, clutching the Greenman's wood with a look of total disgust on her face. But Timothy hurried into the kitchen, returning a moment later with a jar of peanut butter.

"That's right," the ratcatcher said approvingly. "Need to attract 'em." He scooped a glob of peanut butter onto the floor of the trap he had carried into the house, shook the vial, and poured the solution of spit and wood sliver into the peanut butter until it made a gooey mess. He set the trap on the floor next to the washing machine. "That'll draw 'im. Knows a thing or two, I do." And then, motioning for the children to follow, he backed out of the room.

They all three watched through the utility room's doorway. For the first few minutes, nothing happened. Timothy found that he was holding his breath, and Sarah seemed still too stunned to speak, but the little man was fairly bouncing with excitement.

Then slowly, furtively, the rat crawled out from under the washer. Its nose twitched, and its beady eyes surveyed the room.

Timothy heard Sarah's sharp intake of breath, and he knew why: This was easily the largest rat she, too, had ever seen. It must have weighed at least three pounds.

The rat made a dash toward the trap, stopped, and paused again to sniff the air. Finally, it eased itself into the trap and began gnawing at the glob of peanut butter.

Because it was a simple spring trap, the door shut with a satisfying *click*. The rat raised its head and opened its mouth wide in protest, its yellow teeth coated in peanut butter. Then it scrabbled with its claws against the cage.

The little man was bouncing on the balls of his feet. "Works every time!" he cried. "Can't resist the smell of peanut butter and tree, rats can't!"

Just then, the front door opened, and Mr. and Mrs. Maxwell came in.

"How are you, Mom? He caught the rat!" Sarah's words tumbled out all at once as she ran to hug her mother.

"Well, that was fast!" Timothy's father extended his hand toward the ratcatcher, and Timothy could see he wanted to draw it back as soon as he got a good look at the grimy little fellow.

"What will you do with it?" Timothy's mother asked the ratcatcher as she looked squeamishly at the trap and the huge rat inside it.

"Drown it," said the ratcatcher. "I always drown 'em. But I saves the tail. Good fishing bait, the tails is."

Timothy's mother swallowed hard, and Timothy's father took advantage of the sudden lull in conversation to hustle the rodent exterminator toward the door. Timothy hurried after them.

⊹ ⊹ ⊹

"The doctor swabbed the wound, and gave me a shot," he heard his mother telling Sarah as she showed off her bandaged leg. "She said rat bites hardly ever cause any problems. She also said they hardly ever happen in the daytime." She shuddered. "I think we need to keep Prank inside for a few days."

Timothy didn't want the ratcatcher to leave without the chance to ask a few more questions, but by the time he could get out to the porch, it was too late. His father had already seen the little man to his truck.

Just as he threw the cage into the back of the pickup, the ratcatcher turned and looked directly at Timothy. Then he doffed his cap.

RAT-BITE FEVER

ARKELL WATCHED from the top of the poplar. An evil had entered the house. Help had been summoned.

Nom had come. Arkell found it intolerable that this poor, slinking human might succeed where he and Andor had failed. He ruffled his feathers. Nom had trapped the rat and removed it from the house. A third eagle had been summoned now to watch over the house of the girl, Cerridwyn's kin.

An orange cat mewled on the porch. The eagles became alert, ready to swoop down if needed . . . but it was nothing: A light switched on, the front door opened, and the cat sped inside.

Arkell settled his wings.

In the tree opposite, Andor also watched. Andor sent Arkell an image of small rodents, *food*. But Arkell returned the image of the house, rejecting the proposal that they take a little time to hunt for supper. They would not fail again.

Andor sighed. There would be no food until morning.

✛ ✛ ✛

Jessica slept restlessly, her dreams an anxious jumble she couldn't sort out.

There had been three messages from Timothy on her cell phone, each sounding more frantic than the last. All day, Jessica had had a sense of things being terribly wrong, but her parents had insisted that she go with them to her cousin's wedding. Even a research paper, due Monday, couldn't convince them otherwise.

Jessica felt heavy with a sense of dread that she couldn't shake. Ever since the death of her great-aunt Rosemary, it seemed that her intuition had exploded. Her senses were bombarded with messages and feelings she had never experienced before. And it wasn't just emotions. Jessica *knew* things now without knowing how she knew them.

What she knew now was that something bad, very bad, had happened.

✚ ✚ ✚

Sunday morning, Timothy and Sarah met Jessica in her front yard and told her the story of the rat bite and the ratcatcher.

"Are you sure he was the same person?" Jessica asked Timothy for the second time.

"Of course I'm sure. Nom knew about Sarah's wood from the Greenman. And when he left, he tipped his cap to me."

"He was disgusting." Sarah wrinkled her nose. "Just like a rat himself. The worst of it is, Mom's leg is starting to ache. The bite looks red and swollen, even though she went to the doctor."

They sat in a cluster on the grass, letting the late-autumn sun warm their backs. Jessica had grown taller over the past months, while Timothy still measured exactly five feet two inches. He had measured himself again that morning, hoping the long-awaited growth spurt was finally about to kick in.

But Sarah, Timothy thought, had changed most of all. Her appearance was the same, but something in her demeanor was different. After spending three weeks at a dance workshop in New York, she'd returned home more . . . Timothy struggled for the word. He pictured Scrabble tiles and mentally sorted through the smooth letters. *Complex*, he decided finally, twenty points. Yes, Sarah was definitely more complex now. And he couldn't always read her moods the way he used to. Sometimes, she seemed to be thinking about something very far away. Maybe that's what being in high school did to people. But then there were times, like now, when she was his same old sister again.

"I think we need a plan to find the disgusting little man and find out what he knows," Sarah said.

"We can ask Dad which agency he called when we get home," Timothy suggested. "But I don't think we'd ever find him that way again." He rubbed the glass leaf in his pocket. It was cool and smooth. "I suppose it couldn't hurt to try."

Jessica ran inside to get a phone book, but there proved to be at least a dozen exterminators listed in the yellow pages. "Don't worry—I'll call them all. I'll just ask about a man named Nom who looks like a rat."

✝✝✝

By the time Timothy and Sarah got home, it was almost suppertime. But instead of finding anyone in the kitchen, the lights were off and a single sheet of paper lay in the middle of the kitchen table. Timothy recognized his father's large, spiky writing: *Took your mother back to the ER. Leftovers are in the fridge.*

Timothy set out cold chicken while Sarah opened a can of tomato soup.

"She must be feeling really bad, to go back in on a Sunday," he said.

Sarah nodded. "Mom never likes to make a fuss."

They ate the soup and chicken in glum silence, waiting for further news.

Their parents came home well after they had finished. Timothy leapt up from the computer at the first sound of the door opening, and Sarah appeared from her bedroom, wrapped in her robe.

"Such faces! I'm going to be fine!" their mother insisted. But she limped her way over to the recliner.

"I'll fix you some food, Liz."

Their father sounded tired, Timothy thought as he joined him in the kitchen.

"Is she really okay?"

"Rat-bite fever—that's what it looks like. But it can't be. The doctor says it never shows up until *weeks* after a bite. Anyway, they prescribed antibiotics, and she needs to keep her leg elevated."

Timothy said nothing. He stood at the sink, frowning deeply.

"She'll be fine, Timothy," his father insisted. "You and Sarah just need to let her rest for a couple of days. And try not to worry! It worries her to see you worried."

Timothy stared out the window into the bare garden. What was Balor up to?

NOM

J ESSICA WAS AS GOOD as her word. She spent much of the following afternoon, as soon as she got home from school, calling the extermination companies listed in the phone book. Most had very little patience for a girl asking about an exterminator who looked like a rat. When Timothy finally called her with the name of the company his father had contacted, she was out of patience herself. But she was willing to give it one more try.

"I'm trying to get in touch with a rat exterminator who came out to our house on Saturday," she said into the phone for the umpteenth time.

"Saturday . . . hmm," said the woman on the other end. "None of our regulars work on the weekends—we hire independent contractors then. But if you give me your name and address, I can see who we used."

Jessica gave the Maxwell name and address and added, "His name is Nom, and he kind of looked like a rat himself."

Laughter exploded from the other end of the phone. "Well, why didn't you say so in the first place! Nom! Of course! No one's ever put it that way before, but you certainly have a point!" And the lady asked if she could take a message for him.

"I'd like to speak with him directly, if you don't mind," Jessica replied.

"I'm sorry, dear. We don't give out the home numbers of our contractors. But if you leave your name and number, I can get him the message."

"Maxwell, Timothy James—" Jessica left her own cell phone number and then added as an afterthought, "And please tell Mr. Nom it's urgent!"

By Thursday afternoon, Nom had still not returned the call. When Timothy and Sarah arrived home after school, their father was already packing a small suitcase. Their mother, he said, was feeling worse. The calf of her leg was swollen to almost twice its size, and she was running a fever and felt too nauseated to eat.

"The doctor can't figure out what's going on, but she thinks it's best to put your mom in the hospital for a few days, to give her some intravenous antibiotics. Mom'll want you two to keep up with your schoolwork and take care of things here at home." Timothy could tell by his father's flat voice that he was more worried than he wanted to let on.

"I thought rat-bite fever was easy to cure," Timothy said, who had been doing his own research online.

"It usually is, but . . . Look, she'll be home in no time, so don't worry."

"Let me see your leg!" Sarah demanded, bending down to roll up her mother's pants. She gasped when she saw that the swollen area on her mother's calf had darkened from red to bluish-black like a spreading bruise.

"I'm going to be fine," their mother insisted in a weak voice. "And I'll be home by Sunday, promise." She smiled, but the smile didn't convince Timothy.

If only he had captured the rat before it found his mother. If only he had closed the door before it got into the house!

Sarah grabbed her sweatshirt from the hook by the door. "I'm going with you," she declared.

"Absolutely not. I need you to stay here and get dinner ready. Dad will be back as soon as he gets me settled. You can come see me tomorrow, after school."

Neither Sarah nor Timothy argued when she used *the voice*, and she was using it now, in spite of the obvious pain she was in.

✠ ✠ ✠

When both parents were out the door, Sarah found Timothy sitting on the living room floor, head in his hands.

"Get up and help me make dinner."

"This is all my fault!" Timothy exclaimed. "If anything happens to Mom . . ."

Sarah squatted down next to her brother. "If this is really something more than an ordinary rat, there will be help. There always was before."

"What if there isn't this time?"

"You don't think the Greenman and Cerridwyn would leave us here without help, do you? Didn't Nom say that we're being watched? The eagles are still in the poplar. Besides, they know what to do in the hospital about rat bites. And when we get hold of that little ratcatcher, Nom, we'll make him tell us what to do!"

"Oh, you will, will ya?" said a cocky voice behind them.

There, framed in the open doorway, stood the scrawny little ratcatcher. Jessica was only a few steps behind, a determined look on her face. She shrugged her shoulders. "I told him to knock first."

The ratcatcher still wore the same flat cap, but the overalls had been replaced with a threadbare jacket and baggy pants, and on his back was a pack. His bright eyes bored right into Sarah. "No one tells me what to do, princess. I thinks for meself! But I pay me debts, too."

"He called back," Jessica explained quickly, "and I told him to come right away."

Timothy jumped to his feet. Maybe there was hope after all. "You've got to do something," he pleaded with the ratcatcher. "Our mother's very sick!"

"And why wouldn't she be? An evil rat, that one. Rat-bite fever and all. We'd best be off." And with that, he turned and walked out the door.

"Wait a minute—where are we going? I'm supposed to be making dinner! Let me leave a note. I'll say we're with Jessica." Sarah scribbled a note, stuck it on the refrigerator door, and ran after the little man, followed by Timothy and Jessica.

"If you want to help yer mother, you'd best come along. I'll be taking you to where you need to go." Nom moved quickly and stealthily across the yard, skirting the driveway, keeping close to the edge of the flower beds. The three children had to run to catch up, after grabbing their jackets and closing up the house.

✠ ✠ ✠

Days were brisk now that it was November. There was frost almost every night, and the temperature dropped quickly as soon as the sun disappeared. Sarah pulled up the hood of her sweatshirt, and Jessica stuffed her hands in the pockets of her jeans. Timothy wondered with a shiver how far they would be going.

"You need to give us some information," Timothy said, realizing that Nom was headed toward the mountain bike trails leading into the woods. "Where are we going, and how is this going to help my mother?" What he really wanted to ask was, How can we know whether to trust you or not?

"You're always the one asking questions. Too many questions. Got to hunt for it, see, if you want to help her. I'm taking you where you need to hunt." Nom's shoulders were hunched and his head thrust forward. His nose twitched as he left the street and led them into the trees.

✛✛✛

The mountain bike trails cut through the woodland at the edge of town, and Sarah remembered the last time they had come this way, following Mrs. Clapper into the midst of a storm. Thinking of it now, she couldn't help but feel hopeful and even rather excited. It seemed as if another adventure was about to begin. But even a new adventure couldn't ease the constant worry for her mother. She had to trust that Nom knew what he was doing.

She glanced at Jessica, who was plodding along in uncharacteristic silence by her side, her brow furrowed in concentration.

There was a noise overhead like the rushing of wind in the treetops. Sarah looked up. "Look—the eagles are here. And there's a third one. They're following us!"

And then Nom vanished from the bike path. He had disappeared into a tangle of bushes. Sarah saw Timothy follow, bending under low-hanging branches; then he, too, disappeared, swallowed up by the foliage.

"Come on—we don't want to lose them!" Sarah plunged into the undergrowth right where Timothy had just vanished.

The serviceberry bushes were scratchy, but Timothy hesitated only a moment before pushing ahead after Nom. He held his hands high to protect his face, but both hands and face quickly became crisscrossed with small scratches. Jessica and Sarah followed right behind him, and he tried to hold the scratchiest branches out of their way. Where did

Nom think he was taking them? And what kind of name was Nom anyway?

"Do you think we can trust him?" Timothy whispered.

"I don't know." Jessica brushed a shower of leaves from her hair. "But he feels okay to me. I don't have alarms going off in my head, and Cerridwyn said I would if things were terribly wrong."

Timothy deliberately slowed his pace and let Sarah pass. "What do you mean?"

"The last time I saw her—the last time *we* saw her—Cerridwyn promised that I'd develop instincts, a way of knowing, just like she had. What does your leaf say?"

Timothy stuck his hand in his jacket pocket. "Nothing. It isn't even warm." He glanced at Jessica. He could see the gold chain of the necklace Cerridwyn had given her against her neck. She rarely took it off. Without the leaf, without Jessica's necklace, it was tempting to think nothing extraordinary had ever happened.

Then Jessica locked her hand on his arm. "Look. It's getting lighter."

Sure enough, through the tangle of bushes, bright daylight was just ahead.

HUNTERS' GATE

TIMOTHY PUSHED THROUGH the bushes. He could hear traffic: horns blaring, the whir of wheels on pavement. The light grew brighter, and he stumbled onto a sidewalk. A stream of people flowed past him. Jessica still clutched his arm. It was as if they had just surfaced from being underwater and couldn't get enough air into their lungs. Cars honked, engines revved, and taxis sped by on the street. Sarah was just ahead; bits of stray leaves and twigs stuck to her hair. "I know where we are! New York!" Sarah pointed across the busy street. "That's the Museum of Natural History. We visited it when I was here for the dance workshop. But how did we just get here?"

Then Nom was at Timothy's elbow. He looked less out of place here, with his rakish cap, threadbare coat, and small backpack.

"Went through the portway in yer woods," Nom explained, as if it were the sort of thing he did every day. "Another one's just up the street."

They stood at the edge of a very large park. New York? This couldn't be possible. Jessica's fingers dug into Timothy's arm.

"Follow me!" Nom headed toward a large cottonwood tree that spread over a stone wall. "Hurry up now, we don't have all day."

"Hunters' Gate!" Sarah read the name on the opening in the low wall surrounding the park.

"Yes, princess. Twenty gates, there is. One for scholars, one for merchants, one for artists, and so on. The gates always open for them that needs them, and this one's for you. Hunters, that's what yer all today, and this Hunters' Gate will take you where you needs to hunt."

A gate behind the stone wall led them to a gravel path that wound through a canopy of trees. The path was deserted and strangely quiet compared to the city around them.

Nom turned to them and winked. "Now, do what I do." Before Timothy could protest, Nom hurried down the gravel path and disappeared. Timothy's mouth fell open.

"Did you see that?"

Sarah's eyebrows arched in amazement.

Jessica released her grip on his arm. "It *is* another portway!" she said. "I read about portways in the book on myth Cerridwyn gave me." She lowered her voice almost to a whisper. "They don't all appear the same on the outside, and they don't all work the same way, either. They can change where you are in both space and time. You have to be really careful. If you don't know what you're doing, you can end up somewhere you don't want to be."

"But they're not real! There aren't any portals—well, maybe worm-holes, but that's different." Timothy glared at Jessica.

"Portway, not portal. You don't know everything about physics. Port-ways have been around for ages. Most people just don't know about them. We'd better hurry. If we lose him, I have no idea how to get home from New York!" And Jessica stepped onto the path. Her outline blurred like a mirage on a hot day, and in a few steps she was gone.

"Come on, Timothy!" Sarah pulled him by the arm. He was still trying to reconcile what he had just seen with what he knew about phys-ics when he glimpsed a girl behind them at the stone wall. She had long white hair and wore a dress that came to her ankles.

"Sarah—it's Electra!"

But Sarah was dragging him down the path. The trees in the distance began to reel. For a moment, he was sure he would throw up. The colors blurred, outlines shimmered, and his ears began to ring. It was far worse than the portway, or whatever it was, from their woods to New York!

When the world stopped spinning, Timothy found himself once again on a forest path, not quite sitting on the damp, mossy ground. *Sprawled*, he thought: fourteen points played off an *s* with an *ed* ending . . . Always a useful word.

On both sides were trees and bushes. The gravel path was gone, replaced by a muddy track. They must be back in their own woods. Sarah was on her hands and knees in the mud, and Jessica was sitting in a patch of bracken. But Nom was standing with his hands on his hips, looking down at them all.

"Hard to land on yer feet the first few times, I know, but I's been at it for a while, and it don't bother me no more." He strutted around them as if nothing impossible had just happened.

"But what about New York!" Sarah protested. She stood up easily, as if all this portwaying between worlds hadn't bothered her in the slightest.

"Oh, that," said Nom, dismissing New York with a flip of his hand. "We needed the gate for a portway, and that's where it's living."

Jessica rose shakily to her feet.

> "Twenty gates for the needs of men,
> scholar, hunter, enter in.
> Closed until a time of need,
> the gates decide who will proceed."

Nom cocked his head at her. "That's right. Yer catching on. Not as slow as the other two."

"I don't know where that came from," Jessica said with a shake of her brown curls. "It sort of popped into my head and out my mouth." But she looked awfully pleased with herself, Timothy noticed.

"Where are we?" Timothy asked, trying to stand. He had to bend over and rest his hands on his knees. "It looks like we're just back in our woods again."

"Looks like, looks like," Nom said impatiently. "When are you going to learn how to *look*? Do you see any road beyond here?"

Timothy had to agree that he didn't.

"And the trees—is they the same?"

Nom was right. The trees were large deciduous varieties with great spreading limbs, which Timothy didn't recognize.

"Oh, be quiet and listen," Sarah scolded. "I hear music and voices."

" 'Course you do. It's market day, and we're late." Nom bounced on the balls of his feet. "Follow me. If you can stand, that is." He looked pointedly at Timothy.

Timothy forced himself all the way up and hoped he wouldn't embarrass himself by throwing up. Jessica was already following right behind Nom in the direction of the music.

Sarah steadied her brother's arm. "Do you have any idea what we're doing here?"

"Hunting, I guess. For something to help Mom. Sarah, I saw Star Girl by the gate, just before we went through."

"If you saw Electra, then we must be going to the right place."

They walked to the edge of a wide meadow and stopped. The sound of music was closer now. At home, it was already dark and almost time for supper; but here, the sun was right overhead. And what Timothy saw in front of him took his breath away.

THE MARKET

THE FIRST THINGS Timothy noticed were the wagons and the fat ponies. The meadow spread below them was splashed with brightly colored, barrel-shaped caravans parked near dozens upon dozens of tents and stalls. They were arranged in two large circles, one inside the other. The wagons had round windows, like the portholes of a ship, and crooked little stovepipes that angled up for chimneys. The backs of the wagons had arched doors with wooden steps that folded down to the ground, and in the front was a broad seat for sitting on while driving a pony. Tied near each wagon was a pony with a long shaggy mane and tufts of hair covering each hoof.

Each wagon was painted a different combination of bright colors that seemed splashed together without any thought of coordination—purple and yellow, lime and pumpkin, turquoise and mustard . . . But it didn't matter. The aroma of spicy grilled meat wafted through the air! And by Timothy's side, Sarah tapped her feet to the music of drums, flutes, and fiddles.

"The Travelers' Market!" Making a little bow, Nom looked as pleased as if he had invented the whole thing himself.

Banners flew above every stall. There were fish banners and fowl banners and others with pictures of cheese and of jewels, advertisements for the wares being sold, snapping in the breeze.

"Let's go. I'm so hungry!" Sarah exclaimed, plunging ahead.

Nom grabbed her shoulder. "The Market's full of *draíocht*, magic stuff, you know. Got to be careful, not running off like fools! Hunting's yer job, after all."

"Are you sure there's something here to help Mom?" Timothy asked.

Nom continued in the kind of lecturing voice Timothy hated. "Can't say what you'll find, nor where. It was just me job to get you here. But I knows this: Don't trust everyone, and meet back here, by this oak, when it's time to go."

"How will we know when that is?" Jessica said. "And look at us." She gestured down at her jeans and tennis shoes. "We don't fit in at all."

"You'll know when to meet. And don't expect to understand everything you hear—travelers speak their own language when they want to. As for yer clothes . . ." Nom took the pack from his back, and his long, bony hands pulled out a wad of tangled fabric, which he spread out on the ground. There were two roughly woven skirts, one purple and one red with yellow flowers, a pair of blue wool pants that reminded Timothy of pirate pants, and three short cloaks of a drab gray that changed color depending on the way you looked at them.

"That's the best I got." And he sniffed as if he thought they expected more.

"Oh, these are wonderful, Nom!" Sarah said, shooting Timothy a look. He hoped Nom wouldn't see her inspecting the red skirt for bugs. "We can pull them on right over our jeans."

But Nom's sharp eyes were fixed not on them but on the Market. He rubbed his long, thin hands across his face. With his cap set at a jaunty angle, he, at least, looked like he could blend right in with the colorful crowd.

"Now, if you'll not be needing me anymore . . ." Nom said. "It's been a long time since I been to the Market."

But Timothy wasn't ready to let their guide disappear so quickly.

"You've got to tell us what we're looking for—how to find it!"

Nom shrugged his hunched shoulders impatiently. "Too many questions! Just sniff it out. That's all I know, all I do. I'll be around if you need me." And with that he stuffed the discarded sweatshirts into his pack and scuttled through the tall grass as if he didn't like being out in the open too long.

Timothy had a sinking feeling in his stomach as he pulled on the wool pants over his jeans. He wasn't sure if he trusted Nom, but Nom was their only link to home. And now that his stomach had settled, he was hungry. But even the magic of the Market wouldn't make him forget his quest for an antidote to help his mother.

✦✦✦

Walking through the tall grass in long skirts was more difficult than the girls expected, and the pollen was making Timothy's eyes water. But stride by stride, they were getting closer to the tantalizing smells and sounds of the Market.

How would they ever blend into the hodgepodge before them? The long skirts hid the girls' jeans, and the cloaks mostly disguised their T-shirts, but Timothy noticed that Jessica's bright running shoes peeked out at every step. He felt ridiculous in his baggy pants and oversized shirt, as if he were a character in a play. And he couldn't tell what time period they were in. Did traveling markets like this still exist in some parts of the world, or had they gone back in time? From every side, people shouted, bargained, and conversed, sometimes in a language Timothy couldn't understand.

In front of them, a bright yellow wagon sat next to a deep-red tent. Two dogs lazed in the sun nearby and barely raised their heads as the children approached. Overhead, snapping in the breeze, was a blue banner emblazoned with a brown loaf of bread.

"Just our luck!" Sarah complained. "A food tent—and we've no money at all." She eyed a pile of brown loaves and a basket of blueberry muffins that smelled as if they'd just come out of the oven.

Timothy slid off his digital watch and slipped it into the pocket of his pants. If he was going to fit in, he needed to think of all the details.

"Huh? What's this?" He pulled a small silk purse out of his pocket. It was heavy, and its contents clinked in his hand.

"Well, open it up," Sarah demanded.

Inside were a number of silver coins that Timothy poured out into Sarah's palms.

Jessica lifted one of the small coins and studied it. It was octagonal, with a sheaf of wheat on one side and an unfamiliar script on the other. "Do you recognize this?"

Timothy took it in his hand. "Never seen anything like it before. But then, there's lots of coins I don't know."

"Well, I'm hungry," Sarah declared. "Let's see what happens." And she boldly marched up to the front of the tent, where a red-faced woman with a squalling baby on her hip was arranging the stacks of loaves.

"I'd like to purchase a muffin, please." Sarah held out two coins.

The woman paused long enough to wipe the baby's nose on her sleeve and then grabbed up the coins, dropping not one, but three plump muffins into Sarah's hands. Then she bobbed her head and muttered some words Timothy didn't catch at all before disappearing back into the tent.

Sarah gleefully split her prize between the three of them. "Blueberries, and lots of them. I love blueberries!" She sighed with contentment as she ate.

"I think we need a plan," Timothy said around bites of muffin. He was feeling much better now that he had something in his stomach. "We need to find whatever it is that will help Mom as soon as possible. So, we should divide the money, split up, and meet back here."

"Don't you think we should stay together?" Jessica wiped her hands in the folds of her skirt. "What if we run into trouble?"

"And how will we know when we find the right thing?" Both Sarah and Jessica looked at Timothy as if expecting him to know the answer.

"I don't know. I'm sure we'll know it when we find it." He tried to sound much more confident than he felt. "But we do need a signal, a way to get in touch with each other."

"Let's just say that we're all back here in this very spot in two hours," Sarah said, checking her watch. "You both have watches, don't you?"

"Mine's in my pocket," said Timothy. "And I have the leaf. It should warn me when things get dangerous."

Jessica said, "I've got my cell phone. It tells the time."

"Somehow I don't think a cell phone will do any good here," Sarah said. "Do you have reception?"

Jessica checked her phone. "None. That settles it. You and I will go together. I don't like the idea of being on my own. Besides, Timothy has his leaf. That will be his protection."

Sarah gave Timothy a stern look. "Don't do anything crazy, Timothy. Promise me you'll be back here in two hours."

Timothy remembered his mother's pale face, the sheen of sweat on her upper lip, and he swallowed to hold back the panic that rushed at him. "Okay, let's get going."

"Wait, don't forget about the *draíocht*." Jessica flushed. "It's an old Irish word for magic. It's what Nom warned us about." She looked hard at Timothy. "Be careful, and trust your leaf."

But Timothy was already walking away.

JULIAN

THE MAN WORE a short cape of peacock feathers. Bright glass balls flew in a circle from his hands, higher and higher each time. He placed a thin stick between his lips, tilted his dark face up toward the sky, and spun a sea-green ball while his hands never let one of the glass balls slip. The man finished with a flourish, dropping his blue cap to the ground, and Timothy tossed in a coin.

Every sight was a distraction, every sound a chance to explore something new. Focus, Timothy told himself as he turned away from dueling fiddle players. You're here on a mission.

In his pocket, his hand closed over the glass leaf. It was pleasantly warm to the touch, as if it were a living thing. Maybe it will be like a game of Marco Polo, he thought. When he got closer to whatever it was that would help his mother, the leaf would alert him in some way. He already knew it blazed when danger was near.

He scanned the crowd for Nom, irritated that the little man had abandoned them. Occasionally, he thought he spotted him, but it always turned out to be someone else—a young boy or a craggy-faced old man. The ratlike Nom, in his threadbare coat and cap, was lost in the sea of the Market.

An orange caravan with shiny green trim loomed just ahead on Timothy's right. Next to it, contentedly munching on a patch of grass, was a beautiful fat pony with a spotted coat. Its dark tail swished as it ate. Timothy crept closer. The pony watched him out of one eye as it munched. He approached quietly, holding one hand out for the animal to sniff. A pony would be a much more interesting pet than a cat. It allowed Timothy to stroke its warm neck while it continued eating.

Nearby, a tall man with bushy red sideburns and a thick nose stood on a wooden crate. In a loud voice, he hawked his wares: medicines, herbs, and potions. A row of bottles with black-and-white labels glittered on a wooden shelf attached to the orange caravan behind him.

Timothy walked closer to read the labels on the bottles: *Lover's Curse, Breathe Better, Wart Wash, The Invigorator.* Bunches of dried herbs hung around the perimeter of the caravan, like a necklace on a great orange pumpkin.

"Small, weak, need muscle? Try the Invigorator! Two capfuls, morning and night, and you'll be a new man, commanding respect wherever you go!" The redhaired medicine man's voice boomed out through the crowd as he poured a capful of thick black liquid into the open mouth of a short man in a baggy coat. "There you go, sir . . . fit as a fiddle in no time! And there's a bonus—won't be able to keep the ladies away!" The merchant winked broadly. "You'll be the envy of every man in the Market!"

The customer wrinkled a freckled nose and covered his mouth with a grubby handkerchief. "Ew, tastes nasty! Burns me throat!"

"That's the medicine at work. This is a powerful drug, definitely not for the fainthearted!"

Several people in the crowd nodded and pressed close to buy a bottle. Then the most amazing thing happened: The man who had drunk the potion fell to the ground, twitching.

"Oooh! Here, here—what's going on?" the crowd murmured as one. But before the murmuring stopped, the man was still. The woman next to him bent down and offered him a hand. He pushed it away and bounded to his feet, peeling his coat off to display enormous biceps. He flexed them proudly as the crowd gasped in astonishment.

Then the man began to tremble again. Two small lumps appeared, lifting the shirt from his shoulder blades. The humps grew larger and larger as the crowd stared, goggle-eyed, until the fabric on the back of the man's shirt split apart, and with a loud *pop* two small wings unfurled. Small brown wrinkled things. The man swore and grabbed his coat from the ground, and he flipped it over his shoulders as he disappeared into the crowd.

"Well, it makes some like that," the medicine man said with a shake of his shaggy red head. "But that's a rarity. Don't let it frighten ya."

Timothy considered. Whatever the medicine man was selling worked in some mysterious, unpredictable way. Maybe one of the man's potions could help his mother. As he continued to watch, more people came up to consult with the merchant. Most left with a bottle or two clutched in eager hands.

Then Timothy noticed a lady with a baby. She crept up to the man's side and whispered something in his ear. Then she held up the infant, unwrapping him so that the man could take a better look. From the back of the baby protruded a long, thin rat's tail. The medicine man shook his head in pity, and the mother hurriedly wrapped the baby again. He beckoned her back to the side of the caravan.

Timothy moved closer to hear what was said.

"Aye, that's *draíocht*, bad *draíocht*," said the redhaired medicine man, towering over the young mother. "But I can help the wee one."

"Oh, please!" The woman's voice was faint as she rocked back and forth to keep the baby from crying.

"This is a salve." The medicine man unscrewed the lid from a rusty-looking jar. "It comes from the crushed stems of gentian flowers. It's a powerful magic, a rare plant." His voice had dropped to a husky whisper. "I don't let most people know I have it. It goes dear." His fingers were blue with the thick paste.

Once again the mother unwrapped the infant, this time turning him onto his stomach and laying him across her arm. The merchant rubbed the paste into the baby's backside.

Instantly, the baby began to howl.

"You can see it's working its magic already!"

Timothy stared at the tail. As far as he could tell, nothing had changed. Maybe the potion worked very slowly.

The woman held out a small purse, and the merchant poured the contents into his meaty palm, returning the purse empty. The mother tucked the jar into a pocket, rewrapped her baby, and, standing on tiptoe, kissed the medicine man on his cheek before scurrying back into the rest of the Market.

Timothy could hardly believe what he had just seen: A salve that could work against magic! Surely, this was the very thing his mother needed.

He felt his small coin bag, hoping it held enough to purchase the medicine required to heal his mother of rat-bite fever. Glass jars of elixirs sparkled in the sun—love potions, beauty rinses. Nothing was labeled as a cure for rat-bite fever. The big man was bent over a bucket, filling it with water from a barrel for his pony.

Timothy approached him cautiously. "Excuse me, sir."

The man didn't look up, so Timothy repeated himself a little more loudly. "Excuse me, sir."

This time the man straightened and swung around. "Dr. Lachlan McClallahan, at your service, son."

Timothy couldn't quite place his accent—not quite Scots, not quite English. "I was hoping you could help me with a rat bite."

The man's eyebrows shot up and then settled like caterpillars on his brow ridge. "Better show it to me."

"Oh, it's not my bite. A rat bit my mother, and she's very sick." Timothy's voice quavered. "It wasn't an ordinary rat. It was a magical rat."

"A magical rat? What are her symptoms?"

As Timothy explained, the man listened, his eyebrows wiggling up and down.

"Oh, that's bad—very bad, indeed," the merchant said finally. "Lucky she has a son like you, concerned and all. But I can help you. And if I can't, nobody can."

The medicine man ducked through the small doorway into his caravan—and Timothy felt his heart surge with hope. He'd find Nom and the girls, and they'd be home in no time!

Dr. McClallahan came out of the caravan holding a small paper packet in his thick hand. He bent his face close to Timothy so that Timothy could smell onions and smoke on his breath. "This here is crushed powder from a certain deep-sea oyster," Lachlan said. "Rare stuff! Cost you dear, but it's the only thing that can save your mum."

"You mean that, without this, she'll die?"

" 'Course she will, no doubt about it. And with great suffering, too. A terrible death." The man's eyes bore into Timothy. "Three times a day till it's gone. Pour it in a cup of water, swirl it around, and down the hatch before it settles out."

"How much is it?" Timothy wondered if he would need to collect the girls' money as well.

The merchant's eyes narrowed. "Let me see what you got." He pried the coin purse from Timothy's fingers before Timothy could offer it up. McClallahan didn't say a word as he fingered through the coins, apparently counting, but his eyebrows began to wiggle again. "That should do," he said at last. "Should do nicely." He squinted at Timothy. "And what about you?"

"What about me?" Timothy tucked the packet for his mother safely in his pocket. "You'd like to be taller, wouldn't you?" the doctor asked. "Small boys always want to grow!" He drew a packet and a small bottle of clear liquid out of his pocket. "Complimentary, this is. But see that you don't take it until your mother's had hers. Stuff has to ferment for five days before you drink it. And then expect at least four inches." The merchant held his hand four inches above Timothy's head in illustration. Then he slit open the packet and dropped a pinch of the crystals into the liquid. He shook the bottle. The crystals swirled like smoke as they dissolved.

Timothy stared, fascinated. How had the man known how much taller he wanted to be? Timothy clasped the small bottle in a sweaty palm.

Something cold and wet nudged against his arm, and the bottle slipped from his fingers. He made a futile grasp for it, but the bottle tumbled to the dirt.

"Dirty beast!" The doctor's voice rumbled.

In confusion, Timothy bent to retrieve the bottle of growth potion and found himself looking right into the eyes of a great golden wolf.

"Gwydon!" Timothy threw his arms around the wolf's neck, burying his face in the thick fur. How often he had dreamed of seeing the great wolf again! Now Gwydon was here, and everything would be all right.

"I'll thank you not to speak ill of my wolf," said a voice behind them.

Timothy turned. A tall man with a thin face and long hair stepped forward.

"And I think my friend won't be needing this, either." The stranger stomped his boot, crushing the bottle of growth potion into the dirt. Timothy's heart sank.

"You filthy Storyteller, get away from my stall!" But Dr. McClallahan hurried into his caravan, still clutching the money from Timothy's purse. The door slammed hard behind him.

"I think you'd better come with us before anyone else takes advantage of you," the man said to Timothy. As if in agreement, Gwydon pushed his head against Timothy's leg.

Without another word, the man strode off through the crowd, with Timothy and Gwydon at his heels. Timothy could have sworn that the wolf was smiling. And there was something very familiar about the man's lanky frame.

"What about my bottle of medicine?" Timothy exclaimed, half running to keep up with the stranger's stride.

The man stopped suddenly and turned to peer down at Timothy. "How much money do you have left?"

Timothy swallowed. "None. I had to buy something for my mother." He slipped his hand into his pocket and felt the packet of medicine the merchant had given him. Beside it, the leaf rested, uncomfortably warm. With a sinking feeling, Timothy realized he should have checked it before. "I have to go find my sister," he said. "It's urgent."

"If it's about that powder in your pocket, it's not so urgent. It's only alum, used in baking. The so-called doctor is nothing more than a charlatan, adept at separating people from their money."

"But he promised it would help!"

"McClallahan trades in hope. People bring him their sorrows and he sells them false hope. And sometimes something worse."

"But the lady with the baby—"

"Did it have a rat's tail? A cloven foot? She was either a plant working with him or someone desperate for hope. Whatever he gave her will do nothing more than sicken the infant. If she's lucky."

Timothy's shoulders slumped. He felt like a fool. He'd wasted precious time when the cure for his mother was still out there, somewhere. He looked up at his rescuer. His voice was so familiar. "I remember who you are. You're Julian the librarian! How did you get here?"

"Yes, I was wondering when you'd recognize me," he said, with a twinkle in his eye replacing his stern demeanor. "And for now, Gwydon is my companion."

Timothy noticed that Julian didn't answer the other part of his question. What was the librarian doing here in the Market?

"Why don't you come with me? Perhaps I can help you find what you're looking for." Julian, with Gwydon at his side, led Timothy to a nearby caravan and climbed the steps. When Julian opened the blue door, Gwydon padded contentedly in.

"After you," Julian said to Timothy.

Timothy hesitated. "How do I know I can trust you?"

"You're learning, Timothy," Julian said with a slight smile. "All I can say is that Gwydon seems to trust me, and I believe he is someone *you* trust. But you're right to question. And don't forget to check the Greenman's leaf. It was probably blazing hot back at the doctor's stall."

"How do you know about the leaf?"

Again, Julian smiled. "I have some knowledge about the old ways."

Timothy drew out the cool leaf. Resting in the palm of his hand, it was a clear, untroubled blue. Gwydon stood patiently in Julian's doorway, waiting. Timothy looked into the wolf's golden eyes. He could trust Gwydon. He followed the wolf into the caravan.

Behind Timothy, Julian slammed the door shut and locked it.

FERRET LEGGING AND A FRIEND

T HE GIRLS DECIDED to work their way around the Market counterclockwise, visiting the outside ring of stalls first and then the inner circle.

"This way," Sarah said, "we'll be sure not to miss anything."

Behind the wagons on the outskirts of the Market, a knot of noisy people were gathered under a sprawling oak.

"Looks like something important is happening over there." Jessica nodded toward the boisterous group. "I think we should check it out."

The girls approached cautiously. Men of every shape and size had gathered to watch something that made them shout and cheer. Neither girl could see over the circle of heads.

"We'll never see what's happening from here," Jessica said. "Let's try the tree."

The thick oak stood a few feet from the gaggle of men. Its branches hung invitingly low, and under normal circumstances it would be easy to climb into the lowest ones. But these were anything but normal circumstances. Sarah gazed down at her long skirt. Perhaps if she hiked it up to her knees, she could scramble up, but she wasn't sure if climbing trees was the type of thing girls did in this place, and it seemed important not to draw too much attention to themselves. On the other hand, not a single face was turned toward them. A shout went up from the crowd, followed by clapping and whistling. No one would notice two girls climbing a tree. Sarah nodded at Jessica and eyed the easiest ascent.

Jessica went first, her purple skirt wide enough to make the scramble up the branches easy. Sarah kicked off her sandals and hitched her skirt up to her knees. The bark was rough and the first step high. She circled the lowest branch with her arms and threw one leg over. Her skirt caught on a cluster of twigs. As she tugged at it with one hand, she heard the hem rip. Well, there was nothing to do about it. Freed, she scrambled up to the branch where Jessica sat and was able to just see over the tallest heads.

A few women jostled among the men to watch the action in the center of the ring, where a bearded old man tried to stand still. His face was red and scrunched up. Every few seconds, he would open his eyes very wide and twitch all over. Blue baggy pants were banded tightly around his ankles above long and bony bare feet.

Next to the old man was a small, redhaired man holding an empty cage. He was only waist-high to most of the people in the crowd, and his arms were clothed in long leather gloves. Someone in the crowd called out encouragement to the other man: "You can do it, Bruno!"

"Don't mind the biting," someone else shouted. "It's the claws that'll kill you!"

"He's got nothing to lose anyway!" cried a third.

Something moved inside the old man's pants. A bulge traveled quickly down the front of the leg to the ankle, thrashed around a bit, then moved up the back of the leg. The old man gave a yelp, and the small man held up his hands. The crowd burst into cheers.

"Seventeen minutes!" cried the man. "A new record!"

The crowd sent up another cheer. The old man cavorted, bulge and all.

A round-faced woman bent down and undid the bands around the old man's ankles while the small man held out the cage. A dark, sinuous creature poked its head out from an ankle of the pants. In a flurry of motion, the woman and the small man stuffed the thing into the cage as the old man hopped around gleefully. Another man moved forward, reaching down to fasten bands around his ankles.

"It's a ferret," Jessica hissed. "It must be some kind of competition."

"He's going to put the ferret in his pants!" Sarah said, horrified. "It sounds like they're timing how long he can keep it there—the poor thing!"

The girls watched as the small man ceremoniously reached back into the cage with one gloved hand, held the squirming black ferret over his head, and then with a flourish slipped it into the front of the next contender's pants. The woman started a pocket watch. Just like a wooden marionette, the man danced from one long, sticklike leg to the other.

"I've seen enough," Jessica said indignantly as she swung down to the ground, but Sarah couldn't drag her gaze from the spectacle below her—the shouting mob, the sticklike man's legs and arms flailing in every direction. A mixture of disgust and curiosity kept her planted on the branch, lips parted and eyes wide, even though it was obvious to her that this man would not be breaking any records.

At the edge of the crowd, a familiar shape caught Sarah's eye. Star Girl stood watching, too.

"Jessica!" Sarah called.

It was then that the small redhaired man looked up and stared straight into Sarah's eyes as she sat, legs dangling from the thick branch. She recoiled from his gaze as if she, too, had been bitten by a ferret.

"Hey, now, we've got a watcher, ladies and gents! I'm thinking the young lady'd maybe like to tussle with the ferret? We could arrange a challenge for you, missy, spit-spat like!"

"Put it down her dress, then!" the plump woman called out, and the crowd guffawed. Panic beat against Sarah's chest as their eyes bored into her. Grabbing her ripped skirt in one hand, she slid down from the branch, the rough bark scraping the skin at the backs of her thighs.

"Let's get out of here!" she cried, grabbing Jessica by the arm and snatching up her sandals with her free hand. "I saw Star Girl!"

The girls ducked behind a wagon and plunged back into the noisy crowd of the Market. "So much for being inconspicuous!" Jessica exclaimed. "Where is she?"

But the crowd had thinned with the new contender.

Star Girl was nowhere to be seen.

"Come on—she was in that direction." Sarah pointed toward the food stalls. The girls ran.

A different audience, this one surrounding a group of jugglers, forced them to slow their pace, but Sarah's heart still raced. She felt sickened by the ferret legging and a little frightened, too. She could still feel the small man's eyes boring into her. "If Star Girl's here, maybe she can lead us to the antidote for my mother. Timothy thought he saw her, too. Right when we went through the portway."

"You should have said something earlier." Jessica straightened her skirt.

Sarah bent to put her sandals back on. "Sorry, Jess. I guess I forgot once we got here."

Jessica nodded and ran her fingers through her unruly curls.

They were surrounded by food: stalls of apples, persimmons, and oranges, tables heavy with cakes and scones warring for their attention. Three young jugglers tossed fruit taken from a stall, while a vendor shook her fist in mock anger. Apples, pomegranates, and a hard, green fruit Sarah didn't recognize spiraled through the air from one hand to another while jugglers capered, pretending to almost drop an apple and then catching two at once. Children with candy-smeared faces and bright eyes crowded close, and men and women paused their bartering to smile and watch, but Star Girl was not among them.

A boy with long black hair and bright blue eyes lounged against the side of a wagon. His eyes strayed from the jugglers to the girls and rested on Sarah. She shifted self-consciously.

"Don't stare, but I think we're being watched," Sarah whispered.

Then the boy smiled and ambled in their direction. "You're not from around here," he said to Sarah. Up close, his face looked very grubby, but his gaze was steady and his eyes very blue. They took in both girls, but the statement seemed directed to Sarah.

Jessica pulled her eyes from the jugglers. "Why do you say that?"

"Just can tell, I guess. Haven't seen you around before." The boy scratched his nose. "My name's Peter. Where're you from?"

Sarah's mind froze. What could they say? That they'd come through a portway in New York City?

But Jessica seemed to have no problem answering the question. "From a long way away," she said, "and you're right, this is our first time at your Market. I'm Jessica, and this is Sarah." Jessica smiled that dimpled smile that could distract even the most persistent questioner. "You know, I'm awfully thirsty. Perhaps you could tell us the best place to get something to drink and eat—there are just so many choices."

Peter straightened, squinting into the sun. "Follow me," he said in a voice of confidence. "Fiona's pies are the best in the Market, and her drink's not bad, either. She'll know what you need." And without look-ing back, he threaded his way through the crowd.

Sarah elbowed Jessica. "We don't have time for this! We need to find whatever it is that will help my mom!"

"Trust me. I have a feeling about this. He's a friend." And she was away, following Peter, before Sarah could make any more objections.

Dodging knots of people and keeping her eyes on Peter as he wound through the crowd took most of Sarah's concentration. They wove in and out, between overflowing stalls and wagons, in such a circuitous route that she was sure they would never find their way back. She won-dered how her brother was doing, if he was having any better luck than they were. She gave up trying to mark their route and almost bumped into Jessica when she stopped abruptly next to a peacock-blue wagon.

A loosely woven striped cloth was draped from the roof, forming a shady canopy. Fiona's wagon was clearly a popular spot. Tired shoppers refreshed themselves with large mugs of drink and small baked pies. Sarah's stomach complained loudly. How long had it been since she'd eaten?

Peter spoke to the woman who commanded the stall. "They're not from around here," Sarah heard him say. "They could use a pie and drink."

Fiona responded by giving Peter a smile and a quick cuff on the ear. She was a tall woman with long hair, the color of light, caught up in a pile on her head. Tendrils fell alongside her cheeks, softening one of the most interesting faces Sarah had ever seen. Fiona wasn't young, but she didn't look old, either, even though her light gray eyes were webbed with fine lines. Her mouth was wide, her nose long and narrow, but it was her neck that caught Sarah's attention. It was the long, slender, elegant sort of neck every dancer dreamed of having, except for the ragged scar that ran from one side to the other.

Fiona paused, cocked her head sideways, and stared hard at the two girls.

"Morningcrush and kid pie with balsam root," she said with a nod. "Yes, that's what you need to keep you going—to keep you focused."

"Oh, but I was hoping for raspberry," Jessica said, looking longingly at the display of rich fruit pies on a nearby shelf.

"Not for you." Fiona shook her head, brushed a stray tendril from her face, and poured a ruby-colored liquid into two mugs. Then, grabbing two small brown pies from the shelf, she plopped them on the wooden counter.

Sarah felt for the coins in her skirt pocket and drew them out, wondering how much to offer.

"Friends of Peter's needn't pay me," Fiona said brusquely, off to the next customer before Sarah could protest.

"Aren't you going to eat anything?" Jessica asked Peter, reaching for her pie and mug.

"Already have. You can sit back here." He led them to the folding steps at the back of Fiona's wagon.

Sarah sniffed the pie. The smell was spicy and savory, and again her stomach grumbled. Then she remembered Nom's words about being careful of what she ate and drank at the Market. She tried to catch Jessica's eye, but it was too late; Jessica had already taken a mouthful. A rich gravy trickled down her chin, and she wiped it with the back of her hand.

"This is the best! Sarah, you've got to—"

"Don't you remember what Nom said?"

"If it's *draíocht* you're worried about, well, you needn't. Oh, it's *draíocht* food all right, but not the kind that will harm you." Peter looked intently at Sarah.

Why, he's no older than I am, she thought. "How did you know what I was thinking?" she asked, realizing with some surprise that if he were a bit cleaner, he'd be quite good-looking. "And how do I know it's safe?"

Peter merely shrugged his thin shoulders and scratched his nose.

Sarah turned and studied Jessica. She wasn't worried—she was wolfing down her pie. Sarah took a cautious swallow of the ruby liquid in her mug. It was sweet and tart, and more than that. It tasted like ripe strawberries and honey and lemons all at once. It tasted like . . . summer. Her shoulders relaxed, and the noise and dust of the Market faded to the background.

"Yeah, *draíocht* is magic," Peter was saying to Jessica. "You've some of it about you. Light-haunted we call it." He looked at Sarah. "Do you like it?"

"It's great. The best drink I've ever had."

"I told you she'd know what you needed."

"Who is she?" Sarah bit off a mouthful of warm pie.

"Fiona? She's my mam."

How could the tall woman with the fair hair and pale eyes be the mother of this boy with black hair and tan skin?

"I look like my father," Peter explained, as if once more reading Sarah's mind. "That's what I hear anyways. Never met him." He looked at Sarah so long that she felt herself blushing. "Now, tell me—why're you here?"

Jessica spoke up between noisy sips of drink. "We're looking for something we need, something to help someone."

Sarah choked on the pie in her mouth. This was going too far! Jessica shouldn't be giving out information to someone they barely knew.

But Peter didn't press his question further. Instead, he said, "There's many things at the Market. Some can help, some hinder. It's best if you know what you're looking for." He stretched out his long legs and scuffed the dirt with a bare toe. "Maybe I should go with you, just to keep you out of harm's way." And he looked so hopefully at Sarah as he said this that she felt herself blush again. She wished Timothy was there with his leaf.

"We could use some help," Jessica said finally, wiping the last of the drink from her lips and looking around at the kaleidoscope of people, which was the Market. "Especially since we have no idea where we are."

Peter grinned. "Tell me what you want, then. I'm thinking you're in a hurry."

"My mo—I mean, someone close to us needs help right away." Sarah jumped up, wiping her hands on her skirt and brushing off crumbs. The food and drink had given her new energy, and with the energy came hope. The sluggishness of the last hour was gone; she was ready to search, no matter how long it took.

"Which way?" Jessica asked.

"What kind of help does she need?" Peter asked.

The girls looked at each other. Jessica nodded her head.

"We need medicine. My mother's very sick."

And without hesitation, Peter replied, "This is the way I'd go."

38

THE BATTLE OF THE TREES

IT WAS LIKE entering Aladdin's cave. Inside Julian's caravan, bright cushions embroidered with gold thread were strewn across the floor like gems. Rainbows of light from two jewel-paned windows played across the rich red walls and books. At the end of the single room, in the shadows, a wooden rocker sat beside a tiny kitchen cookstove. And books were everywhere: perched in teetering piles on the floor; resting haphazardly on painted shelves that lined the walls; left open on cushions, as if someone in the middle of reading them had stepped away.

Timothy sighed. This was his kind of room. Julian's books were leather-bound volumes with lettering in black and gold. Timothy itched to touch them.

"Sit," Julian said. "Make yourself comfortable. I'll get us some refreshment." He disappeared into the shadowy end of the caravan.

Timothy did as he was told. He chose a thick red cushion, folded his legs, and sat down. Gwydon padded over and lay, muzzle on paws, by his side. Timothy reached down and buried his fingers in the wolf's soft fur, and Gwydon let him. Sunlight filtered across the walls in watery patterns.

Timothy drew a few deep breaths and unclenched his hand. The leaf was a calm, clear blue in his palm. He tried to think of the right word to describe Julian's caravan. *Exotic*, he thought finally and smiled to himself, because the word used an *x*, a difficult letter to play. He put the leaf back in his pocket, gave a gentle stroke to the wolf's head, and picked up a thick brown book from the top of the pile nearest him.

Flipping it open, he saw, rather than the expected familiar letters or even the swirls and dots of Arabic, a series of straight marks that reminded him of tally scores. He'd seen these types of marks before . . . on the back of Mr. Twig's business card!

He studied the marks closely, wondering if it was some type of code. The heavy marks appeared to be grouped in sets, at an angle to a horizontal line. Sometimes they were above the line and sometimes below. Occasionally, they crossed the horizontal line.

It *is* a type of code, Timothy decided, but not one he'd ever seen before. He turned to the next page, looking for patterns. Every cryptographer knew that the secret to cracking a code depended on identifying the patterns. Some of the marks were the same. Repeated words?

Above the marks was an illustration of a tree, a tree holding a spear. A warrior tree, Timothy thought. He ran his finger over the illustration and tried to imagine trees at war.

"This should do." Julian returned, bearing a tray with a plate of cakes, a single glass, and a silver goblet. He set the tray down and looked at the book on Timothy's lap. "Do you read Ogham?" he asked, pronouncing the strange word like "Oyam."

"What did you say?"

"Ogham . . . No, I didn't think so." Julian took the book from Timothy's hands and replaced it with the silver goblet.

Then Julian handed him a dense round cake about the size of Timothy's palm. It smelled of honey, and the pale top was sprinkled with small seeds and nuts.

Timothy took a bite, and a moist sweetness filled his mouth. "Thanks," he said around a delicious mouthful, and swallowed. "Was that a code in your book?"

Julian explained, "It's not a code—it's a language. An ancient language called Ogham."

Eyes wide, Timothy took a sip from the silver goblet. It felt strange to drink out of anything so fancy. "Why did you lock the door?"

"There are things that are best spoken of in secret."

"What things?"

Julian steepled his fingers, resting his pointed chin on his thumbs. "Before you can find what you need, Timothy, you must understand a few things about what you are looking for. Here in the Market, I am a Storyteller. A keeper of history and of words. And what I am going to tell you now is a history worth knowing. It is partly your history."

Timothy's heart beat faster. This was surely it: the secret to curing his mother.

Julian closed his eyes and began to speak in a singsong voice, as if reciting something he had memorized long ago.

"The Filidh are a race of poets, keepers of the word, keepers of wisdom. The rank of a Filidh cannot be earned. It is only by birth and training that one becomes *Ollamh*, master scholar and the highest degree of Filidh, the equal of kings. One shall not slay the Filidh, nor may one ever refuse them hospitality, wealth, or land. Only a Filidh by birth can rule the Travelers, the people of the Market. A Filidh fights in all worlds against the power of the Dark."

Filidh. Timothy had heard that word before. But where? And there was the Dark again. It kept creeping in, and each time, he thought of Balor. The Filidh fights against the Dark. He was just about to ask more about what a Filidh was when there was a pounding at the caravan door. Instantly, Gwydon was on his feet.

Julian held up his hand, signaling silence.

"Come out, Storyteller! You're wanted in your tent!" The voice was loud and nasal. "You know the bargain. The price of living in the Market is your stories. If you have no stories, we'll be throwing you out. Leave you to lions! Tooth and claw!" What Timothy heard then was a high, tittering laugh that made his skin crawl.

Julian stood, threw the bolt, and opened the door. Gwydon stalked stiffly to Julian's side, his fur bristling.

There, framed in the light of the doorway, Timothy saw a small man with a very red face and even redder hair, pulled back into a straggling ponytail. He tapped one leather-booted foot impatiently, and his muscled arms, partially covered by long leather gloves, were tensed at his side. His red face was compressed in a scowl.

Gwydon stepped forward.

"Get that beast away from me!" the man demanded. "He shouldn't be allowed with civilized folk. I'd be having him in a cage with the circus if I was you! Or perhaps you'd prefer to have a little chat with the Animal Tamer?" When Gwydon responded with a warning rumble, the little man added, "It's a known fact that wolves turn on their owners, like vipers." He turned, spit on the steps, and touched two fingers to his forehead.

Julian turned to Timothy. "As you see, duty calls. We must finish our conversation another time."

Timothy's mouth flew open in protest. What about helping his mother? What about the Filidh and the Dark? Why would Julian let this obnoxious little man tell him what to do? Who knew how much time he had wasted, sitting here in the caravan, listening to stories with nothing to show for it?

It wasn't until he heard Gwydon growling softly beside him that Timothy realized his leaf was burning in his palm. He hadn't even been aware of pulling it out. Instantly, Timothy became more alert, every sense prickling. This man was not only obnoxious, he was dangerous.

As he stepped out of the caravan, Timothy squinted in the bright sunlight. Closing the door, he followed Julian, Gwydon, and the redhaired man. Gwydon pushed himself between the man and Julian, who walked behind in heavy silence. Timothy wanted to ask Julian where he thought he might search for something, anything, to help his mother, or if he knew Nom. But maybe it was better not to say anything in front of this man. At least, the leaf seemed to be warning him.

Midstride, the man stopped and pivoted, his hands on his hips. "Am I being followed? What have we here, a visitor to our Market?" His voice was a sneer.

Timothy hesitated.

"Can't you answer when you're spoken to, boy? Shake a leg! Corrie up!" The word *boy* was spit from the dwarf's lips like a curse.

"My name is Timothy James Maxwell," he said to the short man. "I'm afraid I didn't catch yours."

"Everyone in the Market knows the name of Tristan! What wind blew *you* in? You've the smell of a foreigner about you." The man leaned his long nose against Timothy's arm and inhaled deeply. Timothy jerked his arm away.

A few yards off, Julian and Gwydon entered a large white tent set between two stout trees.

"Where I come from's my own business," Timothy mumbled, thinking of Nom's warning not to reveal anything. And where *was* Nom? Wasn't he supposed to be helping them?

"Everything in the Market is my business, boy. *Everything.*" Tristan's eyes continually darted about. "And I'm asking you a question."

"No more your business than mine, Tristan," said a woman's voice from behind.

Timothy turned to see a tall woman with fair hair piled on top of her head. Her voice was lilting but formidable.

"Since when has the Market become ungracious to guests?" the woman continued when Tristan didn't immediately answer. "Don't mind him, Traveler. But come, Tristan, I have a dispute for you to settle."

Tristan puffed up under her gaze like a banty rooster. "I suppose I could be helping you out, Fiona."

She laughed lightly, and Timothy saw it as his chance to slip away. If he went into the tent with Julian and Gwydon now, he thought, he might have a few minutes to ask his questions. As soon as Tristan's back was turned, he dashed toward the white tent, lifted the flap, and slid from the bright sun into darkness.

The air inside was stuffy from the press of many bodies. Men, women, and children sat on rough wooden benches or cross-legged on the floor, their eyes fastened on Julian and Gwydon. Julian, sitting on a small stool in front of the crowd, was beginning a tale in the same singsong voice Timothy had heard in the caravan. Gwydon lay at his feet, nose on paws. When he spotted Timothy, he raised his head as if in acknowledgment and then relaxed again. Timothy found a spot near the rear of the crowd and sat cross-legged on the dirt floor.

"One day, Gwydon, the greatest of all storytellers and magicians, was given a task by the Light. It is often a difficult thing to serve the Light, for at times it involves great sacrifice and courage." An old man beside Timothy nodded vigorously. "He was tasked with securing three creatures that had been captured by the Dark and trapped in the under-world: the dog, the deer, and the lapwing. Just as the Light longs for all to be free, the Dark longs to control each and every thing." Julian spread his hands as if to include them all.

"To fight against the Dark is a terrible task for any man, but Gwydon was not any man. He was a shape-shifter, and now, in the form of a mighty human warrior, he knew he had been set apart for this very purpose. So when he realized how great his task was, to go into the depths of the underworld and free the three—the dog, the deer, and the lapwing—he realized that he would need help. Even in his present form, the task was too great for him alone. Noth-ing less than an army would do if he were to battle the Dark, or seek to outwit it. For the Dark had been gathering fierce warriors and strange creatures who lived under the earth. But where could Gwydon raise an army in time?

"Now, because Gwydon was wise, he was able to see the true nature of things. Before him stood the trees of the woods, and as he watched them, an idea grew in his mind. He would awaken the trees to their oldest form: when they were sentient beings. Once awakened, the trees, in their wisdom, would join him and march as an army against the Dark.

"First there came a great wind. The trees and the grasses began to murmur among themselves. As the wind howled, the voices of the trees joined in. Their voices had been silent for many years, and now they were terrible to hear. They creaked and groaned and shook their leaves. And then a noise even more horrible rose in the forest: a deep moaning and wrenching. The tree trunks began to sway—not just the limbs and the branches, but the thick, muscular trunks of the trees moved side to side. The noise was so great, Gwydon longed to cover his ears, but he needed to be a fearless leader to his army, so he stood fast before them. With a mighty groan, a ripping came from the depths of the earth. The first of the trees, the powerful alders, tore their roots from the soil. And so began the Battle of the Trees.

"The ground trembled violently, as if in an earthquake, and in the blink of an eye, the alders rushed to begin the assault. Never had there been a more terrible sight than hundreds of alders moving as one, trampling any agent of the Dark that stood in the path of their massive roots.

"Then the long-haired willows charged, their arms mighty. As they advanced, the willows shook and rattled their leaves like swords. Despite Gwydon's valiant fighting, despite the help from the trees, the forces of Darkness were winning. The ground shook once more. Birds flew up in a panic. Animals sprang from burrows and shelters, fleeing for their lives."

The crowd listened on the edge of their seats. The tent was completely silent except for Julian's voice.

"Into this chaos, the mighty company of oaks marched forward. No one could stand in their way. They were flanked by the fearsome hawthorn and holly, who challenged the Dark with sharp spikes of thorn. In the midst of the battle, the elm towered over all, flanked by the lofty pine and gloomy ash. Nothing could pass them, not even the Dark's fiercest warriors, men and beasts. Gwydon breathed a sigh of relief. The battle was turning. Now he would be able to set the prisoners free.

"But out of the Dark, there flew a multiheaded creature. Each head was more terrible than the other, and each spouted fire like a dragon, singeing the leaves of the trees. And with a moist, bubbling sound, a great black toad with a hundred claws sprang from a muddy swamp. Hopping in all directions, it slashed at the trunks of the trees. Both toad and beast were guardians of all the Dark held captive. Finally, slithering through the sea of swaying grass, came the many-colored snake—the snake who tormented souls kept prisoner by the Dark.

"Gwydon looked out over the battle, and his courage failed him. He knew that even with his army of trees, he could not complete the task, could not free the three. The battle was lost."

"Oohhh," the crowd sighed as one.

"In this moment of despair, a tree unlike any of the others moved close to Gwydon's side. The tree had the face of a man. He leaned down and whispered in Gwydon's ear, 'Speak a creature's true name. Use the old power of names.'"

The Greenman! Timothy thought. I'm sure it was him!

"And Gwydon considered the many names of the evil force that held the prisoners captive.

"He called out, 'The One-Eyed!' But still the snake advanced, toppling trees with its mighty body. Tree after noble tree fell in its path.

"As the toad slashed through a brave company of birch, Gwydon again called out, 'The Bent!' The name echoed through the battle, good warriors dropped their swords, timid creatures scampered into holes or sought safety high in the branches of trees, but the fury of the Dark increased.

"In desperation, knowing that this would be his last chance to turn the course of the battle, Gwydon reached back to the old knowledge, to a name before many names. 'Balor!'"

When Julian uttered this word, the audience covered their ears. Parents drew their children closer.

"And with the speaking of this terrible name, the whole earth trembled. The snake slithered back into the mouth of the earth, the toad oozed down into the mud, and the multiheaded beast took flight. All was still. The power of the Dark was broken for a time, and from the depths of the earth the deer and the dog and the lapwing sprang free. They frolicked, leapt, and flew to serve man and the Light."

A few spontaneous cheers erupted. Timothy felt like cheering, himself.

"But this was only one victory. The Dark slunk away, remembering, feeding on its bitterness, slowly growing stronger. It returned with new schemes, as it always will until the end of time. But Gwydon also grew stronger as he served the Light, and with each victory he transformed. In the next battle, he wore the shape of another man, a great military leader, emperor of Britain, *Arthur* . . ."

As Timothy listened, he felt like he wanted to do something heroic, too. He longed for the Greenman to whisper a word in his ear. Was this Gwydon of the story the same Gwydon that lay at Julian's feet? The same Gwydon who had carried him on his back in their first adventure? Had Gwydon once been King Arthur? For a long moment after the story ended, nobody moved. It was as if the spell of the story still hung in the air, the bright images slow to fade. Then, one by one or in groups, people stood and stretched, but their voices remained hushed, like parishioners leaving church, until the spell was broken by a loud sneer.

"Are you done with your fancies, then, Storyteller?"

Julian rose, and Gwydon, the fur on his neck bristling again, rose with him. The crowd quickly scattered, and Timothy, sensing danger, crept deep into the shadows.

Tristan strode forward, and once again Timothy was amazed that so small a man could command such presence. He stood before Julian, his feet spread, his gloved hands on his small hips. "This is soft entertainment. If it wasn't for the crowds, I wouldn't have it. Stories? Why do people come to hear lies spun?" He shook his head.

Julian spoke softly in return. "Stories help them make sense of their

lives. Stories provide hope. They promise that the Dark doesn't have the final word. Other people have lived through difficult times, too."

Tristan grunted. "'Sense'? Nonsense. You fill their heads with nonsense, and they come back for more. And you—what kind of person lives this way, by words rather than actions? I'm Master of the Market. I could throw you out today, you and that demon beast. And then where would you be? A lost spinner of tales, begging for food. It's no way for a man to make a living! A man needs truth, not stories fit for old men, women, and children. He needs to fight, get his hands dirty, take what he can get!" As Tristan's voice grew louder, it also grew more strident, more threatening. *Master of the Market* . . . If master meant bullying everyone, then it was easy to believe the redhaired man held that title.

Julian stood with his hands loose at his sides, apparently completely relaxed in the face of the dwarf's onslaught. "Throw me out, and I will still be telling stories, old and new," he said simply. "Sometimes you need to hear truth from another direction before you can recognize it, Master of the Market." Then he shifted his gaze and looked straight at Timothy.

Instinctively, Timothy shrank back farther into the shadows. But Tristan didn't appear to notice.

"Watch yourself, Storyteller. No one tells the Master about truth. In my Market, *I* decide what is true." And he laughed the high, strange laugh Timothy had heard on the wagon steps. Turning sharply on one booted heel, Tristan strode from the tent.

Everything might have worked out quite differently if Timothy had not, at that very moment, sneezed. It was the second time a sneeze had given him away at a crucial moment. The heat and dust were thick in the tent, and Timothy, cursing his allergies, couldn't hold it back.

Tristan spun on his heel. One great hand, splayed like a shovel—a hand that was surely too large for so small a man—reached out and grabbed Timothy by his shirt, pulling him out of the shadows.

"Not only a visitor but a spy! What are you hoping to discover, boy?" Tristan's face was inches from Timothy's, and his breath, warm and garlicky, puffed into Timothy's face with every word. "Never mind what you want." He thrust his chin out. "You're in my Market, and there are no secrets from me here. I have my ways." The dwarf's powerful hand gripped Timothy's shoulder so hard that the boy felt tears spring to his eyes. He looked for Julian and Gwydon, but they were gone. He was alone with Tristan, the Master of the Market.

FIONA'S DRAÍOGHT

RISTAN MARCHED TIMOTHY out of the Storyteller's tent. It should have been easy to break away from someone even shorter than himself, but Tristan was strong. His hand dug into Timothy's shoulder as a reminder that Timothy wasn't going anywhere without him.

"Where are you taking me?"

But Tristan wasn't answering. Instead, he half dragged Timothy along, stopping only when they reached a bakery stall.

"Nothing's hidden in my Market, boy. In a few minutes I'll know everything there is to know about you, whether you want me to or not."

Timothy tried to make one last break for it, but the thick fingers sought the bones of his shoulder. He winced. Why were they at a bakery? Julian and Gwydon, he thought with a desperate look over his shoulder, must surely be following him. He scanned the people clustered around a wooden keg in the shade of a striped canopy. No one paid them any attention. But one face in the crowd was familiar. Nom leaned against the side of the wagon, a flagon of drink in his hand, his face partly turned toward Timothy as he conversed with a man holding a giant lizard on a leash.

"Nom!" Timothy called out. Tristan boxed his ear. The pain, sudden and sharp, made Timothy's head spin. But Nom looked up and, for a moment, his bleary eyes widened at the sight of Timothy being shoved through the doorway of the tent.

The air was sweet with the smell of fresh bread, cinnamon, and ripe fruit. It was also hot. Most of the heavy baking was done in an outside oven during the early-morning hours, but some fresh pies cooled on a rack. "I've brought you a customer, Fiona, but not for bread. Someone who needs his past and future brought to light."

To Timothy's surprise, the same fair-haired lady who had distracted Tristan earlier came forward. Flour smudged her cheek and left white streaks on her red apron. "What have we here?" she asked softly.

Tristan spat and touched his forehead again in the same sign Timothy had noticed before. "I want you to tell me everything about this boy, since he won't say anything himself. I want to know why he's here. Where he came from. Where he's going."

Sadness blurred her pale face. "You know my business is a bakery, Tristan, and I prefer not to deal in fortune-telling."

"You'll use your *draíocht* in the manner I choose." He shoved Timothy forward and then clambered onto a tall stool, where his short legs dangled. He picked up a chopping knife and thumbed its blade. Any thoughts Timothy had of an easy escape vanished.

The lady looked sad, even reproachful, Timothy thought. "*Draíocht* isn't to be commanded by the likes of you, Tristan Quinn," she said softly.

"I'm the Master. You'll do as I say, Fiona, or you'll be back with the Animal Tamer!" As he smiled, Tristan's tongue flicked in and out as quickly as a snake's.

Fiona's hand crept involuntarily to her neck, where a ragged scar ran from one side to the other. She turned her eyes to Timothy and wiped her hands on her apron. "Come closer, child."

Her voice was gentle, and Timothy walked forward, not wanting to cause her any more distress.

"Place your hand here." She took his hand and pressed it to her stomach, over the red apron, then closed her eyes. Dropping his hand, she led him to a large bowl. "Spit into the water."

Timothy wondered if he had heard right. "Spit?"

Fiona opened her eyes. "Yes, spit," she repeated. And so he did.

She watched Timothy's saliva swirl into the clear liquid, then drew a fine gold stick from her hair. Fair strands tumbled down, curtaining her face. She stirred the liquid with the stick, then plucked a curly hair from Timothy's head and dropped it into the bowl.

"Ow!" he exclaimed. "What are you doing?"

"Hush and watch."

A face formed in the bowl. It was Timothy's mother, looking pale and drawn.

Tristan drew close, breathing heavily by Timothy's side. As Timothy looked down at the image of his mother, panic attacked him from all quarters. Her eyes were wide and unseeing, her forehead shiny with perspiration. She writhed in pain. Timothy's father sat beside her, talking on the telephone, distracted with worry. He kept one hand on his wife's shoulder as he spoke, as if afraid she might disappear before his eyes.

Timothy choked back tears. His mother was so thin that her collarbones threatened to break through the skin. "Mom!" he couldn't help but cry out.

Fiona looked even sadder. "Your mother is very ill."

"What will happen to her?" Timothy gasped.

"I can't say more than I can see." She stirred the water again with the golden stick, and another vision appeared: Timothy stood with Sarah and Jessica. Nom was there, too, and Timothy remembered it as the time when Nom was giving them instructions about hunting for a cure.

At this, Timothy felt Tristan stiffen behind him. "So he's not alone."

Again, Fiona stirred the water. This time an image of Timothy's crown formed in the water—the crown given him by Cerridwyn, the one he had traded in a moment of weakness for a drink of water. The circle of vines with a single leaf looked so real that Timothy reached out for it, but his hand met only air and water.

"Please," he said imploringly to Fiona, unable to erase the picture of his mother from his mind. "Please, help me."

She poured the water from the bowl out the door of the tent onto the packed earth.

"So you want something, do you?" Tristan smiled widely. "Something we have for your poor, sick mum? And what will you give for it? A crown?" He began to giggle.

"It's best not to interfere with things beyond you," Fiona said simply.

"Am I not Master of the Market!" Tristan screamed in outrage. "Nothing here is beyond me! I control it all! And I think a crown would be adequate payment for a visit to *my* Market."

"Please, my mother needs——" Timothy faltered. His head was suddenly hurting, and his thoughts were befuddled. He clutched his head in his hands.

"Don't worry," Fiona said. "It always feels that way afterward." She laid a cool hand on his brow.

Tristan eyed Timothy with a speculative air. "You may be worth more than I thought. I wonder what the Animal Tamer would give for you."

Fiona blanched. "Tristan, don't," she pleaded in a low voice.

"Don't you have a boy of your own to worry about?" Tristan countered.

Fiona's hand flew to her throat like a pale bird and rested there. Tristan shoved Timothy out of the bakery tent into the bright sun. The boy looked around frantically for Gwydon or Julian, but they were nowhere to be seen. The leaf in his pants pocket burned through the rough fabric, searing his leg.

THE ANIMAL TAMER

SARAH WAS FOLLOWING Jessica and Peter through the Market when her attention was diverted by the sight of a large crow slumped on a wooden perch. His wings were spread wide, and his head was cocked to one side, beak open. A thin film covered his eyes, and he was so still that Sarah feared he was injured. Falling back from the others, she cautiously approached the bird. His gleaming black breast rested on the perch between the widely spread wings. He did not move when she approached, as most birds would have.

"That's how crows take the sun, lady."

Sarah turned. The handsome man who had spoken to her was very tan, with a mop of golden curls, and when he smiled, his teeth flashed and his blue eyes twinkled. He was so striking, Sarah was afraid she might be staring and hoped she wasn't blushing.

"I thought it was injured, poor thing," she said, trying to look away.

"Crows are tricksters. You can't trust a thing they do or tell you." At that, the crow cocked his head and chortled deep in his feathery throat.

"But now, if you're looking for a pet," the golden-haired man continued, "here's something that would perhaps suit you better." He pulled a thin creature with snow-white fur from his pocket. The animal slid through his hands and sidled up his arm where it posed, looking at Sarah with bright brown eyes. It was one of the most beautiful animals Sarah had ever seen.

"A rare white ermine, lady, and almost as beautiful and rare as you. It keeps its color even when the seasons change." The man smiled with a flash of white teeth.

Now she was blushing. To hide her face, she looked down and stroked the ermine's soft fur. The crow ruffled his feathers and hunched his wings. Then he ducked his head forward and bobbed it up and down, softly chortling.

"Listen, he's talking," Sarah said, glad for a reason to look away from the golden man with the ermine on his shoulder. She moved even closer to the bird, and as she approached, the crow ducked his head even farther. She tentatively reached out one finger and rubbed the top of his head. He pressed back against her finger and chortled. Sarah laughed, and the knot of anxiety in her stomach relaxed a little.

She glanced over her shoulder for her friends. Jessica had stopped to admire a display of glass beads several stalls away. She held a translucent green necklace up to the light. Peter was at her side, but he was watching Sarah. She quickly looked away.

"I see you have a way with animals," said the golden man, once again distracting her. "As you can see, I'm a specialist in rare animals. A tamer, a purveyor of whatever suits your fancy." He smiled his disarming smile and gestured at the fancy cages displayed in his stall. "I am known as the Animal Tamer, and I'm desperately in need of an assistant."

A small monkey clambered up and over the man's shoulder, clutching a red daisy in one paw, and in one unexpected motion jumped onto Sarah's shoulder, offering her the flower.

She laughed out loud. "I'm not here for very long," she said, taking the flower from the monkey's paw. "I'm looking for something for my mother."

"Oh, I'm disappointed," the man said. "But perhaps I can help. Would your mother like some jewelry?" He drew a sparkling gold bracelet from his pocket. "Or a pet, perhaps?" He snapped his fingers, and a bright macaw landed on his shoulder.

"Oh, no. It's nothing like that." The knot tightened in her stomach again as she thought of her mother. She couldn't pull her eyes from the man's gaze.

"Then perhaps she would be interested in one of my rarer finds." Before Sarah could speak, the man took her arm and led her inside a small tent that stood behind the rows of gleaming cages.

The tent was the size her family might have used for a camping trip, Sarah thought. There was only one animal inside, housed in a large and very elaborate cage. She moved closer. Crouched in the back of the cage was a small blue-winged creature with curious brown eyes. Its blue-streaked wings looked as fragile as a dragonfly's. A bushy tail wrapped around the animal's hindquarters. Enormous ears twitched on each side of its head as it followed the Animal Tamer with its large eyes.

An overwhelming desire to hold the strange little creature filled Sarah's heart.

"Venustas," the man said. "A rare find. They are prized, the few that have been captured, for their tracking ability. They're better even than hounds. I assure you, once this animal has been put on a trail, it will find its prey or die trying. Its hearing and sense of smell are unparalleled."

"Can I hold it?" Sarah asked.

"No, lady. This is my crown jewel. It is worth the price of all my other animals combined, and then some. Notice the bushy tail? The little beast survives even in extreme cold by wrapping it completely around its body. And the fur? It may look like a kitten's, but it is as repellent to water as a duck's feathers. I traveled a great distance and put myself at great risk to procure this creature."

The venustas scampered to the cage door to sniff at Sarah's outstretched hand. She tried to poke her fingers through the silver wires of the cage and touch its downy fur.

"However, they do like to be scratched under the chin, and I can imagine an instance when you *might* be able to hold the creature."

Sarah wanted to ask what the instance might be, but that annoying knot in her stomach reminded her that she had another, more important, task.

"What is it, my dear? You look disturbed." And in an instant the man was right by her side, grasping her hand in both of his.

A pleasant warmth seeped through her entire body. Perhaps she should explain everything to him. Perhaps *he* was the person she was meant to find.

At that moment, the crow perched outside the tent began to caw. His call was loud and insistent. Through the flap in the tent door, Sarah saw the crow sidestep back and forth across his perch. Spreading his wings, the bird beat them against the air. The attempt to fly was futile. He was, Sarah suddenly realized, attached to the perch by a thin silver chain.

Peter appeared in the tent doorway. "I think we should go and look for your mam's stuff," he said with a scowl, scratching one leg against the other. In the small tent, next to the Animal Tamer, the boy looked dirtier than ever.

"Peter, I think he can help us," Sarah said, pulling her hand out of the man's warm grasp.

"Wouldn't trust him a bit, I wouldn't," Peter whispered, grabbing Sarah's arm and pulling her out of the tent. "Not one who keeps all his animals caged up like this."

"Whatever do you mean?" said the Animal Tamer, following right behind them. For the first time, Sarah looked closely at the Animal Tamer's wares. He certainly kept a wide variety of animals in elaborate cages of every sort: leopards, bear cubs, a peacock, and a python.

"Perhaps you would allow *me* to show you around the Market," the man said to Sarah in a quiet but insistent voice. "I'm sure we can find something for your mother. I've introduced myself; now it's your turn." The Animal Tamer offered her his arm.

"Uh, Sarah . . . Sarah Marie Maxwell." His skin was warm and very smooth, and her hand felt small resting on his arm. Sarah liked being addressed like a grown-up and unconsciously stood a bit taller. She imagined herself working with the gray-spotted leopard as the Animal Tamer's assistant, or playing with the little bear cub. Of course, that would be after she and the Animal Tamer brought a healing medicine to her mother.

"Don't be a fool, Sarah!" Peter hissed in her ear. But the Animal Tamer took no more notice of him than he did of the crow, which continued to caw on his perch with increasing agitation. Instead, he kept his eyes focused intently on Sarah, waiting for her response.

Sarah slipped her hand from the Animal Tamer's arm and went to the crow's perch, trying to scratch the bird's head again. "Poor thing," she said. "It doesn't like being tied up."

⊹ ⊹ ⊹

The raucous cawing finally caught Jessica's attention. She reluctantly returned the necklace she had been admiring back to its case and wandered in the direction of Peter and Sarah at the nearby stall. She had only gone a few steps when she was stopped by a headache so sudden and severe that she almost dropped to her knees. Her eyes blurred. It was as if her head were being ripped in two.

Just as abruptly, the pain stopped. Jessica's eyes focused, and then she screamed: She saw Sarah take the arm of a hideous one-eyed man. Peter stood nearby looking helpless, surrounded by a menagerie of animals, moaning and shivering in cages much too small to contain them.

"Sarah, Peter! Get away!"

Jessica wasn't sure her voice was working or if anyone had heard her, because Sarah just laughed. The horrible one-eyed man beside her shook his mop of golden curls and laughed in response. It was as if Jessica's feet were nailed to the ground, as if her voice carried no sound.

The crow continued to caw. Jessica began to think of the crow's cawing as *her* voice, and she willed it to caw all the louder. Soon the crow's caw was joined by a cacophony of other cries, and from overhead a cadre of black crows wheeled into view.

✝ ✝ ✝

Andor and Arkell were perched in a large tree on a rise overlooking the Market. The two eagles had been sent by the council of birds to gather news of the children and the Market and to learn more about rumors of a coming battle. Beside them stood a creature both man and tree. It had been some time since the Greenman had listened to the language of eagles. But with concentration, he was able to glean their spare words.

Crows have come. Andor sent the words to Arkell. *Can they be trusted?*

Arkell ruffled his feathers, but it was the Greenman who sent back a reply. He sent a picture of armies of men and animals marching; of councils of the great birds flocked together—eagles, hawks, owls.

But in all of these images, the crows were absent. Crows aligned themselves with no councils, with no armies. They were too busy squabbling among themselves, ready to switch sides with the direction of the wind.

The two eagles nodded. It was as they had always known.

But the Greenman was not finished. This time, even the raucous, unreliable crows would fight for a greater purpose. A true Filidh had returned to the Market. He sent a picture of a boy with his arm outstretched. A single crow flew to him, alighting on his bare arm. Then a dozen more came. Soon the sky was black with crows. The boy wore a simple crown, but his face was hidden in shadow.

That is why we watch him. He has been found. Arkell looked into the distance. *Councils are called.*

Yes. The Greenman's answer carried with it the smell of fire, the scent of danger.

Arkell and Andor rose on a swift current. They would carry the news.

The Greenman looked down at the Market. How he longed to gather all of the people under the shade of his branches, to protect them from what was to come. But he knew that even in the worst of the battle there would be those who would reject his offer of protection. He watched the crows approach like missiles, and bright-haired Sarah, standing with her hands at her sides, face turned upward, listening.

THE COMING
OF THE CROWS

FROM ALL OVER the Market, people watched the birds descend.

"Do you see that? Birds gone mad!"

"It's the end, I tell you! When animals start acting like that, the end is near."

"Never trusted crows. Dirty, sneaking birds, they are."

What looked from a distance like a dense black cloud dropping from a clear sky turned into a cawing mass. Parents remembered folktales, stories of crows attacking children, drawn by the bright young eyes in the same way birds were drawn to glittering baubles. They cried out for their children. Others ran, and a few grabbed sticks or rocks to hurl at the descending birds.

Tristan was nearly to the Animal Tamer's stall with Timothy in tow when the chaos began. He did not like chaos in his Market. He didn't like anything in his Market that he didn't control, and this was definitely something unexpected. But nothing he couldn't contain, he assured himself, tightening his grip on Timothy's arm.

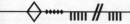

"Walk faster, boy. You've twice the legs I have. Use them!"

The strange behavior of the crows startled Timothy from his thoughts about Nom. It wasn't like anything he had ever seen. He'd once seen two crows chasing a kestrel away from their nest, and another time a crow had gone for his head when he had walked under a tree where a fledgling had fallen, but never like this. Crows didn't attack en masse. Perhaps this was more of the *draíocht* of the Market, but *draíocht* or not, if it upset Tristan, it might be something Timothy could use to his advantage. So he hurried, but kept a look out for Sarah or Jessica, Julian or Gwydon. The leaf in his pocket continued to burn.

The day had become increasingly hot and dry. Every step sent up a swirl of dust, a miniature dust devil, and his throat felt as raspy as sandpaper. People jostled, hurrying from tents and caravans to see the spectacle of the crows around the Animal Tamer's stall. Soon Tristan, dragging Timothy behind, was pushing his way through a river of bodies. As the man and boy drew closer, the noise of the birds overwhelmed the shouts of people. Timothy wanted to cover his ears. Between the swell of curious newcomers, flying rocks, and clouds of dust, this part of the Market was in turmoil.

"The Animal Tamer's gone too far this time," Tristan muttered to himself right below Timothy's ear. "I don't know what he's up to, but this is my Market, and he'll not act as if he owns it."

This would be the time to get away, slip into the crowd, Timothy thought. He knew from watching the other boys in the hall at school that if he kicked Tristan behind the knee, just where it bent, his leg would collapse under him. It was a trick he'd never actually tried before, but now seemed as good a time as any. He watched Tristan's stride for several seconds. Then he drew his leg back, and aimed a sharp kick right into the back of the dwarf's knee.

Tristan's leg buckled. He dropped hard to one knee, releasing Timothy's arm.

Timothy ran. He flew under the arm of a large man dragging a crying child. He stitched in and out between people, not caring what direction he ran so long as it was away from Tristan. He ran until his side hurt, and then ran a little farther, finally stopping behind a faded caravan to catch what was left of his breath.

The sun was still directly overhead. Timothy tried to get his bearings. He was close to the crows but viewing the scene from a different direction. Everyone was so busy trying to see what was happening that no one paid any attention to a boy with glasses and dirty clothes. He knew that Tristan would not regard his escape lightly. Bullies were always that way. They had long memories, and they hated being made fools of.

He scanned the crowd, looking for anyone he knew. If only he had something to drink! Timothy took off his glasses and wiped the sweat from his face, leaving a brown streak on his shirt cuff. His best chance, he thought, was to push forward toward the crows, since it was likely that Sarah and Jessica would be there with everyone else. Of course, that was exactly where Tristan would be, too. He would have to be extremely careful.

✛ ✛ ✛

"Look at the way he's just sitting there like a pet. Shames me to my bones."

"You know it's not his fault. He's kept. Tied up with a sparklie."

"Mind the big cat—thinks he's sumthin', don't he?"

"Oh, look at the sparklies!"

"Focus, Cratcher, we're here for a job."

"Just a sparklie for me nest!"

"Attack! Attack!"

"Who are you calling a birdbrain, Craddoch? I'll pull every last feather from yer tail!"

"You no-good, molting parrot-talker!"

The raucous voices were all overhead, but all Sarah could see were birds, hundreds of black crows swooping and diving. And the voices . . . They seemed to be coming from them! Indeed, there were so many birds talking at once that Sarah had trouble making any sense of their words until she focused on one particular bird, and suddenly the words became clear. She forgot about the Animal Tamer's hand on her arm, about the Market, about the possibility of becoming the handsome Animal Tamer's prized assistant, and even about her mother. She could understand the language of crows!

Sarah had never given crows much thought. They had always

seemed like nasty, squabbling things, eating dead animals off the road and picking through garbage. She had watched them do their funny hop across the school fields after lunch, and heard them cawing in the trees around her house, but she had never heard them *talk* before.

The birds were swirling right above the Animal Tamer's exhibit, cawing and arguing, but so far not a single one had landed. She tried to notice a pattern in their behavior, but she couldn't see one. At the center of the group, there was a particularly large fellow. Sarah focused her attention on him. He seemed to be some sort of leader, or at least he was shouting directions.

"Craddoch, free Crake first! Save our kind! Then, the left flank opens the cages! Right flank, attack the One-Eyed Man! Flight formation!"

Not much of this made sense to Sarah, and many of the birds kept right on chattering over the lead crow's commands. But a strange thing began to happen; some of the birds wheeled around, arcing up together, almost as if their flight was choreographed. Then they separated into two groups. From the center of one group, a motley-looking crow descended fast, landing on the perch next to the crow held by the silver chain. The captured bird, who must be Crake, Sarah thought, began cawing hysterically.

"Stop yer blubbering and hold still so's I can free you!" The motley crow pecked at his comrade's chain. The Animal Tamer immediately left Sarah's side and began flailing his arms, trying to shoo the old bird away. At the same time, a group of ten or fifteen crows dove straight at his golden head. He threw up his arms, covering his face, but the crows were relentless, diving at him from the side, landing on his head, striking again and again in full attack. A bold fellow balanced right on the crown of the Animal Tamer's head, cawing and pecking, holding on no matter how hard the man tried to shake him off.

Sarah wondered if she should come to the Animal Tamer's defense. That was what an Animal Tamer's assistant would do, but something made her hesitate. Meanwhile, some of the crowd lobbed stones at the birds. A small crow fell to the ground, his legs askew. But what, Sarah wondered in confusion, had the crow meant by "the One-Eyed Man"? Wasn't that how Timothy had once described Balor? Was he here somewhere? And where *was* Timothy?

The crow on the perch was not having an easy time assisting Crake with the chain. He pecked and pulled at it with his beak while Crake beat his wings against the air and shrieked.

"Oh, save me!" the bird cried. "Please save me! Mind my leg! Mind my wings! Gotta fly! Save me!"

"Stop yer hollering, you cat meat!"

Now another flank of crows landed on some of the cages. They pecked furiously at the locks. The longer Sarah watched, the more she was amazed. One crow was using a stick as a tool to pry open the lock of an ornate cage holding a peacock. When she missed, she patiently tried again, three, then four, more times. Finally, the lock released and the peacock sprang from the cage, fanning his beautiful tail feathers in triumph as he strutted around in a circle.

"Look here, my feather's bent! Well, never have I been treated like that before. And with my colors—like a common house bird, a parrot, or a mynah!"

Sarah seemed able to understand peacocks as well, and she wondered in amazement if she could understand the language of all birds.

And then someone was grabbing her elbow. She whirled around to meet Peter's blue eyes. His brow was creased with worry, his shirt was rumpled, and a streak of dirt was smeared across his cheek. Sarah had forgotten all about him, too.

"I've been watching you look at the birds. It's like you're listening to what they say."

"Peter, I am. I can understand the language of birds!"

"I knew it! Knew you were *draíocht* the first time I saw you! Better get out of here while you can. The birds'll take care of the Animal Tamer now."

Sarah looked to where she had last seen the Animal Tamer. His head was bent and his arms flailed. Birds covered his shoulders like a fine black cape, stabbing at his neck and face. One large crow pecked persistently just at the base of his skull. "We can't just leave him!"

Peter breathed close to her ear. "He's a bad one—don't you understand? I've been trying to tell you, but you won't listen. Now let's get out of here!"

"Look at my sparklie! Look at my sparklie!" A crow flew close to Sarah's head, a beaded necklace hanging from his beak.

"Give it here, Cratcher." A second crow swooped in close, grabbing the strand in his beak.

Cratcher cawed loudly. "Thief! Thief!"

In the midst of the chaos, a shot exploded, and then another. Cratcher and the crow bearing the necklace fell to the ground. Their bodies hit the dirt with a soft thud, their black wings bent, lifeless.

Sarah turned toward them, but Peter grabbed her arm and dragged her to the ground. "Don't be a fool, Sarah!"

More shots rang out. More birds dropped from the sky.

"Retreat! Retreat!" the large crow shrilled. Gone was the choreographed flight. The crows were in pandemonium—screeching, chattering, calling to one another.

"He'll have to kill me, then!" cried the brave crow still trying to free Crake from his chain.

Another flew in to help. "He'll have to shoot us both!"

While struggling against Peter's strong hands, Sarah could see where the shots were coming from. A short, stocky man with a long nose and a red ponytail was standing atop a barrel. The same man she had seen holding the purse at the ferret-legging competition. His legs spread wide, pistol held with both hands, Tristan aimed into the mass of squawking crows. Peter crawled to the cover of a nearby caravan, dragging Sarah with him. Her skirt was crusted with dirt, and her face was wet with tears. "He doesn't have to kill them!" she cried.

The Animal Tamer, Sarah realized, was now nowhere to be seen.

The two crows were still pecking at Crake's silver chain. Several other birds continued to work at the locks of the remaining cages. Sarah wanted to do something, *anything* to help the crows, but Peter kept a tight grip on her arm.

And then Jessica was there, striding into the middle of the scene as if the man was shooting only a toy gun. Most amazing of all, she looked magnificent. In fact, at first Sarah didn't recognize her friend at all: She looked so much taller and older.

Without even looking at the man on the barrel, Jessica walked up to Crake's perch, wrapped one hand around the crow, stilling it, and broke the chain. The brave crows flew straight up and away.

"Look at her! Look at her!" They cawed in delight.

Crake bobbed his head and chortled low in his throat, as if giving thanks. Then he, too, flew up, obviously delighted once again to have the use of his wings. In a second, he had joined the black retreating mass of crows.

A TRADE

TIMOTHY ARRIVED at the battle of the crows just as Tristan began to fire. Dropping on all fours, he snaked on his belly through the dust, sheltering next to the wheels of a caravan and trying to sort out all that was happening around him. There, in the very center of the confusion, he spotted Sarah, and next to her a shabby-looking boy her age. The boy was trying to drag her away from the most dangerous part of the battle, and she wasn't leaving willingly. Timothy knew how difficult it could be to make Sarah do anything she didn't want to do. He admired the boy's efforts.

But the sight of Tristan standing astride the barrel, armed and his chin jutting forward, sent shivers through Timothy's body. He was thinking he could inch his way around the outskirts of the scene to reach Sarah, when his attention was diverted by the crows. They repeatedly circled overhead like a storm cloud and then darted down into the Market. But it was where they were landing—a stall loaded with elaborate cages—that made Timothy's heart almost stop. He had seen similar cages before, ornate cages with animals trapped inside.

Timothy scanned the crowd frantically, his fear of Tristan nothing compared to the deep dread of seeing Balor once again. And his hip was growing uncomfortably warm. He thrust his hand into his pocket and pulled out the Greenman's leaf. Sure enough, it was a burning, angry red, searing his fingers. No question, Balor must be near.

At that very moment, he saw Jessica at the stall. She's gone mad, Timothy thought. What can I do to save her? He crept forward until he was crouched at the very edge of the caravan under which he had been hiding. He watched Jessica approach other cages, heedless of the gunfire and of Tristan, who had obviously spotted her.

"You there! What do you think you're doing?" Tristan's face was so red, Timothy thought he might explode.

"It's perfectly fine, Tristan. She's with me. Just as this one is," the Animal Tamer said.

Timothy recognized the voice, and it was as if a black pit opened beneath him. Balor was here, at the Market, and he had Sarah. He was dragging her by the arm out into the center of the melee. Sarah had never seen Balor and had no idea at all with whom she was dealing. Where was the boy who was with her before?

"We must stop this horrible slaughter of innocent animals," the Animal Tamer continued in his smooth voice. "Tristan, put away your gun. The crows have left us."

The dark cloud of birds was rapidly receding into the distance, though the bodies of several lay scattered across the ground around the Market.

Tristan jumped down from the barrel. "I'll have order in my Market, Animal Tamer. I am the Master of the Market. And your friend there is wearing something that catches my eye." The crowd of people who had initially fled the crows and the wild shots of Tristan drew back now to watch this new development.

Looking positively regal, Timothy thought, Jessica fastened her eyes on the Animal Tamer, and her lips drew back in a grimace. "You will let go of my friend," she said, her voice as calm and sure as if she were ordering a young child.

"A fair trade, miss," Balor replied with a sneer. "A necklace for your friend. Tristan would like your bauble. Give him the necklace, and I will release the girl. Then perhaps you, too, will consider being my assistant."

Timothy waited and watched. Her arm tight in the Animal Tamer's grip, Sarah eyed the tamer with disappointment and confusion, but her expression betrayed none of the loathing evident in Jessica's face. For the first time, Jessica hesitated. The Animal Tamer strengthened his hold on Sarah's arm. She winced. Timothy clenched his fists.

"See, she is reluctant to leave me." The Animal Tamer ran a finger down the side of Sarah's face. "And she would make a fine assistant." He looked calmly at Jessica. "Come, your necklace for the Master of the Market. He fancies it. And I let your friend go."

Timothy could feel the contest of wills between them. Even Tristan was silent. Jessica dared not give that evil little man the necklace that had been a gift from Cerridwyn; but she had to do something to make the

Animal Tamer let go of Sarah. Timothy wanted to rush in and save his sister, but he knew whatever he did might make the situation worse. He wiped the smudges from his glasses and glanced back to where Sarah and the boy had been sheltering before, but he saw no sign of the boy. There was only a mangy dog, tethered to the side of a caravan.

"It looks like she won't trade, Tristan, so I guess I'll have to keep my young assistant." With that, the Animal Tamer barked a laugh, and in a rapid movement drew Sarah close. He locked one arm around her neck. With the other hand he pulled an emerald chain and collar out of his pocket. He fastened the collar around her neck and chained her to a cage. The mangy dog barked furiously, straining at his tether.

Timothy could bear it no longer. He scrambled to his feet and rushed into the middle of the yard. "Let my sister go!"

But Jessica interrupted him. "Take the necklace, Balor the One-Eyed, though it will do you no good. But remember your bargain!" She snatched the necklace from around her neck and tossed it at him. It flew through the air in a golden arc. Balor leaned forward and caught the chain in his right hand. No one saw him draw a vial from his pocket with his left until he unstopped the cork and, in one swift motion, poured it over Sarah's head.

GHOICES

A WHITE ERMINE on an emerald chain curled around the legs of the Animal Tamer. Sarah was nowhere to be seen.

Jessica advanced on him. "You've broken your bargain!"

"Perhaps you should be more careful with whom you bargain. I don't have your friend—just an ermine. And, of course, your necklace!" He unchained the ermine and scooped it into a sack. He held out the necklace to Tristan, who grabbed for it with a face flushed with pleasure. "Take your bauble, Master of the Market. It will not serve you."

Tristan blustered and strutted as the pendant sparkled on his chest. "Go back to your business, people!" he ordered with an imperious sweep of his arm. "The Market is about to close for the day."

And those who had not left already hurried off, glad to be away.

Timothy stepped forward. He stuck his hands in his pockets so the Animal Tamer couldn't see them tremble. "Let my sister go!"

Balor turned. "Ah. So we meet again, Timothy. And where is the wolf to protect you this time? The time will come when no one can protect you. I have your sister, and I believe you will do anything I want in order to save her." The ermine thrashed in its cloth prison. "Perhaps I shall now make a bargain with *you*. What do you say, boy? Your sister or your mother? Whom do you want to save? She's very ill, isn't she, your mother? And I do know where to find the only thing in this Market that will save her."

"Timothy, let's go!" For the first time, Jessica addressed her friend.

"And leave Sarah—are you crazy?" Timothy turned to Balor. "What do you have for my mother?"

But Balor, who had slung the sack over his shoulder, was already climbing the steps to his caravan.

"She's right; you need to come with us now." Nom appeared suddenly, plucking at Timothy's elbow. "Can't help her like this, you can't."

Timothy felt his anger building like floodwaters about to burst a dam. He shook Nom's hand away. There was no way he was going to walk away and leave Sarah with that man, with that . . . *thing!*

"Free my sister, Balor!" he shouted. "In the name of Cerridwyn and of the Greenman, free my sister!" He didn't know where the words came from, but they apparently were the right ones, for all at once Balor hesitated. And when he turned, Timothy saw the golden man's handsome face melt. In its place, Balor the One-Eyed gaped back at him. The single eye in the middle of his forehead remained hooded.

Nom covered his face. Tristan touched his forehead and spat.

Winds scuttled the clouds across the sky. Again the birds came. They rode the winds and blocked the sun like a living cloud. Finches, hawks, kestrels, fickle crows, and the great eagles. Arkell and Andor flew low. Swooping between the Animal Tamer and Timothy, the two eagles blocked Timothy from Balor's eye, preventing Balor from casting it on the boy. The flap of their mighty wings lifted the hair on Timothy's head. Nom dropped to the ground, cowering facedown, but Jessica still stood defiantly. Tristan ran, arms protecting his head, into the nearest caravan.

Balor measured his enemy. "I see you have friends willing to die for you. They need not worry. For now, I need my strength, and I need you to live a while longer, until I have all I need." He laughed and ascended the steps into the caravan, taking the squirming sack with him. In moments, the sky changed from noonday to dusk.

The air was alive with wings and birdcall. The largest birds swooped down to Balor's empty cages, carrying them off in their talons. Others, the long-beaked species, pecked the locks of the remaining ones until they sprang open and their animal prisoners were released. Timothy remembered the scene in Balor's workshop, when he had frantically tried to free the animals from their cages.

Jessica strode over to the barking mangy dog tethered to a caravan and laid her hand on his head. "Don't worry, Peter."

The dog gave a swift howl and lunged against his tether.

Jessica looked at Timothy. "There's nothing I can do. I thought if I gave him my necklace, he'd let Sarah go. But now we've lost Sarah and Peter both!"

Timothy heard the desperation in Jessica's voice. He thought of the time he traded his crown for a drink of water; the memory still shamed him. "Who's Peter? The boy who was with Sarah?" he asked, but he never took his eyes from the caravan where Balor had disappeared with the bag holding his sister.

Jessica nodded. "He's our friend, and Balor has enchanted him, too."

Timothy watched helplessly as Balor's caravan rumbled away.

"But the battle isn't over." A familiar voice was at Timothy's side, so near it was almost in his ear. "Do not lose heart. Your sister is not lost, nor is your mother, nor even the boy Peter. But your mother is the one who needs you now."

Timothy heard Jessica's quick intake of breath. He turned and looked up in astonishment into the leafy face and warm eyes of the Greenman. Vines sprouted from his ears and nose, and the leaves on his head blew about him like hair in the wind.

"Oh, Greenman," Timothy cried, his voice catching. "Where have you been?"

The treelike man bent over Timothy until his leaves brushed the top of Timothy's head. "Why, here," he replied gently. "In the forests around you. At your house, and in far places. Always near."

A flutter of hope stirred in Timothy's heart. "What should I do about Sarah? I can't leave her here. And my mother, I haven't found any-thing to help her! And the boy—"

"Jessica will stay behind with Gwydon and the Storyteller to look after Sarah. You have another job to do. There is more to your story that you must hear from the Storyteller before you go, and it's late. Your mother will need you before dawn."

"But how can I know Sarah will be safe? And I can't leave because I haven't found anything to help my mother yet."

The Greenman straightened up, shaking all his leaves. His branches stretched into the sky. Suddenly, Timothy felt very small. "Timothy James Maxwell," the Greenman said gravely, "you must have faith in your friends. Once you know what to do and choose to not do it, I can't be responsible."

The Greenman turned toward Jessica, who said, "I tried to save Sarah. But it didn't work out the way I planned."

"Yes, and that was noble." He towered over the dog, who sat and cocked his head as if trying to understand the words the Greenman spoke. A drip of sap fell from a branch, landing on the ruff of the dog's neck. And in that moment he was transformed back into the boy Timothy had seen with Sarah.

"Peter!" Jessica threw her arms around his neck. "Greenman, why did you come now?"

"Because Timothy called my name." And with that, the Greenman receded into the forest that bordered the Market, one more tree among many.

"What was that?" Peter continued to stare into the verge of trees.

"You don't know? That was the Greenman!" Jessica's eyes sparkled once more.

"The one from the old stories? My gram used to tell me about him! Never thought I'd see him myself!"

"Peter, this is Timothy, Sarah's brother," Jessica said.

Timothy nodded at the introduction. "If he could turn you back to a boy from a dog, why didn't he help Sarah?"

Jessica shook her head. "I don't know, but he said you have a job to do; you have to go back. I'm sorry, Timothy, but I'm going to stay and try to help her. And Peter will, too."

It wasn't an answer Timothy liked. Overhead, stars shone in a clear black sky. Timothy thought about Star Girl. Where was she now? Despite seeing the Greenman again, despite being with Jessica and Peter, he felt alone. Ever since the birds' attack, caravans had been leaving the Market. The ones that remained were shuttered tight, lights glowing through curtained windows.

Peter broke the silence. "I have to get back to my mam or she'll be worried, but we'll find Sarah, Timothy."

Timothy turned toward Nom, who still waited nearby. "Where has Balor gone with Sarah?" Timothy asked weakly.

"Away." Nom peered at Timothy and Jessica. "He'll be back tomorrow, and the next day, and the next after that. A sit-down and grub is what *we* need. Come with me."

Heartbroken, Timothy shuffled after Nom. His thoughts ran circles in his head; he'd failed his quest, and he had lost his sister. It didn't get much worse than that.

As if she could read his mind, Jessica linked her arm through Timothy's. "I didn't know what to do, either," she said, "not really. I should have made the Animal Tamer give me Sarah first." She looked just like any girl now, in her long, grubby, purple skirt; not majestic at all.

"I should never have let us split up. I could have warned her," Timothy said.

"Should have, would have—that's no way to be talking." Nom shook his head. "Didn't you just see the Greenman himself? Doesn't he know what to do? And didn't I tell you that the Market was full of *draíocht*?" He stopped in front of Julian's caravan. "Now, *here's* what we're looking for."

KEEPERS
OF THE WORD

J
ULIAN OPENED THE DOOR before they even knocked. His hair was disheveled and stood up in spikes, as if he had been running his fingers through it again and again. Gwydon stood at his side.

Timothy ran forward, burying his face in the wolf's fur.

"Come in and rest," Julian said. "But come in quickly. We don't want to leave the door open long on a night like this."

They were expected. A full pot of tea was already on the table, surrounded by large mugs and plates of meat, cheese, grapes, bread, and dates.

"I know you," Jessica said. "You're the librarian."

"Yes, in your world. Here I'm a humble Storyteller."

"This is my friend Jessica, and Nom. He brought us to the Market," Timothy said.

"Welcome, Jessica. Nom and I have met before. Come and eat."

Then, feeling as if he could no longer stand, Timothy collapsed like a deflated balloon on the cushioned floor, Gwydon at his side. "The Animal Tamer's taken Sarah! Do you know who he really is?"

"Gwydon and I saw what happened. We were at the edge of the crowd. You both were very brave." Julian looked from Timothy to Jessica. "And, yes, the Animal Tamer is more than who he appears."

More than he appears? He's a monster! Timothy wanted to shout.

Jessica sat cross-legged on the floor next to him and poured them both steaming mugs of tea.

Nom, meanwhile, began to shovel fistfuls of dates and grapes into his mouth. His pointy, yellow teeth flashed every time he opened his lips, and he paused every now and then to wipe his mouth on his sleeve. But Timothy's stomach felt as heavy as lead. Only the tea slipped down easily.

"What are we going to do? We need a plan!" Timothy said.

"It is time you heard more of your story," Julian said. "This time we won't be interrupted."

"Don't we have more important things to talk about right now than to listen to stories?" Timothy was on his feet. The last thing he wanted was more fairy tales about trees. What they needed now was a plan to rescue Sarah and save his mother. It was vital. The word *vital* shimmered in his mind.

Jessica kicked him. "Listen to what he has to say."

Nom popped pieces of cheese into his mouth.

Perched on his Storyteller's stool, Julian ignored Timothy, his head back, his eyes half-closed.

"Throughout the ages, the Dark has returned to do battle. Even

Arthur, who battled bravely and managed to hold back the Dark for many years, could not keep it from returning. There will be the Final Battle, but before it occurs, there will be many skirmishes, small ones like today and great ones as well. People will suffer, and others will be misled. And every time that happens, the Dark rejoices. But the Light still chooses to work through humans, no matter how many mistakes humans make or how many times they side with the Dark. And so it is that prophets are sent to remind people of the Light. And like prophets, Filidhs are sent to remind people of the Truth. Without these reminders the narrative can become confused. It's easy to believe that whoever is in power at one time is the victor for all time. And the Dark can be very persuasive."

Timothy sighed and dropped to the floor. He might as well listen because no one else was ready to do anything.

"*File* means poet, learned philosopher. And for many years, here between worlds, the Filidh reigned as Masters of the Market. They were treated as kings. The murder of a Filidh invoked the same penalties as the slaying of a king. And the rank of Filidh was passed through the family named O'Daly."

Timothy sat up straighter. "My mother's maiden name is O'Daly," he whispered to Jessica.

She put her finger to her lips, but her eyes grew very round.

"And in each generation, at least one Filidh rose up to lead the people, to rule the Travelers, the people of the Market, to keep the truth alive. They were assisted by Gwydon and others who remembered the old ways and were true to them. But in the end, the Filidh are only human. Like all humans, their temptations are great, and the Dark is quick to take advantage of that. The Dark wishes to control all things, all people, to pervert the symbols of justice and good. The Dark's assault can come like a rushing sea, a roaring lion . . . or the slightest flicker of a rabbit's ears.

"A generation ago, a Filidh arose who was weak. He turned his back on the old knowledge in return for promises of power and dark magic. It was not enough for him to rule the Travelers and to remind the people of the Truth. He wanted to rule over kings and all the servants of the Light. So he bargained his position away to the Dark for promises of power and wealth. But it is always folly to bargain with the Dark."

Jessica squirmed and looked at Timothy.

"Although the Filidh remained Master of the Market in name, his power was diminished, for the Dark is a harsh master. Eventually, he was forced to leave, and the Dark chose a new master to replace him: Tristan, a man easily controlled by his own greed. Tristan is nothing more than the Dark's pawn, although he doesn't realize it. And with the Dark came the Animal Tamer. He is the one who truly controls the Market."

Balor, Timothy thought. He pictured Sarah chained to a cage.

"Now, Gwydon, being very wise and a shape-shifter, was able to steal the one true mark of the Filidh from the Master of the Market and hide it away until a true Filidh would arise to challenge the Dark.

He who claims this mark is the true Master of the Market, the Filidh of his generation, and can free those the Dark holds captive. *But to do so involves grave risk, even death.*"

Julian sat for a time, staring into space. Even Nom had stopped eating and was staring down thoughtfully at his much-worn shoes. Jessica's eyes were shining, as if she longed to be on a great adventure, on a quest for the hidden mark of the Filidh, the sign of the true Master of the Market.

Timothy sat hunched among the cushions, his mouth open. "My mother's family is O'Daly . . . Does that make her a Filidh? Is that why the rat bit her?" His mother had always seemed a perfectly normal mother, who just liked to paint, and sometimes forgot about regular things like making dinner or washing the clothes.

"Not everyone with the family name is destined to be a Filidh," Julian said.

Timothy shook his head in confusion. "Who in my family would turn to the Dark? And what was the mark of a Filidh that Gwydon hid?"

"Some of these answers you must discover yourself. But I can tell you this. A stone was hidden, a stone that cries out when a true Filidh places his foot on it. It is the most precious of the four treasures of the Market. The other three are a cauldron, a spear, and a sword. These are the things Balor needs to control the Light. But he can't find them without a Filidh to lead him to them."

"But that's part of a story Mrs. Clapper told me. She told me about the missing stone."

Jessica's eyes shone as she looked from Julian to Timothy. "Don't you see, Timothy? It must be you! You must be the one meant to find the stone!"

Timothy jumped at the sharp rap on the door.

"It's a dark night for visitors," Julian said in a low voice.

Gwydon whined and rose to his feet.

From outside the door a female voice replied, "May this door open to the Light."

Julian jumped from his stool and flung open the door of the caravan. There on the steps stood Peter and his mam, the baker, Fiona.

Glancing hurriedly over her shoulder, Fiona slid in like a shadow, with Peter following right behind. Their breath came in quick puffs as if they had been hurrying, and dark cloaks covered their clothes. Cradled in the woman's hands was a small blue ceramic jar. She approached Timothy.

"I've brought the thing you need to help your mother. It's the only thing that will help her. When I saw her face in the water, I knew right away what she needed. And then my own Peter"—she gestured to the boy—"told me you had come with your sister and friend to find a cure. I didn't dare say anything when Tristan was there."

Once more, Fiona looked over her shoulder toward the closed door, and Timothy again noticed the scar across her pale throat. "Rub this on the bite," she continued. "Don't worry about the smell. The odor is healing."

Timothy reached eagerly for the jar, but she still held it close and with a nervous hand tucked a pale strand of hair behind her ear. "It comes with a dear cost," she said quietly. "If you use it, you will never be able to return to the Market as you are now. It will mark you, and no matter how much you wander, you won't find your way back."

Timothy froze. Sarah was *here*, held captive by Balor. If he took this medicine to his mother, how would he ever come back to save his sister? But what had the Greenman said? Something about his mother needing his help before dawn? How could he choose one over the other?

He caught Jessica's eye. She was unusually quiet. "Jessica can take it to her while I help Sarah," he said.

Fiona shook her head sadly. "No, it must be delivered by a kinsman. It is your task, Timothy."

Nom smacked his fist in his palm. "What did he tell you?" he said to Timothy. "Weren't you listening at all? It's not your job to save your sister!"

Jessica reached out and laid a hand on Timothy's shoulder. "I don't know what I'm supposed to do, but I'll do everything I can to save her."

"And she won't be alone." Peter stood up very tall. "I'll help her. No one's going to keep Sarah."

This was *not* the way adventures were supposed to work. Timothy wanted to be the one to save his mother *and* his sister. How could he bear not knowing what was happening here while he was back home? He looked at the floor, unwilling now to reach for the blue jar.

Julian stood. "Did you not hear my story, Timothy? You are an O'Daly. Your work leads you in other directions. Your sister will never be alone. But it is, I grant, a difficult choice, and one only you can make."

Slowly, Timothy raised his head. Something in Julian's face alarmed him. It didn't feel like he really had any choice at all, and it was hard to breathe. Too much was expected of him. The caravan was too stuffy, too close. He needed to go outside to think. He bolted for the door.

THE OLD WAYS

THE AIR WAS THICK inside the dark sack, and no matter how she pushed against it, there seemed to be no way out other than the tied-off opening at the top. But more than anything, she wanted *food*. Finally, it was the emptiness of her stomach that drove her, for when someone tipped the sack sideways and opened the end, she scrambled forward out of the darkness, in spite of the bright light blinding her eyes, only to find herself trapped again.

She didn't know it was a cage at first. It was just a place out of the sack, a place where there might be food, but as she explored every corner of it, she discovered that it was enclosed with metal bars, that there was no way out.

A large hand covered with a mat of red hair opened the top of the cage and dropped three mice at her feet. Seeing her, they scurried in circles, but she drew back her head and then shot forward. In one swift gulp, she consumed the first mouse, fur, bones, and all. The next followed quickly, but the third made her chase him around the cage. The smallness of the cage gave the mouse the advantage, but she could move swiftly as well, and with a quick flick to the right, she caught him by the tail, and in two bites he was gone. The gnawing in her stomach quieted, she curled once around in the corner, and slept.

✦ ✦ ✦

Arkell and Andor watched in silence from the lofty branch of a pine. Timothy was standing below them, alone in the dark. His fists were clenched, and his shoulders shook as if he were sobbing.

In the shadows of the forest, old things moved. Trees shook their branches. A fox startled a brood of quail from their nest. *He is alone.* Andor's words were like the first wind of winter, bleak and cold.

Arkell ruffled his feathers. *Not alone. The Greenman has come, and we are watching. The one-eyed man will not be able to reach him while we are here.*

✦ ✦ ✦

Timothy dropped heavily on the edge of a large boulder perhaps thirty yards from the caravan and wrapped his arms around his knees. His first thought had been to run, but where would he go? He didn't even know where the Market was in space and time.

A vein in his temple began to pulse. Everything was falling apart. *Entropy,* he thought, twelve Scrabble points. Last year he had read about entropy, the tendency of everything to move from order to disorder, and he had liked saying the word. But now it seemed menacing; it felt as if the world were filled with it, and his life was unraveling. Sarah was his first and best friend. He could always count on her. How could he abandon her to Balor, the most evil thing he could imagine? And yet, while he didn't know how to help her, he now had the means to help his mother.

The Greenman's face rose in his mind. He remembered his full laugh and the way he had called Timothy by name. A little of the loneliness subsided.

The door to the caravan opened, and Gwydon padded down the steps. Silent as a shadow, he approached, then stood before Timothy, his face almost level with the boy's. Timothy stretched out one arm to ruffle Gwydon's fur, and the wolf rested his chin on the boy's knee.

"Gwydon, I think I have to leave. Please save Sarah for me. Help Jessica and Peter to save Sarah. They'll need all the help they can get."

And then the wolf did a very surprising thing. He took Timothy's hand in his large mouth and very gently nibbled it. Then he put one paw on Timothy's lap and butted his head against Timothy's forehead.

Timothy stood and returned to the caravan, Gwydon padding by his side. The others turned as one when he entered the room. "I'll go," he said.

Jessica ran to him and threw her arms around him, and for a moment his face was buried in her curls. She smelled of campfires, and sun, and something spicy that made him reluctant to let go.

Julian looked at him over the top of Jessica's head.

"I know the decision wasn't easy, Timothy. But the best thing now is to get you home as quickly as possible. Your mother's life depends on it. In the larger battle, one life may seem a small thing, but to the Light every life matters. And there is something more. Your ability to rule as Filidh is being shaped now. There are still many things you need to learn, tasks you need to perform, and decisions you need to make. Each of these will change you as much as they change the people you help."

But Timothy heard only the words "rule as Filidh." Was Jessica right? Was he the one meant to find the stone?

Jessica let go of his neck, and Nom punched him in the arm. "Now, that's what I calls thinking things through!"

Julian still looked grave. "Nom, you brought Timothy here, but your talents may still be needed. I have another way for Timothy to return home."

Fiona said, "I must get back to my baking or there'll be no loaves for morning, and Peter must be up early as well." She drew a soft leather bag out of her skirt pocket. It hung from a leather loop that she slipped over Timothy's shoulder. "Here's a pouch to carry the jar in. And here is the medicine." She slid the jar into the pouch. "I don't want you dropping it in your travels. Rub it directly on the bite twice a day if you can. But rubbing it anywhere on her skin will help, and she'll be well soon. And, Jessica, we have room to house you for the night, too."

Julian addressed Jessica. "I think it is a wise idea that you rest there. Tomorrow will not be an easy day. And Timothy and I have some planning to do. It's best to say good-bye now."

This was all happening more quickly than Timothy had expected.

He slipped the leather loop over one shoulder. The pouch fit close to his side. Then he jammed his hands in his pockets so no one could see they were trembling. His fingers curled around the cool, smooth surface of the leaf, but still his heart raced. All his doubts and fears roiled. What if he couldn't do all that was expected of him? But before he could say anything, Jessica was hugging him again and promising to do everything she could for Sarah, and Peter was shaking his hand and promising to do all he could, too.

As soon as Peter and Jessica and Fiona had gone, Julian moved quickly, leading Timothy back out into the night before he reconsidered. Gwydon paced by their side.

In the quiet of the night, the only sound was the soft padding of Gwydon's feet. Overhead, the sky was clear with a million—no, a trillion—stars on view. Timothy felt very small under the canopy of sky. He thought of Star Girl, whom he had first met on a night like this, a night wide with stars and the moon, and he wondered if she was watching him now. Even with Gwydon by his side, he felt alone again, cosmically alone. It was a strange feeling, and he thought that maybe who he was and what he was doing were very small things in the plentitude of space and sky surrounding him.

Timothy liked the word *plentitude* and held it in his mouth awhile; rolling it over on his tongue the way he held mints until they dissolved and his mouth tingled. If he listened closely, he could hear the great wolf's breath and a very faint rustling in the trees. He followed Julian and Gwydon blindly, not knowing where he was going. The trees drew closer around them until he could only see the sky in jigsaw pieces and a few stars tangled in branches. Far overhead there was a great flapping, and a shadow passed over him. Looking up, he saw two dark shapes settle on a branch. Eagles, he thought, just like at home. Sarah had called them watchmen. And when he thought of Sarah, he hunched his shoulders and hung his head.

Gwydon stopped as the path forked, right beneath the tree in which the two eagles perched. He sat on his haunches, and Timothy looked into the wolf's golden eyes.

"What is it? What do you want me to do?" Timothy said.

Gwydon lifted his snout, and for a moment Timothy wondered if he was about to howl—the long, mournful howl of a wolf.

But Julian spoke instead. "There is a portway just beyond the stand of birch. A narrow track, an Old Way, is there. Walk on the track."

Timothy didn't want to go alone, but he could see his mother's face, and his heart was torn. He turned and gave Julian and Gwydon one last look.

"That's right," Julian encouraged. "Keep your focus and you won't lose your way." Gwydon nudged Timothy forward with his nose.

Timothy placed his hand on Gwydon's soft head and took a deep breath. Then he strode out toward the birches, which were silver in the moonlight. And between the trees, something more glimmered. Timothy spied the shape of a girl with long hair. He hurried toward her. As he reached the birches, Electra gazed solemnly back. Just beyond was the narrow single track, just as Julian had described. Without stopping or looking back, Timothy stepped onto the track.

Afterward, he found it very difficult to explain the sensation of being on the Old Way, except to say it was rather like trying to balance on a skateboard the very first time. It was as if the road were alive, sinewy and muscular. And then everything blurred.

When he was able to see clearly again, Timothy found himself on his hands and knees in the middle of a dirt track he recognized. It was the exact spot in his familiar woods where an old log made a perfect bicycle jump, and he'd ridden here a hundred times before. He was only about a quarter mile from home.

He felt for the pouch. It was still there, safe at his side. He began to run.

HOME AGAIN

A FEW LIGHTS WERE LIT in the windows of the Maxwells' house. Timothy's mother's car was in the driveway. So was another car, one he didn't recognize. He didn't see his father's car anywhere, and that, Timothy thought, was odd, considering how sick his mother was.

Timothy slowed his pace. He would have to explain where he had been, but he didn't know how long he'd been gone. He stood in the driveway, looking up at his own familiar bedroom window. How was he going to come up with a convincing story to explain his absence? And how would he explain where Sarah was now? He'd have to improvise, he thought. The important thing was to get the medicine to his mother.

He slipped in through the front door. The house wasn't completely quiet; the radio was on, playing some of the classical music his mother liked, but he didn't see anyone.

Quietly, he tiptoed to his parents' bedroom and pushed open the door. What if he was too late? His heart thundered so loudly in his ears that he couldn't hear his own footsteps.

There in the big antique bed was his mother, propped up on pillows, looking very small. Her face was waxen, covered with a sheen of sweat, and the flesh was pulled too tightly across her bones. Her right arm was hooked up to an IV, like Timothy's had been once when his asthma was very bad.

Next to the bed, in a rocking chair, sat a woman wearing a starched uniform and bright orange lipstick. The woman looked up when Timothy entered.

"I told them you didn't need to come right away. Your mother needs rest and quiet." She frowned at Timothy as if he planned to make noise and cause confusion. "But I expect you want to see your mom." Her orange lips softened a bit. "I'm the nurse. I'm here to help out with your mother."

But Timothy had eyes only for his mother. She hadn't even stirred. "Is she—"

"Now, don't worry yourself. It doesn't help anything. Your father's just stepped out to pick up a new prescription. We've everything under control here. Tell your sister not to fret, too." The nurse held an ice chip on a spoon up to his mother's parched lips. She took it into her mouth mechanically and with difficulty. "That's right, dear. Suck on that. You need some moisture."

Timothy crept closer to the bed, his hand covering the pouch at his side.

"Well, since you're here, and if you wouldn't mind sitting with her,

I'd like to use the ladies' room." The nurse gave an orange smile and got up briskly.

"That's fine," Timothy assured her quickly. "I'll stay with her."

He sat on the side of his mother's bed, not even sure if she was aware he was there. As soon as the nurse left the room, he drew out the ceramic jar and took off the lid. Just as he had been warned, the smell was pungent. The cream inside was yellow and thick, and it smelled a little like pine needles mixed with something old and moldy.

"Mom, it's me—Timothy. I've got something to help you." Then he dipped two fingers into the jar and scooped out some ointment. He pulled back his mother's covers, searching for the rat bite on her calf. The leg was still swollen, the affected area green and black. He rubbed the salve in gently. Her skin was very hot, but she didn't flinch.

The ointment disappeared on her skin as he rubbed, and soon only the faint smell of pine needles was left. Despite the Greenman's words, Timothy still worried. What if it didn't help? In fact, what if it was the very wrong thing? His mouth dry, Timothy fumbled the jar back into the pouch.

He heard footsteps outside the door.

"Timothy! What are you doing here?" His father stood in the doorway. Pouches drooped under his eyes, and there were lines on his face Timothy had never noticed before. "I saw the note that you and Sarah were with Jessica, but I knew you'd have a hard time not worrying about your mom."

His father's voice, Timothy noticed, held that false note of heartiness that his parents used around him and Sarah when they were trying to cover something up. "But don't you worry. I've got a new prescription here that should be just the ticket! Fix her right up! Eh, Lizzie?"

Timothy's mother sighed and stirred under the blankets.

The nurse crept back into the room. "Oh, you've got it!" she exclaimed, reaching for the prescription sack. "It really is supposed to be a miracle drug for fighting infection. Something none of the bacteria are resistant to yet." She opened the bag and took out several ampoules of medicine. "I'll just add these to the IV." She wrinkled her nose. "Goodness, what's that peculiar odor?"

"Uh, just some cologne Sarah and Jessica made me try on," Timothy said quickly.

His father looked at him sharply. "Now, give your mother a kiss and run back to Jessica's. I'll call you later with an update."

"I want to stay here," Timothy said, trying to think fast. He knew he needed to be near his mother. "It's just girls over there, and I'll be quiet and helpful here."

"Just girls!" His father snorted. "Someday you might not mind that. But, yes, stay if you want. You'll have to take care of yourself, and no loud goings-on." His father spoke distractedly, as if he didn't even know what he was saying.

"I'll make us some sandwiches," Timothy said, hoping that if he disappeared into the kitchen they might forget all about him.

"Good idea, son . . . I guess I am a bit hungry."

The nurse had already finished putting the medication into the IV. "There, now. We'll soon see some improvement, I suspect." And she settled back in her chair.

✛ ✛ ✛

Later that evening, Timothy was lying on the living room floor, trying to read, when his father came to find him.

"It's the strangest thing . . . The fever's broken! She's resting peacefully." He came over and grabbed up Timothy in a bear hug. "Wow," he added, tears welling in his eyes, "that must be some antibiotic!"

"Can I see her?"

"Well, just for a minute won't hurt, I guess."

But Timothy was already on his way to the bedroom. His mother was still propped up by pillows, but a slight flush of color had returned to her skin. When he entered, she turned her head a little and smiled.

"Mom?" Timothy heard his voice catch.

She didn't say anything, just smiled.

The nurse looked up. She was smiling, too. Then she went back to her magazine.

Timothy snuggled against the side of the bed. "You look better," he told his mother.

She reached out one thin hand and patted his arm.

"I'm feeling better." Her voice was thin, too, and hoarse, barely more than a whisper.

Timothy kissed her on the forehead, and his mother closed her eyes, already drifting back to sleep. Seizing the opportunity, and making sure to screen the pouch from the nurse's view, Timothy again took out the blue jar, scooped out some ointment, and rubbed it on his mother's leg.

"You certainly put on a lot of that cologne!" the nurse's voice sounded behind him. "Did they tell you it would make you more attractive to the girls?" She laughed at her own comment.

"Something like that," Timothy muttered.

"She's ready to sleep, and you should, too. Off with you now!"

Timothy found his father in the kitchen, eating a piece of cold pie.

"Can I stay home from school tomorrow?"

Looking exhausted, his father set aside the pie plate, rubbed his nose, and looked at the clock. "Why not?" he said with a weary shrug. "After what we've been through, we can all probably use the rest." Then he looked up quickly. "Is all your homework done?"

"Yes, sir." Timothy could hardly conceal his smile. He had things to work out, and tomorrow would be his chance.

Timothy climbed the stairs to his room and lay down on his bed, fully dressed. The ointment from the Market seemed to be working. But what about Sarah? He tried to stay awake and make a plan, but he was too tired to wrestle with that puzzle now—it was almost midnight. *Puzzle*—two *z*'s would be twenty points in one play, but everyone knows each game of Scrabble has only one Z. *Puzzle* is a word that could never be played.

THE MAN IN THE WOODS

T HE FIRST THING Timothy did when he awoke the next morning was run down to his mother's room. To his amazement, the blinds were raised and she was sitting upright, eating from a tray balanced on her lap.

He stood quietly in the doorway, watching her eat and thinking how much better she looked in the morning light. She was thinner and paler than before her illness, of course, but a long way from the waxen figure consumed by fever he had seen just last night. He felt for the ceramic jar in the pouch at his side.

Glancing up from her tray, his mother smiled and motioned for him to come in.

"Oh, Timothy, I'm so glad to see you!" She stretched out her arms for a hug. Bending over the bed, Timothy buried his face in her hair. "I hope you weren't too worried about me. Dad tells me you were here watching over me last night. And it's amazing, I feel so much better today. Just a little tired, really." She took a sip of her orange juice.

Timothy found it surprisingly hard to speak. "You look lots better, too," he said, suddenly wondering how he was going to apply more salve now that she was wide awake and aware of what was going on. "Um . . . I've got something for you. From Sarah. It's a new lotion she and Jessica made up. I think it smells nasty, but she and Jessica think it smells great and it's supposed to be good for your skin."

His mother smiled. "Then of course I'll have to try it, no matter what it smells like. Rub a little on my wrist, right here. And tell me what you two have been up to. I suppose Sarah is at school?"

Timothy busied himself with taking out the jar so he wouldn't have to answer her question. He scooped some salve on his fingers and rubbed it on her wrist. His mother wrinkled her nose. "Well, it's certainly an interesting fragrance," she said.

"It's supposed to keep your skin smooth and it's good for cuts and maybe bites, too," he added quickly. "I, um, cut my finger yesterday and it healed it right up!"

"Oh, is that so. Well, then, let's see what it can do." His mother laughed and let Timothy rub some on her calf.

Just then the nurse bustled into the room.

"It's time you rested," she ordered Timothy's mother. She checked the IV and then picked up the breakfast tray. "Oh, and your father had to go in for a meeting with the doctor," she said to Timothy. "He said you're not to tire your mother out and that he'd be home around noon."

"You can fill me in on everything later," Timothy's mother said. She kissed the top of his head, and Timothy gave a small sigh of relief.

Truth was, he wasn't ready to say much yet. Besides, he needed to find out what was happening with Sarah and Jessica.

Timothy quietly shut the bedroom door behind him, thinking that when it came to finding out things, the library was usually the best place to start. Especially if it turned out that Julian—the reference librarian Julian of *this* world—could be in two places, two different worlds, at the same time.

✝ ✝ ✝

It was strange to be at the public library on a school morning, and stranger still to be out and about town. Timothy kept waiting for someone to question why he wasn't in school, but no one did. When he arrived at the library, it wasn't Julian's long face he saw behind the reference desk. Mrs. Torres was back in her usual place.

"I'm looking for Julian," Timothy said.

She looked up from the computer screen and smiled at the interruption. "Oh, Timothy! How good to see you. Julian's on vacation," she said, "but is there anything I can help you with?"

"Do you know when he'll be back?" Timothy said, unable to suppress a note of panic in his voice. Julian, he had suddenly realized, was his only link to the other world, to the Market.

"Two weeks, I think. Has he been helping you with some research?"

"Sort of . . . I just wanted to talk to him," he stammered.

She looked disappointed. "If you change your mind, I'm here."

Timothy nodded his thanks.

✛ ✚ ✛

He sat on the bench in front of the library and thought. He didn't have a backup plan. He'd done what he needed to do, but now he *had* to get back to the Market and help Sarah, and he didn't know the way. Worse, Fiona had said he could never return. But he had to try.

He jumped to his feet. Perhaps he could go back to the track through the woods and find the portway. Why hadn't he thought of that sooner? Perhaps the Old Way would take him back!

He stopped by home to get his mountain bike, and headed straight to the trails on the edge of town. This would be easy; after all, he knew the right path. But when he got to the trailhead, it looked no different than it had a hundred times before: a muddy, well-worn track through the woods. He rode several hundred yards down the path, but nothing happened. Thinking that perhaps he needed to be off his bike to find the portway, he stowed it in some bushes off to the side, then stood in the middle of the path, willing something to happen.

But nothing did. The path was nothing but dirt. In frustration, he grabbed the closest rock and hurled it into the trees with all his might.

There was a loud cry. It was followed by a number of unintelligible words, and for the briefest moment, Timothy thought he was hearing the voice of a tree. The bushes parted, and the red face of an obviously angry man appeared before him. And not just any man. He had hit Mr. Twig.

The professor was wearing a safari hat and had a very large gunnysack draped over one shoulder. In his right hand was a walking stick.

And once again, his clothes were all variations of the same color: green this time, from his jungle-green vest to his many-pocketed sage-green hiking pants. Little bits of leaf and twig stuck to his sleeves and pants. They even bristled from his eyebrows, as if he'd been crawling through the bracken on hands and knees.

"Oh, it's you," Mr. Twig said with a sniff. "You know, if you wanted to get my attention, there are many other, more pleasant, ways." He rubbed at his cheek where a nasty red welt was forming. "You could have taken out my eye!"

"I—I'm so sorry!" Timothy said, suppressing a smile and trying not to show how happy he was to see the man. "I didn't know you were in there at all."

"Then why were you throwing stones at me?"

"It wasn't *at* you. I was just—well, frustrated, and . . ." Timothy's voice trailed off.

"Well, no permanent harm done, I suppose," Mr. Twig said, offering Timothy one last glower before his face relaxed. "I've been out collect-ing," he explained, gesturing at the bag over his shoulder.

"What do you collect?" Timothy said politely, not the least bit interested.

"Oh, juniper berries, laurel branches, pinecones . . . the odd speci-men. Some are good in cooking, some have other purposes." Mr. Twig sat down on a nearby log and took out a canteen of water. "And the woods here give me a place to practice my pipes."

"Pipes?"

"Uilleann pipes," Mr. Twig added. After swallowing a drink from the canteen, he opened his oversized pack and drew out a strange-looking instrument. It had a red velvet bag with a small bellows attached, and something that looked like a flute on one end. "It's my practice set, a bit smaller than my regular one, since it's missing the drones and regulators." He slid the bellows under one elbow and pumped his arm in and out as his fingers danced over the holes carved into the flute. The sound was deep and sweet, not at all like the loud, wailing bagpipe music Timothy had expected to hear.

After playing a few lines of music, Mr. Twig put the pipes down by his feet. "But now, what are you doing on one of the Old Ways, throwing stones?"

"You know about the Old Ways?" Timothy gasped.

"I know some of them. This path, for instance, was once part of the Green Road, an old mail route from the early 1800s. Why do you ask?"

"Because last night I was *on* this path. It took me from somewhere else to here."

"Did it?" Mr. Twig chuckled and pulled a lime-green handkerchief from his vest pocket to wipe his mouth. "Yes, indeed, that's what roads do. Take us from one place to another. Usually we decide where we want to go. But every now and then the roads wake up. It can cause all kinds of havoc." He patted the empty section of log beside him. "Perhaps you'd like to tell me what you've been up to."

Timothy went over and sat down, wondering just how much to tell Mr. Twig and afraid that explaining everything might take too long. "Can there be more than one world at the same time?" he asked instead. "More than one world, but in different places?"

Mr. Twig waggled his eyebrows. "The physicists and philosophers certainly seem to think so. My specialty, as you know, is mythology, but I assure you, mythology would not disagree." He took another drink from the canteen and held it out to Timothy. "Would you care for some water?"

Timothy shook his head.

"For instance, there was a physicist, a Dr. Everett, who suggested we could better understand quantum theory—you have heard of quantum theory, haven't you?—by envisioning parallel universes."

This time Timothy nodded; he'd read about quantum theory on his own last spring. It had been difficult to understand but fascinating.

"He believed that there exist a number of these universes, and that there can even be communication between them. In fact, he believed that what happens in one universe can affect what happens in another."

"But is Dr. Everett right?"

"I assume you mean, is his theory correct? If you find evidence of it, then it's at least probable and worth considering, wouldn't you say?" Mr. Twig blew his nose in the lime-green square of hankie and then folded it up like an envelope and stuffed it back in his pocket. "Mythologies, on the other hand, are stories of the way the world came to be and why things are the way they are. Yet they, too, all say that there is more to the universe than what we perceive with our senses. I expect your own experiences confirm that?"

Timothy squirmed and pushed some dead leaves about with his toe.

"Just as I thought. I also think there must be some particular and perhaps important reason for these questions?"

"There are a lot of things I just can't explain," Timothy admitted with a sigh. "But right now my main problem is that my sister needs help, and she's somewhere else, in a place I can't get to again."

To his credit, Mr. Twig didn't laugh. In fact, he looked at Timothy very seriously. "And do you have a way to help your sister, if you were able to get to her again?"

"I don't know."

"Is there anyone else there who can?"

"Maybe. But *I* should be there. I should be the one to do it."

"Then why did you come back here?"

"I had to come home first. My mother needed help, too."

"And were you able to help your mother?"

"I think so. I brought her a special cream, a healing cream from the other place. But, then, it might just have been the new antibiotic they gave her. I can't be sure."

Mr. Twig nodded and waited for Timothy to go on. When he didn't say anything else, Mr. Twig commented, "Sometimes a task is not ours, no matter how much we want it to be."

Timothy was feeling more and more miserable. This conversation was not going the way he had hoped. "I thought you might be able to tell me how to get back to Sarah," he mumbled finally.

"Timothy, do you believe that you're the one ultimately responsible for your sister's safety? Oh, I'm sure you can help, but that's too large a burden to carry alone for any one of us." When Timothy didn't answer right away, Mr. Twig stood up abruptly and looked at his watch. "You know where to find me. I'd be interested in hearing how this adventure progresses."

Timothy still didn't say anything. He was too disappointed to talk, and here Mr. Twig was leaving him! He watched as the professor lifted the large gunnysack over his shoulder, turned, and, with his walking stick firmly in hand, strode toward the direction of town.

Suddenly, Timothy called out, "What about time, Mr. Twig? If there are other universes or dimensions, would time be the same as it is here?"

Mr. Twig turned back to face Timothy, looking, Timothy thought, like a gangly Santa Claus with a sack over one shoulder. "I believe that things might be able to happen simultaneously," he said. "Our own view of time is rather limited, don't you think? As you've probably read, time is not a straight line." And with a flap of his bony hand, he was off.

Timothy stayed hunched on the log, pondering the problem, and several minutes ticked by before he noticed that Mr. Twig had left his Uilleann pipes behind. Timothy picked them up, planning to return them.

PETER'S PLAN

THE NEXT MORNING, Jessica awoke after passing a fitful night in Fiona's caravan. After scrubbing her face and brushing her hair, she stepped out to the bakery. Fiona had been at work since before dawn. It was one of those crisp fall mornings when the air sparkles and the light is tinted gold.

Despite the events of the previous day, the Market was back in business. Vendors called greetings to one another as they set up their stalls, caravan windows were flung open, children spilled down the brightly painted steps, and fresh wash flapped on clotheslines. Pigs squealed and a rooster crowed. Pyramids of red and green apples, bolts of shimmering cloth, and intricately worked iron caught Jessica's eye. She walked down the caravan steps with a certain spring in her step, feeling guilty about her happiness. She shouldn't be enjoying the morning so much while Sarah was an ermine captured by the Animal Tamer, but sometimes her heart didn't obey her head.

Fresh-baked loaves and pies were stacked in tempting piles on the wooden counter outside the yellow caravan, and plates of steaming muffins cooled on the steps. She could hear a male voice humming from nearby, just behind the caravan. Peter appeared, his shirtsleeves rolled up to his elbows, his face and hair wet with washing. "You're up early," he said.

"Well, we've important work to do." Jessica looked longingly at the muffins.

"Have one. They just came out of the oven. Mam won't mind."

Jessica reached for one plump with blueberries, remembering that they were Sarah's favorite, and she wondered if Sarah had had anything to eat at all.

Peter shook his hair dry and added, as if reading her thoughts, "Don't worry about Sarah; I've got a plan." He grinned and grabbed a muffin.

"What kind of plan?" Jessica didn't mean the question to sound as sharp as it did, but her cheerful spirits were quickly giving way to a gnawing anxiety. All night she had devised plans, only to discard them one by one. Try as hard as she could, she had come up with no plan at all. She had half expected Cerridwyn or the Greenman to appear to her in a dream and tell her just what to do. When she had finally slept, it was a dreamless sleep. No help came at all.

"It's something that occurred to me last night." Peter's cheeks bulged with muffin, and he talked as he chewed. "I know some things about the Animal Tamer. My mam, she was . . ." His eyes shifted away from Jessica. "He enchanted her, too, a long time ago. You've seen the scar on her neck?"

Jessica nodded.

"My mam has the *draíocht* pretty strong. She can tell the future sometimes. The Animal Tamer wanted her gift, and no one knew not to trust him then. He turned her into an antelope, put an iron collar on her neck. Whenever she didn't do what he wanted, he pulled the collar tighter, and"—Peter's eyes glittered—"and that's how she got her scar."

"I'm so sorry," Jessica said. "What happened to you?"

"Oh, I was just a baby. My gram took care of me." He still wasn't looking at Jessica.

"How did she escape?"

"See, that's where I got my idea from. Sometimes even the Animal Tamer has to sleep. I'm guessing you can sneak in and make a rescue if you know how. That's how they got my mam back. We should've left the Market then, but we never did. The Market wasn't always this way. It was a good place once, my mam and gram say. The old Masters of the Market were good people. Sometime before Tristan became Master, the Market changed. Tristan's in tight with the Animal Tamer, and he's as bad as they get. Now Tristan thinks he owns everything in the Market, and he thinks he owns my mam, too." His eyes shining, Peter finally looked straight at Jessica. "But I think it's the Animal Tamer that controls it all."

Jessica was impatient to get to the plan. "How did your mother get rescued when the Animal Tamer was sleeping?"

"There's this draught, see, what makes folks sleep very heavy, so they don't wake for nothing. The old Masters knew how to make it, and my gram and now my mam does, too. If we could somehow trick the Animal Tamer into taking it, then I could sneak in and get Sarah while he's asleep. Then we'll find the right *draíocht* to turn her back." Peter beamed. "That's my plan."

It didn't sound like much of a plan to Jessica. "Don't you think that sounds too simple? The Animal Tamer already changed you into a dog once. I mean, he isn't someone to fool with."

"Don't you think I know that?" Peter folded his arms.

"Well, then, how did your mother get turned back from an antelope?" Jessica persisted.

"My gram used a spell in Ogham. It's an old language some Travelers understand. I can read it a bit myself—my gram taught me—enough to mix up the sleeping draught anyway."

"But enough to turn Sarah back into a girl?"

Peter shrugged. "The important thing is we get Sarah back. Then we can figure out how to get her turned right again."

It all sounded haphazard to Jessica, but she had no better plan. The longer they waited, the more time Balor had to do something dreadful to Sarah. "Okay," she said, "but I don't think we can wait until night."

"Don't worry. He usually takes a midday lie-down. I'll get started on the draught right away."

Peter ran humming into the caravan. Jessica sat on the bench, thinking that he probably pictured himself as some sort of knight coming to rescue Sarah. Shouldn't she know what to do? What good was having Cerridwyn's skills if she couldn't help her friend? Where were *her* supposed powers? She felt bereft of any wisdom. She'd already lost her necklace from Cerridwyn trying to bargain for Sarah, and now Timothy and Sarah were depending on her.

Peter reappeared, interrupting her troubled thoughts. "There are a few things I need to get," he said. "It might be best if you don't come. And I need to think up a plan to get him to drink the stuff."

"What about Tristan?" Jessica offered. "He trusts him."

Peter thought a moment. "They usually eat together, but . . ." Suddenly, Peter smacked the side of his head. "Why didn't I think of it before? I'll be back in a bit!" And without another word of explanation, he hurried off.

Jessica rose to her feet. Maybe Peter's plan would work, and maybe it wouldn't, but she didn't want to wait to find out. She would go to Gwydon and Julian. They would know what to do.

The market was familiar now, and Jessica was able to find her way to Julian's caravan more easily. But the bright, hopeful feeling of earlier had worn off. She dodged by the jugglers tossing pomegranates, past flashing necklaces, and around an old woman making lace in the shade. When Julian's caravan was finally in sight, she ran. She arrived at the steps, hot and breathless. A note was tacked to the caravan door.

Unforeseeable circumstances have called us away.

The Storyteller

Jessica slumped down on the steps, resting her head in her hands. Sweat trickled down her back as she rocked back and forth, trying to calm herself. There was nothing, it seemed, she had learned from Cerridwyn's book of mythology that could help girls turned into ermines. She couldn't do spells or potions. Why was *she*, of all people, the one left to rescue Sarah?

She began to cry. She wasn't used to crying; in fact, she never liked it when girls cried. But once the tears started, it was hard to stop. Her shoulders shook and her nose ran.

After a few minutes, when she was all cried out, she wiped her nose with her skirt and felt a bit better. She stood up. It made more sense to go back to Fiona's bakery and wait for Peter.

Just then a large black feather floated down and landed by her foot. She picked it up, noticing how the sun shone on it with all the colors of a rainbow.

BLUEBLACK'S

PETER WAS NOWHERE to be seen when Jessica returned to the bakery caravan. Waiting was the most difficult thing for Jessica to do when something important needed to be done, and she had been waiting all morning. She dropped to the bench again even though her entire body ached. She watched people come and go, order pies, chat with friends . . . None of them seemed aware that somewhere in the Market a girl was being held captive. She caught whispers about the previous day's attack of crows. But business in the Market seemed as brisk as usual.

The sun was warm on the back of her neck. Oh, why didn't Peter come! Her thoughts ran in circles. Would the Animal Tamer sell Sarah to some unsuspecting customer? If Peter didn't hurry, they might never be able to rescue her!

As if in answer to her wish, there he was, loping through the crowds, looking terribly smug.

"Everything's ready." He patted his pants pocket cheerfully. The top of a cork protruded just above the edge.

All of the anxiety that had been building in Jessica bubbled to the surface. "So what's your plan?" she said, feeling her face flush, hearing her voice loud and sharp.

"Just like I told you," he said. "We'll get Tristan to give it to him in a drink."

Jessica refrained from saying that was *her* idea, crossed her arms, and asked, "And how are you going to get him to do that?"

"Every day at lunch, Tristan takes food and drink to the Animal Tamer's caravan. Then they go over the accounts from the day before. He gets the drinks at Blueblack's wagon. All I have to do is slip the draught in the drink while he's getting the food. Well, come on—we don't want to miss him!"

Peter hurried away, and Jessica matched his stride. "How can you be sure to get it in the right drink?"

Peter didn't seem half as concerned as she thought he should be. He didn't say anything for a moment, nor did he look at Jessica. "That's the tricky part," he finally admitted. "But they each have their own mug, see? We just have to figure out which is which, or maybe I can drug both. Look, I'm doing the best I can."

Jessica shook her head. What if he got the wrong mug? There were so many ways this plan could fail!

Ahead of them arched the ferret-legging tree. Today no raucous crowd gathered underneath its wide-flung branches. Peter stopped a few yards beyond the tree, close to a purple-and-green caravan. The smell of roast chicken and apples filled the air. A crowd was here, gathered around the slab-wood tables and benches, eating and drinking in noisy camaraderie.

It was obvious at first glance why the man serving drinks was called Blueblack. His hair and beard were so deeply dark, they glowed blue in places. Jessica looked closely, wondering if he had rubbed some kind of grease into both his hair and beard to make them shine that way.

Peter nudged her hard in the ribs to get her attention and nodded his head. Just off to their right, near the front of the crowd, Tristan was standing on a bench and leaning into the stall, two mugs clutched in his thick, red hands. Today a short sword was sheathed at his side. Jessica could see her necklace around Tristan's neck glinting in the sun. They moved closer, screening themselves behind the thirsty patrons. "Which mug is which?" Jessica hissed in Peter's ear.

One mug was a coppery brown, made from earthenware. The other glinted in the sun, a silver border ringing the rim.

"The metal one has to be the Animal Tamer's. He's got all sorts of things made from metal. But if I can, I'll drug them both, just to make sure. Stay behind me."

Peter slipped as smoothly as a shadow up to the front of the crowd. Men and women, hungry for their midday meal, pressed around him. Tristan thumped the mugs on the counter to get Blueblack's attention, and the black-bearded man leaned in close. Peter could see his lips move, but he could not hear the words. Then Tristan threw back his red head in laughter as Blueblack poured a thick brown liquid into both mugs.

Peter shifted his weight from one leg to the other. Jessica guessed he must be trying to think of some way to distract Tristan and draw his attention from Blueblack and the brimming mugs.

Peter pulled back his leg and kicked the shin of the tall man to his right as hard as he could. The man yelped in pain. Before he had time to look down and see who had done it, Peter vanished into the crowd.

"Hey, what do you think you're doing?" The tall man looked down at a round-faced fellow next to him, where Peter had stood just a moment before.

"I don't know what you're talking about!" The round man glared up at him.

"I'd say you do. Just kicked me in the shin!"

"I beg your pardon, I did no such thing. You must have bumped against something yourself!"

After a few seconds of what looked to Jessica like a glaring contest, the tall man mumbled something and turned his back on the round man. A small stone came whistling by Jessica's ear—she knew at once who had thrown it—and hit the tall man square in the middle of his back. The man spun around and shouted, "Now, that will be enough!"

The round man glared up into his face. "What is it, you gangly scarecrow? Bark your shin again?"

"Why, you puffed-up little—"

But Jessica didn't hear any more. The crowd had begun to murmur. People turned as one, expecting a good fight. Puffing up his chest, Tristan pivoted his attention away from Blueblack to see what was causing a stir in his Market.

Jessica spotted Peter right behind him, whipping out the vial, uncorking it, and tipping a generous amount of green liquid into the silver mug. But Peter apparently hadn't counted on Blueblack's quick eyes, for instead of watching the brewing fight, the bartender's eyes were fixed on his wares. He reached one thick, hairy arm over the counter and grabbed Peter by the shoulder.

"Look here, Tristan—he's trying to poison you!"

Tristan spun on his heel. "What's that?"

Jessica's heart sank. The crowd, too, swiveled their heads in the other direction.

"He poured something into your drink!" Blueblack said as Peter struggled vainly in his iron grip.

Tristan thrust his red face into Peter's. "Is that true, you little Market whelp?" Tristan drew his sword. "Which drink would you be tampering with? Spit spat, now out with it!"

"That one, Master." Blueblack nodded toward the silver mug.

Tristan pointed his sword at Peter's chest. The tip pricked through his shirt.

"We'll be seeing what the Animal Tamer has to say about this."

Blueblack loosened his grip, and Tristan poked Peter with the sword.

"Get going." He spun Peter around and marched him forward, prodding him from behind every few steps.

Watching from the edge of the crowd, Jessica balled her fists in vexation. Now things were even worse than before! She moved stealthily to follow.

When they arrived at the Animal Tamer's stall, Balor was talking to a couple and holding the end of a chain. At the other end crouched a blue-winged animal with enormous ears. The sun reflected off the Animal Tamer's hair, turning it to gold. The light flashed off the silver buttons on his vest and seemed to fill his deep laugh. "The animal's wings match your eyes, lady. This is a venustas, a rare animal and quite dear to me."

The woman giggled and looked inquiringly at her husband.

Tristan's shout spoiled the sale. His voice cut through the air with a high whine. "Animal Tamer, I've brought you a present!"

Balor looked up in annoyance, but his expression changed the instant he spotted Peter. "Oh, did you, now? And what's the young gentleman been up to?"

"Tried to poison you. Poured some nonsense into your drink." And Tristan gave Peter a particularly sharp poke in the back with the sword. Peter jerked forward. The customer put his arm protectively around his wife and drew back a few paces.

Jessica could see only Peter's rigid back and tight shoulders. She was certain that he was in very deep trouble. Her eyes flew over the cages, looking desperately for Sarah. Maybe, just maybe, she thought, this would be her chance! Perhaps while everyone was distracted by Tristan and Peter, she could do something!

A round cream-colored pony was chained near the tent. The same monkey she had seen chatter in Sarah's ear perched on the pony's back, scratching itself and muttering. Jessica moved quickly around the edge of the stall. The crowd was cheering at something Tristan had said, but she couldn't hear what it was. A thin trickle of sweat ran down her face and prickled under her arms.

And then she thought of something Cerridwyn had once told her: that people rarely pay attention; rarely take the time to truly *see*. Jessica tried as hard as she could to block out the noise of the crowd, her anxious thoughts about Peter and Sarah, and her fear. Finally, she felt her heart rate slowing, and she began to scan the cages.

Behind a large iguana was a very small cage. Inside it, an ermine curled into a tight ball of white against one of the wire sides. Its fur glistened in the sun. Even as an animal, Jessica thought, Sarah was beautiful.

The eyes of the crowd were still on the spectacle of the young boy who had tried to poison the Animal Tamer's drink. It wasn't often that a criminal was caught in the Market, and it was worse when the criminal was one of their own. Everyone in the Market knew Peter. He held his head high; his eyes looked straight ahead. The crowd, hungry for more drama after yesterday's spectacle, drew close to listen. No one noticed when a curly-haired girl opened a cage, drew out a sleeping ermine, and slipped it under her cape. Jessica could feel the ermine's small bones beneath the soft fur, and something else besides: the tautness of muscle beneath the skin. She closed her hand tightly around the animal, wondering if the animal recognized her. Did it still think like Sarah? Would it know it was being rescued?

The ermine squirmed. She tightened her grip, and a hot pain seared her thumb. Sarah had bitten Jessica right in the fleshy part of her thumb! The pain almost made Jessica drop the frantic animal. Hoping she hadn't cried out loudly enough for anyone to hear, she dodged between the cages, away from the crowd, toward the outskirts of the Market.

GAUGHT

I N SARAH'S SLEEP, something warm and firm wrapped around her body. But then the warm thing squeezed her. Adrenaline coursed through her. She sank her teeth into soft flesh— yet still the thing held her steadily in its grip. She struggled but couldn't get free. She was held in a dark place. The scent of human and of fear bloomed around her. They were moving, with a great lumbering gait. Gradually, her need to struggle subsided as the grip that held her relaxed.

When the movement stopped, bright light dazzled her eyes. She was pulled from the warm place and lifted with two hands into the light. A human face peered down at her. A great, ugly human face with two large eyes. Two things warred within her. The strongest was the need to escape, but there was also the feeling of something safe, something reassuring about this human. The human was making a soft, soothing noise, repeating it over and over. Slowly, her bunched muscles eased under the hands that stroked her body.

✛✛✛

Sitting on the ground with her back against a tree, Jessica talked to Sarah, calling her by name, repeating it over and over. She didn't know if Sarah could understand, but she talked anyway, telling her about Peter and how he had tried to save her; about Timothy going home to help their mother; about her own confusion and fears. The ermine had finally stopped struggling and looked at her with curious, bright eyes. Sarah's nose twitched as if she smelled something, and her warm body curled into Jessica's lap.

Now what do I do, Jessica wondered, winding her throbbing and bleeding thumb in the fabric of her skirt. How does one turn an ermine back into a girl?

✛ ✛ ✛

Peter didn't mind so much about being caught. He worried instead that Jessica might not think quickly enough to take advantage of the situation. If only he could send her a message with his thoughts! He concentrated so fiercely that he missed much of what was said to him by Tristan and the Animal Tamer. And maybe that was just as well.

He stood silent and defiant while his mind ran elsewhere. But that didn't suit the crowd or Tristan; they were ready for a fight. Tristan shoved Peter to the ground, and his knee slammed against a sharp rock. The Animal Tamer bent over him, his smoothly sculpted face just inches from Peter's own.

"Now, why would a boy like you want to kill me after he knew what I do to people who cross me? What do people say about your mother's neck?" And he gave a nasty laugh that made Peter think he had never hated someone so much in his life. "If I wanted to, I could turn you into an ermine, just like your friend. But that wouldn't do, would it? You're not so pretty. I think you'd be better as a ferret." He laughed again. "Quite a feisty, fighting ferret, too, I think. Good for sport? How would you like a turn down a pair of pants?"

Peter knew he was being baited, so he bit back his first response. At least this way he might buy time for Jessica. "You believe everything the Master of the Market tells you, don't you?" he said instead.

Balor narrowed his blue eyes.

Peter continued. "He says you're only his pawn. That he can make you do whatever he wants, make you believe whatever he wants."

"Oh, you're good, very good," Balor said after a moment's hesitation. "Just what I need in an assistant. But I want to know more." He jerked Peter to his feet. "Why are you sniffing around here? And where's the boy Timothy?" Then he reached inside his coat and drew out something small, a delicately fashioned crown. Gold vines were woven together, and, in the center, a single gold leaf glowed. "Perhaps you're looking for this?"

Peter's eyes widened. He remembered a crown like this from stories his mam and gram had told him. For years it had been worn by the true Master of the Market, passed from one generation to the next, but during the Dark Times it had been lost. Now, seeing it shining in the Animal Tamer's hand, all the old stories came rushing back. Peter was filled with a longing he couldn't explain.

THE PIPES

A FLOCK OF SPARROWS flew in from the east, filling the branches of the vine maple just behind the log where Timothy sat lost in thought. Overhead, in the limbs of the hawthorn, crows chattered and jeered. Higher still, in the top of the chestnut, two eagles landed.

Timothy puzzled out his thoughts. If there really were parallel universes, and if what happened in one affected what happened in another, then perhaps whatever he did *here* might have some impact on what happened to Sarah *there*. He wished for the comfort of Gwydon or for the Greenman, who would surely know what to do. Sarah would approach the situation like Sherlock Holmes, but, then, Holmes didn't believe in anything other than what he could prove. Still, Timothy wondered what Holmes might say about this situation. Holmes would smoke his pipe or play his violin while he thought the case through. Timothy pictured him in his study on Baker Street, gazing out over foggy London. The word *muse* popped into his mind, only six points.

Absentmindedly, Timothy gazed at the instrument Mr. Twig had left behind, the set of Uilleann pipes. They didn't look that complicated—a bellows, a bag, a flutelike pipe. He placed the bellows end under his right arm, as he had seen Mr. Twig do, then studied the flutelike body. It reminded him of a tin whistle. He tried some random fingering while pumping his right arm at the same time, but it was more difficult to coordinate than he had guessed, and all that came out was a squeak of air. He tried again and again until he was able to produce a few random squeaks in a row.

✚ ✚ ✚

Andor stretched his neck. The sounds from below were like the squealing of vermin when he had them in his talons, and the noise made him hungry. He sent a picture of a small rabbit to Arkell, but the older eagle ignored this message.

Arkell was intent instead on the boy with the pipes. He would have to do better than this, the bird thought, and it might take a very long time.

There was another watcher in the trees. Electra saw Timothy work the pipes. She listened to the random squeaks. And she noticed his two eagle guardians.

✚ ✚ ✚

Timothy tried to remember the fingering for a simple melody he had once played on his father's tin whistle. He and Sarah had bought the tin whistle as a Christmas gift for their father several years ago and left it in his Christmas stocking. For about a month, both Timothy and his father had a contest to see who could learn the most tunes. Neither of them had been very good, and eventually the tin whistle had disappeared somewhere in the house. Timothy still remembered a little of the fingering, and gradually something like a melody emerged. It wasn't much of a tune, but it was better than the first few squeaks.

Timothy pumped his arm harder, continuing to play and not really knowing why; perhaps because it took all his concentration, and he couldn't worry about Sarah or Jessica or what was happening at the Market.

✠ ✠ ✠

At the edge of the Market, a cloaked figure began to play, and at first the music was lost in the jumble of voices. But the figure played on. His instrument was old, and it had been many years since it had been heard in the Market, but the voice of the Uilleann pipes was unmistakable, and when the simple melody finally found its way through the crowd, the oldest merchants stopped at their tasks to listen. They remembered a time when the pipes were part of the Market, a time when the Market was a joyful place, a place of free trade, and of free talk.

Jessica, sitting with the white ermine nestled in the lap of her skirt, heard the music, too. It wasn't an instrument she recognized. But whatever it was, the music slipped through the cloud of despair that hovered over her in the same way that the sun's rays sift through fog, and for a moment she forgot everything else as she listened.

✠ ✠ ✠

Fiona was working a batch of dough when she heard the pipes. The music floated around her like the yeasty smell of bread dough rising in a warm oven. She wiped her floured hands on her apron and straightened up. She began to hum, forgetting the latest batch of pies in the oven until an acrid smell brought her hurrying to salvage what was left of them.

✛ ✛ ✛

Julian breathed a sigh of relief as he walked through the Market. The Storyteller's preparations had not been in vain. A battle was coming to the Market soon. They would need supplies and weapons to survive. And the Light required one last thing: the hope that a new Filidh would bring. Julian had known, absolutely, that he could count on Timothy. Still, he had been holding his breath all morning. Now he returned to his caravan with the few items he needed, Gwydon staying close by his side. As the music of the pipes grew louder, Gwydon pricked up his ears and whined. With a low growl, he bounded off into the Market.

✛ ✛ ✛

Tristan couldn't bear the sound assaulting his ears. What was this horrible noise in his Market? He must put a stop to it immediately, but it was all he could do to focus on the Animal Tamer and Peter, the sneaking son of a wretched mother. Whatever the Animal Tamer was going to do with the boy, he wanted him to do it quickly so that he could track down the source of this cacophony.

✛ ✛ ✛

Peter's only thought was for the crown. It no longer mattered to him that the Animal Tamer might be about to turn him into a ferret or that Tristan probably had some other torture in mind for him. The crown didn't belong in the malevolent hands of the Animal Tamer! Peter didn't know how it had ended up there, but it must have been stolen. He knew that the crown belonged to the true Master of the Market and that he must return it.

✦ ✦ ✦

The wail of the pipes sliced through Balor's head like a furious sword, blinding him with pain. He froze, the crown in his outstretched hand. He never saw the golden wolf until it jumped at him, teeth bared, and snatched the crown from his hand. In an instant, both the wolf and the crown were gone, lost in the surrounding woods!

Balor's face went pale. His lips contracted, and his hands shook with rage. He had been too patient. He should have killed the wolf long ago. He needed the crown to lure the boy, and he needed the boy—the Filidh—to lead him to the stone. But once the stone was found, he would not restrain himself any longer. The boy and the two girls would understand that they had no real choice. They would serve Balor or die. "You fool!" he cried, cuffing Peter hard on the side of the head. "Don't you know who you're dealing with?"

Peter reeled back. Before he could open his mouth to protest, the Animal Tamer had drawn the flask from his pocket with a trembling hand and poured a few drops of liquid over Peter's head.

The boy's body tensed and shook. Fire burned in his veins. In a moment, the boy Peter was gone, replaced by a sinewy, shivering brown-eyed ferret.

A high-pitched squeal of laughter exploded from Tristan's lips. He snatched up the animal in his gloved hands, squeezing harder than was necessary.

The Animal Tamer gazed down at Tristan as if he, too, were no more than a specimen in one of his cages.

"You are an even bigger fool than he is, self-proclaimed Master of the Market! You're useless—allowing that wolf to roam freely!" Balor hissed. "Perhaps it's time I dispensed with you as well."

"H-h-how could I know what that cursed wolf would do?" Tristan sputtered.

But Balor wasn't listening. His eyes had widened into red-rimmed pits. He grabbed the ferret from Tristan's hands and stuffed it into the nearest empty cage.

The crowd, meanwhile, had drawn back in fear, their boisterous chatter muted, and many began to hurry off. The Animal Tamer frowned, and his furious eyes roamed the cages, finally coming to rest on the empty one where the ermine had been. The wire door still hung open.

He cursed loudly, and, for a moment, Balor's handsome face was transformed into a one-eyed visage so hideous that even Tristan dared not look at it.

✦ ✦ ✦

Peter was overwhelmed by his sense of smell. It overrode all his other senses. He was drowning in the scent of humans and animals, and something more—a complicated scent that blew on the wind and carried with it a smell of danger and the nagging sense that there were things that needed defending. He could put no names to the things that needed him, for he no longer had a word for Sarah or for the crown, but the sense of them made him bare his small, sharp teeth.

THE GROWN

IMOTHY WASN'T SURE how long he had been play-
ing, or at least trying to play, the pipes. All he knew was
that his arm was tired and his fingers were sore. He rose
reluctantly to his feet, laying aside the pipes so he could
stretch. Mostly, he was frustrated that he was stuck here
while Sarah and Jessica were still at the Market, well beyond his help.
Perhaps the best thing to do, he thought, would be to go home and
check on his mother. He didn't know what to tell his parents if Sarah
wasn't home by evening.

But first he would return the pipes to Mr. Twig. Cradling the instrument carefully in one arm, he lifted his mountain bike out of the thicket.
A crash in the bushes nearby caused him to stop. The berry bushes
trembled, and Timothy caught a glimpse of golden fur. Before he could
decide whether to make a run for it, an entire head emerged from the
thicket with something glittering between its great white teeth.

"Gwydon!" Dropping his bike, Timothy hurled himself at the wolf.

But Gwydon stopped a foot short of Timothy and dropped a crown at his feet.

Timothy reached out tentatively and picked up the crown. It winked and glinted in his hand. It was his crown! The one he had traded to Balor for a drink of water so long ago in his workshop! The crown given to him by Cerridwyn. The crown he thought he might never see again. "Gwydon, where—how—did you get this?"

But Gwydon only nudged it with his snout. Timothy knew what the wolf wanted. He gently placed the crown on his own head.

"You need to return to the Market, Timothy." The deep voice came from the forest around him, a voice he had been longing to hear. Timothy turned in every direction, but he saw no one.

"But Fiona told me that if I took the salve for my mother, I could never come back."

"Never come back 'as you are now.' And you won't. You are no longer just Timothy James Maxwell. This time you will return with part of your inheritance, the crown. Didn't you listen to the Storyteller's tales? For many years, the Market has been without a true Master, without a Filidh to speak to remind people of the true stories."

"Greenman, where are you?"

"I am near."

At Timothy's side, Gwydon dropped to his haunches and rested there, nose on paws, his eyes on Timothy. "Am I the Filidh?" Timothy asked.

If wolves could smile, Gwydon would have to be said to be smiling at the short, scruffy boy with smeared glasses and hair standing out in every direction, now wearing a crown.

The rumbling voice continued. "Gifts are not given lightly, or by mistake. Your mother's maiden name was O'Daly. The rank of Filidh is an inherited one. The crown is only one part of what you need to claim that inheritance."

Timothy could hardly breathe. The word *Filidh* shimmered in his mind. He wished that he had listened more closely to all that Julian had said. Filidhs were keepers of the Truth, Filidhs were poets . . . There was a stone hidden that would cry out when he placed his foot on it. Still clutching the Uilleann pipes with one hand, he slowly touched the crown on his head with the other. He had no idea how being a Filidh was supposed to feel, but what he felt was more than a little foolish.

"Even now, forces are preparing for battle. It is time to return."

"But what about Sarah? Is she still . . . an ermine?"

"Yes, and you must hurry now. Climb on Gwydon's back."

Gwydon came closer and lowered the front of his broad body. Timothy remembered his last ride on the wolf, when they had been chased through the sky by Herne and his hounds. He threw one jean-clad leg over Gwydon's back and then set the pipes on the ground so he could hang on to Gwydon's neck with both hands. But Gwydon nudged the pipes as well. Timothy picked them up.

And quite suddenly, Gwydon was standing and Timothy was sliding across his back, grabbing the thick fur with one hand to keep from fall-ing while clutching the pipes in the other, the crown balanced precari-ously on his head. In a great bound, they were skyward.

Hanging on to a flying wolf is much more difficult, Timothy soon realized, if you can use only one hand. Luckily, there was no storm this time, no hounds snapping at their heels, no wind and rain trying to pry him from Gwydon's back. The sky was a cold, cloudless blue.

Timothy gripped as hard as he could with his thighs and looked down. As the familiar trees of his town receded behind him, there on the horizon appeared one small puff of cloud. As they approached, the cloud grew larger and larger. The chill air stung Timothy's face, and his hand clutching the pipes was cold and numb. White mist was rising like phantoms on all sides. Timothy could see nothing beyond the cloud. He was adrift in a world of white.

Chilled to the bone, he curled himself into the smallest possible ball on Gwydon's back to keep all the warmth from being sucked from his body. Then it seemed that he could hear voices in the great mist. The words swirled just beyond the edge of hearing, but their tone was plaintive, filled with longing, and the sound sent a further chill through his bones. Was this the same cloud that had been a portway to Balor's workshop? He shuddered at the thought. He was so cold now, he could no longer feel the pipes in his hand. Then, just as the voices reached a crescendo, the vapors began to stream away in tendrils, and light pierced the thick white. The voices faded, and below, Timothy saw a field dotted with trees. Between the trees, bright banners whipped in a late-afternoon breeze. They had returned to the Market!

✣ ✣ ✣

THIS ENDS BOOK ONE OF THE **TIME OUT OF TIME** ADVENTURE.

The story continues in Book Two.

A NOTE TO THE READER

Ogham was a system of writing that developed in Ireland in the fourth century. It looks like a series of hatch marks that cross or are joined to a central line. There are twenty letters in the Ogham alphabet. The hatch marks were easy to carve on wood or stone, and that's where Ogham is usually found. The marks read in the same way that a tree grows, from bottom to top. You can still find stones in Ireland, England, Wales, and Scotland carved with Ogham letters.

Many people call Ogham the "Tree Alphabet" and believe that each letter is associated with a particular tree. For example, the first letter in the Ogham alphabet is Beith, which is associated with the birch tree. Trees are very important in Irish mythology, and ancient Irish law had severe penalties for anyone who unlawfully felled or damaged a tree. A medieval document called the Ogam Tract says that the letters of Ogham represented types of trees important in Irish mythology and life. The tract also says that the Tuatha de Danaan, a race of people from Irish mythology, invented Ogham script.

Where did Ogham really come from? The answer is unclear. Some scholars believe it came from a system of tallies used for accounting. Other scholars believe it was a means of secret communication, employed so that Roman-British forces couldn't understand what was being communicated. And still others believe it was invented by early Christian communities.

THE CODE

By using the key provided here, you can decipher the Ogham script that runs along the bottom of many pages of this book. (Note that in authentic Ogham, the marks read from bottom to top; here, the marks read left to right. Also, Ogham would traditionally translate into primitive Irish; here, it translates into English.) Lastly, the script has been adapted to include the letters J, K, P, V, W, X, Y, and Z to make reading the code easier. Below each Ogham mark is the tree name in Celtic as well as in English, followed by the alphabet letter or letter cluster it represents.

OGHAM

BEITHE BIRGH	LUIS ROWAN	FERN ALDER	SAIL WILLOW	NION ASH	HUATH HAWTHORN	DUIR OAK	TINNE HOLLY	GOLL HAZEL	QUERT APPLE
B	L	F	S	N	H	D	T	G	Q

MUIN VINE	GORT IVY	PEITH SOFT BIRGH	RUIS ELDER	AILM FIR	ONN GORSE	UR HEATHER	EDAD POPLAR	IDAD YEW	
M	G	P	R	A	O	U	E	I	X

K	J	W	V	Y	Z	SPAS	EITE FEATHER	EITE THUATHAIL
						SPACE	START OF SENTENCE	END OF SENTENCE

ACKNOWLEDGMENTS

Thanks to Debra Murphy at Idylls Press, who loves myth and first encouraged this story, and to Howard Reeves, who saw a glimmer of potential and was determined to give the story a larger readership. He has been a wise guide on this book's journey.

Thanks as always to Sandra Bishop, my tireless agent, who believes, as I do, that sometimes "the best way to show people true things is from a direction that they had not imagined the truth coming," which is a quote from Neil Gaiman's acceptance speech at the Mythopoeic Awards and something I believe wholeheartedly.

And the greatest appreciation to my family, who lived through countless revisions, and to my earliest readers: Deb Donahoe, Nat and Nancy Smith, Christine Bian, Michael McCain, Dennis and Brennan McQuerry. Without you there would be no book. And to Claire McQuerry, for bringing me to Oxford, where I first met the Greenman.

TIMOTHY, SARAH, AND JESSICA'S ADVENTURES CONTINUE IN *THE TELLING STONE*, THE SEQUEL TO *BEYOND THE DOOR*. READ THE FIRST CHAPTER NOW!

THE GOOSE
WOMAN

N O ONE HAD ever told Jessica Church how to rescue a girl who was enchanted. Yet here she was, alone in a strange market somewhere in time, trying to help her friend Sarah Maxwell, who had been turned into an ermine. Jessica sat on a bench away from the bustle of the Travelers' Market. A beautiful white ermine lay curled in her lap. The bench was hidden behind a cartload of apples, and she was glad for the temporary cover because she had stolen the long, sinewy animal from its cage when the Animal Tamer was distracted. Now she had no idea what to do next. As she worried, she absently stroked the animal's lithe body. "Don't fret. I'll think of something soon." Did ermines worry? She had no idea. "Sarah, can you understand anything I'm saying?"

A leg twitched. Did that mean anything? Jessica didn't know. She considered the animal's bright brown eyes. She'd never had a pet. She didn't particularly like animals; they were smelly, and many of them drooled. If only the Greenman was here to help.

A shout dragged Jessica from her thoughts. She startled, almost dropping Sarah. The ermine squirmed. A man's voice boomed, followed by a steady stream of curses. Jessica's fingers tightened around the ermine's narrow body. She could feel the rapid heartbeat, the small bones beneath the silken fur. The animal twisted in her hands, and Jessica loosened her grip, just a little. She didn't want to get bitten again.

"I'm sorry, but I don't know what else to do." It felt ridiculous apologizing to an ermine, even when that ermine had once been one of her friends. Jessica shoved the still-squirming Sarah into a burlap sack. The bag bulged and wiggled. Claws scrabbled at the fabric. She eyed the thumb her friend had bitten when she'd grabbed her from the cage. In no time at all Sarah would chew or claw her way through the sack. Jessica needed a safe place to hide her friend and fast.

The shouting subsided. Sarah stopped thrashing, and the bag on Jessica's lap lay still. Jessica brushed a curly strand of hair from her eyes and took slow, deep breaths. She needed to put some distance between herself and the scene of the crime.

Peering out from behind the apple cart, she considered her next move. Any minute now the Animal Tamer might find her, and then what would happen? Her memory replayed the Animal Tamer's laugh as he turned Sarah into an ermine and locked her away. Their friend Peter had tried to save Sarah. He'd caused a distraction so Jessica could get to the cage. And it had worked. But distraction hadn't worked so well for Peter. The last Jessica had seen of him was as a slinking brown ferret. She shuddered.

As Jessica watched the crowd, an idea unfolded. The Travelers' Market was bustling with men and women bartering wares, buying apples, filling their bags with green and gold squash, arguing over the price for a cheese. Her best hope would be to blend in with the crowd, a curly-haired girl carrying a dirty bag that might be full of a day's purchases. She'd get far enough away from the Animal Tamer's stall that she'd be able to think clearly and come up with a plan. Dusting off her skirt and with a firm grip on the sack, Jessica walked briskly into the crowd, looking straight ahead as if she had somewhere important to go. No one noticed how fast her heart was beating. It took great effort not to run.

Was it only a day ago she'd come to the Market with Sarah and Timothy Maxwell to find a cure for their mother, who was desperately ill with rat-bite fever? No, she reminded herself, they hadn't *come* to this market between worlds; they'd been led there through a portway by a scrawny little man called Nom, who looked like a rat himself. He had promised this was the place to search for a cure. And they'd be given an ointment, something that Timothy could take back to his mother. But nothing had gone as smoothly as Nom had promised. The Dark was already there waiting for them: Balor the One-Eyed disguised as the handsome Animal Tamer, and Tristan, the Master of the Market, who was his pawn.

Behind her something hissed. Jessica froze. Had she been discovered? Before she could turn, something pinched the back of her thigh right through her long skirt and twisted. Jessica screamed. She grabbed for her leg. The bag spilled open.

"Sarah!"

In a flash the ermine was out of the sack, a white streak winding away behind a barrel of grain. Jessica dove after her, but the ermine was too fast. It disappeared from sight. Jessica swore in frustration, then screamed as something else took a pinch of her backside. She swung around. A large white goose thrust its serpentine neck forward, yellow beak and shiny black eyes just inches from her nose. Spreading its wings, it hissed a threat. In response Jessica rose up to her full height. The animal thrust its neck forward.

"There, there, my pretty boy, leave the young lady alone!" A short gray-haired woman in a red bandanna tapped the animal's neck with a stick. The goose straightened up, head wobbling but still hissing. Then she rapped him again, more sharply this time. The animal turned and waddled back to its gaggle. "I expect you'll have a rare bruise there by morning." The woman turned to Jessica. "And you've lost your pet, too," she added with a cluck as she tucked her stick back under her arm.

"She's not my pet!" Jessica sobbed. Her leg stung like fury. Where was Sarah? She dropped gingerly to hands and knees, peering beneath tables of fruit and behind baskets of nuts. With every movement, she winced.

It was no use. Sarah was gone. Jessica collapsed in the dirt with her nose running, a waterfall of tears coursing down her cheeks. She wiped her nose with her sleeve, but the harder she tried to stop crying, the more she cried. She cried because she had lost Sarah and Peter, because Timothy was gone, but mostly she cried for herself, stuck in this miserable Market.

"Oh, my, this isn't good, isn't good at all." The old goose woman bent over and peered into Jessica's face. Her gaggle crowded close behind her, strutting and honking. "It can't be that bad, now, can it? Well, I suppose it can. But how can I help you, since it was my dandy boy who caused the problem in the first place?" The old woman took Jessica's arm and with surprising strength pulled her to her feet. "Suppose you tell me the whole thing, eh? Get *back* there, Minerva!" She wielded her stick at a big gray goose with a bulbous beak that was about to help itself to a barrel of grain.

Too miserable to resist, Jessica found herself being steered by the arm to a bench beside a large pen.

"You sit here"—the goose woman pushed Jessica onto the bench—"while I put my beauties away." With a series of clucks and a few well-timed taps of the stick, the old woman managed to corral the entire gaggle into the pen. The geese fretted and honked in protest for a few seconds and then settled down to drink from a metal trough in the shade of an oak tree. She dipped a long-handled cup into a wooden barrel.

"Here you go, Jessica," the woman said finally, wrapping Jessica's hand around a cool cup of water.

"How do you know my name?" Jessica asked between sniffles. She was sure she had never seen the goose woman before.

"So, you've forgotten me already?"

And as Jessica watched, the lines in the woman's old, round face softened, and her gray hair lengthened and cascaded into red waves around her shoulders.

"Cerridwyn?" Jessica gasped. Could this be the same fierce huntress who had led her, Sarah, and Timothy into their first adventure? The same woman who had once been disguised as Jessica's elderly great-aunt?

"Yes, it's me. Do you remember your first lesson? After the night of the storm when the Wild Hunt rode, you and I traveled together. Remember the first rule I taught you? Things aren't always as they seem."

"But I didn't know if I would ever see you again."

"I have had many names in many places. I told you that you would never see me again as I was in your world, your great-aunt Rosemary Clapper."

Nothing could have prepared Jessica for the events of the past few months: traveling through portways, fleeing from flying wolves, and discovering that her great-aunt Rosemary wasn't just an old family friend but Cerridwyn, a character right out of Celtic mythology. Now here she was, just when Jessica needed her! Cerridwyn would help her, would tell her what to do.

"It seems your friends have had a very difficult time of it."

"My *friends?*" Resentment sharpened Jessica's voice. "*I'm* the one having a hard time! Timothy's gone home with an ointment for his mother, and *I* got left behind to help Sarah. And even if I do find her, *I* don't know how to turn her back into a girl. And Peter tried to help, but—"

"Yes, he needs help, too. It can't be pleasant being changed into a ferret! Nasty, slinking creatures. Always stealing eggs." She glanced fondly at her gaggle, then turned back to Jessica with a solemn face. "I'm afraid things may get worse before they get better; they often do. But things won't get better if you keep thinking of yourself first."

Jessica's face flamed at Cerridwyn's words. It was hard to think about how her friends felt when she felt so alone herself.

Cerridwyn watched her with sharp eyes. "You are *not* alone."

How did Cerridwyn always know what she was thinking?

At Cerridwyn's urging, Jessica took a swallow of the sweet water. She wiped the back of her hand across her lips. "I think the Animal Tamer knows I've stolen Sarah."

"*Balor.* It's important to call evil by its true name. But here in the Market it might be safer not to mention it. You never know who might be listening."

Jessica looked over her shoulder. A prickle of fear ran down her arms.

Cerridwyn peered closely into Jessica's face. "Of course, we live in a world noisy with evil. History is nothing if not a story of the long battle between good and evil. So we shouldn't be surprised when we find it. Now, clean yourself up." She handed Jessica a handkerchief.

Jessica wiped her nose. None of this was reassuring. "But what can we do to help Sarah and Peter? What should I do?"

Cerridwyn held up one knotted hand. "I can't tell you what to do. What I *can* tell you is that the Market is on the verge of a great battle. News of it has been abroad for some time, and many are preparing for it even as we speak. Even Balor will be preparing."

The small hairs on Jessica's arms stood on end, and her heart beat faster. "A battle? Here?" She looked wildly around the Market, where people haggled and laughed, gossiped and sang. Already some merchants were putting away their wares, closing up their caravans for the day.

Cerridwyn's face remained grim. "Things have not been right in the Market for a long time. The balance of power has turned toward the Dark. But now something has happened that threatens that power, and the Dark will not stand for that."

"What's happened?"

Cerridwyn spoke carefully, as if weighing what she would say. "The next in the true line of Masters of the Market has come of age. As you've seen, Tristan is nothing but an imposter. He's controlled by the Animal Tamer. The true Master of the Market is always a Filidh, one of a long line of people who are keepers of the truth. And that is why a true Filidh is a threat to the Dark and to the lies it weaves."

Jessica thought about the stories of the Filidhean that she and Timothy had heard from Julian, the Storyteller at the Market.

Julian had told them, "The Filidhean are a race of poets, keepers of the word, keepers of wisdom. Only a Filidh by birth can rule the Travelers, the people of the Market. A Filidh fights in all worlds against the power of the Dark." And then he had added the most remarkable thing of all: All Filidhean shared a common ancestor with the name O'Daly.

Timothy had looked at Jessica and said: "My mother's maiden name is O'Daly!"

The very thought of Timothy Maxwell, a small brainiac, being in the line of the Filidhean was hard to believe, but maybe it wasn't any stranger than everything else that had happened to them.

Cerridwyn was still watching her closely.

"Julian said that the true Filidh has to find something to prove his birthright." Jessica furrowed her brow and squeezed her eyes shut, trying to remember. "A stone! The Filidh must find a stone that cries out and something else, something about four treasures."

Cerridwyn smiled. "You listened well. Yes, the rightful Filidh must find a very particular stone, but it will be a difficult quest."

"But it is Timothy, isn't it? He must be the Filidh!"

"Time will tell you that and more. Right now we must prepare for the coming battle."

"Is the stone here at the Market?"

"No, it's not in time out of time. This stone has a long history in your world. It's been part of the coronation of many kings."

Feeling as if the conversation were spinning out of control, Jessica pressed for an answer. "If there's a battle, what am I supposed to do? And what about my friends?"

"You will have help when the time comes. It won't be easy; battles for the Light never are. But the first thing you must do is get your necklace back."

Jessica's hand flew to her neck, her face flushing. "My necklace?"

Cerridwyn nodded. "The one I gave you with my trust."

"I didn't mean to lose it! I traded it for Sarah. Tristan wanted it, and the Animal Tamer said that if I gave it to him, he would let Sarah go."

"A noble attempt to help a friend, but the Dark never keeps its bargains. Don't you know that by now?" Cerridwyn laid a hand on Jessica's arm. "It's time you retrieved it."

"But how? Tristan's wearing it, and he's a friend of Ba—I mean, the Animal Tamer."

"You'll have to figure that out with help from another friend." Cerridwyn looked past Jessica's shoulder.

Had Timothy returned? Jessica swung around, only to see Nom standing there, cap in hand, looking as skinny and dirty as ever.

"But he's just a ratcatcher!" Jessica cried, her hopes dashed as quickly as they had risen.

"Rodent exterminator," Nom corrected her with a smile that showed too many of his yellowed teeth.

Inwardly Jessica fumed. So far, what had Nom done to help? He'd come to Timothy and Sarah's house when their mother was bitten by a rat. He'd trapped it, and then, when Mrs. Maxwell became seriously ill with rat-bite fever, he'd gotten them to this Market between worlds to search for a cure. But that was the last they'd seen of him. He'd abandoned them here when they needed him the most.

"Your first lesson again," Cerridwyn said. "Everyone is more than meets the eye. For example, I know a very brave girl who once did a terrible deed out of anger. But she is more than that one deed, is she not?"

Jessica blushed, remembering how she had once betrayed her friends.

"I think Nom will be of more help than you might expect."

Jessica looked again at the little ratcatcher in his baggy pants and shabby vest. He didn't look like anyone who could be of help. She didn't know why a necklace, even a necklace from Cerridwyn, was so important when her friends were missing and a battle was about to be fought. When she turned back to Cerridwyn, it was the old goose woman she saw, round-faced and smiling. The questions died on Jessica's lips.

"I hope that bit of a sit-down did you good. You're looking as fit as a fiddle! And now I have to get back to my geese and eggs."

White and brown eggs overflowed baskets. Others, painted with vines and flowers, were balanced on small wooden stands. The most intricate had entire rural scenes ringing the eggs. On one, a village nestled under a starry canopy.

"I paint them myself," the goose woman said proudly. "And we haven't been properly introduced. In the Market, my name's Brigit, and over there's my brother, Nom." She leaned close and whispered in Jessica's ear. "Black sheep of the family, but not a bad sort once you get used to 'im."

"Now, Brigit, don't be telling secrets on me." Nom's cap was back on his head at a jaunty angle.

"It wouldn't hurt you to help out in the stall occasionally, you know. But right now you can help Jessica retrieve her necklace."

"I suppose it's the one I've seen around Tristan's neck!" Nom took Jessica's arm in his thin, sharp hand. Jessica tried not to cringe at his long, dirty nails.

"Off with you, then. I've work to do." And the goose woman gathered a bucket of grain to toss into the pen.

"She's right—usually is," Nom said. "Now we'd best be off to see to that necklace of yours."

"But we can't go without finding Sarah first!" Jessica cried.

Nom scratched his head. "Oh, she'll be long gone by now. Not as smart as rats, but ermines is tricky in their own way."

And Jessica, not knowing what else to do, allowed Nom to lead her in the direction of the Animal Tamer's stall.

Maureen Doyle McQuerry is a teacher specializing in young adult literature and writing. She has written poetry and nonfiction and is the author of *The Peculiars*, a YALSA Best Fiction for Young Adults book. Maureen was a McAuliffe Fellow for Washington State. She lives in eastern Washington, on the banks of the Columbia River.